Sixpence in her Shoe

Also by Frances McNeil

Somewhere Behind the Morning

Sixpence in her Shoe

FRANCES McNEIL

First published in Great Britain in 2006 by Orion,
an imprint of the Orion Publishing Group Ltd.

1 3 5 7 9 10 8 6 4 2

A CIP catalogue record for this book is
available from the British Library.

ISBN-13 (hardback) 978 0 7528 6852 3
ISBN-13 (trade paperback) 978 0 7528 7432 6
ISBN-10 (hardback) 0 7528 6852 7
ISBN-10 (trade paperback) 0 7528 7432 2

Typeset by Deltatype Ltd
Birkenhead, Merseyside

Set in Adobe Caslon

Printed in Great Britain by
Clays Ltd, St Ives plc

The Orion Publishing Group's policy is to use papers that
are natural, renewable and recyclable products and made
from wood grown in sustainable forests. The logging and
manufacturing processes are expected to conform to the
environmental regulations of the country of origin.

The Orion Publishing Group Ltd
Orion House
5 Upper Saint Martin's Lane
London, WC2H 9EA

www.orionbooks.co.uk

Acknowledgements

Thanks to Evelyn Phelan for her youthful memory of carrying a baby through town one long ago Sunday in May. I'm grateful to Tom Horace Alderson, Member of the Boot Trade Association/St Crispin's Shoemaker's Society, Denise Clarkson, Bob Etherton, Edith Farrar, Frank Hartley and to Michael Phipps, Archivist at the Henry Moore Foundation. Thanks also to Jill Hyem for listening; to my agent Judith Murdoch, and Yvette Goulden for being such a sensitive editor.

I

Fractures

If I hadn't paused on the church steps, had stayed inside longer, or paid more attention to what was going on around me, it wouldn't have happened the way it did. But my attention was on the baby.

I stepped out of the church feeling so proud. Me, a godmother. Leila Catherine McBride, fully baptized and wrongly named, slept again, snuggled against me. A six-week-old baby can be heavier than you expect.

The scent of church incense and carnations, pinks and lilies came with me into the warm May Sunday afternoon. I could hear a brass band in the distance, going away from me. In the road, a motorbike weaved around the tail end of the miners' procession. A couple of policemen on horseback clip-clopped along.

As I stepped onto the pavement, a man brushed by me, his clothes smelling of coal dust. Two others raced after him calling, 'Scab!'

I pulled the baby closer, shielding her. One pitman grabbed the cowering man, the other threw a punch to the head. I tried to step back but someone was in my way. The police horses mounted the pavement. One of them crashed against me.

When I screamed, Leila started to bawl her head off, either because of my scream or the jolt from the horse.

The next minute I was back in the church porch, still holding Leila in my right arm, my left arm hurting like mad and hanging in a funny way, making my blazer sleeve poke out in the middle.

I opened the church inner door by pushing my body against it.

Father Flynn must have been praying near the front of the church. He came hurrying up the aisle.

'What happened? Come and sit down.'

Leila was still crying. Was it because she was hurt, damaged for ever by the horse and my stupidity? The priest took her from me and laid her on the pew, which seemed to me a dangerous place because she would only have to move a fraction, roll an inch, to crash onto the stone floor.

'Stay still, my child. I'll fetch you a glass of water.'

It had all happened too quickly.

My left arm hung useless. I put my right hand by Leila, to keep her from rolling off the bench. That seemed to quieten her. I stroked her and told her everything would be all right. Father Flynn came back, carrying a glass of water from the vestry.

'I can't take you home. I'm saying Benediction shortly. Let me fetch the housekeeper.' But he didn't move, just stood looking down at me, as if he were waiting to take the glass back in case I dropped it.

I did not notice the sound of footsteps. Father Flynn looked up. I turned my head to follow his gaze.

Wilf stood awkwardly at the far end of the pew, his sketch book in one hand, absent-mindedly holding the end of his art college scarf in the other.

'I was drawing the statue in the Lady Chapel.' In the dim church I couldn't be sure, but I thought he blushed. He didn't say, 'I was drawing the statue, Father.' Or, 'I hope that's all right.' But then I wouldn't expect him to. He gave up all religion last year, even though that side of the family are only Unitarians, which, according to Mam, is no religion at all and hardly worth giving up. Mam says Wilf has bad blood and it is coming out at last, as she always guessed it would.

'This is my cousin Wilf Price, Father,' I said.

Father Flynn nodded at Wilf. I thought for a moment he would reprimand him in some way and say the church was for praying, not for practising your drawing, but he said nothing.

Wilf edged his way along the pew, walking sideways, looking at my arm. He put down his sketch book and looped the scarf over his head as if he were about to begin skipping with it. 'I'll do you a sling, Jess.'

Father Flynn frowned. 'Careful!' he said, as Wilf fastened the scarf around my neck and lifted my arm into it. I tried not to cry out, but I couldn't help it.

'Sorry,' Wilf said. 'It needs to be a bit more . . . If you could . . .'

He looked to Father Flynn to support my arm while he made the scarf sling shorter.

Neither of them looked at Leila. She and I stared at each other. *Are you all right?* I wanted to ask her. *Have I done some terrible damage to you?*

I had released my hold on her while Wilf fastened my sling but reached out to her again. Father Flynn moved away as I accidentally touched him. He sounded annoyed. 'We should have gone into the vestry. More room.'

'I've done it now.' Wilf picked up his sketch book. 'Let's get you to the dispensary, Jess. See to that arm.'

The priest seemed both relieved and uncertain. 'Will I fetch the housekeeper?'

Wilf ignored him.

'We'll manage, Father,' I said. 'If you'd please just put Leila on my right arm, I can hold her well enough.'

She screwed up her face when he lifted her, but almost seemed to sigh when he placed her against me. I drew my arm around her. She looked at me once more, then shut her eyes, as if to say, *I know the worst is over now.*

That didn't make me feel better. What if she slipped into a coma? By the time I got her home she might have stopped breathing. It would be no consolation to her mam and dad that her soul would whizz straight to heaven.

Wilf put his hand between my shoulder blades when we left the pew, as if he didn't trust me not to fall over.

Father Flynn walked us to the church door. 'You get that arm attended to, Jess. I'll say a prayer for you both at Benediction, and for you, too, Wilf. See them home safely.'

'I intend to.'

My arm throbbed. I felt dizzy. Even so, the thought came to me that Father Flynn must know I had an atheist for a cousin. Wilf could at least have sounded more polite.

In the church porch, Wilf said, 'Why aren't the baby's parents here?'

'Tommy had to go out with the handcart, selling fruit. Heather looked worn out. I said I'd manage on my own.'

Outside there was no sign of the miners, and no sound of their band, only a scruffy lad slouching along, kicking a stone and whistling to himself. On the corner, a gypsy hawker with a couple of children in tow tried to flog us a piece of lucky heather.

'Bit late for that,' Wilf said, giving her a coin.

She tried to hand me a piece of lucky heather. Wilf took it for me.

'Bless the wee bairn.' The gypsy peered at Leila and looked back at me. 'You're so alike.'

We walked on.

'She's dark and you're fair, but I know what she means,' Wilf said. 'Must be to do with the planets. Weren't you born on the same day? Didn't you tell me you share a birthday?'

I nodded. He was trying to take my mind off the pain but I just wanted to concentrate on putting one foot before the other. My arm throbbed. With every step, a sharp pain shot through me. I didn't speak, putting all my energy into striding carefully, keeping steady.

Wilf stopped by the dispensary on North Street. 'Jess?'

I kept walking. 'I have to take her home first.'

As we turned into Benson Street, the girl who rides bareback came galloping out of Creasey's Yard onto the cobbles. Fear stopped my breath.

Wilf took my good elbow. He rapped on the McBrides' door.

Heather McBride's smallness made me feel like a looming giant. I stepped back off the clean donkey-stoned step, one foot on the pavement. She had tied her thick wavy black hair with a long ribbon made from the belt of a cotton dress. Ribbon and hair draped over her right shoulder down to her waist. She wore a dark-red cotton frock with a broad elastic belt and a black, silky apron patterned with brightly coloured flowers. Twenty-two years old – seven years older than me – she looked like a pixie or an elf from a story book, or the tiny gypsy girl I'd seen at Woodhouse Feast one blustery autumn night.

'Come in, Jess. Wilf. Tommy's still out on his fruit round.' As she spoke, a tortoiseshell cat miaowed and dashed past, brushing my ankles as it escaped into the street.

'We won't come in,' Wilf said.

I stepped inside, needing Heather to know that I had brought

Leila back safe and sound. She took the sleeping baby from my arm. Leila moved a little. Still alive, then.

Wilf stayed in the doorway. 'We're not stopping. Jess took a bump and hurt her arm. She needs to get to the dispensary.'

'Poor Jess!'

'Leila didn't take any hurt,' I said quickly.

Heather placed her infant in the wooden drawer that sat on the table. 'I'll feed her in a minute.'

With Leila lying in the drawer, it was easy for me to lift the white shawl, check her arms and legs, and make sure they were all in one piece. They were. After that, a lightheadedness came over me.

Heather rinsed a mug under the tap. 'You look really pale, Jess. You'd better have a cup of tea if you're off to the dispensary. They think nothing of keeping you waiting the day long and if you've had a shock you need summat.'

Wilf made an impatient little noise and gave me a look, telling me to get up and get out of there.

Heather poured a cup of tea and spooned sugar in. 'That's good for shock.'

Wilf refused tea.

I wanted Heather to pick up the baby, look at her, and make sure Leila really was all right.

But she was more interested in having an account of the christening.

'Will you take the baptismal certificate from my right inside blazer pocket, Heather?' With my left arm in the sling I couldn't have got it myself.

She took the certificate but did not look at it immediately. 'If you've the strength, tell me all about it,' she said, picking up the baby, settling herself on the straight-back chair, her back to Wilf, the baby at her breast in a clever way with her dress open, shawl pulled round, so you could not see anything 'untoward', as Mam would say.

I refused to meet Wilf's eye, not able to go until she knew about the mistake in the name. Heather took my stillness as the sign that I felt comfortable and was in no hurry.

'The good thing was that I found a shilling in the aisle and lit twelve candles for her. You'd better just look at the name on certificate before I go.'

As she read the baptismal certificate, she raised her dark eyebrows.

5

The baby sensed a change in her mother and waved her little red fists in the air.

Heather let out a long sigh.

'I'm sorry. I did *say* Catherine Leila. Father Flynn turned it round, both at the font and in the vestry when he wrote it in the register. I don't know why he did that.'

'I do,' she said. 'After you'd left the house, a sign came to me. I knew all of a sudden that my mammy, Leila Lee, would be there, watching over. My mammy turned the names in Father Flynn's mouth. She guided his hand in the register. She led you to the shilling so you could light candles.'

She'd made me shiver.

Wilf reached out his hand and helped me up. He set my cup on the draining board. 'Can we get to the dispensary now?'

'You do look pale, Jess. Best do as Wilf says.'

'When Tommy comes back, would you get him to tell Jess's mam and dad where we've gone, Heather?'

'You look after her, Wilf,' Heather called as we left.

As Wilf pushed open the dispensary doors, he glanced up and pointed out the carving above the doorway. A pair of stone cherubs gazed down, one fearful – perhaps with a chubby broken arm – the other superior-looking, as if it had never in its cherub life got into an argument with a police horse.

Lifting my head made me feel sick, though I knew he was again only trying to distract me from the pain. As we walked across to the desk, I groaned at the sight of rows of people waiting to see a doctor.

'We should have been in here half an hour ago,' Wilf said.

I recognized the straight-backed man behind the desk as someone who brought his shoes to Dad to be mended. He picked up his pen.

'You're Paul Price's daughter.'

'Yes. Jessica.'

'What number Benson Street?'

'Thirty.'

'Date of birth?'

'Thirtieth of March nineteen eleven.'

'Age?'

'Fifteen.'

'What's the damage?' He looked at my sling.

'I got bumped by a police horse.'

He frowned, wrote something, then looked at Wilf. 'And you are?'

'Wilfred Price. Cousin.'

Wilf gave his address, Blenheim Square.

'I served with your dads, in Leeds Pals Regiment. You'll have a bit of a wait today, I'm afraid. Only a couple of doctors on duty.'

A granny with a sick-looking child on her knee budged up to make room for us on the end of a bench. Wilf took a pencil from his pocket and opened his sketch pad.

'I'm going to do some drawings for our story book.'

'You don't have to stay here with me.'

'Yes, I do.'

He sketched a large shoe. Peeping out of it came the face of an old woman and a pinched-faced child. As the afternoon ticked away, all the children in the waiting room found their way into that shoe.

2

The Shoemender and the Elf

My sister Bernadette says that with the pot on my arm I did not toss and turn so much in bed last night. That's because shifting my position is too awkward. I slept by the wall as she gets up first, to go to her job making corsets.

Even pushing myself up out of bed with one arm wasn't easy. Bernadette wouldn't help me with my clothes. She just stood, fastening her skirt. 'If you're to be in plaster for six to eight weeks, you better get used to dressing with one hand.'

I managed to dress, very slowly, like some old lady. We have no banisters but I usually run down our steps. Today I trod carefully.

Mam said, 'You'd better rest. We'll see what you're fit for when you're over the shock. You might just turn the mangle for me today.'

Dad had already eaten his porridge. I could hear him working in the cellar. When Mam went in the scullery, I called that I'd be back in a minute. She would object to me going the length of the street to check on Leila. I left our house and went along to Heather's door. She was at the dolly tub, lifting out a sheet.

'Jess! Your arm! I thought it was nobbut a bruise.'

'It's fractured in two places.'

'You poor thing.'

Leila lay in her cot drawer on the table, looking up at a fly paper hanging from the gas-mantle in the centre of the ceiling. She looked well enough, but a baby wouldn't be able to let you know if she'd been so shaken up from police horse joltings that she would lose some vital function in her limbs or brain and fail to develop in a proper way. Then one day Heather would think, *She was all right till I let Jess take her to be christened.*

I was still in the house making sounds and linking fingers with Leila when Heather went out to hang her washing on the line.

'Isn't that your dad whistling?' she called to me.

I went to the door and listened. Lots of families have whistles, to call for each other, or for the dad to let everyone know at the end of the street that he is nearly home. Our whistle is a long note and a short.

'It'll be Mam wanting me.'

Heather called ta-ra to me as I hurried along the pavement, dodging Mrs Blumenthal with her basket of washing and half a dozen little Blumenthals, the biggest one solemnly holding a bag of clothes pegs.

Mam had sent Dad to the corner to whistle for me. She was in the cellar, not at Dad's shoemending end but her own mangle end.

'I know you can't frame much, but you can turn the mangle with your good hand,' she said in a peeved way.

Mam has a bad temper. The least thing I do sets her off. Dad says it is because she has one leg shorter than the other and a gammy foot. I do not see the connection between a short leg and a short temper. If it had not been for her short leg I might not have been born. Dad, when he worked for old Mr Poole's company, made her special boots, one built up, and that is how they met. She also has a hernia that must be set in place each morning.

I stood turning the mangle with my right hand while Mam fed washing through, folded it and put it in the basket. She liked to have her washing out early but I had set her back. 'I helped you with your shoes and stockings,' she said accusingly. 'Where did you bounce off to?' As if she didn't know.

Hanging out the washing was usually my job but all I could do was pass the pegs. Mam said then that I could do what I liked, so long as I didn't go out and about, putting myself in harm's way. And for heaven's sake to keep away from that Heather McBride and her infant. She had nothing against her for being a gypsy, but I had to understand that a godmother did not need to move in with the child's family.

9

It was awkward for me to pull my box from under the bed. This contains my exercise book of stories. Changing the pen nib and unscrewing the top off the ink bottle gave me trouble.

I am writing up all the fairy tales I know that feature footwear: red shoes, glass slippers, seven-league boots and so on. With Wilf's illustrations we will make a book. Mam says once we improve our lot in life and move to Premises, she will have the books printed and ready for sale around a Christmas time.

I told myself the story of the Shoemender and the Elf before starting to write it down. Mam says the story is the Shoe*maker* and the *Elves*, but I intended to write it as Dad told it to me when I was small.

When Dad came home from the war I was seven years of age. Our Bernadette did not have much to say to him. She did not want to be kissed. Straightaway I liked him, and not just because Mam told Bernadette that Dad had a big hurt and we must be kind to him. She told Bernadette, not me, because Bernadette and Mam talked a lot to each other. They left me to find things out by earwigging.

Dad burst in, carrying his army knapsack and a suitcase. I used to sit under the table sometimes, out of the way of Mam and Bernadette's busyness. From under the table I could only see their legs; Bernadette's thin and white, Mam's covered by her long skirt, not hiding her bony knees and one high boot. I was under the table when Dad came home from the war.

'How's my Jess?' Dad picked me up. He whirled me round and round till I was dizzy with whirling and the scent of his hair and scalp. I combed my fingers through his hair.

I watched him, to see where his war wound was. When he took off his vest and stood at the kitchen sink to wash, I saw that the hurt was a hole in his back. I could put my fist in it. The hole came about because of shrapnel. The surgeon gave Dad the piece of shrapnel, which sat on our mantelpiece next to the clock.

Mam wrote a notice on the back of a piece of card cut from a shoebox got from Uncle Bill and Auntie Irene's shoe factory. She set the card in our downstairs house window: '*High-Class Boot and Shoe Repairs*'.

Soon everyone knew Paul Price had come home.

'Take your shoes to the soldier,' people said.

We had the end house. The small window at ground level went

directly into the cellar where he worked in puttees, braces and army shirt and trousers. He wore a large apron so that he could keep a boot or shoe on his lap without it falling between his legs. Under his foot he slid a broad leather strap with an adjustable buckle, so that he could hold a shoe firmly on his knee. He sat on his buffet, a small bench in front of him, his tools laid out.

As people hurried to work early in the mornings – pressers and cutters, tailors and tailoresses, engineers and mechanics – they passed their boots and shoes through the cellar window to me as I stood on the table to reach, until Mam sent Bernadette to fetch me for school.

Every Saturday evening I helped him sweep and mop the floor, clear cobwebs, dust shelves, lift boots and shoes, and dust them, too. Monday mornings, before I went to school, I would check the cellar. It was always neat, clean and welcoming, with its smell of old boots, new leather, black-ink stain, russet-brown stain, heady wax and dizzying cow glue.

'We will never let anything go out that we would not wear ourselves,' Dad said as he took a stick of wax and put a drop of oil on it. He gave me the wax to work in my hand, like putty, into a ball. 'Don't ever let anyone say your father is a cobbler. A cobbler is a crude workman, with bits and pieces. Seven out of ten men will mend their family's boots and shoes with a bit of machine belting and a last. Here we repair shoes grandly, bringing them to glory.'

When the stick of wax became a ball, ready to make thread waterproof and strong, he pulled the thread through, two arms' lengths of it, 'Till it's a whisper.'

Mam did not like me to go in the cellar, because I am a girl. She said to Dad, 'You'll have to employ a helper some day, when we have Premises.' But I was his helper. I was not allowed to touch the small sharp knife that he used to trim round the edges of heels, but I polished the wooden lasts, I put lead in the bottom of the tin where we held the hemp, to keep the tin firm.

'Come up from that cellar!' Mam yelled. 'You'll catch your death.'

But I put on my coat and hat and said, 'I like it in the cellar.'

Dad made me a buffet, just like his but smaller. I sat beside him after school and watched him work by the light of the oil lamp and by candlelight. The gas that lit our house above did not come down to the cellar. I watched him set out the tools in a row on the bench. He lay the stabbing awl by the sewing awl. I knew the use of all the tools. He gripped with the pincers, tap-tapped with the hammer and, with his strong fingers, folded and lasted the uppers, stabbed, sawed and clicked.

Sometimes he collected boots and shoes for repair from high-class shops. I would go with him, sitting on the special seat he made for me on the back of his bicycle, with sides and a back to hold me in, and a buckled strap so I wouldn't slip. After a while, the work was delivered to him. Dad was given smart brogues and riding boots for mending, from a big store in town.

'Sniff that leather,' Dad said to me. 'Feel that stitching. These boots and shoes were made by Lobbs, Shoemaker to the Royal Household.'

One night we had finished working. Mam and Bernadette were on with their knitting. I sat on Dad's knee by the house fire and he told me a story of the Shoemender and the Elf.

'Did you see the elf?' I asked Dad. 'Did an elf help you?'

'I don't need elves,' Dad said. 'I have you; you are better than a hundred and one elves.'

Then he brought out a pair of shoes made of softest leather, polished to a high brown sheen. 'These are for you, Jess.'

Every day I walked to school looking at my feet. At school, I stared at my shoes, feeling so proud. Some children had no shoes. Others wore wellington boots or pumps, but I had fine brown leather, elf shoes that almost had a pointed toe, as if one day the toes might make a turn towards the sky and take me somewhere else. Always, after that, I liked stories about seven-league boots, Puss in Boots and magic slippers. I knew that my brown leather shoes would one day whisk me somewhere magical and far away.

Dad said, 'I hope I haven't given you itchy feet.'

'You're a big girl now, Jess,' Mam said. She held my arm as I went to open the cellar door and go down. 'You can help me put jam in the tarts.'

I could tell by her voice that this was meant to be a treat. Usually Bernadette would have the spooning of jam job. 'I don't want to,' I said.

She pulled her mean face and hit me on the legs with her long wooden spoon. 'It's time you helped me. You spend too much time in that cellar.'

When summer came and a shaft of light made the dust in the

cellar dance, Dad took a bag of pear drops from his pocket and winked at me. 'Your mam says you've to have fresh air today.'

'I'm stopping with you,' I said.

Dad went upstairs but I wouldn't follow. I heard them talking, Mam, Dad and Bernadette. Mam whispered. Bernadette said, 'Oh, all right, then, if I have to.'

Through the cellar window, I watched Bernadette mount her bike and ride off.

Dad came back downstairs. I set out the tools in a row on the bench, the stabbing awl by the sewing awl.

Dad said, 'This Sunday I'll take you on the back of my bike to Gargrave. We'll visit your Aunt Bella who keeps chickens. Soon you'll have a bike of your own.'

Bernadette came back. She looked through the cellar window and waved. Cousin Wilf was with her. He put his dark head through the open cellar window and called to me. 'Will you come to the Lido? It's a great day for a swim.'

Dad said, 'You go, little one.'

Upstairs, Mam pushed my swimsuit into the bone-handled leather patch bag, with an apple and a slice of bread. She whispered to me, 'Share Wilf's towel.'

I climbed on the back of Wilf's bike, holding the bone-handled bag. He knew the way to Roundhay Park, to the Lido, without getting lost once, even when we did not follow tramlines but went along sunny streets with trees and houses that had gardens and long paths leading to their doors.

Wilf knows a lot. I asked him, 'What's a hindrance?'

'Something that gets in the way,' he said.

All around the pool was crowded with children, big girls in charge of groups of smaller children. The stone steps where people sat about and shivered felt warm to my bare feet. *I'm not a hindrance*, I thought, as the sun made me want to stretch out like a cat. *Mam can say what she likes to Dad, I'm not a hindrance.*

'Race you to the pool,' Wilf said, and did not give me a chance or say one-two-three-go, he just ran.

The word *hindrance* tripped me up. I went flying, splat flat on the stone.

Wilf looked worried. 'Where does it hurt?'

'All over.'

13

He rubbed my leg. 'It'll turn to a bruise. Could be brown, or yellow and red.' He took my hand. 'Come on. The water will make you better.'

He slid in first. 'Come on – it's freezing! Don't say I didn't warn you!'

The water was so cold it was like biting on an ice cream. My jaw turned numb. Shrapnels of ice shot up behind my eyes and danced under my skull. I went under and came up again, to make the feeling pass. I floated, watching the sky, half shutting my eyes against the bright sun. I kicked my legs to move, and flapped my arms, wondering about the birds. I could hear them but not see one.

At first I wasn't able to keep in a straight line, swimming along on my back, making up movements as I went along. Wilf did not swim on his back. He splashed a lot, doing the crawl. Sometimes I had to turn over, to see where I was going. So I kept to the deep end, out of the way of other children, especially boys, splashing.

When I got out, Wilf had dried and dressed himself. The towel was wet all over, not a dry edge or corner.

'I invented a new stroke,' I told him, trying to get myself dry, shivering, my teeth chattering.

He held up the towel for me and turned his head while I dressed. When I had finished, he said, 'That new stroke you invented, it's called the Old English Backstroke.'

I grabbed the towel from him and flicked it at him, catching his legs, making him run for his life.

A big red-faced man with sticky-out eyebrows and a walrus moustache shouted at us to behave and said, 'Young uns today don't know they're born.'

When we got to the 'Way Out', I turned back and yelled, 'I do know I'm born, or I wouldn't be here!'

The look on that man's face – as if he would burst! Then we jumped on the bike and Wilf pedalled like fury till we were well away, up by the bandstand.

'You're too cheeky,' Wilf said. 'You could have got us barred.'

'He wasn't an attendant,' I said, 'just some rich kid's granddad.'

We each had a pear drop. Cousin Wilf went quiet. The funniest little things make him go quiet sometimes. He is a rich kid because his mam and dad – Uncle Bill and Auntie Irene – have a big business, but the shoes they supply are not first class, according to Mam.

At the drinking fountain, I put my mouth to the water.

When Wilf drank, I asked him, 'Did our Bernadette tell you to bring me here? So I would be out of Dad's way?'

He wiped the back of his hand across his mouth. 'Yes. But I would have come anyway. You're a better swimmer than any of the boys at school.'

It started to rain. From the bandstand we ran to the shelter that has seats, the wheels of his bike making marks across the grass. Some bigger boys were there already, and they looked at us and at Wilf's bike. Without speaking, we changed our minds about the shelter and wheeled our way back to the path, cycling uphill to where the trees grow and you would not know a stream ran by unless you went to look. Wilf leaned the bike against a tree. It had stopped raining. We skimmed stones into the stream, seeing who could make the most splashes.

'I'm adopted,' Wilf said, picking up another stone. 'Mam and Dad said they chose me. But it means they chose me because I wasn't wanted.' He skimmed the stone all the way across. 'I don't care.'

'What does it mean?' I asked.

He said that his true mother could not keep him, or did not want him, in Wilf's opinion. Nor did his true father. They gave him away, and he did not properly belong to anyone except himself.

I told him then how Mam would never let me stop in the cellar, yet she did not want me. She had Bernadette, and they always talked and left me out.

'Well, then,' Wilf said, 'it's not the same, but still, we have each other.'

That was when he took out his penknife, and he cut his thumb and I cut mine. We let our blood run together and swore a sacred vow that he would for ever be my blood brother and I would be his blood sister.

Then we each had another pear drop and exchanged pebbles.

Here is the story I wrote in my book on the day after Leila Catherine McBride's christening. It is called 'The Shoemender and the Elf':

A poor shoemender came back from the wars. He needed to mend boots and shoes so that he could buy food for himself and his wife and children, and to pay their rent. A fine lady brought a pair of excellent shoes to him. He had only scraps of leather left, and placed them this way and that on his bench, looking to see how best he could repair the lady's shoes. 'How can I mend fine shoes from such scraps?' he asked himself sadly, and with a big sigh went to bed.

The next morning, when he came down to his cellar, he rubbed his eyes and blinked. There on his workbench stood a pair of perfectly mended shoes, fit for a queen. He held them in his hand one by one. Such perfect tacking on of a sole. Such neat, decorative stitching. The shoes were even more splendid than before.

Moments after he set the mended shoes in his cellar window, a crowd drew near. Everyone in the town wanted him to mend their shoes.

With the money he got, he bought all he needed to do the best repairs in the town. Everyone respected his fine workmanship, so that even slaughterhouse men and building workers cleaned the filth off their boots before they brought them to him for mending. One day he had so many shoes to mend he despaired of getting through the work. He went to bed and dreamed of being smothered under a mountain of shoes. But when he got up the next morning, the work was done. The elf had called again.

The shoemender and his wife were kind-hearted. They wanted to know who had helped them, so that they could repay the kindness. One night, as the church clock struck midnight, they crept down the cellar steps and peeped round the door.

Sitting on the workbench was a tiny elf, wearing not a shred of clothing and no boots. The elf whistled and sang happily while mending shoes, then disappeared with a mighty flash and a bang when the work was done.

The next day, the shoemender made a tiny pair of boots of best leather. His wife made a set of elf clothes. They set them out on the workbench.

On the stroke of midnight, the shoemender and his wife tiptoed downstairs and peeped round the cellar door. How the elf smiled as she put on her new clothes and boots! How she laughed.

The elf did not come again, but the shoemender and his wife and family prospered and lived happily.

'Did you see the elf?' I asked Dad when he had first told me the story. 'Did an elf help you?'

'I don't need elves,' Dad said. 'I have you; you are better than a hundred and one elves.'

Then he brought out a pair of shoes made of softest leather, polished to a high brown sheen. 'These are for you, Jess.'

When I put on the shoes, I felt something hard underfoot.

'Take a look-see,' Dad said. 'Perhaps the fairies have left you a present.'

It was a sixpence.

'That's for good luck, and to say you have far to go in life.'

3

A Pair of Oxfords

Dad stood at the sink, washing his hands. Mam swears Father Flynn smells her baking. He came just as she took a pie from the oven. 'Get another plate, Jess.'

'No need at all.' Father Flynn stayed in the doorway, raising a hand in protest. In his other hand he held a brown paper carrier bag. 'I only came to see how Jess fared after her terrible ordeal outside the church, and to bring Father Baxter's shoes for mending.'

'Sit down, Father,' Dad said. He dried his hands and nodded to me to take the bag from Father Flynn.

The priest tut-tutted and shook his head when I told him about the facture. He held my left hand, made the sign of the cross over my plaster and blessed me for a speedy recovery.

I put out an extra knife and fork, and he sat down.

Dad has not been to church since he came back from the war. He said war cured him of religion. When he says such things Mam gets upset, closes her lips and sends me off to refill her bottles with holy water from the big jar in the church porch. When the priest blessed me, Dad said, 'Blessing or no blessing, it'll be an eight-week job to mend that arm, I daresay.'

Mam sat down last. 'Would you say grace, Father?' she asked in that over-polite voice she uses when the priest calls.

'For what we are about to receive, may the Lord make us truly thankful.'

We all amen-ed, including Dad, who passed the sauce to Father

Flynn, who passed it to Mam, who passed it back to him as she believes sauce is vulgar and unnecessary.

Father Flynn shook a goodly dollop of Daddy's Sauce onto the side of his pie. 'I'm relieved to see you looking so well in yourself today, Jess. You had me worried for a while there. Such a crying shame to round off your first day as godmother with an injured limb and a visit to the public dispensary.'

'Better than a visit to the public house,' Dad said cheerfully.

Mam glared, but Father Flynn smiled. He usually smiled at Dad's jokes. But his attention stayed on me. 'You won't be able to cycle round on Saturday nights collecting the altar money with me.'

'No, Father.' I found it awkward to eat with him sitting there in normal times, much less with only one hand of use to me.

Dad took my knife and fork and cut up my pie.

'Do you know,' Father Flynn said to Mam and Dad, 'Jess here is probably too modest to mention this, but she only had to be taken round once to know every house in the parish that contributes to the altar fund. The Saturday before last when I was administering the last rites to a poor soul, she did the whole round entirely on her own and came back with a collection that topped the lot.'

He was probably trying to cheer me up, but I felt embarrassed by his praise.

'I can't cycle round, but I could walk.'

'No, no. I wouldn't hear of it. I shall have to struggle on alone.'

I don't know what made me suggest Madge Hanrahan for the collecting. Only she is very devout, can borrow her brother's B.S.A. bike, newly painted red, and has not given up hope of being accepted into the Little Sisters of the Poor.

Mam frowned.

'I think that's a very good idea,' Dad said. 'Please do follow that up, Father Flynn. In fact, I've a pair of shoes for delivery to the Hanrahans, I'll mention it myself.'

Father Flynn looked as if he wished he hadn't spoken. Mam glared at Dad but said nothing. After the priest had gone, Mam said to me, 'You've done yourself no favours there. Madge Hanrahan will jump at the chance to make summat of herself in the parish.'

Well, then let her,' Dad said. He sat on the outside step having a smoke.

Sometimes his back hurts where the shrapnel lodged. He will

stretch his arms to the top of the door-frame which he says does a favour to his spine. When he had done that, he flicked his tab end into the fire. 'Come on, Jess. You can spit and polish some footwear.'

He picked up the brown paper bag containing Father Baxter's shoes.

Mam shot Dad a look. Ever since she stopped me going in the cellar as a child she has been keen to keep me out of there, as if working with Dad would somehow make me unfit, or unwilling, to help her.

But for once she did not object, perhaps realizing I would not be much use to her.

All the brushes have their names painted on: brown applicator, black applicator, brown polisher, black polisher. Holding a pair of boots steady with the fingers that emerged from the pot on my arm, I held the polisher brush with my right.

Dad tapped a heel onto a shoe, taking tack after tack from his mouth. He trimmed at the heel.

I said, 'You know why Father Flynn didn't hand over his own shoes to mend?'

'No.'

'He thinks they're past mending. And he only has that one pair. He'd have to do his rounds in stockinged feet.'

Dad whistled while he worked. After a while he said, 'We'll do something about it, then. It ought to please your mam as she likes to make priests happy, and I reckon he's a good man. He seems genuinely concerned about you.'

'What will we do?'

'You and I will go up to our Bill's factory this afternoon and buy Father Flynn a new pair of shoes. When he comes to collect his superior's shoes, we'll present him with a pair of his own.'

'We don't know his size.'

Dad tapped his temple. 'It's all in here. Never forget a customer's shoe size.'

'Don't tell your mam I let you get on the back of the bike,' Dad said. 'And hold on with that one arm for your life or *my* life'll be worth nothing.'

Dad cycled steadily and slowly along the cobbles. Balanced on the hard, narrow seat, I held on, circling his waist with my good arm.

The bumps jolted me a little but with my arm so well encased in plaster it was no more painful on the bike than off.

We reached East Street. The hum of the Wright Shoe Company created a music all its own: cutting, humming, stitching, tap-tap hammering, and above it all the voices, light, laughing, indistinct. In the yard two men loaded boxes onto a cart.

The ground floor of the factory is given over to shoes, divided into sections for the different shoe-making tasks. The floor above is devoted to boots. To reach the offices, you climb a staircase to the wrought-iron enclosed balcony that runs the length and breadth of three of the ground-floor walls.

Uncle Bill is two years younger than Dad, and a little stouter, even though he plays golf as well as cycling out on Sundays. Dad says his extra flesh is due to his businessmen's suppers, events that would not suit Dad at all. Bill sat at his desk, which faces the partition separating his office from that of his typist-book-keeper. In this position he does not stare out at his workforce on the ground floor but only needs to turn his head to see their activity.

Bill was pleased to see us. He and Dad say I look like their side of the family. The aunt who died and the cousin who went to Canada were such blondes as me – a strain of natural blondes whose hair never did go dark. Bill insisted on making us cups of tea in mugs stained dark brown on the inside, tea-streaked on the outside. It tasted like shoe leather, and with that everlasting milk that comes in bottles with serrated metal tops. He sympathized about my accident and said of Wilf, 'He tells me nothing these days, but he told his mother that Jess fractured her arm.'

He and Dad took different sides over the miners' strike. Sometimes I wondered why they bothered to discuss any topics as each knew where the other would stand.

'Blooming miners. Want to get back to work. Cutting off gas, cutting off electric. I can't operate my machinery as I want. Don't know what we'll do if this strike drags on. Hope you and Dolly have got a good store of candles, Paul.'

'We'll manage,' Dad said. 'Pit owners should settle. The miners have to live, just like you or I.'

I stood looking down onto the shop floor. Heather McBride used to work there. She had told me how she started – putting laces in shoes and shoes in boxes. She was so quick, eager to learn and dextrous that in no time at all she had become a skiver, a most skilful job, trimming the edge of the shoes.

Bill told Paul he wouldn't hear of him paying for a pair of shoes for a man of the cloth. We must go to the reject room and pick a pair that only the closest inspection would reveal as less than perfect, and I must find a pair for myself and for Bernadette, too.

We walked through the shop floor, surrounded by the scent of new leather, glue, blacking and the sharp metal tang of boxes of nails, to the room where imperfect shoes stood row upon row.

Dad chose a pair of black Oxfords for Father Flynn. I waited until he went to talk to one of his old workmates from Poole's before choosing shoes for myself and Bernadette. He seems to think we should wear flat shoes with laces, like kids or old ladies. 'Better for your feet,' he says.

I chose T-straps with a tiny heel, peep-toes for Bernadette, and found a bag for them.

As I climbed the stairs back onto the balcony, I could hear Bill still arguing, but with a different sound, as if he and Dad were really falling out. But it wasn't Dad. It was Wilf. Bill and Wilf were having a fierce row. I stayed on the balcony.

Bill said, 'You can put it out of your mind entirely. I'm not shelling out so you can become unemployable.'

'Why do you think I've been to art college? Why do you think I've completed three years' work in two years? Not to sit here and count shoes.'

'Counting shoes, as you put it, paid for your expensive education and your art school, too. I would have had more gratitude if we'd let you struggle at the Ragged School.'

'I see. I get it. I'm supposed to be grateful because you adopted me.'

'I'm not asking for grateful. I'm asking you to see sense.'

'There's nothing else I want to do in my life. To be a sculptor, I have to go to the Royal College of Art. Do you know how many hundreds of people will be envying me my place?'

They had seen me standing on the balcony just outside the office. There was nothing for it but to open the door and go in. I wondered whether I might be doing Wilf a favour if I changed the subject and showed Uncle Bill my choice of footwear. But there was no pause in the argument.

Bill said, 'Well then, let one of the envious multitude have your place, because your mother and me we're coughing up no more fees. Yer what? The cost of London for how long? Three years? *Three years*? You can wipe that idea from your mind.'

I should have kept out of it. But I didn't. 'Uncle, you know from when he was small he was always going to be an artist. He has the talent. It's in him to do it. It's a gift. It'd be a sin not to use his talent.'

'Then he mun draw and paint on Sundays like the civilized folk his mother and me have brought him up to mix with.' Bill picked up a long box containing jockey's boots. 'Just get across to York with these Wilf. I haven't time to be arguing with you.'

'I know I said I would—' Wilf started to say.

'Yes, you did, so on your way.'

'I have an essay to finish.'

'An essay? An essay? Since when did essays pay for a loaf of bread? Burn the midnight oil over your essay like the rest of us have had to do over hard work.'

'All right, all right, I'll deliver the boots.' Wilf grabbed the box as if he intended to wrestle it to the floor.

'You're damn right you will, pardon my language, Jess. And if you've any sense, as soon as that college breaks up, you'll be in here, earning your crust. I'd been earning my living—'

'Four years when you were my age,' Wilf finished.

'Get outta my sight before I really lose my temper,' Bill said.

When Wilf had gone, Bill took the bag of shoes from me, glanced at them and said, 'Good choice, Jess. You'll look grand. Now, do me a favour and go after that lad. Calm him down before he jumps on that so-and-soing motorbike and storms off. I'll have to answer to Irene if he ends up in a ditch and cracks his thick skull.'

Outside Wilf was sliding the box of riding boots into the pannier.

'Are you upset?' I asked him. 'Because he won't let you go to art college in London?'

'No one will stop me. If I've to live under a bridge and beg, borrow or steal to buy pencils I'll do it.' He fastened his black leather helmet and climbed on the bike. 'If they adopted me thinking they'd have a successor for the firm, they picked the wrong orphan.'

'Wilf! It's not like that.'

He revved the engine. 'You're the only one who understands me, Jess.'

The motorbike snorted and a plume of smoke burst from the exhaust.

'Thanks for speaking up for me,' he called as he disappeared out of the yard.

Early the next morning, I stood by the cellar window to take shoes from people hurrying to work, or to hand over a mended pair and take payment. Father Flynn must have decided to make us his first call. Mam sent him down the cellar steps. She knew about the surprise shoes.

Dad showed him Father Baxter's beautifully mended shoes before putting them back into a brown paper carrier bag. Then he said, 'And here are yours, Father.'

'But I didn't bring any.'

'Then the fairies must have left them, eh, Jess?'

Father Flynn sat on Dad's buffet. He unlaced his shoes and took them off, his right sock neatly darned at the toe and heel.

'Ahhh, bliss!' He slipped his feet into the new Oxfords.

Dad picked up the old pair. 'We'll have these as good as new by the end of the week.'

He passed them to me and I set them on the shelf for mending.

'Thank you.' Father Flynn gazed at his feet.

I looked away because I thought I saw a tear in his eye. He bent to fasten his shoes, then strolled about the cellar. 'These'll put a spring in my step.'

Dad said, 'The shoes were Jess's idea.'

'It was your idea, Dad,' I said.

Father Flynn laid a hand on my shoulder. 'Ah now, Jess, it's a sin to tell a lie, even if it is out of modesty.' He stroked my hair. 'Bless you, my child. You, too, Mr Price. God bless you all.'

4

Grand Designs

Wilf had known Jess would be coming to the church that afternoon and hoped to see her. Once the papish ceremony ended, perhaps she'd sit for him, on the stone steps, holding the infant – a Madonna and child.

He stood in the dim light of the church, sketch book resting on his hand, pencil capturing the outline of the Virgin Mary. The first time he had sketched this figure, she had been cloaked in purple for Lent. This, his cousins told him, was to make the congregration more sharply aware of the object concealed and so give it a more powerful reality. That idea appealed to Wilf. It fitted with the way he liked to seek the essence of a thing through its sweep, not in its detail. The figure's shape under the purple shroud had held a more ominous and mysterious quality than the uncovered figure on its stone plinth. Once it must have been part of an altar's rood-screen. In her original context the figure would have turned her head to look up at her crucified son. Other figures would have shared the space with her, but now she stood alone, in an alcove, with only a bank of votive candles – some flickering, others unlit – in brass holders in front of her. She looked up not at a crucifix but past the alcove's stone walls at a vaulted ceiling. As he sketched, he decided to bring in the nearest stone pillar, two pillars, creating the perspective he had intended to avoid. At least the shadow would not comply to the 45-degree requirement. Not enough candles flickered for that. Following narrow rules of technical proficiency irked him sometimes; architectural drawing, drawing from life, perspective, drawing from memory, shading at an angle of 45 degrees; it turned what he loved into something mechanical and dreary.

Only when the priest walked up the side aisle and began to speak by the door, not in a low church voice but lively and conversational, did Wilf become aware of Jess. Unmistakeably Jess. Suddenly he felt awkward, an intruder. As he watched from behind a pillar, the figures took on a significance outside themselves – the priest in his vestments, Jess holding the infant. They stood on either side of a tall font, forming a perfect balance of shapes, imbued with an emotion Wilf could feel and draw, but not name or experience from the inside as they did. For Wilf, art was his religion. Churches were fine places to draw. Only that morning he had cycled to Adel and drawn grotesque gargoyles, devils and saints. They spoke to him of the skill of generations of craftsmen, sculptors from the Middle Ages, long dead, but still crying, *Look at me. See what I achieved!*

He watched his cousin with an artist's eye. He also looked at her as a young man looks at a young woman. She puzzled him sometimes. How could a person as smart as Uncle Paul let his daughters be indoctrinated with papish superstitions when Paul himself never went near a church? Perhaps he thought it would keep them out of trouble. Wilf wondered what Jess would have become if not such a good, obedient Catholic girl, browbeaten through pity of her crippled mother into following her every wish. She could have swum the channel, become an athlete, certainly at the very least a teacher. He could imagine a class of children held in her spell, jumping and leaping to her calls in a school yard. Here he was, with the world opening up to him, and she seemed caught like a fly in a web. He pushed these thoughts from his mind so that he could view the scene only as an artist, seeing primitive shapes, like some ritual where the relationship between the parts had to be exactly so.

Rapidly, Wilf's pencil sketched the lines onto the page. He flicked to a new sheet as the shape changed. The man held the baby. The woman leaned forward, speaking, the murmur of her responses echoing through the church. The priest and Jess walked together down the aisle and disappeared into the vestry. Wilf realized she would be surprised to see him there. Perhaps annoyed that he had concealed himself. He tucked his pencil into his top pocket and closed the sketch book. He could finish the statue from memory later. He pulled out a hanky to wipe a smudge from the front of his book. As he did so, a coin rolled along the floor and out of sight. Damn! His shilling. He thought it had come to rest near the second pew. As he scrabbled about looking for it, she emerged from the vestry door. When he heard her footsteps, he stayed crouched in the pew, feeling ridiculous. He had left it too late to show himself. Where she came to worship, he came to draw. Her footsteps paused for a moment and then she went towards the statue. A coin dropped in the box. He watched her light one candle after another. One, two, three, four, five, six. Still she lit candles. All the other candles were burnt almost to stubs. Hers flamed tall and bright. Now he could definitely not let himself be seen. But that was silly. He would go after her, catch her up and walk her home. His body would not let him. He watched her tread lightly towards the side door. The priest hurried after and detained her, prattling on, keeping step until she reached the door and left the church.

He turned back. She had lit so many candles that the shadow thrown by the statue onto the wall had shifted. Was it 45 degrees? A little shiver went through him. He opened his sketch book. He would meet the requirements. He would draw the statue and its shadow at 45 degrees, and the bright candles.

Sounds broke his concentration. The door swinging open, a kind of gasp, the priest's footsteps, voices. Jess.

He closed his book and followed the sounds to the back of the church. There she sat, the priest standing over her. Wilf couldn't see the baby, only hear its cries.

As he reached the pew, he saw the infant lying on the seat, Jess's right hand keeping it safe. Her other arm dangled at an odd angle. The idiot priest hadn't even noticed. A great surge of feelings he could not define rushed through Wilf as he edged hurriedly towards her, seeing she needed first aid, for once glad of his enforced membership of the Boy Scouts.

As he made a sling for Jess with his art college scarf, Wilf knew that leaving her behind would be the greatest loss. His pal. The one who knew him best.

At one o'clock in the morning, Wilf was still working at the desk in his room. Jess's injury had upset and disturbed him, slowed him down. He wrote his essay by candlelight, wanting to keep that certain feeling candlelight brought. He had chosen to discuss the work of Michelangelo, yet a scream rose inside him at having to produce words. The language of sculpture was form, material – and magic. The meaning and drama of sculpture came from the quality of the wood or the stone, or even from the purple cloth that covered a statue in Lent.

When he had finished the rough draft of his essay, he put his work together, ready for the class in the morning. His mouth felt dry. He poured himself a glass of water from the jug. What if all these forced technical requirements, these dry demands of aged tutors, led him away from his aim and his love? What if it killed the thing inside him that had led him to want to be an artist?

'You don't get it from me,' his dad had said, 'and certainly not from your mother.' Well, obviously not! Wilf sometimes wondered how they could say these things, as if pretending he was not adopted.

A tap on his door disturbed his thoughts. 'Wilf?'

Bill wore blue striped pyjamas under his plaid dressing gown, and slippers in a woollen check. He carried a candle in a brass holder. 'You burning the midnight oil again, son?'

'I've finished now, Dad.'

Bill nodded. 'Get yourself to bed or you'll be fit for nothing in the morning. Remember, an hour's sleep before midnight is worth two after.'

Wilf unbuttoned his shirt. For a moment, he thought Bill would go over the old arguments. Why did he have to rush through the art course? No one was chasing him to finish.

'Henry Moore did it in two years,' Wilf would say. 'And so did Barbara Hepworth.'

'Who're Henry and Barbara when they're at home?' Bill had asked.

Wilf did not say that the sooner he finished his course, the sooner he would go to London where he would come into his own, leave the strait-jacket of Leeds College of Art behind and become the artist he knew himself destined to be.

'There'll be no money in art. You'll have a good life in the firm. Be as artistic as you please. Design shoes.'

Wilf didn't answer. He would break the news tomorrow, that he had a place at the Royal College of Art.

Bill sighed. 'Paul and me cycled out on us own today. Bernadette was out with her young man, and Jess at a christening.'

Wilf sat on his bed. He felt tired now. He wanted Bill to go away and let him be.

'We cycled by the spot where Jess took a tumble the other week, when you pulled over and she ran into the back of you. What was it you were going to show us that day?'

'Just an unusual tree,' Wilf said.

A drop of hot candlewax trickled onto Bill's finger. He turned away, knowing that was all the answer he would get. 'Goodnight, Wilf.'

'Goodnight, Dad.'

Wilf threw his trousers over the back of the chair and draped his shirt across them. As he climbed into bed, he could not decide whether to be sorry or glad that they had none of them seen his carving in the tree that day. Sorry because he had meant it to be his way of saying, *I shall miss these Sundays, when we searched for beauty in the hills and dales of Yorkshire. I shall remember these days all my life long.* Glad because in the end, when he went back and looked again, the figure in the tree was not as good as he wanted it to be. It had taken him by surprise to see who emerged from his chiselling and carving. Though imperfect and rough, it was unmistakeably Jess. He had gone back a week later with a mixture of fish glue and chalk and given her a finishing coat because he could not bear to think of her buffeted by wind and rain.

As he drifted into sleep, a pang of hurt seeped through him. Someday soon he would leave this place he had called home, soar into his new life, and he would leave Jess behind. That would be the hard part. He fell into a dream where he changed the afternoon's events; in the hush of the church, he spoke Jess's name. She turned and smiled at him, and a glory of candles formed a halo behind her.

The next morning at the breakfast table, Wilf slid the letter from the Royal College of Art to Irene. Sometimes he wondered what Irene had been like when she first adopted him as a baby. She looked slim and lovely in the wedding photograph on the sideboard. In later life she had developed a small hump on her back, which must always have been there, waiting to become more pronounced. Her neck came from her shoulders, thick as a small tree trunk. He knew she had some medical condition she would never name. It did not keep her from all her charitable works. A fond memory was when he was off school with some childhood illness and had sat for hours on her lap, being nursed and hummed and sung to.

Irene smiled. 'Well done, Wilf. You've worked hard for this.'

'Worked hard for what?' Bill looked up from his paper.

'I've been offered a place at the Royal College of Art in London.'

'Well, I hope you'll tell them you already have a place at the Wright Shoe Company, a place that'll pay your way in life.'

'No, Dad. I'm going to be a sculptor.'

5

St Crispin Comes Up Trumps

Old Mr Hardy served in the war and is shell-shocked. Only Dad knows how to hold his head still, wash and cut his hair, and lather and shave his big jowly face.

When he is awake, and not afraid and cowering in a corner, Mr Hardy won't let his daughter, Gladys, open the door. He shouted, 'Friend or foe?'

Dad called, 'Friend, Mr Hardy.'

I muttered, 'Foe.'

The old soldier opened the door fiercely, as if he expected the person knocking to be there for some foul reason: robbery, murder or selling Irish sweepstake tickets. He cannot control his movements but stood in the doorway with a long brass poker in his shaky hand. The poker is in case the person who said 'friend' turns out to be an imposter with murderous intentions. Sometimes Mr Hardy holds a gun by its barrel, to smack you with the handle end. Dad says it's a starting pistol. If it's a starting pistol, I think it's the pistol that started the war. It looks mean enough.

Inside, Mr Hardy returned the poker to its stand. 'Heavy,' he said. he had held it in his right hand, but he rubbed his left arm.

'Perhaps you should stick to the gun, Dad,' Gladys Hardy said.

She made me smile, till I realized she meant it. Now that I am used to him, it is not so horrible being with Mr Hardy as when I was small and afraid of him.

Mr Hardy's wiry, tufty hair grows fast, as if it knows the inside of his head is demented and it can't wait to escape. His bright blue eyes, like a doll's eyes, have a glazed, puzzled stare that sometimes turns normal when he looks at Dad.

He glared at me, then at his daughter. 'What's she to you, Gladys?' he asked sharply. 'Another mouth to feed?'

She has the same blue eyes in a face that's worn and tired. When her father spoke, she looked down as if she could hardly bear to answer.

Dad said, 'Jessica's my lass, Cedric, You know that, old chap.'

I handed Miss Hardy her mended boots. She admired them, as she always does. Dad put a towel round Mr Hardy's neck and tucked it in his shirt. He stood at the kitchen sink and leaned forward while Dad wet his hair with warm water from the jug. For a few moments, Miss Hardy and I sat at the table, not speaking but feeling relieved because the mad eyes had shut for a moment, to keep the soap out.

Miss Hardy sympathized about my broken arm. She is the one person who encourages me to do things and not stay at home, helping Mam. She says that even though I can't sew – and that is a great disadvantage in a city full of clothiers – I could turn it to my advantage and perhaps find an office job. She said going to commercial college in the evenings would set me up for life and I must be sure to consider learning typewriting once my arm is better. She relies entirely on pen and says it would be a boon to be able to write her reports for the local children's holiday charity on a typewriter. I asked her if she had been to college.

'Yes, but not commercial college.' She took a quick look at Mr Hardy. 'I was a teacher once, a long time ago. And you must call me Gladys now. You've known me long enough.'

I like to listen to how she does her work for the Leeds Poor Children's Holiday Camp – Auntie Irene's main charity. Gladys goes from house to house taking details of the families whose children go on holiday to Silverdale every summer. Hundreds of children have gone there over the years.

Dad rinsed the soap from Mr Hardy's hair and for a while the old man sat still, letting Dad dry his ears and rub his head with the towel. Dad combed and fingered Mr Hardy's hair, snip-snipping with his barber scissors. The hair fell onto the newspaper.

'Gladys! Get the soldiers down from the mantelpiece for Paul's lass,' Mr Hardy barked.

She stood up to reach for the little wooden soldiers. Mr Hardy had whittled the figures when he and Dad were in the war together. When I was small, I used to march them up and down the hearth rug or the table while Dad gave Mr Hardy his shave and haircut. Six of the soldiers belong to the West Yorkshire Regiment. Then there is one each of a Canadian soldier, an Australian, Indian and South African, and also one German and one Austrian, all with their different hats and uniforms. Miss Hardy set the soldiers out on the table in rows. I helped her. It seemed to calm Mr Hardy to see us place the soldiers in lines.

Mam would like a house like the Hardys', with no bikes cluttering the doorway and everything just so. I told Miss Hardy that and she smiled.

Dad picked up the newspaper of hair clippings, made a funnel shape and poured the hair into the coal scuttle.

'Look, Dad, your hair's made a wig for the coal,' Gladys said. She was always trying to say some little thing to amuse or divert him. He ignored her.

Dad placed the towel under Mr Hardy's chin, ready to lather him for a shave. But Mr Hardy waved Dad away and asked for the soldiers. One by one I passed him the West Yorkshire Regiment soldiers. He handed them back to me, saying each one's name: Harold Pickles, James Deverell, Ebenezer Briggs, Clifford Watson, Horace Baker, Ernest Varley.

Dad waited patiently. While we waited, Gladys poured us tea. I had to give Mr Hardy all the soldiers and then he would pass them back. He shook his head at the German and Austrian as if he did not really know their names. 'It could be Wilhelm or Hermann. I'm not sure.'

When I passed him the Commonwealth soldiers he looked at Dad. 'Name them, Paul. You name them. You knew them.'

Dad took the soldiers one by one. The names did not seem to me to fit. He called the African Lawrence, the Indian Lou, the Australian Fred, the Canadian Bert. By then I was re-arranging the West Yorkshire Regiment on the mantelpiece. But of course I had put them in the wrong place and Mr Hardy began to re-order them in his shaky fashion.

He does not join in with tea drinking. This is because he cannot keep still and does not want us to see that he sits at the table sipping from a straw. I dunked a Rich Tea biscuit. Dad says you should only dunk a biscuit once. On a second dunking it is in danger of collapsing to the bottom of the cup, which does not make a good impression in company.

Gladys undid a piece of tape around a sheaf of documents that sat at the back of the table near the wall. She took a sheet of paper from the top and smoothed it with her long, thin fingers. 'Mr Price, my committee has authorized me to buy one hundred pairs of serviceable clogs for the holiday camp children – sizes one to thirteen. Would you be willing to undertake the work for us?'

'I don't usually make clogs these days,' Dad said.

'But you can!' I said. I know he worked for a clog firm as an apprentice, before he worked at Poole's, and then at the Wright Shoe Company, which had belonged to Auntie Irene's father.

He looked uncertain. 'It's a different kind of work to what I do now. And I'm not sure I'd get hold of the right machinery.'

'Dad!' I kicked him under the table. Reading Miss Hardy's sheet of paper upside down, I could see that it had a price per pair. I had no idea whether that was a good price or a bad, but it was money. I kicked him again.

'Yes, thank you,' he said to Gladys. 'I'll do it. Thanks for thinking of me.'

Gladys smiled. 'Good. I'm glad it's going to be you.'

'I'll help,' I said. 'How soon would you like them, Gladys?'

She wanted them as soon as possible. Mam would have made a good business woman, as we all know, because she tells us. I tried to think of what she would say in this situation. 'Is that your budget, Gladys?' I asked, seeing that it said 'Budget for Clogs' on the top of the paper.

She slid the sheet to Dad across the spotless linoleum on the table.

Dad glanced at it. 'We're in business,' he said.

They shook hands.

Dad looked at me with a smile in his eyes. 'Wait till your mam—'

But he didn't finish because Mr Hardy had sat himself down and tucked the towel under his chin. His big old face had the look of a little boy, waiting for someone to pay him attention.

Dad poured some water from the kettle into the jug, dipped in his

34

brush and ran it across the soap stick. Very gently he made circular motions on Mr Hardy's cheeks and chin, turning him into Father Christmas. With one hand, Dad held the crown of Mr Hardy's head to keep it steady. With the other he scraped the cut-throat razor across the jowly cheek. Miraculously, Mr Hardy's head stayed still. Dad stretched the skin taut and scraped down to the chin. You never knew what would set Mr Hardy off and so I stopped watching and concentrated on the pattern of the table cover. Gladys had reached for pen and ink and was writing out an order to Mr Paul Price for one hundred pairs of clogs in assorted sizes.

So neither of us saw it happen. I heard the groan and Dad's intake of breath and, 'I've got you, old chap. I'm here.'

Mr Hardy had gone very still. His hands no longer twitched, his arms did not fling out, his legs did not kick. Dad took hold of his wrist. Gladys did not move. She sat with her mouth open. Dad felt at the base of Mr Hardy's throat, where the towel was tucked into his collar. Suddenly Gladys stood up and went to her dad. She put her hand on his heart. With one cheek and his chin still covered with soap, it seemed to me unbelievable that he was dead.

Dad looked at Gladys and shook his head. He put an arm around her shoulders. She is tall and thin and in that moment, with Dad's arm around her, she looked to be made of wires. She holds herself very straight and seemed like some mechanical thing that had stopped.

Dad sat her down in the rocking chair. He patted her hand. He looked at me as if I should do something. I spooned some sugar into her tea, topped it up from the teapot and passed it to her.

'Don't leave him like that,' she said, 'with bubbles on his face. He looks ridiculous.'

Dad shaved Mr Hardy. He held his hand on top of the dead man's head and I watched, half expecting movement – the wave of a hand, his leg to tremble. After he had finished the shave, Dad sent me to fetch the doctor and old Mrs Claughton, who does the laying out for that street.

She grumbled about the time and how tired she was, but came with her bag. When we got back, Dad had carried Mr Hardy upstairs to his bed. The old woman went up there, taking a basin and hot water. Gladys followed her. They were gone a long time, but Dad said we must not leave.

Later, when Mrs Claughton had left and the doctor come and gone, Dad said, 'Jess will stay with you tonight, Gladys. Won't you, Jess?'

That left me no choice. But Gladys shook her head. 'It's all right, Mr Price. I'm not afraid of my own father. Not any more.' She reached for my hand. 'But will you come up with me?'

I followed her to the stone steps that led to the bedroom. It was dark by then and she carried a candle.

She set the candle on the dresser by the window. I could scarcely see Mr Hardy. Just a shape lying there, his hands meeting on top of the cover.

Gladys fumbled with the locket at her throat. She asked me to bring the candle near. A drop of wax slid down from the flame. I would have to hold it steady. It would be a disgrace and an outrage to drop burning wax on a corpse. He would probably leap up and pull a poker from under the pillow.

In the locket were some strands of hair, wound into a sort of plait, fine and dark in the candlelight. When Gladys took her father's hand, I saw that she had made a ring of the hair. She slid it on his finger.

'Is it your mother's hair?' I asked.

'His grandchild's. My baby's hair.'

I said a stupid thing: 'I didn't know you were married.'

'I wasn't. That was the trouble.'

She leaned over her father. I couldn't see her face. She touched his forehead with her lips. I wondered whether I was expected to do something. She stepped back to leave me near him. I touched his smooth old cheek with my fingers.

Dad went upstairs to pay his respects, leaving me downstairs with Gladys in a thick silence, only the clock ticking.

I did not know what to say, or whether to say nothing. Mam says a rule of conversation is that if someone introduces a topic you must Take It Up. 'What age would your baby be now?' I asked.

'He'll be seventeen, on the sixth of June.'

She reached for a shawl from the hook behind the door. I wished I had thought to hand it to her.

When Dad came down, he said, 'One of us will gladly stay.'

She shook her head and stood up to see us out. 'I'm best alone tonight. Really.'

When we got home, Mam said, 'Where on earth have you been till this time?'

Dad said, 'Don't.'

I said, 'Mr Hardy died.'

'What happened?' she asked. 'How did he die?'

Dad said, 'He died of the war.'

I said, 'Dad, how could he have died of the war? The war ended years ago.'

Dad said, 'It's not just me and thee that cast shadows. All sorts of events cast longer shadows than thine and mine.'

'Gladys Hardy's given Dad an order for one hundred pairs of bairns' clogs,' I said.

Mam crossed herself. 'Eternal rest grant unto Mr Hardy. And thank you, St Crispin, for heeding my poor prayers.'

And neither of them knew that Gladys Hardy has a son who will be seventeen on 6 June, exactly the same age as Wilf.

Why had she told me her secret?

But so many boys must have been born on that day. The Hardys weren't from Leeds originally, so perhaps he was born somewhere else. I couldn't sleep for thinking about it. When we were children, Wilf had once told me how he imagined his mother and father, and how one day he would meet them. His mother would be beautiful, but poor. His father would be rich. He would lose his legitimate child, and see that Wilf was all he ever wanted. Wilf would then come into his inheritance.

It seemed to me that Gladys Hardy did not fit the bill of a mysterious, beautiful mother. I hoped I was wrong. Then Wilf could hold onto his dreams.

The next day, Mam baked, with me helping in my one-handed way. She sent me along to take a pie and a couple of teacakes to Gladys.

I had to ask, as we sat at her table, just the two of us. 'Gladys. Your son. Was it my cousin Wilf?'

She nodded. I didn't know whether to be sorry or glad when the Unitarian minister knocked on the door and we could not talk any more.

I had said I would walk up to town and meet Wilf in his college dinner hour. But how could I tell him such a thing? And how could I not? The best thing would be to stay out of his way until I could think what to do for the best.

Instead I went to see Heather and Leila, and took Leila for a walk in the pram I got her from Mrs Hanrahan.

When we got back, Heather said, 'My little one has no aunties or grannies or even cousins. I'm glad she has you, Jess.'

6

Tram Conductor Wilf

Wilf went along with them, just for the lark. Two of his fellow college students had been taken on by the tram company, to drive and conduct the Roundhay tram. Someone had to break the strike and put the country on its feet.

'I always wanted to be in charge of a ticket machine.' Wilf borrowed the cap, too, and set it at a jaunty angle. He hung the money satchel and ticket machine round his neck, and walked along the gangway calling, 'Tickets, please!'

The tram trundled along North Street on Saturday morning, sparks flashing from the overhead wires.

When he had issued tickets, he stood on the platform, holding the bar with one hand. Three other students stood with him, wearing their grey flannels and blazers. One of them raised his straw boater to a girl on a bike, calling, 'Do your patriotic duty, miss! Leave your bike at home. Take the tram and break the strike!'

'Shut up pestering her!' Wilf said.

It was Jess, cycling with one hand. She turned off towards Poole's, probably on an errand.

A group of workmen standing on the corner of York Road jeered at Wilf and his friends. One called, 'Miserable strikebreakers! So yer'll be down't pit next, will yer?'

Wilf felt uneasy when the men ran after the tram, calling names. 'Put your foot down!' he called to the driver.

Too late.

The men jumped on the tram. One landed a punch on Wilf,

knocking his cap off. They moved on through the tram, heading for the driver. Wilf removed the ticket machine and set it on the floor. The tram continued for a few more yards, onto Briggate, then screeched to a shuddering halt.

Passengers began to get off, quickly. Wilf helped an old lady who was carrying a heavy bag. There was something about the men on strike – a wiry hardness, boiling over anger.

The driver had been pushed out onto the road. Wilf ran to help him while his fellow students fled. Wilf freed the driver but took a punch to his jaw and a blow to his solar plexus. He wished he'd taken up boxing when he had the chance. Suddenly Wilf's attacker yelled in pain. Wilf saw a flash of the ticket machine being wielded like a whip against the man's legs.

'Wilf! My bike!'

It was Jess. Her bike leaned against a shop window. Before the angry striker had a chance to recover from his surprise at being hit by an angelic blonde with a pot on her arm, Wilf had mounted the bike and Jess was behind him.

'Faster! Let's get out of here.'

He pedalled like billy-o, all the way back to North Street. Only when he calmed down and his breathing went back to normal did he realize that he still had the money satchel around his neck.

'Idiot!' Jess called. 'It wasn't your fight.'

'You're the idiot. You shouldn't be riding your bike with a broken arm.'

He slowed down at the top of Benson Street, leaned the bike against the wall of the Eagle and stopped to get his breath. 'Where were you last week, Jess? I waited for you two dinner times and you never came.'

'I couldn't, that's all.'

'You've fallen out with me, haven't you? And you're not telling me why.'

'If I'd fallen out with you, I wouldn't have come rushing to help you just now.'

'How did you know to come?'

'A customer in Poole's said he'd seen a couple of striking miners jumping on the tram.'

'Thanks for riding to my rescue.'

'Well, you took me to the dispensary, now we're even.'

That made him certain. Something was wrong. She wouldn't look at him. Somehow, he would find a way to keep her with him for a while longer, then it would come out, and they could be friends again.

'What am I supposed to do with this, do you reckon?' He put both hands under the money satchel, testing its weight. 'It's full of fares. I suppose it ought to go back to the tram company.'

'I don't see why. They don't need it.'

'What, then? I'm not off back to hand it to the chap who tried to murder me.'

'Put it round my neck. I'll take it to Father Flynn for the St Vincent de Paul Society. They do a lot of charitable work.'

'Not likely. Not to a priest. I wouldn't trust any of them.'

'Wilf! That's a terrible thing to say.'

'Even if he did pass it to a charity, they'd only give it to good practising Catholics.' Wilf felt pleased. The argument kept her beside him. 'I'd prefer to give it to some miner, so long as he didn't try to bop me on the chin.'

'Come on, then. Let's give it to a miner.'

'Who?'

'My goddaughter's father.'

'I thought he worked in a fruit shop.'

'He's friendly with the chap next door who is a miner.'

Leila lay in the drawer on the hearth rug, watched over by a whippet and the tortoiseshell cat. The whippet wagged its tail.

'I didn't know you had a dog, Heather,' Jess said.

'It won't bark yet because it's not sure this is its home. Tommy came by him from a feller that left Leeds to seek work elsewhere. He's valuable, that whippet.'

'What's his name?' Wilf wished he had brought his sketch book.

'Dempsey.'

'Seems a fierce, fighting name for a timid young lad of a dog.' Wilf put the conductor's satchel on the table. 'We brought this donation for you or Tommy to give to the striking miners. In a roundabout way, it's from the tram company.'

'Thank you very much,' Heather said. 'Tommy will see it gets into the right hands.'

Wilf remembered why he liked Heather. Unlike the other women at the Wright Shoe Company, she had never called him Young Mr

41

Price, in that slightly mocking way Bill Price's workers had of making Wilf feel an intruder, an irrelevance.

Heather stacked the money on the table. 'Will you take this satchel with you? Coppers might be after it, and they'd come here, but not to you.'

Wilf wasn't so sure of that. He thought coppers might be more likely to question him. He'd have to say it had been stolen.

He took the satchel, not knowing what to do with it. His jaw hurt all of a sudden and he felt a little sick.

He wheeled the bike along Benson Street, Jess walking beside him. As they neared Jess's end of the street, Wilf saw Dolly standing at the door looking out. He slowed the bike and gently leaned it against the window sill.

Jess said, 'Hello, Mam,' in the same moment that Wilf said, 'Hello, Auntie Dolly.'

'Don't you hello me, either of you. I might have known who you'd be with.' Dolly stepped aside for Jess to go in.

'Wilf wasn't with me. We just happened—' Jess spoke from inside the house.

'Don't you interrupt while I'm talking. Inside, Wilf.'

The cellar window stood open. Wilf was conscious of Paul, still working in the cellar, listening. Wilf followed his aunt's orders and went into the house. He had fancied a cup of tea. The fancy left him. He turned on the tap and ran water into a cup, taking a drink and passing it to Jess.

'What malarkey have you been up to today? Don't you know she shouldn't be on a bike with a broken arm? Don't they teach you anything at that college?'

'I went out on the bike to try it out,' Jess said. 'I'm used to riding single-handed. Ask Dad.'

'Single-handed when you've a spare hand to bring into play. Not when one arm's in a sling. You were only off to Poole's. You should have been there and back in under half an hour even if there were a queue. You dad was waiting for that wax.'

Jess brought the wax from her pocket and moved towards the cellar.

'Leave it!' Dolly ordered. 'It's too late now. He's packing up and tidying for the weekend. And you're off to confession. Now!'

'Mam!'

'Don't Mam me. Here.' Dolly passed a navy beret to Jess. 'And don't leave any of your transgressions out, either.'

Jess took the hat and left the house, without looking at Wilf. He moved to follow her. Dolly grabbed his arm.

'You stay here till she's well on her way. Then I want to see you going in the direction of home. I was sad when I heard you were going to London, after all Irene and Bill have done for you. He's an ungrateful child, I thought, and he's missing a great opportunity to make a good life for himself. But you're trouble. And I'm glad you're going. The sooner the better.'

Wilf wanted to speak, say something, object. No words came. He felt his mouth turn down, his strength fall away, like a small boy being told off, even though he towered over Dolly. He turned and left. Something made him look down to the cellar window. Paul was looking up at him. For a moment, Wilf thought Paul would speak. But Paul looked away.

Wilf felt he was burning. His solar plexus hurt from the punch; his jaw, too. But that wasn't what hurt him most. He felt such a longing to know who his father really was. Someone with spirit, Wilf felt sure of that. Not a man like Bill who only counted his takings and measured profit and loss. Not a man like Paul, a weakling who let his wife rule the roost and didn't have the gumption to be more than a miserable shoemender.

Yet Dolly and Paul had the power to keep him from Jess. And Bill had the power to keep him in penury.

Well, damn them all. None of them would get in Wilf's way. He'd show them.

7

Keeping House for the Clergy

Mam has a walking stick but would rather lean heavily on a person's arm. We made an odd pair on the day of my dispensary appointment to have the pot removed from my arm. Me with my sling, she linking my good arm to aid her progress.

Something was in the air. She and Dad had talked about it when they thought I wasn't listening. It concerned my future. I hoped the order for clogs meant a good enough improvement in the family fortunes so that something would change for me. 'She's been less use with her arm in a sling. I've had to manage,' I'd heard Mam say to Dad.

Mam broke the news as we sat in the dispensary waiting room. 'I've spoken to Father Flynn. They're in a bit of a pickle at the priests' house since the housekeeper took sick. I've told him you'll go along there and help out.'

For a minute I just stared at my arm. 'Why?' was all I could say. I must have said it loudly. She shushed me and whispered, 'It'll be good for you. Good experience. And not hard work. There's a cook and a maid.'

'Well, can't they do it, then?'

A man with an eye-patch sat down next to her.

She spoke in a hushed voice. 'Not now. I'll tell you about it later.'

That was a bit rich. She was the one who chose to tell me in the public dispensary.

Without the plaster, my poor, itchy white arm looked unfamiliar, like someone else's limb. I felt light and free walking back along North Street. Mam stopped and bought me an orange. 'That's for being a brave girl.'

As I sat at the kitchen table peeling my orange, she took her leather patchwork bag from its hook behind the door. 'You'll need a few items to take with you.'

'Today? I'm going today?'

'No time like the present. Listen to me, Jess. We have to do something. You're a good girl but too easily led, too impulsive. And you're accident prone because you don't pay enough attention. In a place like the priests' house, you'll have to pay attention. This'll calm you down. It'll be a nice steady job for a short time.'

'What doing? How will I know what to do?'

She hesitated. 'Well, answering the door to people who want a mass said, making cocoa, that kind of thing. Go get your nightie, underwear and a clean blouse.'

I walked slowly upstairs. There is not space for a chest of drawers in the room I share with Bernadette, the little room above the outside passage. I pulled my box from under the bed and took out what I would need. I couldn't believe she'd volunteered me. Housekeepers for the clergy are old – priests' unmarried nieces, ancient ladies with no one else to take them in. A dozen biddies from church would be only too glad to step in for Miss Molloy.

She slid my nightie and underwear into the leather bag. 'Where's your toothbrush?'

I could see it was no use objecting. I slapped my toothbrush, hairbrush, comb, soap and flannel on the table.

She took the soap back. 'They'll have plenty of soap.'

'I won't know what to do.'

'You'll find out. Learn to mix with the right people. You've spent too much time with Wilf and them McBrides. You'll broaden your outlook.'

'How long will I be there?' I asked.

She wrapped my toothbrush in a clean white handkerchief. 'Until Miss Molloy gets better.'

'That could be for ever.'

'Nothing's for ever.' She clicked the handles of the bag shut. 'We must say yes to everything, Jess. One day we'll say yes to something that turns our fortunes around. This is temporary.'

Dad came up from the cellar, not smiling, not looking at Mam or me. He went to the sink to wash his hands.

I said, 'Dad—'

He did not turn round but said softly, 'Do as your mam says and you won't go far wrong.'

I rang the doorbell at the priests' house. When no one answered, I rattled the knocker. After a moment I tapped again, and tried the door. Locked. I walked through the alley and yard to the back of the house and looked through a half-window into the cellar kitchen. A face the colour of unbaked pastry looked up at me. When she stepped back, I saw a roly-poly woman in black dress and white pinny, her grey hair pulled back in a bun, a white cap perched on top. She turned and hobbled out of the kitchen, not giving me any sign, though I knew she had clocked me. I listened for footsteps but heard none. After a long while, the back door opened. She glared at me. 'Did thah just ring't front doorbell and rattle't knob?'

'Yes. I'm Jessica Price, here to stand in as priests' housekeeper while Miss Molloy's badly.'

'Then thah'd best come in.'

The kitchen smelled of baking. A row of pies stood along the dresser. A bluebottle danced around them. The cook eyed it. 'Pass me a newspaper.'

I handed her one from the pile folded by the side of the range. It had a headline about the sorry state of miners' children. She folded the paper, and waited for the bluebottle to land on the dresser. Missed it. She swatted the bluebottle on her second attempt, as it landed on the distempered wall. Tearing off a corner of the newspaper, she scraped it up and tossed it onto the fireback saying, 'Depart from me, ye everlasting bluebottle, into the eternal flames.'

She washed her hands under the tap at the big flat sink by the window.

'What am I to do?' I asked.

For a moment she didn't answer. I supposed she was thinking out some long explanation of my duties. She looked for a clean spot on the roller towel, then began to dry her hands slowly. 'What are any of us to do? We're born, we suffer and we die, hoping for the Resurrection into eternal life.'

'I mean about the housekeeping.'

'You could change this slop-rag of a roller towel for a start. It's been getting muckier since King Dick were a lad.'

'Where's Miss Molloy?' I asked, thinking the poorly housekeeper might groan instructions to me from her sick bed.

'Gone to convalesce. All right for some.' The cook eyed my patchwork bag. 'Ah, now I know who you are. Prices. The cobbler's daughter.'

'He's not a cobbler,' I explained. 'Cobblers bodge. Dad's a high-class shoe repairer.'

'And the other branch of your family owns a shoe factory. They're the well-off ones, only they're not Catholic,' she went on, as if I hadn't spoken. 'They're some peculiar thing, what is it they are?' She took off her pinafore and hung it on a hook behind the kitchen door.

'My Auntie Irene's Unitarian.'

I hoped she would have the sense to stop, and not say what I could see in her face – that Uncle Bill turned his back on his religion to get his hands on the shoe factory.

'Thah best follow me and I'll show thee. Priests are all out on parish business.'

I followed her along a dark hallway and up twelve stairs dimly lit by a stained-glass window on the landing. A second set of twelve stairs led to the attics.

'I don't know why they picked a kid for't job,' she said.

'I'm fifteen.'

'Oh well,' she puffed, out of breath, 'that makes all't difference in't world.'

She pushed open the attic door, telling me that was where I would sleep. It smelt of sickness and some other smell I couldn't place. I opened the curtains. The sash window had been painted shut and wouldn't budge. The room had not been cleaned. She watched me as I stared in disbelief at the room, and for the first time I saw a look like sympathy or friendliness cross her stony face. 'Room shoulda been cleaned,' she said. 'This is what happens when you've no housekeeper. Stuff doesn't get done.'

'Am I supposed to clean it?' I asked.

'Happen you are if you want it clean and they leave you time to do it between now and bedtime. Cleaner waint be in till tomorrow now.'

'I'll want clean sheets,' I said.

'I'll show you,' She turned to go. 'And you'd best pick up that piss pot. My hands aren't steady for that kind of thing.'

A chamber pot under the bed brimmed with blood-red pee. I felt sick. She handed me a small grubby striped towel that lay across the bottom of the iron bedstead. Before I put it over the chamber pot, holding the handle on one side and the rim on the other, I gave her my bag to carry. I didn't want to leave it in that dirty room. When she took it without a word, I thought perhaps I could get on with her.

As we went back downstairs, she kicked a basket-weave box on the first landing. 'You'll find fresh sheets in there.'

She opened the back door and pointed out the privy. Onto my little finger she slid the key on a piece of string weighted with an empty bobbin reel. I had difficulty placing the pot on the ground without spilling any, so that I could unlock the privy door. I pushed it open with my foot and emptied the pot into the midden.

When I came back, she was buttoning her coat. 'Don't rinse that thing in my sink. There's a sink in't cellar for muck.'

'You're going?' I asked.

For answer, she pulled a black felt hat down on top of her bun.

'When will you be back?'

'Tomorrow's soon enough for me, lass. Pies for their supper and porridge ready to cook for breakfast. Send it up on that there dumb waiter, see?' She demonstrated the contraption.

'What if someone knocks on the door?'

'Open it and ask what they want.'

She left by the front door. I locked it after her and hung the key on the hook.

As I was halfway down the cellar steps to rinse the chamber pot, the doorbell rang. A ragged little boy, about seven years old and with arms like clothes pegs, stood on the second step without speaking.

'The priests are out,' I said when he remained silent after my hello. He stepped back. 'What is it you want?' I asked gently.

'You're to put us down for summat.'

'What?'

'Yerve to writ it down.'

48

I left him sitting on the step and found a pencil and pad on the hall table. He told me his name, Thomas Riley, but started to cry when I asked his address and what else I had to write. The tears streaked down his dirty face.

'I don't know me address now we've flitted. Me mam didn't tell me.'

I asked him inside and took him into the kitchen, not wanting some passerby to report the priests' housekeeper for making a child cry. At the kitchen table, with half a cup of mik and a bit of bread, he calmed down.

'Do you go to St Charles's?' I asked.

He did and could tell me his class and teacher. I wrote it down. 'We'll find your address from school.'

When he had drunk the milk, he remembered what he had to say. I was to put the family down for a visit from the St Vincent de Paul Society. I had to make sure SVP knew that there wasn't a crust in the Riley house.

I said, 'Tell your mam you'll get a visit.'

He wasn't looking at me. His eyes seemed fixed on the pies on the dresser. The cook hadn't said anything, but even I knew that three priests didn't need four pies. I wouldn't be doing my job if I left them sitting there.

'How many in your family?' I asked.

'I'm oldest. There's six kids and me mam and dad.'

I slid a pie off its plate and wrapped it in a tea-cloth. 'You take this home,' I said. 'Bring the cloth back tomorrow.'

His eyes widened. 'Everyone'll know it's a pie. Someone'll tek it off me.' He looked at the folded potato sack by the pantry door. 'Put it in that sack, miss. Then no one'll guess.'

By four o'clock there was just one pie left on the window sill, and a list of requests for prayers, visits and the like on the hall stand. I thought I had done very well because there would be a pie for the priests' tea that evening, and the cook would be back tomorrow.

The bell rang again. A woman with hair parted in the middle, and plastered down so well it looked like a wig, stood back from the bottom step. A couple of paces behind her, holding a bowler hat to his chest, stood a balding chap with a moustache like Charlie Chaplin's. He held a walking stick at a jaunty angle.

'Is Father Baxter in?' the woman asked.

'All the priests are out. Can I take a message?'

She turned to the man, waiting for him to speak next.

'You'll not know about us, the Treasures, hmm-hummmm?' the man said. He leaned towards me as he brought his words to a humming close.

I stared blankly. I could not answer at first. They waited, a sad look crossing her face, as if I must be a little slow. But I have never before met a person with that particular speech habit or impediment, where at the end of a sentence comes a short hum which takes off into a long hum, as though the words expressed something so important they needed musical accompaniment.

I shook my head.

'Mr hummmmhhm Treasure, Richard Treasure, and his er-er humm hmmmm cousin, Miss Treasure.'

'Mr Treasure and Miss Wynifred Treasure,' the woman repeated, smiling and showing one front tooth shorter than the other, but both very good teeth.

In the pause, a whispered conversation took place between them. The man spoke again. 'Did any of the priests mention word coming from the Holy Father, giving a er-hummm-hummmmmm, certain special type of, er, dispensation? Humm, huuuuummm.'

'Or not,' the woman added. When he glared at her she said quietly, 'We must be prepared for the worst, Rich.'

'You're the one who wanted to come hummm-hummm specially,' he whispered.

'I don't know anything about that,' I said, trying to sound both helpful and not as stupid as they thought me to be. 'I only started today.'

'A powerful feeling seeped through me early this morning, that today might be the day,' she said. 'Would there be any item of post in today's delivery that has the smack of a papal edict in its appearance?'

They each had a way of holding their heads to one side, she to the right, he to the left. I thought from the way they spoke they must be very well educated.

'My cousin means, is there a letter from the Vatican in Rome hummm, hummm, hummm?' the man explained.

'I'll go and see. Excuse me.'

I turned my back as she was saying to him, 'Rich, dear, there is no Vatican anywhere other than Rome.'

I looked through the small pile of letters on the hallstand. Feeling sure that such a letter would not bear the King's head or an Irish harp, I went back to them and said, 'None of the letters has a Vatican stamp.' I was pleased with this answer as it seemed better than a plain no. I think they were impressed.

Miss Treasure's face filled with disappointment. Mr Rich Treasure took her arm.

'Thank you for your time, young humm-humm lady, humm.'

'Good day to you, miss,' she called back to me. 'No doubt we'll see you again. We call on a regular basis. Time is running out for us.'

I was about to shut the door when Mr Treasure cleared his throat urgently and asked my name. 'Just a moment,' he said when I had told him. Before I could refuse, he slipped a coin into my hand. 'We're here for the seven o'clock mass every morning, praying for news. If you hear any hummm-hummm-hummmm thing . . .'

I could feel without opening my palm that it was half a crown. If they went to mass every day, why not put it in a box themselves? But before I got a chance to ask him, he said in a confidential voice, 'That's for you to put towards your own special intention hum.'

Father Flynn arrived first. I felt relieved to see him and not Father Baxter, who is extremely old and has a stern manner, or Father Walmsley, who never looks directly at you but always glances sideways as if there is something faulty about you and he is not sure what. But I recognized the tuneful whistling of 'The Last Rose of Summer'. Everyone says Father Flynn could win a prize for his whistling. I went into the hall. He was looking through the messages on the hallstand. I waited. He looked across at me as though he had never seen me before, then smiled broadly.

'You look different in your pinafore, Jess.'

'I'm here to stand in for Miss Molloy, Father.'

'Of course you are,' he said, nodding his head. Even when not whistling, his lips formed a whistling shape as if he were just about to begin again. 'How's your arm now?'

'Better, thank you, Father. I had the plaster off this morning.'

I handed him the list of names and details of requests for prayers for the sick, dying and dead, a mass, a set of marriage banns and three charity cases to be visited by the St Vincent de Paul Society.

I hoped Mam had not given the impression I was looking for a job and wanted this one. I opened my mouth to speak again. He waited. 'Any news of Miss Molloy, Father?' I asked, adding all in a rush, 'Because the minute she's well she'll be wanting to come back. I'm only here till then.'

'Then you will be here till eternity, my child.' He crossed himself. 'May she rest in peace.'

'But I thought . . . she's convalescing . . . ?'

He shook his head. 'Convalescence for Miss Molloy was not part of Our Lord's plan.'

The hall seemed to get darker. I crossed myself and felt a sense of panic. What if I would be there for ever?

'Don't upset yourself, Jess,' he said. 'She had the last rites three times from two different priests, one of them sure to be a future bishop. Go across to the church now. Say a *de profundis* for her.' He reached for a little black mantilla from the coat peg. 'She kept this here for just such an emergency, in case she had to make a dash for the church. Put that on your head and go.'

It was the kind of lace that feels crocheted from steel wool. I took it between my finger and thumb. He opened the door for me saying, 'We'll eat at six o'clock. The priests are on their way back now.'

Since it was quarter to by the grandfather clock in the hall, I knew it would have to be a quick *de profundis*. All the way through the prayer I thought Miss Molloy was the one who had the lucky escape. I was the one in purgatory, tormented by callers who were starving, bereaved and half mad. No wonder Miss Molloy took ill. No wonder the priests went out the whole day long.

While the priests dished out their own cold potatoes and sliced tomato, I cut into the pie. Apple squidged out from the first slice. Old Father Baxter smiled, which he has done excessively since he got a new set of teeth. 'You've brought the wrong pie, child. We'll have a slice of meat and potato pie first.'

'I'm sorry, Father. That's the only pie there is.'

A lot of discussion took place between them, but only Father Baxter addressed me. I explained about the number of pies cook had left, about the callers and their hunger. The priests decided they would eat tomato and potatoes, followed by apple pie and cheese. I had to explain that there was no cheese. I did not say why. They did not ask.

I can't remember which of them gave me my chance to escape by asking me to fetch a jug of milk for the tea. I gave a little curtsy and left the room. Inside, Father Baxter was murmuring grace.

I stood outside the dining-room door. Should I go back in straight away and say that there was no milk? I had given it away. Half a cup to the little boy, half a cup to the woman who fainted on the doorstep and a drop in the cups of tea for each of the tramps who called for a drink and a bit of bread and dripping. I didn't know how to go in and explain. Perhaps I should pretend to look, then say the milk had gone off. Or just appear very surprised and say, 'Sorry, no milk.' Or tell the truth. I had not properly shut the door. At least they weren't talking about me and the unsatisfactory supper. Father Flynn had kindly changed the subject. He was talking about a family he had visited where the father was a sleepwalker. Father Flynn is very knowledgeable about almost everything. A sermon of his once brought in the fact that in the Eastern Orthodox Church people cross themselves with their left hand. That surprised the congregation. I stood for a moment, listening to what he had to say because Bernadette had sleepwalked, but I did not remember seeing her do it because I was too young at the time.

I decided to do nothing about the milk. Left to themselves without it, they would probably offer up the sacrifice of black tea to gain indulgences for poor Miss Molloy's soul and shorten her time in purgatory.

The gas-mantle in the attic room had shattered. I lit a candle. Even by candlelight I saw that the sheets were sweat-stained and marked with blood. I ripped them off the bed. The mattress was stained, too, and damp.

I folded one of the blankets and lay it across the mattress, then reached for a clean sheet I had taken from the linen chest. It was a table-cloth. I had fetched two table-cloths, one pillow case and a tea-cloth. That decided me. I grabbed my bag, shoved my toothbrush in and went downstairs as quietly as the creaking stairs would allow. I let myself out the kitchen door, locking it behind me, then unfastened my bike from the railing and pedalled home.

The house was in darkness. I put my hand through the letter-box, pulled out the key and wheeled my bike into the house.

Bernadette gave out such a yell I'm surprised she didn't wake Mam and Dad. 'You scared me half to death, our Jess.'

I snuggled into our own bed.

She moved over reluctantly. 'What are you doing back here?'

'I'm going to sleep before I go mad.' I grabbed the clean sheet and held it close, never wanting to let it go.

She was wide awake then and wanted an account of everything that had happened.

'You can't just come home,' she said, snatching at the sheet. 'If you're a housekeeper you sleep in the house. That's what a housekeeper does.'

We tussled a bit over the sheet till it came out even. 'I'm not a housekeeper. Now that Miss Molloy's dead, they'll have to find someone else. I'll give them their porridge in the morning and that's it.'

'What about the five shillings?'

'What five shillings?'

'Didn't Mam tell you? We'll be getting five bob a week and your keep. She's banking on that. As long as you're there, you won't be eating her out of house and home.'

I told Bernadette about the window that wouldn't open, the stench of the room and the state of the mattress.

'All mattresses have stains,' she said, yawning and turning on her side.

'I know. It's different if it's your own family's stains.'

'Give it another try. I won't tell Mam you came back. Go back in the morning, before anyone wakes up. Think yourself lucky. At least you don't have to fit up old women for corsets.'

I banged my head five times on the pillow, to tell myself to wake at five o'clock.

I let myself in quietly, but already someone stirred in the priests' house.

'Jess?' Father Flynn called me from the dining room.

'Yes, it's me, Father.'

'Come in here a moment.' He sat at the table, his missal in front of him. 'Sit down.'

'Where have you been at this time?'

It suddenly crossed my mind that Mam had told him I was wild and impulsive. She'd probably asked him to keep an eye on me. At the thought I felt myself turn red and uncomfortable from my head to my toes.

'I went home, Father.'

'Why?'

I couldn't anwer.

'Are we so terrible here?'

'No, Father.'

'Did anyone upset you?'

I shook my head.

'Speak, child.'

'No, Father, no one upset me.'

'What, then? Take your time.'

'It's that room . . .'

He stood. 'Show me.'

I walked up the stairs slowly, feeling embarrassed about the room, its smeared windows, cobwebbed ceiling, its sick old-woman smell.

I believe he was two steps behind me. I did not feel comfortable with him so close and wished I had let him go ahead of me. As we reached the first landing, I stopped and turned to say, 'You won't want to see it, Father.'

He had not expected me to stop, and bumped against me then drew back. 'Just show me the room.' I opened the door and stepped aside for him. He strode across to the window, raised the blind and looked round. He walked to the bed. 'It's not so terrible. But then young women are more sensitive to these matters. I'll have it seen to, Jess. The cleaner must come and speak to me the moment she arrives. She will do nothing else until this room is fit for a girl from a good home.'

'Thank you, Father.'

He left the room. I stood there feeling foolish.

I went back to the kitchen, lit the fire, boiled the kettle and, although none of the priests had got up, took Father Flynn his tea and porridge. He smiled. 'Now you'll be spoiling me.'

8

Sleepwalking

Now I know why priests' nieces become housekeepers. They do not feel so ill at ease around the men in black as I do. It was different going out and about with Father Flynn to collect the altar money, both of us on our bikes. Perhaps it is something about this house I do not like, or that does not like me. I cannot be myself here. I tried to explain to Dad on Sunday. He said, 'Tell your mam.' I did. Mam said, 'You aren't there to "be yourself". You're there to make yourself useful, just for a short time. Can't you even do that?' So I tried to make the best of it. If it were not for Father Flynn being so kind, I would go mad.

When Mam said it was 'temporary', I hoped she meant a few days, or a week. I took a dictionary from the bookcase in the priests' dining room while they were out. Temporary means lasting, or meant to last, only for a time. That 'meant to' made me feel very uneasy.

The breakfast porridge creaked up to the dining room in the dumb waiter. While the priests ate, I picked up the letters from the mat in the hall. One envelope felt heavier that the rest – a cream bond written in a flowing, foreign-looking script. A Vatican stamp sat crookedly on the corner. Could this be the envelope Mr Treasure had given me half a crown to look out for? I set the envelopes on the hall stand.

Mr and Miss Treasure had left the church after the seven o'clock mass and were walking slowly down the street, sharing an umbrella. I did not like to call out so ran to catch up. I tapped him on the arm, 'Mr Treasure. Miss Treasure. An envelope came this morning.'

Their faces looked anxious and hopeful at the same time. 'Shall we . . . er hummm-hummm?' he said to her.

She adjusted her hat pin and looked at me.

As I spoke it came to me that I shouldn't really be telling people about what post had arrived. I said, 'It's a bit early to call. The priests are having breakfast. Half-past nine would be a good time, before they go out.'

Mr Treasure must have read my thoughts. He tapped his big snitch with his forefinger. 'Mum's the word! Mmmmmum.'

Miss Treasure nudged him but before he had chance to put his hand in his pocket and give me a coin, I turned and ran back to the house. I did not want them to think I was after their money.

Because I gave away too many pies during my first day, the cook had reluctantly taken to answering the door, so long as I agreed to peel spuds and veg and do the marketing, which she loathed and I loved. After a few days she said that the word had probably gone round, and people must have got it into their thick skulls: they couldn't just come and ring the bell for a slice of pie and a cup of milk. It seems Miss Molloy's practice was to stand in the doorway and make a note of requests. She did not ask people in and feed them. Tramps would come to the back door and get a cup of tea and a slice of bread and dripping, but only once in the season. Real tramps moved on.

On my first morning of being allowed to answer the door again, when the cook was up to her elbows in flour, I stood face to face with a thin, agitated woman with drawn-in lips and sad eyes. She held a baby in her arms. 'I need a priest to come to the house. Dad's near his end. I want him to have the last rites.'

I wrote down her name and address. 'Father Flynn's in church. Shall I find him for you?'

She nodded. 'If you will, love. I have to get back to Dad.'

An old woman knelt in a rear pew, beating her breast. No sign of Father Flynn. Hearing a noise from the sacristy, I tapped on the door. Before I had a chance to speak, he beckoned me to come in. He stood with a chalice in his hand, sniffing at its contents. I explained the request and gave him the address.

'Ah, old David Ryan. I know him well. You're doing a grand job, Jess.'

'Thank you, Father. I wish . . .'

'What do you wish?'

Having spoken without thinking, I now felt too embarrassed to say.

'Go on. Speak, Jess.'

'I only feel happy to talk to you, Father Flynn. The other priests make me a little nervous. I feel out of place.'

'Sure you've nothing to fear. You can always come to me. Now, sniff that altar wine. Wouldn't you say it's turned sour?'

I hesitated.

He looked at the wine and then at me. 'It's all right. It's not Our Lord's blood yet.' He held it under my nose. 'Take a whiff. What would you say?'

I tried not to breathe in. 'I can't tell, Father. I have no experience of wine.'

'Of course you haven't, child.' He sniffed the wine again, took a sip and spat it back into the chalice. 'As I thought.'

'His daughter says Mr Ryan's fading fast.'

'I expect he is.' Father Flynn picked up his stole. 'He wouldn't be seeking Extreme Unction otherwise.'

He returned the wine to the cupboard and locked it. Under the tap, he rinsed the chalice and placed it in another cupboard. From there he took the little silver pyx in which he would carry the host.

'Will that be all, Father?' I asked.

He locked the cupboard. 'You see, Jess, some of these chaps know they should have died a dozen years or more ago, in the Great War. They've had the extra time. I'd say most are glad when the day comes. Now, go say a prayer for the old fellow, for a good and speedy death.'

I remembered old Mr Hardy's speedy death as I prayed; then the secret Gladys Hardy had confided in me. I still needed to find a way of telling Wilf that his mother was not some mysterious beauty, or a wayward countess wearing a hood in a wood.

On leaving the church, I made my way to the market to shop for the cook. People were hurrying through town, going about their business, some on their way to work in offices. Cart and van drivers delivered to shops, heaving boxes across the pavement. A baker's lad carried a tray of teacakes with the warm oven smell still on them. I envied people who had proper jobs in shops and offices. Even our Bernadette's work of making corsets seemed to me a fine thing to do, with no pestering from needy souls and no having to watch how you spoke, trying to play the part of a creeping old creature, polite and respectful all the while. If it were not for Father Flynn, the place would have driven me to distraction.

It might have been more bearable if I could have escaped to a decent room, shut the door, and felt safe and sound. Although the cleaner had done her best, nothing would improve Miss Molloy's stifling attic. That night, using a hammer and fish-knife, I chipped away at the paint that kept the window tight shut. When I gave it a good shove, it still would not budge, though I cracked the pane. I wanted to cry with fury at that damned window. An attic in summer is unbearable, with heat sizzling through the roof and turning it into an oven. I thought of Father Flynn. If I asked him, he might get someone to make the window open, or even do it himself.

I had made the bed in a thorough way, turning the clean sheet back over the eiderdown so that nothing that had touched dead Miss Molloy would touch me.

The iron bedstead creaked as I climbed into bed. I could hear a scuttling in the eaves. Once I woke, sure something had run across my face, but I could see nothing so perhaps it was a dream.

Even with clean sheets, Miss Molloy's bed felt like Miss Molloy's bed. I lay on my back, and realized I'd slid into the hollow in the mattress where she must have lain. I turned on my right side, but that meant looking at the wall. I turned on my left side, but could not feel comfortable, because of worrying about my heart. Mam said you should never sleep on your left side, always on your right side so as not to put weight and a strain on your heart. I turned and turned and turned. I thought I might sleep better sitting up. I missed hearing Dad snore. I missed hearing Mam get up in the night. I missed Bernadette beside me, telling me her plans for when she and Michael Mooney married. Finally, I fell asleep.

I woke with the room still dark, one of those sudden wakenings when you do not know whether you have slept for five minutes or eight hours. I lay on my right side, with my back to the room and my face to the wall. My body felt anchored to the dip in the centre of the bed.

Before I opened my eyes, I knew I was not alone. I lay still, hardly breathing. I half believed in ghosts. You hear so many stories. Part of me waited, and dreaded, to see the ghost of Miss Molloy.

Laying very still did not make my fear go away. If it were a ghost, it was breathing like a man who smoked. I felt a heaviness somewhere near my feet. Would a ghost weigh heavy on the bed? After a long time, I opened my eyes. In the dim light I saw a white shape out of the corner of my eye.

I forced myself to look. Not Miss Molloy. A man, in a nightshirt.

I blinked. Looked again. In the age since I woke, the room had grown a little lighter. No mistaking. Father Flynn. He sat as still as a church statue.

Something made sense now. On my first night there he had talked to the other priests about a sleepwalker. That was because he was a sleepwalker himself − or perhaps had been at some time, and now again.

I lay wondering what to do. If one of the other priests had sleepwalked, I would have had no hesitation but to knock on Father Flynn's door. But I couldn't see myself knocking on one of the other doors. I'd be too tongue-tied.

I could have left him there, gone downstairs quietly and hoped the cook would come in good time, but what if he walked back, still in his sleep, tripped down the stairs and broke his neck?

I had only one choice. When Bernadette sleepwalked, Dad had taken her arm gently, turned her round and took her back to bed. If you woke a sleepwalker, it could be dangerous. There would be a lot of explaining to do if I made some sudden movement and gave him a heart attack.

I slid softly from the bed. Taking his arm, I whispered gently, 'Come on Father. I'll guide you back.'

When he didn't move, I stood in front of him, took both his arms and drew him towards me. He stood. Once again I took his arm. This time I led him onto the landing. On the wide staircase, I put his left hand on the banisters. Holding his right arm, I guided him down the stairs and along the landing. The door to his room stood open. I led him in and to the bed, turned him round, saying, 'Sit on your own bed, Father.'

He sat down, and then something in him changed. He blinked, shook his head and looked at me. I let go of his arm.

'Jess? What are you doing? Is something wrong?'

'No ... I ... you were ... sleepwalking.'

He looked puzzled. It had come out wrong. I felt sure from the look on his face he thought I was sleepwalking. He looked alarmed.

'Go back to your room!'

I turned and hurried back upstairs, feeling ridiculous, mortified.

The cook arrived as usual at nine, grumbling about another warm day. She hung her coat and hat on the hook behind the door and slipped her pinny over her head. 'What's up, Jess?'

I just shrugged and said, 'What's up? Umbrellas when it's raining, parasols when it shines.'

By eleven o'clock I had answered the door three times – for a mass to be said and for charity visits from St Vincent de Paul.

'Don't let it upset you,' the cook said as she kneaded the dough. 'The poor are always with us.'

I tried to remember what Mam had said about Bernadette's sleepwalking, which was after Dad came back from the war. It happened twice.

Maybe Father Flynn did not even know he sleepwalked. But what if he did it all the time? What if he always sleepwalked in my direction? How could you tell someone that a priest walked into your room at night? You just couldn't. Mam would say I dreamed it, had too much imagination. Bernadette would agree with Mam, of course. People might begin to think me mad. I could be put away. 'Oh, she was all right till she got to fifteen. Then she went crackers. Imagined the most disgusting things.'

The kitchen clock struck noon. I wet my hands and smoothed down my hair.

'I'm going for some fresh air,' I told the cook.

I ran to Cookridge Street, to the art college. Although it was the summer holidays, Wilf had enrolled for an extra life-drawing class. If I hurried I might catch him coming out. I just needed to talk to someone, to stop the thoughts going round and round my head.

Some students were already walking towards the Headrow in twos and threes, chatting and laughing. One girl came out alone, yawning. I looked out for Wilf in his serge suit. But he wouldn't wear his serge suit on such a warm day. Perhaps he would leave by a side door. I stood on the top step, keeping to one side. The students were my age, some a little older. I wished I were one of them, coming out arm in arm with another girl, laughing and talking, looking forward to eating my sandwiches on the steps of the Town Hall.

Wilf came through the main door with three other people, two chaps and a girl. He was holding forth, waving his arms to explain something. One of the chaps contradicted him and took his arm to stop him. Suddenly I felt awkward, out of place. The others saw him look at me and they carried on down the steps. 'I'll catch you up,' he called to them. 'Hello, stranger. Is something wrong at home?' he asked me.

I shook my head, and heard myself explaining that I was nearby and had come to say hello. Wilf looked away from me, towards his friends heading in the direction of the Headrow. 'Look, I know your mam thinks I'm bad company, but come with us for a cup of tea and a smoke.'

He knew I didn't smoke. I shook my head. 'I'd better be getting back.' We walked down the steps together and since we were going the same way fell into step. His little crowd was just ahead of us, walking slowly to give us chance to catch up.

'I've been drawing all morning, your head doesn't come out of it very easily. My brain's full of perpendicular lines.'

'Must be very uncomfortable,' I said.

'What's up, Jess?' Wilf frowned.

'Umbrellas when it's raining! Got to get back now.' I didn't give him a chance to answer but turned off behind the Town Hall and made my way back. It was mad to think I could talk to anyone about what had happened.

The voice boomed at me, as I dodged a horse and cart and crossed the road. 'Miss! Miss Price!'

They looked so different, Mr and Miss Treasure. Even though they stood a little apart from each other, they seemed joined by an invisible thread. Something struck me about their ugly faces. People with attractive faces often look happy. The Treasures' faces reminded me of the maps of countries – full of river lines, their noses a bumpy mountain range. No, you would not expect to see joy in the Treasures' faces any more than you would find glee in a map of the British Isles. But there it was. Pleasure.

The cook had left for the day. They came into the kitchen. We sat at the well-scrubbed deal table and drank stewed tea. Their story surprised me out of my worries.

'We have decided to confide in you,' Miss Treasure held her cup in a dainty way, gripping the handle between her fingers and thumb.

Mr Treasure gulped at his tea, nodding encouragement. 'Be truthful. Tell Miss Price why we hummm-hummm have decided to confide in her. Mmmmmm.'

The tea tasted foul.

'We are first cousins, Rich – Richard – and I. We share paternal grandparents, and hence a name.'

He leaned towards me across the table. 'We work together, too, teaching at a college. Wynifred unveils the hummmm glories of commerce. I myself instruct the uninitiated into the mysteries of double-entry hummmmm book-keeping, at all levels.'

'We are very close,' Miss Treasure continued carefully, looking at her tea, wondering how much of it she could leave in the cup without offending me. (All of it, for all I cared.) 'But of course, as first cousins, we were not permitted to marry . . .'

'*Were not* being the operative words,' Rich Treasure smiled, tilting his head. 'Until that important missive from the Holy Father that you kindly chased after us about. You see, we hummm-hummmm asked for a dispensation from the Holy Father, because, you see, there is a very good reason why we two should marry. In his wisdom, and guided by the Holy hummmm-hummmm Spirit, the Pope has granted a papal dispensation to allow us to mmmmmmmm marry.'

Miss Treasure nodded. 'Of course, what must have weighed greatly with the Holy See was the fact that there will be no children, due to our age and station, that and our vow.'

Between them they were so determined to make something clear to me that I began to find it more and more difficult to know what they were talking about.

Miss Treasure took a deep gulp of tea, pretending to down the lot, walked to the sink, poured it down then rinsed the cup under the tap. 'Shall you tell Miss Price about our obligation, Rich, or shall I?'

Mr Treasure considered. 'How should I describe it?'

I hoped they would not describe anything to me. I marvelled at the way they could talk about such private matters to someone they hardly knew. I wished they would stop.

He drummed his fingers on the table thoughtfully, as if it helped him to think. 'More a mmmmm stipulation – not our own, but one that we took to our bosoms as seriously as a vow, huumm?'

I was beginning to feel dizzy. I realized I couldn't just go and cut a slice of bread. It would seem rude. I wondered if I could break a piece off and eat it in the absent-minded way Miss Treasure had tipped her tea down the drain.

He was talking to me again. 'We are fortunate in owning some properties, a modest number. In marrying we shall combine our resources. The hummm properties come to us with a condition, arising out of our joint grandparents' last will and ummm testament. Today we have today signed an affidavit to that effect, agreeing to the condition, and we have arranged our marriage – but not in Leeds because we are not yet ready to let the world know of our hummmmm wedlock.'

'I'm sorry,' I said, 'I'm not really understanding. I don't understand about wills and affidavits.'

'Try to be straightforward, Rich, dear.'

He shook his head as if this might be impossible. 'You do it, dearest. You are so much better at talking to humm females.'

'Very well, dear. Miss Price, Jessica if I may, we want to ask you not to mention that we are to be married. We do not intend to announce our marriage yet. Not until we retire in two years' time. At the college where we teach, my cousin and husband-to-be . . .' They exchanged a smile. 'My cousin and husband-to-be shall continue to be known as Mr Treasure and I shall continue to be known as Miss Treasure.'

There were little phrases for this kind of thing. Mam and Bernadette knew them all. Fortunately, I remembered one. 'I wish you every happiness in your future life together.'

It was not the end. I tore off a piece of bread and pushed it in my mouth so my cheeks popped out. Watching me chew, they thanked me for my good wishes, he with his head to the left, hers to the right.

'What do you understand by the word perpetuity, Miss Price?' he asked, without humming.

They watched me closely, waiting for my answer. I swallowed my mouthful of bread before answering. 'Like perpetual,' I said. 'For ever. "Let perpetual light shine upon them."'

'You see,' he said, standing up and reaching for his bowler hat, 'we have sometimes debated whether our grandparents knew the meaning of the er-hummm word.'

'I'm sure they did, dear.' Miss Treasure picked a loose cotton thread from his jacket sleeve.

'But Miss Price is a practising Catholic. In a manner of speaking, our grandparents . . .'

She glared at him as if he had gone too far. 'They were Catholics, Rich, dear, no ifs and buts. But, to come to the point, we had to promise that we would care for their grave in perpetuity. By marrying, we allow ourselves to inhabit one property and rent out another, and also make ourselves eligible to adopt a child who will be able to keep up the good work on the cemetery front.'

'We thought if you knew the extent of our story and our obligations, you would hummmm do us the courtesy of keeping q.t. about our nuptials. Hummm.'

'Of course,' I said. 'I won't say a word.'

They each thanked me twice for the tea. He put on his bowler hat. Miss Treasure thanked me again for the tea. 'Now, we mustn't detain Miss Price any longer. She has her duties to attend to.'

After they had gone, the kitchen and the house above it seemed to press in on me. It was so hot in there. Stew for the priests' supper simmered on the range. The cook had told me to stir it every now and then so it would not stick to the bottom of the pot. It already had. A thick black gunge clung to the tip of the wooden spoon. It would be two hours before the priests came home. If I were at home I could have worked on my fairy tales. Sitting there looking at the surplices that wanted ironing, the cassock for mending and the woollen socks left for darning, I wondered how Snow White felt when the Seven Dwarfs went off to work and left her hard at it.

Once I threaded the needle, I thought I might as well sew on the button that had popped off my blouse, so I undid my blouse, slipped it off and sewed on my button. I felt cooler without the blouse in that oven of a kitchen. The tear in the cassock did not take much mending so I did that next. Mam had tried to show me how to darn. It entailed sliding a wooden mushroom into the sock and working wool across and up and down. I thought I would have a go at that. I stabbed with the darning needle, making a crazy sort of cat's cradle.

My best hope would be that Father Flynn thought he had

dreamed me coming into his room. After a bit of cat's cradle crazy darning, I convinced myself of that.

I turned my thoughts to the Treasures, and what he meant when he said their grandparents were Catholics 'in a manner of speaking'. Did it mean, like my father, not at all? He had not been to mass since coming back from the war. Uncle Bill had not been a Catholic since meeting Auntie Irene and marrying in the Unitarian Church.

I had never understood how someone could turn their back on the Church. I jabbed the darning needle through the black wool sock, across the hole in the toe. A new feeling tingled through me, a kind of relief that at last I understood something. Being in a house full of priests, who were grumpy, greedy, put their toes through their socks, washed, wore big nightshirts and slept and snored like other men, I could understand how a person might stop believing that priests had special powers. The one exception would be Father Flynn.

It was at that moment that the bell above the kitchen door rang. I looked to see which room the call came from. It was the dining room. Father Baxter, being so old, usually came back from his rounds early and wanted tea. Might as well make a pot and send it up. Cook kept the kettle permanently on so it did not take me long to warm the teapot, spoon in the tea and find the tray.

After I put the tray on the dumb waiter, and sent it upstairs, I picked up my blouse, just as someone opened the kitchen door from the house side.

Father Flynn seemed hardly to glance at me, then turned away. 'Didn't you hear the bell?'

'Yes, Father.' I held the blouse to my chest.

'Would you come upstairs, please? Straightaway, Jess.'

I quickly put on my blouse and tied on my apron.

I knocked on the dining-room door and he called for me to come in. I hoped he hadn't properly looked at me in the kitchen. Mam would be furious if she knew he'd seen me in my vest.

He had put the tray of tea on the table. 'Will you pour, please?'

I poured him a cup. He took a drink. 'Sit down, Jess. I need to speak to you. About last night, and just now.' He pulled out the chair next to his.

My mouth went dry.

'What were you doing last night, shortly after you went upstairs?

66

Only you seemed to be moving about an awful lot, and knocking. You know your room is above mine?'

'I was . . . the window won't open. I was hot.'

'And did you open it?'

'No, I thought of asking you, Father.'

'Is that why you came to my room in the night?' He took a sip of tea.

'No . . . You came to my room, sleepwalking.'

He put his cup down carefully. 'No lies. I'll have no lies from you. You would have alerted one of the other priests if that had been the case.'

'I didn't know what to do, I didn't dare wake anyone. If it had been anyone else—'

'I think I understand. I thought you were young and innocent, and a good girl. Now I see that you're a young woman of deep feelings, and some of those feelings are for me, feelings you shouldn't have for a priest. I know you admire me. You can answer.'

'Yes, Father.'

'You chose me as your confessor, you came round faithfully on the altar collections.'

'Yes, Father, but—'

He put his finger to my mouth, and drew it down my lip. 'Last night, you were in my room, in your nightgown, undone at the neck. This afternoon, after I rang the bell, you disrobed in the kitchen, hoping I would see you.'

'No!'

'Did you or did you not stand there without a blouse, without an apron, in your, your undergarments, your breasts free?'

I shook my head, not meaning no, but meaning he was wrong.

'Don't compound your fault by denial. I understand your sin, it's human. Temptation must be resisted, such blatant flaunting . . .' His voice was kind and soft, as if he were not chastising me at all.

'I didn't expect—'

I stood up to go, wanting to run from the room. He stood, too, putting his hands on my shoulders. 'Kneel and pray, Jess. We'll pray together. Ask for God's help to overcome this temptation.'

I felt rooted to the spot. I thought he was going to push me to my knees, but he drew his hands over my breasts, whispering, 'Is this what you hoped I would do?' I shook my head, trying to say no. He put his lips on mine, his mouth tasting of cigarettes. I pulled away from him. As if he were dancing with me, he grabbed my wrist with one hand and put the other on my back, walking me to the corner of the room so we stood by the tall bookcase. I was pinned against the wall. 'Just this once I'll do what you want, touch you where you want me to touch you. You're an innocent, Jess, you don't realize a priest is also a man like other men. Can you feel me against you?'

Just for a moment, this is my shame, I didn't want him to stop. In the seconds he held me there, I saw that room so clearly. The old volumes in the bookcase, the frayed carpet square on the floor, a ray of sunlight through half-shut blinds making the dust dance. 'Touch me, Jess, touch me.' He relaxed his hold on me for a moment while he fumbled with his trousers. I broke free and made for the door. He cried out, 'You can't stop now. You need to learn where your actions lead.'

The front door was nearest, and unlocked. I daren't stop to get my bike from the railings round the back. I ran. Only when I was far enough away did I realize I couldn't go home. Mam might send me back. Father Flynn could come looking for me.

I was out of breath then, and had to slow down. Keeping to the back streets in case he came after me, I made my way to Blenheim Square.

Wilf opened the door. 'Twice in one day . . .' he started to joke. 'Jess, what's wrong?'

I was in the hall. 'Is Auntie Irene in?'

He nodded and led me into her William Morris sitting room, which is very peaceful and would usually make anyone feel calm, with green-blue wallpaper and the chairs and sofa covered in throws. Irene sat at the writing bureau. She turned to look at me, then put down her pen. There was something reassuring about her heaviness, her solidity.

If I looked alarming, she showed no sign of being alarmed, but got up and asked Wilf to fetch some tea and a toasted teacake. She led me to the big upholstered chair and sat me down.

'What's the matter Jess?'

'Don't let them send me back to the priests' house. I won't go back.'

'It's all right. No one will make you go back. Shhh. It's all right.'

'I don't want to go home. He'll know where to look.'

'You can stay here tonight.'

Not until she had sent Wilf with a note to my mother did she ask me what had happened.

'I don't like it there.'

'Why not?'

I couldn't say the words. I didn't know what to say.

She waited, but did not press me.

Irene took me upstairs. She found me a nightie and a toothbrush. In the bathroom I stood at the sink and washed myself from head to foot with a white flannel and Pears soap. My clothes lay in a heap on the floor; I wanted to kick and tear them, but I left them lying there.

Irene was waiting in the bedroom for me. Although it wasn't a cold day, I felt shivery. She had brought a bed-warmer, wrapped in a knitted cover.

She looked as if she would ask me something else. I snuggled into the bed and turned my head away.

She tucked the bed covers behind me, leaned over and kissed my forehead. 'You'll be all right now. I'll look after you. You mam's mad to send you to such a place, though don't say I said so.' At the door, she turned. 'Is there anything you want to tell me?'

I shook my head.

'Now, don't you worry. Leave things to me. Sleep, that's the healer. Sleep.'

I did sleep, for hours and hours, until the afternoon of the next day.

Hilda the maid brought me tea and toast. She put the tray on the bed. 'I kept looking in on you,' she said. 'Mrs Price has gone to Benson Street to talk to your parents.'

'Where's Wilf?' I asked.

'Gone to his life-drawing class. He said to tell you he'd come up and see you when he gets back.'

I still felt worn out, though I had done nothing. Usually I can eat anything that's put in front of me, but I managed only half a slice of toast. I slid out of bed and put the tray on the dressing table.

As I got back into bed, Hilda popped her head around the bedroom door. 'You have a visitor. It's your priest.' She opened the door wide, practically bowing to him in her politeness. Before I had chance to protest, she was gone.

There he stood in his shabby black priests' clothes and black reject Oxfords. Father Flynn. How did he know where to find me?

As if I had asked the question aloud, he said, 'I'll always know where you are. I'll find you, wherever you try to hide.'

'Hilda!' I called.

'Don't bother to order tea for me. I'm only here to say one thing. If you ever mention what happened yesterday, no one will believe you. You see, I've already explained to Father Baxter the real reason for my dissatisfaction with you. He knows you behaved like a slut. He had a similar experience himself as a young curate, a married woman throwing herself at him. For the sake of your family, I shall say no more about it, but if you say one word, I won't hesitate to denounce you.'

'It wasn't me. You came to my room. You touched me.'

He shook his head. His lips curled, one nostril twitched. 'They put girls away who have fevered imaginations. Oh, it happens frequently. That's why your sex is called the weaker vessel. Read St Paul. He'll show you how to guard against your own nasty sinfulness. You'll keep silent, Jess, or you'll regret it for the rest of your life. Your mother will never hold up her head again. And do you think the Mooneys would let Michael marry Bernadette if they knew the truth about you?'

If he had stayed at a distance from me, I might have said nothing, but he came closer and closer, so I could feel his breath.

'Dad and Uncle brought guns back from the war. I know where they are. If you touch me ever again, I'll shoot you. I'll kill you.' At the top of my voice, I screamed, 'Hilda!' Hanging above the bed was a bell cord that linked to the kitchen. I grabbed it and pulled.

'You won't always be able to call on your rich relations' helpers.' He took a step back, shaking his head. 'Repent soon, or you're on a fast road to hell.' He made a cross in the air. 'Bless you.'

I felt as if I had been cursed.

When Mam and Dad came to see me late in the afternoon, I did look poorly, and felt it, too.

'I told you she was too young for that sort of palaver,' Dad said, and it was rare for him to go against Mam.

'You stay here,' Mam said. 'At least you made a move, and you tried. Trying always leads somewhere.'

I didn't want to think where it might have led.

Dad said, 'Bill wants you to work for him, in his office, when you're fully better. How does that sound?'

'I'd like that,' I said.

8

Glass Slippers

Wilf learned everything he knew about cutting and shaping stone from the mason who worked in the yard next to the cemetery. At Leeds College of Art, the teachers had insisted Wilf should model from clay. One said to him it would be soon enough to carve when he started at the Royal College of Art. Wilf did not want to wait. He wanted to carve now. He loved the discovery of some creature, shape or being within a material that ordinary mortals would simply see as a lump of wood or a slab of stone. It was his way of losing himself, of escaping from tedium or from those thoughts that sometimes went round, an escape from his deep disappointment at growing up to find so little magic in the world of the shoe factory, the organized charity of the Unitarian Church and the academic rigour of the grammar school.

Growing up, knowing himself to be adopted, Wilf had liked to imagine parents thwarted in love. A high-ranking officer who worshipped a titled lady, promised to a duke. Bill and Irene would have answered any questions, but he preferred to create his own stories and did not know how to form mundane enquiries such as: Where was I born? Who was my mother? By the time he could give shape to such words, he did not want to speak them, preferring his own versions of romantic family histories, sometimes involving a backdrop of castles, battlements, moats and wide tracts of heather and gorse-covered land where deer grazed and his cloaked mother kept a midnight tryst by an ancient oak with a handsome young man, whose breath grew quicker when she dropped her hood and turned her face to him, lit by the moon.

Drawings of his childhood imaginings filled page upon page of sketch books bought by Irene. She encouraged him to sketch not just what he imagined but what he saw. Slowly he had found that by looking hard at the landscape of the dales and moors he could find the shapes and textures that echoed his own feelings. In this way, his art took on a harder edge until he came to the point where only sculpture would really do. Only the grappling with some hard thing – a grappling that was both a contest and an embrace – could give him satisfaction.

He wheeled a cracked headstone which the mason had given him home on the borrowed cart, with no particular form in mind, but he knew something lived in there and he would release it.

He set the stone in the yard and went to see Jess.

She was up and dressed, sitting in the William Morris sitting room. Irene sat at her letter-writing. Jess had Wilf's illustrations by her: the Shoemender and the Elf, Puss in Boots, The Red Shoes, Cinderella in old felt slippers full of holes, and then waltzing in magnificent peep-toe glass shoes with twisty, twirly heels.

'I wasn't sure how Rumpelstiltskin featured as a boot and shoe story,' Wilf said. 'That's why I gave him fool's shoes with bobbles and bells.'

Jess looked suddenly younger as she talked about Rumpelstiltskin, and how he must have had sturdy shoes or he would not have been able to dance around his fire without scorching them. Wilf nodded gravely. 'You think the bobbles and bells are wrong?'

Jess frowned. 'The bells would get hot and the bobbles scorch. Perhaps I shouldn't have included Rumpelstiltskin in the stories.'

'Well, there they all are, for you to decide.'

Wilf hadn't noticed his mother leave the room until she came back with glasses of dandelion and burdoch. 'I'm glad you're here, Jess. I don't always get to see Wilf's work.'

Wilf left Jess and Irene together and went up to his room. He could not start to chip away at the marble headstone without a vision of what the stone might yield.

He picked up a stick of charcoal and let it stroke the page. The tilt of her head, the slope of her shoulder, her arms as she reached out to dive into the Lido; Jess, but not Jess. On the opposite side of the page he drew a male figure that did not seem like himself at all but had arms stretched in a mirroring movement, reaching for the female. The moment swept over him and through him. Longing to be with Jess overcame his desire to work, to create. For a long time, Wilf lay on his bed and stared at the ceiling. He wished that he had a lock on his door. Not that anyone would come in, but as he thought that, he wished someone would. Jess. And slide into bed with him, just to hold each other, to be close. That she was downstairs, here in his house, only brought home to him what he had known for such a long time.

He filled his sheet of paper with sketches. Another male and female figure, close enough to embrace but only their hands touching. He liked the reach, the stretch of their arms.

The day broke fine and clear. It was Irene who suggested Wilf give himself a day off from his art and the two of them cycle to Otley Chevin.

'I should go and see Mam,' Jess said.

'Your mam wants you to get well so you'll be fit to start work and earn your living. The fresh air is just what you need.'

They sat in pale sunlight at the foot of the Cow and Calf. 'I've drawn the two of us together, Jess. We're on a sheet of sugar paper in my room, reaching out towards each other.'

'What like?'

'Like two swimmers ready to dive towards each other.'

'Show me.'

'Stand up, then.' He reached out a hand and tugged her to her feet. 'Watch me. Raise your arms like this.'

She lifted her arms above her head. 'That's it,' he said, 'just a little more curved. It's easy to draw. It'll be harder to carve.'

She lowered her arms. 'I'll miss you, Wilf.'

'Will you? Will you really? I can hardly bear the thought of leaving you, Jess. It'll be three years.'

'You'll come back, though?'

It was in her voice more than what she said. He knew, or hoped, she felt the same. They stood facing each other, the hard rock beneath their feet, wind blowing through her hair. He reached out, held her arms gently and kissed her very lightly, almost as if he didn't dare. 'I love you, Jess.'

74

'I love you, too, Wilf.'

They sat down, the rock behind them.

'I really mean it. I want us to marry, Jess, when I finish my course. Would that suit you?'

'Yes, that would suit me very well.'

'Now I'm going to worry all the time.'

He had a sudden glimpse of her succeeding where he had turned away. She would become a business woman, sure of herself, clever, matter of fact. She might come to despise the boy who could draw glass slippers, an old woman in a shoe, a cat in boots and red shoes aflame. Would the new heir to the Wright Shoe Company care that, with the deftness of his fingers, he could turn a piece of wood into a shape that screamed against comfort, self-satisfaction and the shoe trade which had so far supported him towards becoming a fledgling artist.

In a matter of weeks he would be leaving Leeds for ever. It seemed strange that as he left she would be taking up the life that Bill had meant Wilf to follow; ledgers, orders and wages; profit and loss, and stocks and shares. But all he said was, 'When you go to that commercial college to learn accounts and typewriting, don't let any of those business students carry your bag.'

She laughed. 'You're the one who meets models and artists. I'll probably meet the book-keeper from the pickle factory.'

'There'll never be anyone else but you for me. I think part of me has known that since we were children. It was always the two of us against the world.'

She pulled away suddenly. 'We'd better go, Wilf. The sky's getting dark.'

'What? What's the matter?'

'Nothing.'

But Wilf felt that she was holding something back, and he wished he knew what.

The next morning, Jess cycled home. Wilf went into the yard where he had sectioned off an area to work, covered with corrugated iron to form a roof. He worked all day on the marble. He worked until dark, not hearing Irene's calls about food or cups of tea or a glass of Tizer. It would not come right, would not yield. He wasted so much, the marble turning to chips. Then it came, a narrow figure with a round head, barely any neck, sloping shoulders, round arms raised to heaven, breasts just a little misshapen and lop-sided.

'That's nice, dear,' Irene said, bringing him a glass of lemonade and a cheese and pickle sandwich. 'Shouldn't you stop now? It's getting dark.'

He lit two oil lamps.

The next figure had a more oval head, a touch of neck, straight shoulders that looked odd when the arms were raised. He had expected this male figure to have arms reaching out, as in his sketch, but the marble had a different idea. He left the piece unfinished.

The next morning, he stood the female figure on the kitchen table. Bill looked at it, searching for something to say. Now that Wilf had been awarded a bursary to attend the Royal College of Art, Bill's opposition had evaporated. If people thought what Wilf produced merited two hundred pounds a year, it could not be a complete waste of time. 'Marble must be hard to carve, son.'

'Yes.'

'It's lovely,' Irene said uncertainly.

Wilf could tell from her voice that she wanted him to say it was for her. A parting gift before he left for London.

9

Chin Up, Bernadette

Bernadette had lain in the same position all night, knees tucked up, chin down, arms clasped around her chest. I climbed over her to get out of bed. She still lay in that position when I had pulled on my clothes.

I buttoned my shoes. 'You'll be late for work.'

She didn't answer.

As I washed my face at the kitchen sink, Mam stood at the foot of the stairs. 'Bernadette! Do you know what time it is?'

No answer.

'Go up and see what ails her,' Mam ordered.

I carried my cup of tea with me, not wanting to be late myself. She wasn't interested in the time. No movement.

A sudden scare ran through me. I pulled the sheet from her, half fearing she'd died in the night and I'd slept next to her corpse and stepped over her mortal remains.

She groaned, 'Leave me alone,' and snatched the sheet back. Her eyes looked red. She must have been crying in the night and I hadn't heard.

'Have I to tell work you're sick?' She really did look pale and poorly. 'I could call on my way to the office.'

I liked saying that, 'to the office'. It made me feel I had found my own way in the world at long last.

She fished under the pillow and pulled out a hanky. 'Go away. You don't understand.' She wiped her nose then slid into the centre of the bed, hunching herself more tightly than before.

'I'd better do that, then,' I said. 'I'll say stomach cramps, so don't you go in saying headache tomorrow.'

I don't know what it was about the word 'tomorrow', but the minute I said it a great sob came racking out of her and under the sheet her body started to shake. I sat on the edge of the bed and reached out a hand to her.

She shook me off. 'Leave me alone. You don't understand. Nobody understands.'

'Have a drink of tea.'

She hit out at me and I had all on keeping my cup steady. I drank the tea myself. 'I have to go to work.'

No answer.

'Mam'll be up yelling at you. She's going frantic.'

This was a new experience. Usually I was the one who drove Mam frantic, not Bernadette, Mam's friend and ally.

'I just want to be left alone.'

Slowly, I walked back downstairs. Mam stood at the bottom of the steps, watching me. She turned and walked into the kitchen. 'Well?'

I rinsed my cup under the tap. 'She's not budging. She's still upset.'

'What am I going to do?' Mam asked. 'How long is she going to be like this? Your dad says let her be. We can't let her be.'

'I said I'd call in to her work, say she's got stomach cramps.'

'Cramp in the bloomin' brain, if you ask me. Does she think some rich moving picture star would cry for her? And what do we do tomorrow? Send word that she's taken to her bed heartbroken because Rudolph Valentino's dead?'

Bernadette must have been listening. She set up a great wail, followed by a sob.

'I have to go,' I said, moving Dad's bike to get at my own. 'I'll do that, then; call in and say she's poorly.'

I had forgotten to pick up my sandwich. Mam handed it to me. 'And for heaven's sake, think of something. It's ridiculous. I'll leave her today, but if she's like this tomorrow, I'll drag her by the scruff of the neck myself and pull her all the way to work in her nightie.'

I spent the morning marking up unpaid invoices that needed statements, trying not to think about Bernadette or Rudolph Valentino because Mrs Crawford, Uncle's real office clerk, is very quick to jump on me if I make the least error, and she always finds a tactfully triumphant way of letting Uncle Bill know my mistakes.

Mrs Crawford smells of cigarettes and keeps a moth-eaten black cardigan on the back of her chair. When I passed her the marked-up invoices, she studied them carefully, hoping to spot a paid one and draw it to my attention. She sniffed magnanimously. 'Look again, you mighta missed one.'

I hadn't. When she couldn't find fault with me, she mentioned Wilf, who used to work in the firm in his holidays. 'At least you're not like your cousin, on the shop floor sketching the workforce and forgetting to do the filing.'

I ignored her.

When it came to dinner time, I cycled like fury to Blenheim Square, to see Wilf. He was in the yard, chipping away at an old piece of marble cadged from the stonemason who worked in the yard next to the cemetry.

He left off what he was doing to fetch us each a drink of Tizer. We sat on the grass in the square, talking about Bernadette grieving so much for Rudolph Valentino that she couldn't leave her bed.

'She needs to be able to mark the occasion somehow,' Wilf said. 'If we were millionaires, she could go to America for Rudolph Valentino's funeral.'

I finished my sandwich and threw a bit of bread to a thrush that pecked on the grass and fixed me with its beady eye. 'I suppose that's why it's so hopeless for her,' I said. 'If a real-life person dies, well, it would be difficult but people know what to do. Mam even says she could have a mass said – anonymously, so as not to show us up.'

This sent Wilf into a fit of laughter.

Auntie Irene waved to us from the front window. 'She's back from one of her committee meetings,' Will sighed. 'They've been arranging for a photographer to go over to Silverdale and take pictures of the civic visit, when the Mayor visits the Leeds Poor Children's Holiday Camp, and all the bairns will be wearing Price clogs.'

I changed the subject, because talk of the camp made me think about Gladys Hardy, her father's death and the secret that she had told me, which made me feel a little uneasy every time I was with Wilf. Why couldn't I bring myself to tell him? Perhaps because I knew he imagined his real mother as some mysterious beauty, not a plain everyday sort of woman who tramped the streets for a charity, carrying a small notebook and a silver-topped pencil. But Wilf was still thinking about Bernadette and Rudolph Valentino.

'What will Michael Mooney make of it, with his sweetheart brought low and broken-hearted because of a Latin lover?'

We had lain on the grass, turned towards each other as we talked.

I said, 'Poor Rudolph.'

Wilf said, 'Poor Bernadette.'

Very meanly, we exploded and rolled about, laughing like billy-o.

When we had laughed ourselves silly, we just lay there and gazed at the sky. I knew I'd have to get back soon, and with still no solution to Bernadette's grief. 'You're not taking this seriously at all, Wilf. You're just waiting for me to hop it, so you can get back to chipping your marble.'

'I am taking it very seriously,' Wilf protested. 'And I've got an idea. You know Mother used to be in amateur dramatics, and she's got all sorts of costumes.'

'The ones we used dress up in, from the suitcases in the attic?'

Wilf stood up and reached out a hand to me. 'Genius resides in seeing the connection between two quite separate ideas. In this case, dressing up and photography. It's just a thought, but if I'm right and Bernadette needs somehow to mark Rudolph's exit stage left feet first, we could get her to dress up as one of his leading ladies, and have her photograph taken holding a lily.'

'A lily?'

'It's an emblem of death,' Wilf said, bending down to pick up a buttercup and holding it to his chin. 'Do I like butter?'

I looked for the buttercup's reflection on his throat. 'No. And how do you know that the lily's an emblem of death?'

'Because I'm an artist, Jess. It's my business to know.'

'It's worth a thought,' I said. 'If she'd get out of bed. I wonder which of his leading ladies she'd like to be.'

'Come on. We'll find the clothes. You can be Vilma Banky, you have the same nose and eyes.'

We ran across to the house. 'It's Bernadette who's in mourning,' I reminded him.

'Well, she's probably in a swooning mood so she can be Agnes Ayres.'

Auntie Irene had so many costumes to choose from that I had no difficulty in finding something suitable. I knew very well that Bernadette favoured Vilma Banky, so I thought she'd better have the stripy headdress.

I was late back for work and got a glare from Mrs Crawford, but she forgot as the afternoon wore on. When I offered to deliver the statements by hand to save postage, she let me go early. It did not take long to cycle round the shoe shops dropping off envelopes. Then I raced home.

She was still under the covers in our little room where there is hardly space to turn round. Bernadette did not look up at first, but curiosity got the better of her. She peered over the top of the sheet, keeping it up to her nose. 'What are you doing?'

I slipped on a short-sleeved lacy blouse, edged with binding at the neck and sleeves, and pulled on pantaloons, tying a check silk scarf around my waist to make a skirt. The black cotton shoes couldn't have belonged to Auntie Irene because they were too tight a fit. I slipped a long double row of imitation pearls over my head. I like stage jewellery as it shouts about itself, unlike Auntie Irene's real-life jewellery, which is very tasteful and dull.

'Why are you getting dressed up?' Bernadette asked.

I said, 'I wish we had a big mirror. How do I look?'

She said, 'Are you meant to be Vilma Banky?'

And I said, 'No. That'll be you. I'm Agnes Ayres.' One by one, I held up the stripy headdress with bobbles, a silk blouse with big sleeves, cotton pantaloons and little silk shoes.

Slowly, Bernadette sat up and swung her legs over the edge of the bed.

'Come on, Vilma,' I said. 'You and Agnes have an appointment at the photographer's studio. We're doing this for Señor Rudolph Valentino, because we can't go to his funeral.'

She dressed without speaking, very clumsily, and I had to button her shoes and fix the headdress for her.

I heard the motorbike come to a stop outside, and waved to Wilf through the window.

Dad almost spoiled it when we went downstairs. 'You can't go out with feet shod like that,'

'No one's going to see us,' I said. 'Wilf's taking us in the sidecar, to the photographic studio.'

'I'm not thinking of folk seeing you,' Dad said. 'Them sort of slippers give no support. That's just what leads to fallen arches in later life.'

Mam nudged him to shut up.

At the studio the photographer's assistant dabbed powder on our faces. 'Would you like a little lip rouge?' she asked eagerly. I guessed she liked painting faces. She was wearing rouge herself. Bernadette said no, being in mourning, but I said yes that, we wanted to look our best and very dramatic. Afterwards we looked at ourselves in the mirror, and I truly thought that Rudolph would have been happy to act or share his tent with either of us.

Wilf had brought a lily as promised, and in one pose, Bernadette stood alone beside a tall candle, holding the lily to her chest. But my favourite pose was when we sat side by side, cross-legged, as if we were just outside the desert tent of the Sheik of Araby.

The next morning, when Bernadette left for work before me, Mam said, 'Perhaps I was too hasty judging Wilf. He's not such a bad lad. He won a bursary, you know.'

'I know.'

'And the fact that he's not going into the Wright Shoe Company, well, that's given you your opening.'

'Yes.'

'It's just a pity he draws filth.'

'What do you mean?'

'You know very well what I mean.'

I knew very well that Wilf and I were right to keep our love a secret.

11

On a Bicycle
Made for Two

Wilf laid out the map on his bedroom floor: Yorkshire, Lancashire and Cumbria, ten miles to the inch. He felt sure he and Jess could do the journey to Silverdale for the camp's civic ceremony without staying overnight in Gargrave, but both Irene and Dolly insisted they should break their journey and spend the night there with Aunt Bella.

He traced the route from Leeds to Gargrave; so far, so familiar – through Apperley Bridge, Bingley, following the route of the Leeds and Liverpool Canal beyond Skipton. From there they would cycle up past Giggleswick, across to High Bentham. Or perhaps it would be better to go on to Kirby Lonsdale and drop down into Carnforth and then on to Silverdale.

He folded the map and took the stairs two at a time to ask Bill's opinion on the route. Bill sat smoking in the dining room. Wilf spread the map on the table. Bill picked up his glasses, pored over the map and said he was sorely tempted to join them. *Don't*, Wilf said in his head. *Just for once, let me and Jess do something on our own.*

On the day, Wilf checked the tandem's puncture outfit, filled bottles of water and tucked sandwiches and apples into the saddlebag. They set off at daybreak.

Jess had not ridden a tandem before and claimed she'd never get used to it – like being the rear end of a pantomime horse. She couldn't see where they were going, get her bearings or feel in control, as if she were missing something.

As they cycled up out of Headingley towards the Wharfedale road, Wilf started to sing. 'Daisy, Daisy, give me your answer do. I'm half crazy, all for the love of you . . .'

Jess joined in. 'It won't be a stylish marriage, we can't afford a carriage, but you'd look sweet upon the seat of a bicycle made for two.'

'We're finding beauty!' he called. 'By the end of today we will have cycled through beauty and some of it will stick to your heart and soul.'

Early-morning hedgerows wore spidery webs of silver thread. Two blackbirds perched on a branch watched them pass by.

'It's too soon to stop,' Jess said when he pulled onto the verge near a ladder stile in the dry stone wall.

'Don't you recognize it?'

She looked at the gnarled roots of the elm, at the stile and the loose stone. 'It's where I took a tumble that Sunday.'

'I want to show you something.'

She followed him across the stile, along the edge of a field of wheat. When they reached the boundary edge, he said, 'I have to blindfold you now, because it's a surprise.'

'How can you have a surprise in the middle of nowhere?'

He took out the square cotton hanky, folded it and placed it across her eyes, tying it at the back of her head. 'No cheating, no peeping!'

He creaked the gate open and led her across uneven ground. This field lay fallow and smelled of meadowsweet and fern. A brackeny scent tumbled down from the nearby hill. Blackberries ripened in the hedgerow.

'This had better be good,' she said, reaching out her arm and touching prickly hedge.

'Can you see?' he asked.

'No!'

'Wooden stile,' he announced, as they reached the wall at the field end. He climbed up first, guiding her over behind him. At the other side he held her waist and helped her down.

'Reach out and touch,' he ordered.

She said, 'If someone's made off with the tandem while we've been clarting about, I'll brain you.'

But she stretched out her arm and touched the tree in front of them.

'Can you tell what sort of tree it is?' he asked.

She ran her hands over the bark. 'A wooden one?'

'Jess! It's a poplar. I was out on my own one day, exploring. I found something in it.'

'Can I look now?'

'Not yet. Walk backwards, just a few steps.'

He undid the blindfold.

Behind the tree, the sun was rising. She shielded her eyes, blinking at the light. Above her, from the tree, a female figure loomed. Its feet merged into the trunk, legs rising to meet the drapery of a skirt. Bare arms seemed barely to protrude from the carving. The swirls of the skirt continued up over her almost flat-chested body. Her shoulders jutted sharply. The neck seemed too long but graceful. Something about her pose, the shape of the head and the bobbed hair made it unmistakeably Jess.

'What big shoulders,' she said. 'Are my shoulders that big?'

'I suppose it's the swimming,' Wilf said, trying to keep the disappointment from his voice. 'Swimmer's shoulders.'

She bit her lip but said nothing.

He said, 'It's probably the way I did it. Your shoulders are perfect. Just that when you're gouging from a tree, working with a chisel and a knife—'

'How did you reach?'

'I fetched a tall buffet, fastened on the back of the bike.'

After a long moment, he said, 'Say something, then.'

'She has no feet.'

'It was just the way it came out. I'm not very good at feet and hands, not yet.'

This exchange was not going how he imagined.

'Did you get permission?' she asked.

'It's a dead tree. And I didn't ask *you*, because I didn't know it was going to come out as you.'

'I meant from the farmer who owns the field.'

'No.'

After a long time, she said, 'I suppose it's good. It's not like me, is it? But it is like me, too. I don't want anyone else to see it.'

'I'm not going to dig it up and take it to Leeds, am I?'

'People will see it, though. Farmers, walkers, children playing.'

Wilf looked round the empty expanse of fields and hills. 'Even if they do, they won't know it's you, sort of you.'

'Well, I've seen it now, then.' She turned back to the stile.

As they walked back across the field, Wilf said flatly, 'It was just to show you I'm an artist now. If I do nothing else ever, I'll know that I'm an artist and you helped me to become myself.'

'You talk a lot of rubbish sometimes, Wilf Price. I'm just glad I fell off the bike that day so no one else would see how big you think my shoulders are. I'd never hear the end of it from Bernadette.'

'Please yourself.'

Back by the roadside, Wilf righted the bike and held it at an angle for her to mount.

'Anyone else would be flattered.'

'At having their likeness in the middle of a godforsaken field? Well, not me.'

'I didn't know you were so vain or I'd have asked for you to be a nymph on a plinth in City Square.'

'Shut up. If you can't say owt sensible, shut your gob.'

Leaves blown by the weekend winds darted about the road, dancing across the tandem's wheels. He began to suspect she was taking revenge by not pedalling hard when they were going uphill and pedalling too strongly on a downhill. But after a few more miles she must have relented. Wilf began to feel lulled by the movement, by the way in which his feet and legs worked of their own accord, and the road wound through his brain, hypnotizing him so that he no longer had to think. Soon they and the tandem moved as one, like a single creature, slowing to glide downhill, pedalling faster as the ground beneath the wheels began to rise.

They passed men in fields who sometimes stopped to watch them go by and waved. Sheep strayed onto the road, then scrambled out of the way when Wilf rang the bell and called out. Once a flock of birds flew right in front of them, to light on a field where some sharp-eyed bird leader had spotted insects to be pecked or seeds to be gobbled.

On reaching Aunt Bella's stone cottage in Gargrave, they dismounted. Wilf leaned the bike against the wall. He thought Jess must still be annoyed with him as she didn't speak, just stretched her legs and rattled the sneck on Aunt Bella's door. Breathing in the scent of lavender and honeysuckle, Wilf watched bees flit between stems and dart about on blossoms. He wondered how to break the silence.

He ducked through the doorway of the low-ceilinged cottage. After the heat of day the cool, empty house seemed to welcome them. Wilf watched Jess kick off her shoes and pad across the flagged floor.

A note on the table directed them to two plates in the cold press, and a jug of cider on the pantry shelf. Bella had left them cold sliced mutton, lettuce, tomatoes, new potatoes and a loaf of bread. Wilf set out the lunch on a small square table laid with a clean check cloth. Jess poured two glasses of cider from the jug.

Wilf knew Jess always felt better for something to eat and drink. He broke the silence. Sniffing at the strong-smelling tomatoes, he said, 'Do you think Aunt Bella grew these herself?'

'And slaughtered the sheep?'

It was the family joke that there was nothing Bella could not do. She kept bees, hens and a goat. She cleaned the vicarage and the church and 'did' for a retired mill owner. In the evenings she hand-knitted sweaters sold by post to a firm in London.

So it took Wilf by surprise when she came in and asked if he would mind distempering the pantry walls and ceiling for her, if she and Jess cleared the shelves. Her shoulders weren't up to the job any more. Wilf could have bit off his tongue when he joked, 'Jess'll do it. She has a fine pair of shoulders on her.'

Jess glared at him. She chatted to Bella as the two of them cleared the pantry, then they left him to it. Jess went with Bella into the village to pick up the knitting wool she had ordered.

Wilf slapped on the distemper, thinking that this outing was a great mistake. He should have stayed at home, got on with his carving and let Jess travel to Silverdale by train or charabanc with their parents and Bernadette. He wished he hadn't shown her the figure in the tree. Perhaps they should have just cycled on without breaking their journey. The distemper splashed onto his hair and the floor, making him despair. If he couldn't distemper an old woman's pantry, what hope would there be for him at the Royal College of Art? Jess was the one person he could always get on with, the one he loved. Now even that was going wrong.

*

Wilf liked Bella's cottage. He lay in the smallest bedroom. He had fallen asleep for an hour or so, then woke up suddenly feeling it must be morning. In the darkness he stared at the shapes of the dresser and wardrobe, too big for the tiny room. He imagined someone must have removed the window and brought the furniture up on ropes, as the winding stone staircase would be too narrow. The church clock struck one. Although he had washed, still he could smell the distemper on himself, as if it had entered his pores. To help himself back to sleep, he imagined the kind of studio he would have one day: large, well lit, big doors to take materials through, a bench for his chisels and knives, like the workmen of the Middle Ages.

A sound disturbed his thoughts and scattered the images of his perfect studio. Footsteps. Jess, padding downstairs; the rattle of the pipes as she turned on the tap. He pictured her filling a cup with water. After a few minutes, she had not come back up. The awkwardness between them seemed to swirl around him. He wanted to clear the air, ask her what was wrong.

Wilf swung out of bed and picked up the dressing gown that had belonged to Bella's late husband, the uncle they had never known.

The stone stairs chilled his feet. Jess was sitting in the chair by the dead fire in their aunt's long white nightie, sipping water.

'I couldn't sleep, either.' Wilf sat on the buffet on the opposite side of the fireplace.

'Why not?' she asked.

'I don't know.' He did not like to say it was because of the awkwardness between them.

After a long time, she said, 'I know why I can't sleep. I keep thinking . . .'

When she did not say what she kept thinking about, he said, 'Is it my fault? Did you hate the carving?'

'No, idiot! Trust you to think that.' She waved her hand. 'You always think it's . . . I don't know . . . you come back to that all the time, your art.'

'Because it's important.'

'Other things are important as well.'

'Your shoulders? I didn't mean—'

'No. It's not your fault if I have big shoulders.'

'You don't!'

She took another sip of water. 'Look, it's not that. Nothing to do with that.'

'What, then?'

'Something I've known, something I've wondered about, thinking: Shall I say it or not?'

'What?'

'About you.'

The wool of the dressing gown felt prickly against his thighs. His back itched. 'What about me?'

They spoke quietly, so as not to disturb Bella, but Jess's voice became a whisper as she told him about Gladys Hardy, and that Gladys had a boy, the same age as Wilf, with his birthday on the same day. 'I wondered whether ... I thought maybe ... I mean, because you're adopted ... And so I went back and asked her straight out.'

'Is she my mother, you mean?'

Jess nodded in the darkness. He waited for her to speak. An emptiness seemed to fill him. He wanted to reach out and touch her.

'Yes,' he said simply. 'She is.'

Jess forgot to whisper. '*What?* You knew? All this time I've been treading on eggshells, wondering how to tell you, and you knew all along?'

'Why did she tell you?'

Jess stood up and took the cup to the sink. 'How long have you known?'

'Two years. Since I saw my birth certificate when I enrolled at college.'

Jess turned from the sink and walked to the bottom of the stairs. Wilf was quicker and grabbed her arm. 'Jess, why are you being like this? It doesn't matter. Irene's my mother. How can Gladys Hardy mean anything to me? I've only ever thought of her as the woman who tramps round for the children's charities – if I've ever thought of her at all.'

She shook him off. 'Let go! I don't understand you. She's such a nice woman.'

'Nice? Nice? So damned nice, she told you so you'd tell me. She's trying to make me feel guilty.'

'It wasn't like that. Her father, your granddad, he'd just died.'

89

'And I'm supposed to care? She gave me up.'

Jess pulled free and went upstairs.

They did not speak over the very early breakfast. As they cycled out of the village, Bella watched them go. On the corner, Wilf turned and waved to the tiny figure, who looked so lonely now to him.

Had Bella looked forward to seeing them and feeding them up? Wilf wondered. She had always been there for them. When they were children, he, Bernadette and Jess had spent summers there, squeezed together in the tiny bedroom. One summer Bella put up a tent in the back and they slept there, looking at the stars through the open tent flap. Bella meant more to him than Gladys Hardy.

The beauty of the Trough of Bowland seemed to taunt him, as if to say, *You'll never capture beauty, not my beauty.*

A few dark clouds gathered. Wilf didn't care. Everything was spoiled now. What did it matter if they ran into lashings of rain? But the sky cleared.

People travelling by charabanc and motor car from Leeds planned to stop on their way, for a midday meal at the Red Lion, their arrival timed for an afternoon start to the civic ceremony when the Lord Mayor would make his speech. Wilf began to dread it, and wished he could turn back.

They had cycled all the way to Carnforth without stopping, neither he nor Jess prepared to speak to each other. Jess reached into the saddlebag for water. He couldn't see her, but knew she was taking the cork from the bottle for a swig. He wouldn't ask, though his mouth felt parched.

'Here.' She passed him the bottle.

'Thanks.' He took it, keeping one hand on the handlebars. He wished she had said, 'Here, *Wilf.*'

Wilf was not sure of the route once he reached Silverdale village. They passed a leafy lane. Then he remembered. A left turn up a steep hill to the holiday camp. He hoped he was right. Jess had never visited before and he had come several times over the years, as Irene played an active part on the charity's committee.

As they cycled stubbornly uphill, neither prepared to say they should get off and push, he was aware of Jess turning to look at the sea and the shore. He looked himself, seeing the long stretch of sand through the trees.

Then he saw the sign: Leeds Poor Children's Holiday Camp. They turned into the opening through wide metal gates, and free-wheeled down the dirt track towards long huts. Outside a wooden chalet-style house with steps to the door, a woman emptied a teapot onto the roses. Children played in the wood, running and climbing trees. Groups of girls appeared, staring at the bike, calling out to them.

An ageing man in dark serge trousers, blue shirt-sleeves and braces came from one of the huts, pulling an official-looking cap onto his head. He recognized Wilf and greeted him, ignoring Jess on the back of the tandem. Wilf explained that they were early. The superintendent told Wilf that the visitors' bungalow was open, and no one was there, so they could rest and change. His wife would bring them a pot of tea.

Jess got off the bike and walked towards the other wooden chalet in the clearing of trees.

Wilf followed, wheeling the bike and leaning it against the wall of the bungalow.

The superintendent called after him, 'Let me or my wife know if there's anything you need.'

She had gone into the bathroom. Wilf needed to stretch his legs. He walked to the wood where the children played, saying he'd give a penny to any girl who could find him a branch or a stone that looked like something, a person, a creature, or any object alive or dead.

One girl came with a stick and said, 'It looks like a stick. Give us a penny, then, yer said yer would.'

When he saw the superintendent's wife carrying a tray of tea to the bungalow, Wilf went back. He poured two cups. Jess did not appear. He knocked on the bathroom door. 'Jess?'

No answer.

Suddenly, he knew where she had gone. She must have gone for a swim.

He had not thought to warn her about the treacherous bay, about the quicksand. He leapt down the bungalow steps, ignoring the skinny girls calling to him about their finds, and ran along the gravel path towards the clifftop. The only sign of life was a white gull pecking at the far-off point where the tide ebbed. No sign of her. No footprints on the ridgy sand. But then, footsteps here could disappear as the sands shifted. He remembered the story he had heard last year. A cockler out with horse and cart saved himself, but the horse and cart went down. He should have told Jess and almost did, but then stopped himself because he thought she would dream about the struggling horse, as he did, seeing the terrified creature dragged by its cart below treacherous sands.

The track dropped away, sloping into sand and rocks. On either side, cliffs rose. He walked along the shore, seeing no one. Perhaps she had just gone to explore, or to talk to the superintendent's wife. At first the movement in the near distance seemed as natural as a gull alighting on the shore, and as low. The outgoing tide had left a pool. Like a mermaid she had found her way to it. *My cousin, the champion swimmer*, he had sometimes said if he met someone he knew from school at the Roundhay Park Lido.

He gasped for breath as he saw for sure, it was Jess. Swimming. He made himself stand still, take deep breaths, but the panic did not lessen.

He wanted to call a warning but dared not. By his foot lay a couple of branches of driftwood. To test his fears, he picked a piece up, flung it onto the loose, wet sand to his right. It sank like a stone, swallowed up by quicksands. She had made a beeline for the pool, across light, dry sand. But what if she tried to touch bottom? What if she dug her foot in the sand at the side of the pool to clamber out? He could not tell from here, but by the shading around the area where she swam it looked dangerous. She might sit down for a rest, or to pull on her shorts and blouse.

Fearing to startle her, he walked slowly across the track of light, dry sand. What words should he say? If he said the wrong words, she would flounce away angrily and get out of her pool as far away from him as possible. Worse, she might dive to the bottom to prove him wrong. This quicksand was not the soft agreeable stuff of the deserts in the Rudolph Valentino moving pictures, where someone could be pulled out as easily as chewed in. This sand turned hard as stone once it grabbed and sucked.

Jess had not seen him. She floated on her back, gazing at the sky, her naked breasts and thighs just breaking the surface of the water.

'Jess.' His voice came out so soft he wondered if she heard him. 'Jess, keep swimming, keep floating, and please listen to me.'

He had startled her. She turned quickly, using the water to hide herself, looking up at him, 'Get away! This is private!'

'Don't touch bottom.' He heard the fear in his voice but she did not. 'Jess, don't be scared, but you're swimming above quicksand. And it's all around.'

She looked round. 'Clear off! You don't trick me that easily. And where've you put my clothes?'

'Keep swimming, Jess, till we work out what to do. But watch if you don't believe me.'

The driftwood arced from his hand, landing on the gobbling-up sand. 'That's where your clothes have gone.'

Jess's mouth opened in a gasp. 'Sweet Jesus!'

'Did you dive in?'

'I jumped.' She paddled on the spot, arms moving, body still. 'Oh, hell. Why didn't you tell me?'

'I'm coming to the edge. When I reach out, grab my hands. I'll pull you free.'

She nodded. He stepped carefully to the edge of the pool, crouched on his haunches and reached out. Her hands were icy.

'Steady.' He noticed the whiteness of her shoulder, slope and curve. He tugged at her, leaning back, stepping back to make room for her feet.

A look of fear filled her eyes. 'My foot's stuck.'

He tugged hard. 'Pull. Pull!'

'I can't. It's stuck fast.'

He pulled her so hard he lost his balance. One of her hands slid from his. He righted himself and made a grab for her wrist. Hands locked, with everything in his being, he pulled at her, willing her to be free of the sands.

She was out. Naked. Standing in front of him; round breasts, flat belly, small mound of hair. She started to shiver. He took off his shirt but dared not give not give it to her in case, in moving, she splipped.

He hardly trusted himself to know what to do next. 'Jess, when I turn round, take my waist. Follow me along the path. I'll lead us back.'

She nodded.

'Like the tandem,' he said. 'We're the tandem without the bike.'

He kept his eyes on the sand, watching for a change of colour, for the grey sand that shook if you stood on it. Under his bare feet he felt the reassuring firmness of soft dry sand. For long moments they walked in silence. Only the gulls wheeling above them cried out to each other.

They reached white sand, strewn with seaweed. His hand trembled as he handed her the shirt. She took it. It fell from her hand. Neither of them moved. He could hear her breathing, short, shallow breaths.

'You did champion,' he said, picking up the shirt.

She put it on. 'I'm so cold.'

Neither of them moved.

'Idiot, idiot. Why didn't you tell me? You never speak. You could have said. All those hours on the bike, not speaking. You must have known I wanted to swim. All you had to say was, "*There are quicksands.*"'

'I'm sure I told you once. I'm sure I mentioned it.' He knew he had not.

She started to pound his chest with her fists. 'We could both have been killed.' She did not stop aiming blows at his chest, arms, anywhere her hands would reach. Then his arms were around her and she was crying.

'Can you imagine, if I'd had to tell them: "*Oh, by the way, you won't be seeing Jess again. She disappeared in a pool on the beach.*"'

She started to laugh. He did, too.

'And I would have gone straight to hell,' she said, 'because I didn't go to mass on Sunday.'

'You would have gone straight to paradise because heaven needs champion swimmers.'

For some reason this made them laugh even more. She couldn't speak for laughing and fumbling to fasten the buttons of the shirt. He felt he was looking at her for the first time.

They stopped laughing. 'Your feet and legs are covered in sand,' she said.

'So are yours.' He wanted to say that her feet were on the earth and her head and heart touched heaven every day of her life. Then he did say it, not knowing whether the words were his own or he had read them somewhere. Afterwards he did not know who made the first move, perhaps they had moved together. He liked to think so. Sand against their bodies, seaweed touching their thighs, they embraced.

'You taste of salt, Wilf.'

94

'So do you. I never knew how much I loved salt.'

She pulled him close as his hands touched her body, sliding across her breasts and thighs. When they kissed, she ran her tongue over his lips. His hand moved between her legs. Suddenly she felt him stiff against her and in an instant she changed, pulling away, saying no. No.

'Jess, Jess, it's all right.'

She was crying. He put his arm around her. 'It's all right. I've stopped.' He stretched out his arms and turned his palms skywards. 'Look, no hands!'

She gave a little sigh or a moan. 'It's not you, Wilf.'

'What, then? What is it? What are you thinking?'

She looked past him, glimpsing the road through a break in the cliffs. 'I'm thinking I better do up this shirt quick. There's the blinkin' charabanc.'

He followed her gaze. 'We'll cut round the back of the bungalow. I know the path. They'll all be going into the main building for cups of tea.' He took her hand. 'Bernadette will have brought you a change of clothes. We'll do it, don't worry.'

'Will we, Wilf? I'm not sure we ever will.'

'Five minutes, we'll be in our hidey-hole bungalow before anyone spots us.'

Only as they reached the path did he realize they might have spoken at cross purposes.

12

Saying Goodbye

On Wilf's last full day in Leeds, we went to the market café in the dinner hour and ate a slap-up lunch of roast, potatoes, two veg and treacle pudding with custard. Then the waitress brought us a teapot, and when she took our pudding dishes away, Wilf placed two brown paper parcels on the table, pushing one towards me. Below the paper was a covering of beef sheeting and under that a small, starkly white figure. He unwrapped the other and we set the pair on the table, pushing the Daddy's Sauce and the salt cellar aside.

'She's for me, and he's for you. They're marble, Jess, and as solid as our feelings for each other.'

As they faced each other, their arms outstretched, it made me want to cry.

'Do you like them?' he asked.

'They're beautiful. I just hope they're not in that position because someone's pulled a gun and said, "Hands up, give us the money." ' I picked up the smooth, heavy figure. He was lovely to hold. 'I'll take him out and look at him every night.'

'What do you mean, take him out?'

'You don't imagine I could keep a naked figure on display in our house. Mam wouldn't stand for it.'

'One day, when we're together, we'll place them either side of our mantelpiece for all the world to see.'

'One day.' I stirred the tea, let the leaves settle, and poured. Bubbles on top of our tea made me think we'd have good fortune. One day. But when? 'Three years is such a long time, Wilf.'

'It'll soon pass. We'll see each other. Holidays. We'll write. Don't ever doubt me, Jess. You do love me, don't you?' he whispered.

'Of course. And I'm glad you're going to art college. You deserve it. You'll be a great success.'

'Don't *you* be too successful, though! If you climb the greasy ladder of business, push Dad off the top and take over the firm, you won't want to know me.'

His train left early the next morning. I cycled to the station and met him at the barrier. He had bought me a platform ticket.

'Jess! I thought you weren't coming.'

We walked through, found a seat on the platform and, for a few moments, sat holding hands. But we couldn't stay still, and walked about, not seeing anyone else, only looking at each other. I hated the moment when the train drew in. We put our arms around each other and I didn't want to let him go.

'I'll write straightaway,' Wilf said. 'I'll write every week, whether there's anything to say or not. Promise me you'll write back.'

'Yes!'

'And I'll see you at Christmas.'

The train didn't go immediately. We looked at each other for a long time through the carriage window, smiling, not knowing what else to say. Then the guard blew his whistle, the engine roared and clouds of smoke filled the platform.

I went into the ladies waiting room to rinse my face.

Getting to work early, I chained my bike to the railings. Neither Uncle Bill nor Mrs Crawford had arrived, but the workers were busy on the factory floor. I took the cover off my typewriter and made a start on typing the September invoices, wondering whether it showed in my eyes that I had just experienced the saddest and gladdest parting of my life.

13

Controlling Skeletons

For two years I worked in the office of the Wright Shoe Company, saw Wilf in the holidays and wrote letters every week. My college course had almost ended.

I felt a little uneasy seeing the Treasures out of college hours, but had made the mistake of mentioning their offer to Mam. As college teachers and good Catholics, they are the Right Kind of People and might Do Me Some Good, she said. I must accept their invitation to tea. There I sat, waiting for their comments on my thousand-word commerce composition. 'The Boot and Shoe Industry with Particular Reference to a Leeds Firm.'

'We were left two houses and it is our ambition to buy a third. Hm. Mmmmmmah!' Mr Treasure smiled.

'Oh. How interesting. Mam is very keen for us to have a new place. Premises.'

He nodded towards the door of the cellar kitchen where Mrs Treasure had gone to make a pot of tea. 'I know this parlour may seem a little dark to a young person, but Mrs Treasure holds a fervent belief in double net curtains. "We must Hang Double Net Curtains," she says, in my view ranking it alongside church commandments, such as Visit the Sick, Comfort the hummm hummm Bereaved.' He gave me a confidential smile, then slapped his lips shut as she came up from the cellar kitchen, teapot and cups rattling on a rose-covered tray, set with a lace doily.

'The adage is this.' Mr Treasure watched his cousin-wife place the tray on the circular polished table. 'Leave the land in good heart hmmmmm-hummmm. Where one blade of grass grew, ensure that two-mmm-mmm grow after you are gone.'

I did not say that we do not have grass in Benson Street, and if we did I would not be in charge of it. I tried to think how his 'adage' might apply to me but had no ideas. I could not think of anything to say, which is what I had feared and one of my (many) reasons for not wanting to be there. *Comment favourably on some item of furniture or an arrangement of ornaments*, Mam had said. *If they have birds under a glass, admire them.*

The furniture had nothing about it worth commenting on. They had the usual holy pictures on the wall, the Sacred Heart and Our Lady, and a tall brass crucifix on the mantelpiece. No stuffed birds.

'What pretty cups,' I said. 'What a lovely tray. I like roses, too.' Immediately I regretted using three comments when one would have done.

'Thank you.' Mrs Treasure poured milk into the cups. 'One lump or two?' she asked. I have a sweet tooth so asked for two and wondered whether I would be able to snaffle an extra one if they turned away. But I decided against that because I am sure that a teacher of double-entry book-keeping and a teacher of commerce must count their sugar lumps before and after visitors.

'This is a very nice tea service,' I said, at the risk of repeating myself. 'You don't often see green roses.'

'It was bequeathed to me by my Aunt Harriet.' Mrs Treasure placed a spoon on my saucer. 'Yes, we have been fortunate in our inheritance, my erm, my husband and I. We were left two houses—'

'I've explained that,' Mr Treasure spoke to her more sharply than I remembered. He did not hum after his words.

I looked at the clock on their mantelpiece. Quarter-past four. Mam had said that I must stay an hour. Any less would be impolite. Any more might be a compliment or not, depending. She did not say depending on what. I wondered how soon to mention my composition.

I was saved the trouble. 'Most creditable, your piece on the boot and shoe trade, most creditable indeed. Hm. Hmmmmm. Huummmmmmm.' He waved the sheets of paper back and forth across the teapot. 'A few more commas would not have gone amiss. You write in a most breathless fashion. Hmmmm. Hummhummm.'

'Commas. Thank you. I'll look out for places to put commas in.'

'A dot in the margin. Look for the line where there is a dot in the margin and read that line hmmmmm-hummmmmm. Do not put commas in the wrong place.'

'You have a great future ahead of you. Please take a fig biscuit.'

I was partly relieved that there were no other comments on my composition. I would have felt a bit of a cheat because, so far as I knew, no other student of the commercial college had been invited to tea to discuss their written topic.

Mr Treasure slid my essay into a used brown envelope and handed it back to me.

Mrs Treasure topped up the teapot with hot water from the rose-covered jug. She waved her free hand about, as if giving a demonstration. 'This house was one of the properties bequeathed to us. Another, in Peel Street, is rented out to a reliable family who have only twice fallen into arrears.'

'It is our intention to rent out this property and buy a house for ourselves in Hanover Square. Mmmmm. Hummmm. Hm.'

'Hanover Square is very nice,' I said. 'I think all squares are . . . All squares have grass growing. And most of them have railings.' The clock said twenty-past four. 'You'll be able to sit in the square. That will be very nice.' I was pleased with my goodly outpouring of words and felt I could risk leaving the conversation to them for a little while. I helped myself to another biscuit. I did not want to have to ask for the key to their lavatory so decided to slow down my tea drinking.

Mrs Treasure re-filled my cup. 'You may remember, when you were so aptly taking on the role of housekeeper for the priests—'

The biscuit stuck in my throat. As I choked, and stopped the proceedings, Mr Treasure hurried, humming, to fetch a glass of water from the cellar kitchen. When I had recovered, I took a careful sip of tea.

Mrs Treasure continued. 'I mentioned to you why it was imperative that we marry. A condition of our grandparents' will stipulated that we must keep up the tending of their grave in perpetuity. We decided to marry so that we could adopt a child who would undertake that duty and pass it on generation unto genera-tion.'

There was a long pause. They looked at me intently. I felt I was being tested and must say something. But what? 'I see.' They waited for me to say more. 'I remember. And, erm, you asked me did I know the meaning of the word perpetuity.'

'And of course you did, mmmm-hummm-hum. Being a good Catholic. Hmmmm.'

Mrs Treasure smiled at Mr Treasure, and I understood that they had something to say to me and had decided in advance that she should be the one to speak. Did they want to adopt me? It is very awkward when you think you are going to get the giggles and there is no escape.

'We wonder now, whether it will be necessary for us to go to the trouble of adopting a child. It is not something in which either of us has experience. We have experience of young people, naturally, being employed in our capacity as educators at the commercial college. But neither of us has had much . . . well, much to do in a personal way with younger and more impressionable souls.'

The clock on the mantelpiece struck half-past four. I felt my face freeze into a kind of misery and tried to force a cheerful, listening expression, as I had done during his lessons that week on double-entry book-keeping, or her talks on the art and craft of modern commerce. She seemed not to know how to go on. *Don't let there be awkward gaps in the conversation*, Mam had said. *Say something.*

'I should think it would be quite difficult to bring up a child to tend a grave,' I said carefully.

'Oh no. We could do that. We were brought up ourselves to tend graves. Teaching a child to tend a grave is an easy thing. You take it to the cemetery every week. You teach it to read from gravestones. You introduce it to the whole of its family and to others with interesting names or who died in pathetic or arresting circumstances. Soon, the graveyard becomes the most real place in the world. It can be a source of great beauty, insight and peace.'

'Have you visited Killingbeck Cemetery on a Sunday, Jess? Mmmm. Hummm.'

I shook my head.

I had a sudden picture of the two of them as children, looking just as they did now but smaller, playing tig in a graveyard, chasing round the stones. But the child that they jumped on to say, 'You're it!' was me.

'Would you like to visit Killingbeck Cemetery on a Sunday, Jess?' Mrs Treasure asked.

Be polite, Mam had said. *Say yes to everything in life. Refuse nothing but blows.*

'No, thank you. I er, I do things with the family on Sundays.'

She leaned closer. 'Let me put it another way, more directly. We have discussed the matter between us and we believe you may be the answer to our prayers. We shall never have children, but you will. We feel sure of it. When we die, we have no one to whom we are obliged to leave our worldly goods. If you would be willing to undertake the care and upkeep of our grandparents' graves, and – if you felt kindly disposed, the graves of our parents – we should be much obliged and would make you our beneficiary.'

Mr Treasure had not spoken but began to hum all the same. I listened to his humming while I thought how to answer.

'Thank you for asking me. But I can't.'

'It would not be so hummmm arduous as it sounds. Three graves at the mmmmmost.'

'You don't have to decide now. I meant to say that, didn't I, Rich, dear? We do not want to rush you. Think about it. Think about it for six months, if you wish.'

'I can't. I'll probably go to live in London.' It had never occurred to me that I would live in London instead of Wilf coming home, but suddenly it seemed a good idea. 'Even if I stayed in Leeds, I couldn't make such a promise for myself, and not for people yet unborn.' I stopped myself from saying I thought them mad.

Afterwards, Mam said I was the mad one, and I must consider their proposal. This was a great opportunity to be a woman of property, and perhaps it was not too late. I called to tell Bernadette, who, now that she is Bernadette Mooney, spends her days behind the drapery shop counter. She said I must promise faithfully to tend the graves. She would do it for me, on Sundays. It would be an opportunity to escape the house. If I would share the booty when the Treasures snuffed it, she would be an independent woman, not answering to her in-laws, dancing attendance at their beck and call.

Dad said the Treasures were dotty and I should steer clear. He said that of course the living have an obligation to the dead, but not when the dead put it in writing and demand a signature above a penny postage stamp.

Wilf wrote to me that when he came home we should cycle to the cemetery and see the graves that held these controlling skeletons. He wanted to sketch the gravestones. I said he could go if he wanted, but I wouldn't. The Treasures would be lurking somewhere, ready to jump out on me and scream, 'You're it!'

14

The Summer Exhibition

When Auntie Irene enters the Wright Shoe Company works, older employees especially show her great respect. They remember her from years ago when she was Miss Wright, the boss's daughter. The door to the office was open. Before I heard footsteps on the iron staircase to our balcony, I knew she had arrived. The chatter from the ground floor died down. One or two workers called a greeting.

It was a summer evening, so still light. I had just put the cover on my new Imperial typewriter when Irene came into the office. She almost sat on Mrs Crawford's chair, until she spotted The Cardigan hanging on the back.

'I've told Bill you should have your own little office,' she said. 'You shouldn't be sharing. You could make it pretty, make something of it. We should all have beauty in our lives.'

This is the kind of thing Irene says since she took a night school course on the designs of her hero William Morris. Things like, 'You are what you look at.'

Bill also says I should have my own office, but that's because after qualifying at night school I took on responsibility for doing the firm's wages and costing orders.

The Wright Shoe Company premises are not just cramped for the amount of footwear produced, but damp and old. You open a drawer and a dozen silver fish scuttle about; you open a ledger and a black clock marches across the page to inspect the figures. I tried not to smile when Irene asked if you could get typewriter covers in a

William Morris print. She thought possibly we might find one in London.

She wanted us to see Wilf's second-year exhibition at the Royal College of Art. She hoped I would come, for the company and because she would feel less awkward with Wilf's young friends if I were there. I also felt uneasy about meeting art students but did not admit it. Irene was the only person in the family who knew how Wilf and I felt about each other. Mam would have raised the roof at the thought of me with Wilf – artist and agnostic.

Now I know what it feels like to be well off. When people think you have money they cannot do enough for you and treat you with great respect. On the train we travelled to London first class. We sat in the elegant dining carriage with linen tablecloths and best china. The waiter practically bowed as he took our orders and set down the soup. Irene has a way of catching a porter's eye, and our cases were whisked to the cab at the London end without my having to lift a finger.

Wilf came to our hotel. What a joy to see him! He made us laugh, talking over tea and cakes about the food his landlady cooks. For breakfast she gives him kippers or finnan haddock, no matter how much he says he would prefer toast or an egg. One evening he had the cheek to ask what type of meat was in the pie. She looked very put out and said, 'Best meat.' This has become one of his jokes and so for tea in the hotel we ate best buns and best biscuits with our pot of best tea.

Afterwards, Irene went for a lie-down, saying she'd have a bite to eat sent to her room later, and that Wilf and I should go off on our own and explore. We went to a stall on the Embankment, where he eats pies and drinks tea if his landlady's food has been too bad to stomach.

No matter how long it is since we have seen each other, within a second of meeting again things are just as they were between us. That is how I know we are meant for each other. I think London must be the most romantic place in the world. We walked by the Thames, watching lights twinkle in the water, waiting for the moon to rise. He walked me back to the hotel, and I got back so late that Irene was fast asleep. I tiptoed into our room quietly so as not to disturb her.

I felt a pang of envy as we made our way to the exhibition the next morning, sure that the art students would say smart, funny things to each other and be dressed in a clever Bohemian way, or in the latest fancy fashions. Bernadette had insisted on making me a skirt, long at the back. Definitely the latest thing. Of course I am always well-shod, and not in rejects. Irene said I looked fine and would knock any art student into a cocked hat.

Wilf had his back to us and was being talked at by an important-looking couple. Irene thought they might be potential buyers and we must not interrupt. As we stood for a moment, wondering where to begin, a total stranger bounded up to us in a wild way, as if we were his long-lost friends.

'You must be Mrs Price and Miss Price?'

Irene agreed that we were and held out her hand.

'I'm Ralph Moxon, Wilf's fellow student.'

He looked too old to be a student but explained that he had done a stint in the Guards Regiment. 'When I saw the most stately matron and the most beautiful young woman in the room, I knew you must belong to Wilf.'

We couldn't help but smile.

'You have the charm to be amused by me, which is all I ask.'

He was perhaps not as old as he looked but was prematurely balding. Lively, corkscrewing reddish hair sprouted from either side of his tonsure, making him look like a mad professor, except that a mad professor might be shabby and not care about his appearance. This man dressed – as Irene said afterwards – as if he belonged in the late years of the previous century, like a young dandy, with a long scarf and a sensationally large carnation in his buttonhole, as if he had been to a wedding.

'You must let me show you round. Up to now I've only envied Wilf his talent but now I envy him his friends and relations.' He looked at me and shook his head, as if with great regret. 'I wish I'd met you first. I hope you'll both sit for me, for your portrait. Wilf said you're staying the night. If you'll come this afternoon, I'd be very glad to do preliminary sketches, and try not to take up too much of your precious time.'

Irene shook her head. 'Really, I don't think—'

'Please. There'll be a day when a portrait of Wilf Price's mother will command a high price, not to mention a place in the National Portrait Gallery.'

Just at that moment, Wilf rescued us. But even as Wilf began to talk to me, Ralph held onto Irene, pressing his card on her, extracting a promise to have her portrait done by him.

Wilf walked us round the exhibition, saying what materials were used and which were hard to work and which not so hard. He came out with lots of words to describe the work, such as 'three-dimensional' and 'close observation of natural objects'. Thanks to her course on William Morris, Irene commented on the drawings for fabrics and how original some pieces were. I know that in his first year Wilf took four prizes in different categories, including dress design.

Both Irene and I felt a little apprehensive when he would not say which was his work and that we must discover it for ourselves. The work is to be judged without identification. He hoped we would be able to spot his pieces. I felt as I used to when a little girl and Mam would give Bernadette and me a photo of a football team of big fellows, or a huge group of soldiers, and say, 'Can you pick out your dad?'

Wilf left us to walk round. He chatted in a corner with a small, slim, dark-haired girl. I deliberately ignored them because seeing them so free and easy together got in the way of my concentration. Irene kept saying, 'Which is Wilf's piece, do you think? Is it that one?'

The sculptures were set out at one end of a long room, which had an open window. A white curtain blew in the breeze so it seemed that the room was breathing. Mam would not have liked it at all. Not one of the human figures wore clothes. Of course, it did not matter for the heads. One exhibit was very beautiful, a head of an angel with a short fringe and thick hair, exquisitely carved from wood. I knew it was an angel because of the title Angel's Head – but it had a look of a film actress, perhaps Vilma Banky, which made me say, 'This is Wilf's, Auntie.' Irene immediately hoped it was because it was the best piece in the room, according to her. There were mask-like figures, a carving in the shape of spear and shield, and a figure like an egg cracked open.

Irene said, 'What a lot of mother and child pieces.'

If I had not known from Bernadette, who knew it from Mam, that Irene once had a still-born child, I may not have heard the sadness in her voice.

I did not immediately recognize Wilf's second piece, not from a distance. Only when I looked close and from different angles. From the side it looked like a single figure, an athlete bending over to touch the ground. From the front I saw a bridge, then realized it was two figures touching hands, fingers to fingers. It had a sadness about it, too, because it seemed like two swimmers about to dive, but they never would because they met in the middle and became something else. I pointed this out to Irene and said that once you see these are like human figures, you see the shape of a calf, a thigh, a round shoulder, the curve of the arm. Long feet formed the base. But you could squint – half shut your eyes – and see just an arch, or even the entrance to a cave. The card said it was made of elm wood, which Wilf had mentioned was difficult to carve and had to be taken slowly. It had such a sheen to it and the grain seemed to bring it to life. 'This is Wilf's,' I said, and felt so sure; perhaps he had shown me a sketch of the ideas on his visit home during the Easter vacation.

I thought it looked like a young cat, arching its back, saying, 'Stroke me.'

'I'll take your word for it,' she said. 'So if we think it's the angel head and this, which are the other two?'

When I did not answer, she wandered off to look round, wanting to see everything, muttering about how they should have put names on the pieces. She came back to me after a moment. 'I've found one,' she beamed. 'He did a little version of it a good while back, a swimmer with her arms in the air.'

She led me to the swimmer, a bigger version of the tiny figures Wilf had chiselled out of the cracked marble gravestone. This figure was about two feet high. A card said it was cast in concrete. I did not like it half as much as the little marble figure. This looked as though it would never swim.

Wilf's drawings were easy to spot. Among them was a sketch of Dad, heeling a shoe on his last, hammer in hand and a mouthful of nails. He had caught just so the way in which Dad's hair swings when he tilts his head.

When we saw Wilf again, the dark-haired girl stood nearby but laughing and talking with someone else. He asked if we had spotted his work.

'Yes,' Irene said. 'Now you can tell us if we're right.'

We were. As we looked at the angel head, I said, 'She's no angel. Angels don't have bobbed hair and look like Vilma Banky.'

'That's how exactly how angels look.' Wilf admitted he took the idea from a film magazine and said he would not invite me to any more exhibitions of his because I would be too quick to give the game away.

Irene chose it as her favourite piece in the whole exhibition, and wanted to buy it. Wilf refused. It would be a sad day, he said, if, in an account of his work, when he became famous, he had to say that the very first piece he sold was bought by his mother.

Over lunch, Wilf told us of his plans to visit Venice with Ralph. He touched my arm. 'I wish you could come.'

Irene sighed. 'I've always wanted to visit Venice, especially Murano, to see the glass.'

'Let's all go,' Wilf said. 'It'll be a great adventure.'

But I knew that wouldn't be possible. 'Wilf! Some of us have to work for our living. I'm back in the office on Monday.' I wondered whether there would be a time when I could feel as free as Wilf.

Irene said, 'Since Ralph is your friend and you're going to Venice with him, we'd better keep our promise to sit for him.'

That afternoon, Wilf led us to Ralph Moxon's tall house in Chelsea. A servant let us in and showed us into a large downstairs room with a big chandelier. Minutes later, Ralph bounded in, like an excited child. 'I didn't think you'd come when you gave me the slip at the exhibition.'

He led us up to a studio at the top of the building, with skylights specially added to give him more light. Paintings hung and leaned against the walls, some finished, some only part done. Many were country scenes, with horses and dogs, and there was one of a race course. The figures in the portraits smiled or looked serious, but all looked affluent and delighted with themselves.

He had placed two chairs on either side of a tall, spindly table. 'I have a camera, too, so I'll sketch and photograph you, if that's all right.'

'I'm happy to sit and rest my legs,' Irene said. 'But I'm sure there'll be other opporunities for you to paint Jess.' She looked at Wilf. 'You two go off for a couple of hours. Leave me and Ralph to get to know each other.'

I was about to ask her if she was sure, but Wilf grabbed my hand and called, 'See you later, then.'

As we went down the stairs, Wilf grinned. 'That was very mean and very clever of Mother. You were the one Ralph took a shine to, but of course he couldn't say that.'

I expected him to head for the door, but he led me back into the downstsairs room with the chandelier, shut the door behind us and we began to kiss.

When we had kissed until our faces were sore, we went out for a walk, and to a café.

'Ralph's offered me accommodation in his house. Rent-free.'

'That's very good of him.'

'It's nothing to him. As he says, the house is there and he doesn't use half of it.'

'So you'll say yes?'

'I don't know.'

'Why not?'

'He can be a bit overpowering. He might get in the way of my working.'

'Nothing will get in the way of your working.'

'He has a yard at the back. That would be useful.'

When we went back to collect Irene, she and Wilf looked at what Ralph had done so far. Ralph came up to me as I looked at one of his portraits – a man with a whippet.

'It's good,' I said. 'Whippets are funny little dogs. You've caught it perfectly.'

He twinkled at me. 'I would rather have captured you. But I don't mind waiting to paint you, Jess. I'd wait for years.'

15

Clenched Knuckles

Once, not so very long ago, I thought I knew everything. The facts of life, the mystery of modern art, what it is to be a traveller boarding the London train, how people fall in love, how a person makes her way in the world.

It came as a shock to me that I did not even know Heather was expecting another baby. I had not been to see her and Leila very much during the summer. When I looked back on those times, though, my picture of her was resting with her feet up. When I asked her if she was tired, she said Leila had kept her awake in the night with tummy ache.

I called on a fine Saturday in October, my half-day off work. Dempsey barked and made a great fuss till I came inside and spoke to him. Heather was standing near the window, clutching the edge of the large shallow sink. Beads of sweat stood on her forehead and she looked in great pain. Leila sat on the hearth rug where Dempsey resumed his licking of her hands, as if she were a pup he had to wash. Heather clenched her jaw. Pressed hard against the sink, the back of her hands grew white as porcelain. I asked if she was ill. She said the baby was coming, as if I knew about it all along. Run for the doctor, she told me. I asked if I should fetch Tommy and she said no in a definite way. I was to tell the woman opposite, Mrs McDermot at number twenty, and to take Leila with me. Leila did not want to leave her mammy. I had all on loosening her grip on her mother's skirt. As I did so, Heather held herself stiffly and bit her lip. She managed to say, 'Go with Jess, little darling.'

And I said, 'Come on, I'm going to give you a ride in the basket of my bike.' I put my head back round the door and asked Heather again: was she sure about not wanting me to fetch Tommy? She did not speak, just shook her head at me and leaned forward as if a great pain gripped her.

I did not know what to do first. I ran to the house opposite and opened the door without knocking. A tumble of children turned to look at me. Their mammy had taken Stanley to the dispensary, one of them said, because he had fallen and broken his nose. They would give her the message to go to Mrs McBride just as soon as she came home.

With Leila in the basket on my bike, I cycled along the street. In spite of what Heather had said, I nearly called to Tommy as I passed the fruit shop, but saw that he was serving a customer and I feared losing time.

Pedalling nineteen to the dozen, I reached Dr Steinman's surgery just as he came out carrying his black bag. He wore his bicycle clips and was obviously on his way to a call. I didn't even dismount from my bike but pulled up in front of him, barring his way. 'Please, Doctor,' I said, 'Mrs McBride, on Benson Street, says you're to come straight away.'

He tutted and put the black bag in his pannier. 'I'm on my way to someone who's dying. I can't be in two places at once.'

Leila let out such a cry, calling for her mammy, but she looked at the doctor. It made me think that at two and a half years old she knew more about how to persuade people to do things than I did.

The doctor ignored her. 'Why didn't the woman go to the hospital? I arrange these things. I booked her in. They're all the same. Don't like the hospital, leave it till the last minute and then it's too late. Well, I've another call.'

'She couldn't leave the little one,' I said. 'Her arrangements went wrong.' I hated to say it because Leila listens to everything you say, but I had to. 'She looks so bad and she's on her own.'

He sighed. 'Well, I suppose the dying have a stronger way of holding on than an infant struggling into the world.'

He mounted his bike and cycled off ahead of us. I called after him, telling him the number. 'I know the address, young lady! It's the one with the cleanest curtains and best kept doorstep.'

That surprised me. Mam always said men didn't notice such things.

I followed the doctor on his bike back to Benson Street. Tommy had come to the doorway of Deakin's Cash Fruit and Veg Shop. He watched the doctor cycle up the street. I had to tell him. Leila put out her arms to him. When he didn't go to pick her up she said what her mammy says, 'Come here, little darling.' He lifted her up and rubbed noses with her, while watching the doctor pull up at their door.

'Do me a good turn, lass.' Tommy handed Leila back to me. 'Keep an eye on the bairn and give a call up to Mrs Deakin to mind the shop.'

He pushed his rough hessian apron into my hands and was gone before I could answer. I walked through the shop and tapped on the door at the back, calling, 'Mrs Deakin?'

'Just a minute,' a quavering voice called down.

I waited in the centre of the shop, looking round at the fine displays of fruit and veg, trying to think how to divert Leila, who looked so sad and a little scared.

'Do you like plums?' I asked.

She shook her head.

Two customers came in one after the other. I recognized the mother of the girl who rode bareback. The other, with neatly pinned grey hair, was the baker's sister.

'Where's Tommy?'

I hesitated, not wanting to say too much in case I upset Leila. Before I had a chance to speak, Mr Deakin, the ginger-haired son, came through the shop door. He looked at me and Leila, bag and basketless, and me holding Tommy's apron. Mr Deakin scowled.

'The doctor's just gone to Mrs McBride,' I said, handing over the apron. 'Tommy won't be long.'

He rolled the apron in a ball and flung it onto the sack of potatoes in the corner.

I turned to go. From the shop doorway, I said, 'Heather's having a baby. That's why Tommy had to go.'

He scowled. 'Midwife as well as barrow boy?'

I left the shop. The baker's sister came out behind me. 'That man's a disgrace.'

*

I didn't see any choice but to keep Leila with me. I should have known what Mam would be doing on a Saturday, with the house to herself for once. She would sit by the fire, examining first one bare foot then the other. She liked absolute peace and quiet for the job of tending her corns. One false move with the scissor point and she could be in trouble, she would say. We had heard often enough of Mam's aunt – poor-Auntie-Nellie-God-rest-her-soul – who trimmed and chipped her corns too fiercely, with mortal results. She died of blood poisoning within the week. Mam would begin by edging the scissor point into the dark heart of her least troublesome corn and probing gently.

So when I burst in, pushing my bike with Leila in tow – 'Laughing and talking like some giddy schoolgirl', according to Mam – she was not pleased. At first she shifted her feet to the fire side of the Tizer crate to hide their nudity, slipping the scissors up her sleeve, point first, nicking her wrist as she did so and pulling a face.

I could see Leila felt upset about being in a strange place, so I raised her up in my arms so that she almost touched the ceiling. I felt proud of her, as she has a lovely smile. And how she can laugh!

I said, 'This is Leila Catherine, Mam, my goddaughter.'

Mam glared and gave me that 'as if I couldn't have guessed' look. It didn't matter in the least bit to her if some urchin toddler saw her feet, so she placed them squarely back in the centre of the Tizer crate and ignored Leila.

'I'm doing my corns. I would have had them done by now if I hadn't kept your soup warm for the past hour and a half. Where have you been?'

Mam put down her scissors and took her feet off the crate with a very definite movement, stamping them on the floor. 'I need concentration for this job, not an audience. And have you forgotten we're going to see your sister?'

'No, I haven't forgotten. Come on, little Leila, have some soup with me.'

Leila clutched my leg, hiding her face in my skirt.

'She's wiping her nose on your skirt.' Mam slid a stocking over her misshapen foot. 'Try and keep a bit respectable-looking. What will your in-laws think of you, your clothes creased to blazes and streaked with snot?'

I wanted to bounce out of the room. I imagined myself kicking the

Tizer crate across the floor. She made me furious. How could she be so mean, scaring the child? But I kept my voice light and cheerful. Surely, if she knew the situation, even she would be a bit more sympathetic. 'Leila's going to have a baby sister or brother. The doctor's with her mammy now.'

Mam played with her stocking, as if she had not entirely decided whether to go on with the work of trimming her corns. Her eyes narrowed suspiciously. 'She'll have made an arrangement, then. Unless she made the arrangement with you weeks ago and you didn't tell me?'

'No.'

'Well, the child can't stay here. You marched her in without a by your leave, so you can march her out again.'

'Mam!'

'Don't mam me. You heard.'

'But—'

'It's the thin end of the wedge, people like that. You have to learn. You have to be cruel to be kind. I won't have you taken advantage of just because you stood for her at her baptism. We've no obligation to that family.'

I picked Leila up. 'It's just for a short while and—'

'Did she make an arrangement for the child?'

'Yes. With a neighbour.'

'So there's your answer. Take her to the neighbour. We're not getting caught up with them and that's final.'

'The neighbour had to go out.'

'Well then, go and see if she's in now.'

Leila started to cry. 'I want to go home.'

Mam called after me, 'You be back here in ten minutes!'

As I shut the door, I realized what must have annoyed her. Before Bernadette married, she was always there on a Saturday afternoon to fill a basin with hot water for Mam to soak her feet. That was supposed to be my job now.

No matter how peevish Mam gets, I try to see things from her point of view because I think it must be hard to have bunions that twist your feet out of shape, one leg shorter than the other and a hernia that has to be set in place every morning before she puts her corsets on. But all the same, it was difficult to know just why she had such a down on Heather. She had only ever seen her once, at the

Christmas midnight mass. Even then she made a big point of saying that was the only time she'd seen Heather in church and that she 'knew the type'. The woman, according to Mam, was nothing but a little gypsy. Just because she had fetched up from who knows where and once found herself a job in the Wright Shoe Company, working in the sort of low occupation she was fit for, that didn't mean she could insinuate herself and her little family into the Price household. Some people were just on the lookout to suck their way up in the world at the expense of others. Well, Jess hadn't studied and qualified to work in an office to be a baby minder for a gypsy woman and a barrow boy. That's all Tommy McBride was, a barrow boy. Oh, he thought he was the business, the bees knees, when old Mr Deakin got poorly and put him in charge. But young Mr Deakin had put him in his place all right. He had marked his card. Mam knew for certain that the world was full of people ready to take advantage of a kind heart. Well, two kind hearts in one family were two too many if you planned to prosper. She had tried to save Dad from himself all those years and she certainly did not intend to see my good nature taken advantage of. Looking out for other people did not take you any nearer to acquiring Premises.

I had no choice but to walk Leila back along the street to her own house.

Tommy opened the door and swept Leila into his arms. It took him a moment to force a cheerful look on his face. Leila looked round for her mammy. 'She'll be back soon. Daddy's looking after you tonight.' The tortoiseshell cat sat on the chair. Under the table Dempsey the whippet thumped his tail on the floor.

Tommy said, 'These doctors, once they've got it into their head that a woman should go into hospital they like to stick to it.' He put Leila down. She and the dog began to talk to each other, Dempsey licking her face, as if her toileting had been interrupted and now he could start again. When Tommy thought Leila wasn't listening, he said quietly, 'A boy. I won't tell yon, yet, she won't grasp it and she'll only worry.'

Of course, Leila missed nothing. 'A baby brother?' she asked. 'Where's Mammy?'

'She's gone somewhere to have a rest and be taken care of, just for a little while. Daddy will look after you.'

'Won't Leila be staying with the neighbour?' I asked. I knew that on Sunday mornings Tommy usually went out with the barrow of fruit and veg. I expected he would be doing so the following day.

'I don't work for Deakins after today.'

'He sacked you? He sacked you for leaving the shop?'

'That weren't no sort of job for a grown man, not since Ginger showed his nasty bloated face. I'll get summat better, summat more fitting for a man with a little family of his own.'

It was all my fault he had lost his job. Heather had told me not to tell him. She must have guessed what would happen. I wished that we shopped for our fruit and veg at Deakin's, so that we could stop going there.

When he asked me to stay with Leila until he went to the hospital to enquire after Heather and find out her patient number, I had to say yes. He took a small ruled writing pad from the drawer. Slowly and carefully, he wrote a letter, touching the indelible pencil against his tongue, turning his mouth purple from its lead. He wrote her name on the envelope and slipped the pencil in his pocket so that he would be able to add her patient number when he got to the hospital.

I guessed it would take him at least twenty minutes to walk there, twenty minutes back and fifteen minutes to be kept waiting by a porter. I was meant to be going to Bernadette's. Mam would be like thunder; she set so much store by our new in-laws and their drapery business. As usual, I would let the side down. Leila saw me looking at the clock on the mantelpiece and asked me to tell her the time.

While her daddy was gone, we said the numbers from the clock and sang nursery rhymes.

Tommy seemed more cheerful when he came back. I borrowed his pencil, licked the point and wrote Heather's hospital number on my wrist. 'I'll buy the paper tomorrow as soon as it comes out,' I said.

'Oh, her number won't be in it,' Tommy said. 'They only print the numbers of them who's very poorly. If someone's fine, they just say, "Everyone else satisfactory," or some such thing. They've only taken her in to feed her up.'

Michael came to the door to let me in. I like my brother-in-law because, even when he plays all formal and tries to be his father's son, I cannot help but remember his twenty-first birthday party when he drank too much rum at the church dance and sat in the corridor crying to me about how much he loved Bernadette.

They had pulled out the leaves on the table, brought a tall buffet from the shop and a chair from the bedroom so that all seven of us could sit down. Dad, Mam, me, Bernadette, and Michael and his parents. Mr Mooney senior looks every inch the draper, so well turned out in his dark suit, white shirt and striped tie with a golf club tie-pin. He has smoothed-down hair, turning grey, and an alert manner, as though any second he will jump to attention and show you a length of ribbon or lay out a card of hooks and eyes for inspection.

Mrs Mooney – the mother, not Bernadette, who is now also unfortunately a Mrs Mooney – has fair hair, frizzed out with curling tongs and always slightly burnt at the ends. Her main characteristic is a distinctive laugh that tinkles in a high register, not unlike the sound of their shop bell but continuously and more loud. She apologizes for her laugh and says she cannot help it; her mother and sister have it, too, she tells us, it runs in the female line.

She smiled at me and passed a plate of salmon paste sandwiches. 'Your mother tells me you've been on an errand of mercy.'

I caught Mam's eye. She smiled at me with a glare.

'Yes,' I said, playing for time, taking a sandwich onto my plate. The silence told me I was meant to say more but I didn't know what to say.

'She's godmother to the child,' Mam said, 'and you're kind-hearted, aren't you, Jess?'

This sounded like an accusation. I decided to keep to the facts, just a few of them. 'Mrs McBride and the new baby have been taken into hospital.' I did not mention that Tommy had lost his job.

Mam and Mrs Mooney exchanged looks.

'Is Heather going to be all right?' Bernadette sounded anxious, although she never usually showed any interest in the McBrides. I had once asked her to come to the park with us but she said no, not even bothering to think of an excuse.

Mam and me are not in company together very often, but when we are she frequently sends silent messages to me in very subtle ways, so subtle that I cannot work them out most of the time. She was putting a finger to her tongue and touching it to her wrist. What was that supposed to mean?

'Well, who is going to announce our news?' Mrs Mooney asked, smiling all around the table.

Mam put down her sandwich and rubbed one wrist against the other while nodding at me.

Mr Mooney inclined his head towards his wife. 'Why don't you, my dear?'

Mam glared at me, nodding at my hands. Were they dirty? I didn't think so.

'Well,' said Mrs Mooney, 'we are expanding.'

Mam and Dad turned their attention to Bernadette. While eyes were averted from my direction, I looked at my hands. So that was it. Mam wanted me to clean the number off my wrist. I had better do what she wanted. I looked at Heather's hospital number and said it over to myself before erasing it with spittle and my thumb. Because of that, I missed some of the details. The 'expansion' means that Mr and Mrs Mooney, the parents, will move to a new shop on Harehills Lane, leaving Bernadette and Michael to take over the present shop.

'Well, isn't that just wonderful,' Mam forced herself to say. It was the kind of news she would have wanted to announce for herself and Dad, but our removal to Premises seemed always to hover on the horizon, just out of reach. Mam fixed a smile on her face. Dad tried to swallow his mouthful of potted meat sandwich. He knew the pressure to move up in the world would be on him more than ever now.

Bernadette motioned me to follow her into the pantry. She handed me a plate of buns. 'I'll go mad, Jess, I swear I'll go mad. This is how they are. All they ever talk about is who came in the shop and what they bought. They snort about girls who buy velvet ribbons, and suck up to people who order quality liberty bodices for their daughters. I'm glad they're going to another shop and leaving me and Michael to this one, but how will I stand it? They've even got in a range of corsets and I'm to specialize in corsets. At both shops!'

'Did you make the buns?' I asked, not knowing what to say.

'Yes. I put a few in a bag for you to take to Leila.'

'That's kind.' I took the buns to hold onto them until it was time to go. 'I'm supposed to be the soft-hearted idiot. You're supposed to be the hard-nosed business woman.'

'That's their plan for me. I'd rather go back to being Vilma Banky.'

It had gone quiet while everyone waited for the buns.

'I'm going to have a baby,' Bernadette whispered, 'So I'll put the damper on all their plans. I can't tell you how many times Mrs Mooney's said babies and business don't mix. But what am I supposed to do? Send it back?'

I marched in with the plate of buns and she followed carrying a wobbly jelly in a blue glass dish. Michael took the dish from her and held her chair as she sat down. He knew. I felt really proud and properly grown up for the first time. Bernadette had told Michael and me, but no one else.

Mrs Mooney dished up the jelly.

16

Endings

Every day at twelve noon – rain, sleet or shine – Mrs Crawford would take her mackintosh from the peg, arrange her hat by touch, and go out, carrying sandwiches in a small brown paper carrier bag with string handles. Uncle Bill guessed she walked to the grounds of the parish church and perched on a gravestone, feeding crumbs to crows. He once asked did I want to place a bet with him and follow her. I said if he was right and she took to an open space, I would not have much success in tracking her unnoticed.

When she had gone, I went to his office and asked if he could spare me a moment. He looked up from his doodlings and said to pull up a chair. By the way he made space on his desk, I knew he thought I wanted to go over some costings.

When I explained my request, I thought at first he would be sympathetic. He listened when I said I knew a good worker who needed a job. He had worked in the fruit and veg trade, was taken on to manage Deakin's store, but the job had come to an end. When I said the name Tommy McBride, still he seemed inclined to listen. But when I said his wife Heather, who used to work here, was in hospital, Bill suddenly changed and became full of questions. Who had said to ask him? Was it Heather? Did people think he was running a charity for former employees' spouses and relations? He calmed a little when I said it was my own idea. Bill asked if the man was experienced in the shoe trade. No, he thought not. Well, he was sorry if the family had come on hard times, but the Wright Shoe Company was a business, not a charity, a business that would have gone under long ago if he listened to every sob story. The best day's work Irene ever did was to marry him, and the old man knew it. Old Mr Wright knew on his deathbed he had left his daughter and his business in good hands. If Irene had married my father, then there would be no business left by now.

I said nothing. So long as he ranted and raved, he had not turned down my request and I thought there would be a chance for Tommy.

It was no good being sentimental. I would have to learn to develop a business head to balance my tender heart, something my father had never done. Oh, he wasn't criticizing my father. No man could want a better brother. If it hadn't been for my father picking him up on the battlefield at Ypres when others left him for dead, he would not be here today.

I ignored the story of Paul saving Bill's life, I had heard it before. It was the first time Bill had mentioned there may have been a time when Paul, not Bill, may have married Irene. I did not let him drag me away from my main point, as I knew that any moment the foreman might come in.

Bill asked why, if this Tommy McBride fellow was such a steady chap, he did not have a job already. I told him how Tommy lost his job, with Mr Deakin, the fruit shop son, wanting to be rid of him. Bill said nothing for a moment. Then he seemed to soften. He said that when Wilf had worked in the firm during his holidays, he had taken a liking to Heather. Wilf had sketched all aspects of the works and workers, but Heather seemed to have a particular fascination for him. I said I could see that she would, because she is different and striking. But still he would not offer Tommy a job. Out of the goodness of his heart, he would help the family out, just this once, and I was not to ask again. He opened the safe, took out the cash box and counted five guineas into my hand. 'Don't say it comes from me, or he'll be round with the begging bowl. This is just until the man can stand on his own two feet.'

I wondered how I could explain to Tommy. I decided to say it came from the firm, and just be vague. After all, because Heather had worked there, a collection could have been taken. Five guineas would be a large collection, but not impossibly large.

I tapped on the McBrides' door. Dempsey recognized my tap and whined a greeting. There was no one at home. Uncertain what to do, I cycled to the end of the street and back. Deakin's Cash Fruit and

Veg Shop stood satisfyingly customerless. I couldn't think where Tommy would be, not when he had Leila to look after. He had said hospital visiting was once a fortnight and so it was too soon for him to be visiting. Much as I didn't want to, fearing to be seen as a busybody, I called at the neighbour's and asked Mrs McDermot if she had any news. She had not. Reluctantly, I cycled home.

Dad had left a copy of the *Evening Post* on the table. For the first time in my life I turned to the hospital report page. Number 397 was very poorly. Well, they would have to say that, to justify taking her into hospital.

We sat down for my favourite tea of veg fry-ups with the leftovers from the Sunday joint. Not until after tea did Mam tell me to stay sitting down, she had some bad news for me. Sad news. Earlier, Tommy had called to say his wife had died.

'Heather?' I said stupidly. 'No, not Heather. She was all right. They just took her in to get her strength up.'

Mam leaned forward, her arms resting on the table. 'They say things like that, about keeping strength up. They don't tell you the truth. You only had to look at her. There was nothing to her.'

I flicked through the paper and pointed out her number. 'That's her, number three-nine-seven, poorly.'

'It's an early edition,' Dad said, taking the paper and folding it up small.

Mam said, 'She wasn't made for having family. She had no hips to speak of.'

I wished I hadn't eaten. The food turned to iron in my belly. 'Poor little Leila. She's too young to understand. And what will Tommy do, without her?' I stood up to go.

Mam caught my arm. 'You're going nowhere. Sit down!'

Dad said, 'I'll go with her. She has to go. You know that.' He sliced the loaf and put a piece of meat from yesterday's joint between two slabs of bread, then wrapped it in greaseproof paper.

When we got to the door, I remembered the money in my purse at the bottom of my pocket. I handed it to Dad. 'I don't know what to say. Uncle Bill said not to mention it's from him.'

Dad took the money.

This time, Dempsey barked.

Once we went to a boxing match at Hescott's Gym, to watch a couple of lads Bernadette knew. They were well-matched for size, but one boy landed punches with the fury of hell in his fists. The loser staggered on the ropes, looking as if he wouldn't be able to tell you whether it was day or night, or even answer with his name. That was how Tommy looked.

It took him an age to speak. 'They let me in to see her. She said she felt the ward spin. The ceiling looked so far off. She said, "Please God, don't suck our breath away." I held her hand. I kissed her. I touched the baby's fingers and told him to look after his mammy. Heather said, "We'll look after each other, and so must you." My poor wife. She looked like some creature knocked down by the wayside.' After a long silence, he said, 'Leila's in bed. Go and look in on her, Jess.'

Dad nodded to me. I went upstairs. Leila lay in the centre of the bed, the blanket thrown off her, tear stains on her cheeks, thumb in her mouth. I lifted the covers over her, wondering how many times she would ask for her mammy, the mother who would never hold her again.

When I went downstairs, Dad had made tea. He put the meat sandwich on a plate. 'You eat it, Tommy. Get something down you for the sake of the little one upstairs.'

I don't know how long we sat. I didn't want to look at the clock. It seemed to mock us, tick-tocking when Heather's heart had stopped.

I wanted to ask about the new baby, but Dad stopped me, shaking his head. Tommy took small slow snaps at the sandwich. He had difficulty swallowing. Dad kept saying, 'You need it. Go on. There's no more than a couple of bites left.'

He lit two cigarettes. Tommy seemed to find his voice when he had smoked a bit. He would say something such as, 'We didn't want much, me and Heather. Just our two bairns.' And Dad would say something back. After a long time, Tommy would speak again, saying what they had hoped for, and so the words seemed not to hang together. 'Summat of a roof over our heads . . . Not to clem, not to see the bairns clem . . . Just to look out for each other . . . where did we go wrong?'

'You didn't,' Dad said. 'You went right. You did everything right. Your world went wrong.'

'I'll never get over this.'

'No,' said Dad, 'you never will. Never, and how could you?'

I didn't have any words. I don't even know what I said when we came to leave. I think I just put some water in Dempsey's cracked basin.

Outside, Dad told me that the baby had died, too. Tommy had said it when I was upstairs. 'What bairn wants to be in a world without its mam?' Dad said. 'The child was bound to follow.'

'What will Tommy do?'

'It's too soon for him to know. And it's not as if he has a lot of choices.'

I was glad we left when we did because moments later I heard the jaunty footsteps that always fill me with dread. Dad turned to see who stopped at Tommy's door. 'Father Flynn's visiting.'

I had been so good at keeping out of his way, but like a dark, threatening shadow he would appear when I least expected.

17

You Took Their Breath Away

On the day of the funeral, I expected to see Heather there among us, not dead but saying, '*What are you doing here? It was all a mistake. Go home now. Blink your eyes and know it was a dream.*'

They shared the same coffin, she and the newborn infant, together for all eternity, like two angels who would watch over each other. Dad said the baby boy was baptized Thomas, in an emergency by a Protestant hospital chaplain. But I somehow knew Heather herself would have put her finger to her tongue and blessed his tiny forehead, knowing it's the intention that counts.

All her pains were over now, but she must have longed to stay on the earth with Leila and poor Tommy, who looked like lost souls. The dull October day threatened rain, like damp fingers stroking my cheeks.

How will we help you remember her, Leila? I wondered. Was there even a photograph? I must ask Tommy. It must be treasured and saved.

Leila stood between me and Bernadette. My sister was crying and whispered to me, 'All any mother would want would be to take care of her child until it grows.'

I told her to shush because she does not seem to know how much Leila understands.

Tommy's burial policy ensured a proper funeral, but no headstone. He is a small man but held himself to his full height, though he looked drenched in pain. I have never seen a man weep, but he wept as the coffin swayed down and down. He had come without a handkerchief. Heather would not have let him leave the house for a funeral without a handkerchief. Dad slid a large white hanky with blue striped edging into Tommy's hand. He blew his nose.

When Tommy threw earth on the coffin, I took Leila a few feet away, to show her some greenery in a vase on a nearby grave – a couple of branches of privet, trimmed to fit.

I would not let myself cry for Leila's sake. Bernadette, with her tiny hat and oh-so-sleek, shiny hair, wept as if her heart would break, and she didn't know Heather at all.

When it was done and we all turned to go, I took Leila to Tommy and he held her hand. Dad walked beside Tommy, guiding him towards the cemetery gates.

I dropped behind. When Bernadette blew her nose and took my arm, saying, 'Come on, Jess. You did your best,' then I had all on not to cry. I said to myself, Don't cry. Don't cry yet. You have to be strong.

18

The Treasures
Make an Offer

On Sundays, Mam makes Yorkshire pudding in individual, rectangular tins. When I was small, Dad made us all feel happy and silly because he cut doors and windows in our puddings. He did that again today when I sat staring at my plate. So then I had to eat; but the food lumped itself in my throat because of what Dad had told me earlier, when Mam was out at church.

Dad said, 'Tommy asked if you'd go round there after dinner. The priest's going to call.'

'Which priest?'

'I don't know.' He gave a grim smile. 'You're the one with the inside knowledge of priests.'

'Why does Tommy want me there?'

'To be with the child. Perhaps to take her attention. It'll be hard for her to have her future discussed.'

'Her future? Her future's with her dad.'

'Not unless he marries again. A man on his own can't take care of a child.'

'Then we'll take her,' I said. 'Let us give her a home. Tommy will get another job. We're close enough by. She'll see him all the time.'

Dad let out a long breath. 'You'd have to ask your mam about that.'

We both knew what the answer would be.

All the same, I asked, as I picked up the gravy boat. I knew I must at least ask.

Mam paused, knife and fork in her hands. 'Jess, we can't take a child. Your poor dad working all day, you with a real chance to better yourself. You see how I have my work cut out. And I'll be helping Bernadette when she has the baby. People have to put their own family first. We could have had Premises by now if we were more ruthless in the way we go about things.' She paused again. Dad avoided her look. 'But we're not ruthless. No one wants us to be. But let's not be ridiculous, either. All right?'

I did not think I was meant to answer, but my sigh seemed to offend her.

'And you can stop all that sighing and long-facing about the place. You don't know you're born with the good luck of having a decent job and your college education.'

Tommy had kept the blind down, as a mark of respect. I went in expecting to see Leila, but he had taken her across to Mrs McDermot. I asked should I go over there, because so far as Dad had explained I was meant to be taking care of her while Tommy talked to the priest. But Tommy wanted me to stay with him. He had intended to keep Leila by him, but the thought of discussing her future while she sat there, asking for her mammy, was more than he could bear. I must be there, to help him do the right thing. Heather set a great deal of store by me and she would want me to play a part, he said.

Dempsey barked ferociously at the rap on the door. I opened it.

Tommy held the whippet back, saying to Father Flynn, 'He's not usually this fierce, Father.' He lifted the cat off the chair and dusted it with his hand.

The dog calmed down once the priest was seated. I did not calm down. I sat on the buffet by the far wall and lifted Dempsey onto my lap, stroking him, keeping him between myself and Father Flynn.

He said, 'Bless you, Tommy, and I'm sorry for your loss. Our Lord works in mysterious ways. He takes the ones He loves the best.' He scowled at me, waiting for me to leave. Tommy did not think to explain my presence.

I could not bring myself to look directly at Father Flynn. We had avoided each other carefully. Yet that day had come into my mind so many times, like a set of pictures flashing through my brain. For a time I had begun to believe that it was my fault, that I had led him on. But slowly, as time passed, the dread I felt told me he was the one who made the moves. He was the culprit, the guilty man. I convinced myself his sleepwalking was a game to worm his way into my room. I should have been thinking of Heather, Leila and Tommy. But sitting there, clutching Dempsey, I felt so filled with loathing and anxiety that I could hardly hear what was said.

My mouth felt dry. Father Flynn stopped speaking. Tommy seemed to forget we were there.

The priest looked at me directly for the first time. 'There is no need for you to be here. You can go now,' he said coldly.

I tried to keep my voice steady. 'Mr McBride asked me to be present because, as you know, I'm Leila's godmother.'

He brushed his hand in the air, as if what I had said was of no account.

Tommy seemed to come back to the present from wherever he had gone. 'Yes, I want Jess here, Father.'

Ignoring Tommy's remark, and ignoring me, he said. 'Let us kneel and pray.' He put a hand on Tommy's shoulder. The two of them knelt on the hearth, facing the low fire in the grate. Behind them, I stayed put, holding Dempsey.

He raced us through the *de profundis*, ending with 'Eternal rest grant unto Heather and Infant Thomas, O Lord, may they rest in peace.'

We joined in the amen. At least he hadn't suggested a rosary. When we rose from our knees, he indicated Tommy should take the chair. Father Flynn sat on the high stool, crossing his ankles.

He would state matters as he saw them, as he was sure Tommy would not be thinking clearly now, and indeed how could he be after such a severe blow?

The matters as Father Flynn saw them: Tommy would need to earn his living; he could not stay at home looking after a child, which was an unnatural occupation for a man and of course they would both starve within the fortnight. He asked Tommy questions, such as would he be able to pay the following week's rent? When he asked that and Tommy bowed his head, unable to answer, I wished myself anywhere but there.

Little Leila would be accepted into the orphanage where she

would want for nothing; her spiritual and physical welfare would be a matter for parish funds. Father Flynn himself visited the orphanage on a weekly basis and could testify to the loving care meted out to its charges.

Tommy did not speak.

The other possibility, Father Flynn explained, was that Leila might be put up for adoption by devout Catholics. In this way she would enjoy the blessings of family life.

Tommy raised his head. 'I was in the orphanage myself, Father. No one wanted to adopt me.'

Father Flynn looked at his fob watch. He had taken the liberty of inviting a Catholic married couple to meet Tommy, he said, and of course they would need to see the child. He had asked them to be here for three o'clock, but if Tommy did not wish to pursue this possibility then Father Flynn would meet the pair at the end of the street and explain to them their visit was not required.

I looked at the clock. Five to three.

It was as if the breath ebbed from Tommy's lungs. His breathing turned noisy and shallow. He could not seem to speak. Finally he managed a choked whisper. Father Flynn leaned forward to catch Tommy's words.

'They might as well come.'

I set Dempsey down. 'I'll fetch her.'

How pleased she was to see me, holding out her arms for me to lift her and twirl her. 'Is my mammy home?'

I crossed the street, saying, 'Mammy's not there.' I had explained about death as best I could, and so had Tommy. Each time, we thought she had understood. But she did not believe me about Heather until we got into the house. The priest frightened her. He tried to give her a kindly look, but she was not fooled, hiding her face in my neck and whispering, 'Take me to my daddy.' I crossed the room, passing Father Flynn on his high stool.

The strangest sensation came to me. Holding Leila in my arms, I was not afraid of Father Flynn. Holding her, I felt like a woman who knows instinctively how to protect. When I let her go to Tommy, the feeling stayed with me. As long as I had to keep her interest at heart and look after her, no one could hurt me. I felt fearless, even towards the priest.

There was a knock on the door. Every sound now seemed to make

Leila think Heather had come home. Dempsey started up again, growling and baring his teeth. I took hold of his collar and shushed him.

Tommy opened the door to the devout Catholic couple: Mr Treasure and his cousin-wife, Mrs Treasure.

The cat made a dash for the street.

Father Flynn introduced them to Tommy. 'I'll go now, and leave you to get to know each other.' He glared at me. 'No doubt Miss Price will wish to leave, too.' He held the door open, as if I would go through and let him follow me out.

'Jess can stay,' Tommy said.

Father Flynn glanced at Mr Treasure.

'We know Miss Price is the soul of discretion and a good hummm friend to all parties.'

Father Flynn wished the room good day and left.

'Hello, Leila,' Mrs Treasure said hopefully, touching Leila's cheek.

Leila set up a howl. Dempsey joined in.

Over the din, Mr Treasure said, 'We had thought to ask her some catechism questions, but obviously she's too hum-young.'

'Young is what we want, my dear.' Mrs Treasure touched his arm.

'You look a healthy man yourself,' said Mr Treasure to Tommy. 'Is there any history of disease in your family, or your late wife's? I'm sorry to be so blunt hummmm.'

'And you do have our heartfelt sympathy and prayers,' Mrs Treasure said in a very definite way. She had taken the stool vacated by Father Flynn.

Tommy said, 'Excuse me, I'm forgetting my manners. Please take this chair.'

Mrs Treasure moved to the chair, Mr Treasure moved to the high stool, Tommy paced the room speaking softly to Leila, holding her because she would not let him put her down. She was crying more quietly now.

'I'm healthy,' Tommy said.

'We understand the child would go into an orphanage, in the normal way of things,' Mr Treasure said. 'We would be honoured to take her and bring her up as our own. She would want for nothing. We are well placed, as I believe Miss Price understands.' He turned to me for confirmation.

Since I fell off the bike all that time ago, my leg can still go into cramp from sitting in an awkward way. I shifted my weight on the buffet. 'Mr and Mrs Treasure are well placed,' I said, rubbing at the pins and needles in my thigh.

Tommy did not have far to pace in such a small room. Leila had stopped crying and clung to his neck, refusing to turn her face to the company. Each time Tommy passed Dempsey, the dog licked his trouser-leg.

Mrs Treasure nodded at Mr Treasure. He cleared his throat. 'We know that you have fallen on hard . . . that's to say . . . well . . . you have a fine child, a credit to you hummm.' He took a blue cloth bag from the inside pocket of his coat. It jingled with coins as he placed it on the table.

No one moved. All of us, even Dempsey, who stood on his hind legs, looked at the bag on the table. At that moment, the clock stopped ticking. Tommy began to wind it, first with one key, then the other.

'I'm sorry,' he said eventually. 'I . . . Father Flynn didn't give me time to . . . My wife had sisters. We must first see if one of them . . .'

'Of course.' Mr Treasure stood up and reached out a hand to his wife. She took it. 'We're so sorry to have troubled you,' she said. I heard the disappointment in their voices. Tommy had his face buried in Leila's hair.

I walked with them to the door, picking up the bag to give back to them.

Mrs Treasure shook her head and pushed it back into my hands. 'We are not heartless, my dear. Mr Treasure and I agreed before we came that we should bring this . . . this help regardless of the outcome.'

They were gone. Tommy took the chair again. I sank to the floor by the fireplace, stretching out my legs across the rug. 'That's good about Heather's sisters,' I said. 'I didn't know you were in touch with them.'

'I'm not. I never met them. I have no idea where they are. No more did Heather.'

'But—'

'It was the money. I didn't like the look of them, too old and grey, but I might have risked it, if not for the money. How could I let my child go to people who come with a bag of coins?'

'You did the right thing,' I said. Somehow I would find a home for Leila. I put the bag of money back on the table. 'They want you to have it anyway.'

I was not sure that he heard me, or that he could see. He spoke, but almost to himself. 'I did well enough in the orphanage.' He raised his head to me. 'You'd visit her there?'

Leila wriggled from his arms and came over to me. I sat on the chair, lifted her on my lap and swung her back and forth, singing. 'See-saw, Margery Daw, Johnny shall have a new master. He shall have but a penny a day because he can't work any faster.'

'Again,' she said.

And I sang it again, and again, and again.

Leila does not like to miss anything and tried not to give in to sleep, but she has the habit of an afternoon nap and soon Tommy carried her upstairs.

When he came down, he said, 'I can't believe Heather's gone. I felt so sure when I woke this morning she lay beside me. I didn't want to open my eyes and find it not true. If only she'd tell me what to do.'

'What made you think of her sisters earlier? Is there any hope we'd find them?'

'All I know is what she told me.' He took a packet of gold leaf, with finger and thumb spread the tobacco across the thin paper and rolled it. Not until he struck the match and inhaled did he start to speak, pausing now and then as if to recall and piece together what Heather had told him of her past.

'Heather came from travelling stock. She were the youngest, and mebbe not much older than Leila is now when they was left to fend for theirselves, though who knows because she remembered in snatchy bits and pieces, and sometimes she said her own young life seemed like a misty dream. Her mammy, Leila Lee, died while they were on the road, in the horse-drawn wagon. Heather was too young to understand, but afterwards thought it must have been consumption. Her daddy was called Joe. He died not long after, of a broken heart, she said.

'There were older sisters and brothers, and for a while the children lived like wild animals – eating berries, catching rabbits, getting ill on wild rhubarb. Another travelling family come by and they took the older children. Heather wasn't sure why she was taken to a farm and handed over. She never saw her sisters and brothers again, and for a long time held it against them that they never come back for her. Only not so long ago did she let them off for what they done to her. It were after you and her went to Temple Newsam that day, and a little lad asked you for yer bus tickets. Well, Heather, when she come home and told me, she said that little lad were no older than the biggest of her sisters, so how could they have known to come back for her? She nearly told you of her sisters that day, because as the two of you and the bairn sat on the grass, she wondered to herself, did her sisters ever have the pause in their days to smell the grass, look at the sky and say to themselves: once I had a little sister called Heather, and how sorry we are that we lost her?'

Tommy finished his cigarette and stayed quiet for a good while. 'They worked her hard on that farm, clearing hot ashes, setting the fire, sweeping, scrubbing, beating the rugs. Outdoors, too. Weeding, scaring birds. Only when one of the children from the village come to help in the fields, and afterwards told the schoolteacher about Heather, did she get fetched to school. And when they left school, that girl – Catherine – she went into service in a big house. She were the one what said to Heather, "Go to Leeds, Heather. You are not happy so go to Leeds and tek your chance." This girl, young as she were, she could name a cousin or two who had gone to Leeds and done well.

'So that's how we come to meet. I were out in the street with the hand-cart, up by where your uncle has his shoe firm. Heather had a good job there. She come out in the dinner hour. Asked me how much for one apple, a Worcester Permain. The first time our fingers touched were over that apple.'

'It may be some of her family did find their way back to that place. Did she name it? The place she came from?'

Tommy shook his head. 'Back of beyond. But I know she once had a letter from Catherine, for she kept it ever so long and would sometimes read it.'

'It's worth a try,' I said. It had grown dark outside and I knew I had best get home. 'If you can put your hands on that letter, perhaps we could find out where she lived and whether her family ever tried to find her after they grew up.'

Even as I said it, it sounded unlikely that something would come of it, but I was glad because Tommy looked interested and nodded. 'I'll look it out. It's in the biscuit tin.'

'There's some hope, then,' I said, as he walked me to the door.

He said, 'If I can frame meself to get a job that'll pay me enough to keep body and soul together, I'll find some good person who I can pay to take care of the child, then we won't have to be parted. And thanks, Jess. I don't know what I would have done without you and yer dad.'

We had done so little. I wondered what else I could do.

19

A Piece of the Jigsaw

I cycled up from the Wright Shoe Company to Blenheim Square with my packed lunch. We sat in Irene's William Morris room. I held my plate carefully, trying not to drop crumbs. My doorstep of a cheese sandwich seemed out of place in such an exquisite setting.

'Why on earth did Tommy McBride turn down the chance of having the child adopted?' Irene asked. 'If the priest brought the couple round . . . You influenced Mr McBride against them?'

'No! It wasn't that at all. Tommy came to his own conclusions. The Treasures are ancient. They turned up with a bag of money.'

'They can't be that old. Jess, to you, anyone the wrong side of twenty-five is ancient. Presumably they would live long enough to see the child grow up?'

'I suppose so . . . But it's not just that they're old. They . . . how can I explain? When they're not teaching at the college, they practically live in the cemetery.'

'The woman works?'

'I expect she would have given it up. Honestly, Auntie, if you'd met them you'd think the same as me.'

'So it was you who put him off?'

'No!'

'Your intentions are good, Jess. But really you did a wrong thing by putting Mr McBride off the adoption. It seems to me you both let your hearts rule your heads. I can understand him being loath to part with the child, but how can an orphanage be better than a loving home?'

'I've been to their house. It's dark and silent. They have two lots of net curtains at every window.'

'For heaven's sake! What is wrong with you? You should see some of the children we have to turn down for holidays at Silverdale. We can't let them go because they're eaten up with lice, and have styes on their eyes, infected ears, scabs, rickets. I don't have to tell you, Jess. You can see them all around you. Why do you think your mother is the way she is with you? Because she's kept you from falling back into the gutter where she came from. I'm sorry to be so blunt, but really it's time you stopped meddling and let the man make up his own mind.'

I had come to say it and I would, whether it fell on deaf ears or not. 'I thought you might take her, Auntie.'

'Huh! Haven't you noticed, Jess, I'm old!'

'Not in the same way as the Treasures.'

'There aren't that many ways of being old. You have a bit of energy for certain things, and you decide what those things are. The Treasures are willing to give their time and energy to a child. I've done that. And now I've lost him. Oh, we'll see him from time to time, and the bond will always be there. I know he writes to you every week and I'm glad of it, but he writes to us when the mood takes him, which isn't very often.'

She stopped herself and I felt sure she was going to say that he only wrote when he wanted something.

'Jess, I have no regrets about adopting Wilf. He's been a joy to me, and I'm glad we helped him find his vocation as an artist, though Bill isn't always quite so charitable about it, as I'm sure you know. But we can't go through all that again. Now, finish your sandwich and I'll top up your tea.'

She came back with a plate of biscuits. 'Sorry, Jess. I didn't mean to be unkind. I know your intentions are good. But if you're trawling round Leeds looking for the perfect home for your goddaughter, you'd better ask Roman Catholics. No one else would be allowed to take her.'

Gladys Hardy's everyday boots are almost as familiar as any of our own. They stood in front of the cupboard at the side of our kitchen range: soft black leather, a little battered, size five, highly polished, taking the shape of her feet. They come to be mended often because she tramps the streets, visiting the families whose children go on holiday to Silverdale each year.

The boots sat with three more pairs that Dad had tried to deliver and brought back. He saw me looking at them. 'She was out when I called.'

I picked up the boots. 'I'll take them round.'

Mam did not definitely forbid me to go, just frowned and said it was too late in the evening for me to be out on my bike. I'd lose my way.

'It's well lit, isn't it, Dad?' I turned to him but he was looking at the paper.

Mam frowned again.

I put the boots in my bike basket. 'Gladys must find it very lonely without her dad.' I did not say that if I were Gladys I would be delighted to be rid of the mad old soldier. My words had the right effect. Mam raised no more objections. The visit then came under heading Comforting the Bereaved, which is a church commandment. So off I set, cycling along Regent Street onto Roundhay Road by the light of the gas lamps.

Gladys put me in mind of her father when she called to me through the closed door, 'Who is it?'

When I called back, I heard the door chain slip off its hasp and the key turn in the lock. She was glad to see me and to have her favourite boots back.

I sat down at the table with a cup of tea. A large jigsaw showed a country scene with many shades of green. She and Irene both like jigsaw puzzles and exchange them with each other. What a strange friendship between Irene and Gladys. They worked for the same charity, and shared the same son. Yet somehow, they made things work. I could understand why Wilf didn't want to involve himself with Gladys. It all seemed a bit too complicated. Pieces of jigsaw sky, green grass and the darker green of the trees lay in separate groups around the edge of the puzzle. While she poured me a cup of tea, I slotted in a couple of pieces of sky.

She said that when her father was alive she had all on to finish a jigsaw puzzle. It upset him to see an incomplete picture. Sometimes he would swipe the lot from the table. She commented on how fast I found three pieces of tree in quick succession, so I thought I would stop and let her do the branch herself. While she placed a leaf on a tree, I told her about Heather's death, and Tommy not being able to look after Leila.

She stopped doing the jigsaw and turned towards me, listening until I told her the whole story, except for the part about the Treasures' intention to train up some poor child to tend graves all its life.

I expected her to say the same as Auntie Irene, that any child would be better in its own home. But she said there were worse places than orphanages. At least in an orphanage a child would be fed, clothed, schooled and properly brought up, with the company of other children. She knew some of the nuns at the orphanage and had not a bad word to say about them.

'I wish I were older,' I said, 'and things were different for me. I would look after her myself.'

In my haste to find a home for Leila I had not thought that talking to Gladys might upset her and remind her that she had given up Wilf.

She spotted a piece of jigsaw – a top piece of the sky that had fallen on the floor – and bent to pick it up. 'You never know what the future holds. What age are you now?'

'Seventeen.'

'The little girl's two—'

'Two and a half.'

'Who knows? If you marry in a few years' time, she'll still be young enough for you to adopt her. And I'm sure as her godmother you'll be welcome to visit her in the orphanage, and perhaps take her out sometimes.'

I doubted my welcome at the orphanage. If Father Flynn had a say, I would never get to see her once she was in their clutches. But why shouldn't I adopt her myself?

As I reached for a piece of pond, she said, 'I'll leave the jigsaw for now. Evenings can be very long on my own. I'm glad I'm going away for a few days.'

She showed me details of the conference she was to attend, the Invalid Children's Association annual meeting in London. 'Honestly, Jess, if you could see some of the sick little children it would break your heart. It's terribly sad about your Leila, but at least she has people to worry about her.'

She went to the mantelpiece, took down the soldier figures her father had made and stood them in a row alongside her half-done jigsaw puzzle. 'I'd like you to choose one, as a keepsake. It always pleased Dad that you enjoyed playing with them when you were little.'

She thought I had difficulty deciding because I did not choose immediately. But I was thinking about what she had said.

She went to the drawer to find tissue paper to wrap my soldier. I put just one more piece of sky in the jigsaw puzzle while her back was turned.

Wilf and me planned to marry when he finished his course. But what was to stop us marrying now and adopting Leila? Nothing that I could think of.

'When are you going to London?' I asked.

'Friday.'

'It's my Saturday morning off this week. If I can take Friday off, can I come with you?'

20

Blind Man Preaching

'Wilf, did you say something about needing a hand? Only I've coloured in as much of my portly-city-gent as I'm going to today.'

Ralph did not usually work into the early evening, but that October Friday had promised himself that he would spend longer on the bank director's portrait so that it would be ready for the old chap's birthday the following week.

'Through here!' Wilf called. 'I've got a piece of Portland stone arriving.'

Ralph walked along the wide hall and out through the back door. The gate stood open. Two men, a father and his middle-aged son, wheeled the heavy cart into the yard. A large piece of stone showed through a hessian covering, secured to the cart with ropes.

In his serge trousers and big sweater, Wilf could have been taken for a workman rather than artist. Together the father and son labourers tipped the cart carefully. With Wilf's guiding hands, they slid the stone onto the flagged yard.

Ralph made as if to help. 'Why didn't you warn me it was a labour of Hercules? I would have held onto my paintbrush for another half-hour until you'd done.'

Wilf thanked the delivery men and handed the older man a coin.

Ralph shut the gate behind them.

Wilf gazed at his acquisition from this angle and that.

Ralph dashed at the white flecks on his trousers. 'Does this mean you'll be lost for the weekend, admiring this bit of Stonehenge and making sketches?'

Wilf nodded. 'Of course.'

'Pity. We're invited to a party tonight.'

'Well,' Wilf said slowly. 'I won't be doing too much looking by lamplight. It can wait until tomorrow.' He walked around it, slid his hands across its breadth, holding and pushing at the same time. He did not take notice when the front doorbell rang.

His butler had the evening off. Ralph went to answer it himself.

He did not call Wilf straightaway, but made a fuss of Jess in the hallway, helping her off with her coat.

'Jess!' Wilf walked towards her, mouth open with surprise, eyes lit with pleasure.

'I suddenly thought you might not be here, or have gone away for the weekend.'

'We have no plans whatsoever,' Ralph said. 'Now, let me sort out some refreshments. I'm sure you need replenishing after your journey.'

'I had something at the hotel. Perhaps just a cup of tea.'

'With the greatest of pleasure. I'm sure you two have a lot to talk about. I'll leave you to it.'

Wilf led Jess into his sitting room. She stood in the centre of the room in her cream blouse and black skirt. He drew her onto the saggy brown sofa and sat beside her. In an instant, the room lost its shabby look. Her hair smelt of the steam train. His lips on her neck tasted the soot of the station.

'Is everything all right at home?'

'Yes, everyone's well. I had the last-minute chance to come to London with ... well, with Gladys Hardy. She's here for a conference.'

'And she invited you?'

'Wilf! Why are you always ready to think she's chasing after you? She could have done that long before now. I invited myself, because I wanted to see you. I have something to ask you, and I'd better not put it off or I'll lose my nerve, because it's not something a girl normally has to ask.'

'Ask me anything.'

But Jess could not because he was kissing her again.

Ralph tapped on the door and walked straight in, bringing a tray of tea. 'Oops! Sorry. I'm interrupting. I don't usually do this sort of thing, Jess, but my man has the evening off. I hope I've done you justice on the cake and biscuit front.'

He had put a cup on for himself. 'Now, you must let me be mother, but I shan't stay, just long enough to make sure Wilf offers you all necessary hospitality. You will let us put you up?'

'Thanks, no. I'm in a hotel nearby, the Chelsea Gate.'

'Then you must promise to come back tomorrow and sit for me. Milk or lemon?'

'Milk, please.'

'Milk it is. And I insist that I paint your portrait. It will be part of my wedding gift, if you like. I've made Wilf promise I can be best man.'

Jess looked at Wilf, uncertain how to respond to Ralph's request to paint her.

'Oh, sit for him,' Wilf said. 'I'll never hear the end of it otherwise.'

When Ralph finally left them alone together, Wilf asked, 'What is it? I can't imagine what you want to say to me that's so important you wouldn't put it in a letter.'

'Show me round first. I didn't get a proper look in the summer.'

He led her round the ground-floor rooms that Ralph had given over to him, and back to the front room. She flicked the light switch, for the ceiling light and the lamp. 'Will he let me come here, too, do you think?'

'I suppose so. But by next year, when I've finished my course, we probably won't want to. I'd like to have a place in the country where I'll have room for a decent-sized workshop, space for my carving.'

'But for now, there's enough space for us – and for a child.'

'A child?' He could not keep the alarm out of his voice. 'I hope we won't have children yet.'

'I want us to bring the wedding forward, Wilf. I don't want to wait until next year. We could have a child. Within nine months we could have a child.'

'Of course we could.' He took her in his arms.

He went to his desk and picked up a book of poetry. 'Remember me talking about the English master at school? How he carried the torch for Laurence Housman. Well some lines kept coming back to me, and I couldn't get them right. I picked up this book in a second-hand shop yesterday, to find the piece because it so expressed what I feel about you. Listen:

To sleep with you, and wake with you,
Lie down with you, and rise,
And let you feel the sunshine through
My love upon your eyes.'

'Wilf, that's beautiful.'

'Of course we'll bring the wedding forward. I wish it were tomorrow.'

He led her back to the sofa and they embraced. The way she kissed him, her mouth slightly open, inviting, he wanted never to stop kissing her. He ran his hands over her body.

'I'm so glad you said yes, Wilf. But don't you want to know why?'

'Because we love each other.'

'Yes, but there's something else.'

'What? Tell me. Are they sending you mad at home? Is it your mother? Is it my dad over-working you?'

'Mam's her usual self. Uncle Bill really appreciates me. He said he doesn't know how he ever managed the firm without me.'

'What then?'

'I told you about Heather's death.'

'Yes. I was so sorry.'

'I want us to adopt my goddaughter, Leila.'

'Jess! That's mad. We're in no position to adopt a child.'

'Why not? What difference would it make?'

'Well . . . I need to make my way, so we can live properly, not in some hole-in-the-corner set-up. No one can be a successful artist with babies screaming and toddlers to fall over.'

'It wouldn't be like that. If money's tight, I'm sure I could get a job and we'd find a nursemaid. We're ready to start our own life together, Wilf? Aren't we?'

'I can't wait.'

They kissed again. He kissed her eyelids, her cheeks, her mouth, and ran his hands over her breasts. 'Jess.'

'Yes?'

'Take off your blouse.'

She hesitated.

'Jess, don't say no to me.'

Slowly she undid the buttons on her blouse as he watched, then helped her slide it off her shoulders. He kissed her breasts. She undid his shirt.

'Do I stop? Do we wait?' he asked.

She sighed. 'Wait for what? Wilf, we began this on the beach at Silverdale over two years ago, and I couldn't then . . . I have to know . . . Perhaps I can't.'

'Jess, what a thing to say!'

'You don't know.'

'What don't I know?'

But she didn't say, only shushed him and said they had talked enough.

And when they had made love, Wilf felt he had not been slow enough, or tender enough, so he kissed her again and again.

The sky turned dark. He went down to the kitchen and found some food and made another pot of tea, realizing Ralph had gone out to his party. When he went back to the room, she had dressed again. He did not know why they spoke in almost whispers as she poured tea.

For what seemed a long time they sat together quietly, looking out into the darkening street.

'Come home next weekend, Wilf. We'll tell the families together, then we'll do what we said, and come to London to be married in Chelsea Register Office. Mam can tell people what she likes.'

'And this child . . .' Wilf suddenly sounded less sure of himself. 'I hope Ralph won't mind a toddler pottering about.'

'She'll be no trouble, honestly. You're not having second thoughts?'

'No thoughts at all! I don't have to think. Jess, if it's what you want, it's what we'll do.'

Arm in arm, they walked back to the hotel. A light shone from the fanlight above the hotel door. 'Shall I come in with you?'

She shook her head.

'I love you, Jess. I'll call for you in the morning. I'll never hear the end of it if you don't let Ralph do your portrait.'

'Goodnight, Wilf. I love you, too.'

As he walked back, Wilf felt sure he had made the right decision. When he qualified, he could teach, as well as get commissions. He would make a home for them. True, he had not intended to leap into teaching. He and Ralph Moxon had talked about putting on an exhibition. They were sufficiently different to team up, and share exhibition and gallery space. If he worked hard, made the right choices, perhaps he and Jess and the child – and any other children of their own – would live well enough. It was just not what Wilf had planned. But the thought of having Jess by his side made any other plans dissolve.

Alone in his room, he began to sketch, wondering what he would find in the Portland stone. And much as he wanted no words, only images, he hated his old English master who had fought in the war and carried the torch for Housman because another verse bounced about in his mind:

> You hear a blind man preach the light
> Wherein he never dwelt,
> Because his hands can handle right
> The darkness that is felt.

A sudden rush of fear caught Wilf by surprise and made him catch his breath. What if, with a wife and child to think about, he could not 'handle right'? Perhaps his career as a sculptor would be stillborn. He would become like some of the older tutors at the art school: a man who had stopped hoping.

Early on Saturday morning, Wilf pushed open the door of the Chelsea Gate Hotel. It was time he grew up, he told himself, time he introduced himself to Gladys Hardy. His mother. After all, if it had not been for her, Jess may not have come to London this weekend and given him the most blissful hours of his life yesterday evening.

He asked the clerk at the desk if he would take a message, but Jess came down alone. Gladys Hardy had breakfasted early and left for her conference.

As Wilf and Jess ate breakfast together in a café on the King's Road, Wilf reached out to her and they held hands across the table. 'We'll do this every day of our lives, Jess. You and me, having breakfast together.'

She smiled, and he was glad she did not mention that there would be a child sitting there – a small, dark-haired child he found difficult to imagine.

They made their way back to the house, where Ralph had his

studio on the top floor. Ralph had already prepared for Jess to sit for him, placing a rattan chair by the window and beside that a table set with a vase of flowers.

As Wilf went back downstairs, he heard Ralph say, 'I'm going to take your photograph, Jess, so I'll have something else to work from. Because I know you won't want to spend all your precious time in London sitting in here for me.'

Wilf sketched circular shapes; something biblical like a stone being rolled from the mouth of a cave. He remembered the shape of the Cow and Calf rocks in Ilkley, big and small, unequal but balanced. When his pages were filled with shapes, he realized that there had been sounds on the stairs and voices, and he came back to the present. Ralph had released Jess from her sitting. He was glad Ralph had so quickly wanted to paint Jess. Everyone would. He would have to protect her, guard her from the cronies who were always on the lookout for an attractive female. She must not sit for anyone else, only Ralph, whom Wilf trusted implicitly.

'We were just about to call you,' Ralph said, when Wilf emerged and followed the sounds to the kitchen.

Ralph laid the table with plates, dishes and spoons. He set out a bowl of fruit.

Jess did not meet Wilf's look. Something had happened.

'What's wrong?' Wilf asked. 'Are you tired? Ralph, you shouldn't have kept Jess sitting so long.'

'It's not that,' Jess said quietly.

'What then?'

'Ralph's told me. About your award.'

'Yes. Well, you knew about that. It's no secret.'

'But not the conditions. That it's for a single man. And it will open all sorts of doors for you, because it's a very prestigious award to have won.'

Wilf knew what was coming. He glared at Ralph. 'You had no business . . .'

Ralph spooned soup into dishes. 'Yes, I did. Jess had to know. It wouldn't be fair to keep her in the dark.'

Jess looked so beautiful as she gazed at him, her head slightly tilted, a questioning look in her eyes. 'We can't do it, Wilf. We must wait till next year, as we said all along. You'll lose the opporunity if you marry.'

'I don't care,' Wilf said. 'Besides, who'd tell?'

Ralph put Jess's soup on the table, then Wilf's. 'You wouldn't keep a girl like Jess a secret,' he said. 'It would come out.'

'Let it.' Wilf sat beside Jess and took her hand. 'I said we'd marry now and we will.'

'No.' Jess pulled her hand away. 'Don't try to persuade me, Wilf. All that work at Leeds College of Art, doing so well now. It's too important to risk throwing it away.'

And Wilf loved her more than ever in that moment, knowing she was right, and he hated himself because a great relief swept through him. Some months of freedom, in which he'd prove himself; some months of freedom without another man's child around his neck. Jess saw it in his eyes.

'And I know, you can't hide it. I know you don't want Leila. Perhaps by next year . . .'

'Of course I want her, if you do,' Wilf said, unsure whether he lied or told the truth, and in that moment he wanted to hurry back to his sketch book because he saw that the great boulder rolling back from the cave, rolling out of his Portland stone, had a hole running right through it that matched the emptiness he felt at the thought of having to wait for Jess for months and months.

He closed his eyes, kept the image steady and knew he would come back to it.

'Come on, Jess. I'm going to show you the sights of London and make you change your mind.'

'You won't change my mind, Wilf. We're going to wait until next year, even if Leila has to stay in the orphanage until then.'

21

March of the Orphans

'Go to the nine o'clock mass,' Mam said. 'You'll see the orphans and how much company Leila will have, bigger girls who'll look out for her.'

I heard their clogs before I saw them, tap-tapping on the tiled floor. Leila spotted me straightaway, as if she sensed my presence.

The big girls came first, heads bowed. She stepped out as best she could although the clogs looked too big and must have weighed heavy on her little feet. Her eyes fixed on mine. No words came from her mouth but she slowed her halting steps. Her lips moved, saying, *My mammy?* The nun behind her put hands on Leila's shoulders and moved her along towards the front pews where the orphans take their places.

Afterwards, when I thought about everything, I felt it must have been to do with seeing her, so tiny, dressed top to toe in black. Black dress, stockings, coat, bonnet and clogs, all black, like a baby widow. I did not know they made black serge coats so small, and with buttons too big for tiny hands.

I sat for the epistle, stood for the gospel, knelt for the offertory, up and down like a mechanical creature. The mass was no different from any other. Father Flynn gave a long sermon, explaining in confusing detail how an allegory is different from a parable. The Old Testament story about the man who tended his vineyard with great care, yet even so only wild grapes grew, that was a parable. I thought he glared at me when he spoke of wild vines. I kept thinking that Leila might want to go on her potty, or have a drink of water, or need a cuddle. The second collection was for the orphans, Father Flynn said. Mam nudged me. She put her hand in her pocket and passed me an extra penny for the second collection plate.

For two years I had tried going to another church, to a mass where he would not officiate. Putting it off. Not wanting to admit to myself that everything I once believed in had fled. Loss of faith once seemed a thing to dread. Now all I felt was relief, and a sense of how ridiculous it all seemed.

When the mass ended, along came the orphans in reverse order. The big boys led the way, followed by little boys, then big girls and little girls. Mam knelt with her face down, not looking, busy pestering God, praying for whatever she prays for. Premises probably. I sat, watching the orphans go by. When little Leila drew near she smiled a kind of desperate smile, reached out her arms to me and cried, *Come here, little darling.* I moved towards her, but the nun cuffed her lightly and half lifted half pushed her along. What a wail she set up, hitting the roof with her cry.

I said to Mam, 'We have to take her.'

Mam had not been praying at all for she had missed nothing. 'She'll settle in. Even the cat took a week or so to settle. She's young enough to forget.'

I couldn't eat my Sunday dinner. It would not pass the lump in my throat. Dad did not cut doors and windows in my Yorkshire pudding. Mam said I must eat, and what a waste to leave food on my plate like that with people starving all across the town and the world. I said I would eat it later and put the plate in the oven. She said it would spoil and what a waste and a sin.

Walking along the street in the drizzle, I thought surely something else could be done. In spite of the rain and grey seeping damp, Tommy sat on his doorstep, Dempsey beside him. 'I can't bear to be inside on me own,' he said. 'I won't be for much longer.'

The biscuit tin on the table was full of papers. He dipped his hand into it, as if running his fingers through water. But his hand came out empty. 'I can't stand to look. It's our marriage lines, the young un's birth certificate. It's . . .' His voice trailed off. 'You mun take them. They need a birth certificate for Leila at the orphanage. Will you keep the rest? Keep them for her.'

'Where are you going?'

'On the tramp. I've chance of a lift part way down the country. There's nowt here for me, lass. I mun try my luck...'

The word luck seemed to stop his mouth.

'Yes, of course I'll take them.' I wanted to ask if he had looked through the stuff. Perhaps there would be a clue about Heather's sisters, or someone who might help.

'And Dempsey,' he said. 'I don't like to ask, especially since your mam took the cat for me. But it's cruel on a dog to take it tramping till its paws bleed.' He took a piece of string and tied it to Dempsey's collar. 'I know it's a lot to ask.'

The dog looked at me expectantly. I stroked its head. It seemed to me the cruelty was in how easy it could be to say yes to a cat or a dog, and how impossible it seemed to say yes to my little Leila. 'Perhaps there's someone ... someone's address in among the papers...'

For a moment he looked all brightness, as he had when I first met him and he was full of hope. But quickly the brightness slid away and he sighed. 'I don't think so. No. I'm sure not.'

We walked together to North Street, Dempsey trotting between us. 'There is summat else. When I talked to't baker, Mr Barker, he sent me off to his solicitor. I used some of the money they sent from the Wright Shoe Company to get a lawyer's letter off him. It's among them papers, giving you authority over Leila when you reach eighteen, or marry.'

On the corner of Benson Street and North Street he shook my hand. 'This is the parting of the ways, Jess love. I know you'll do what you can for our little lass.'

'But you'll be back?'

He sighed. 'It's hard for a working man to have good intentions. I can't muster any just now. Given a choice, I wouldn't go. It's a matter of seeing what life throws at me.'

The whippet wanted to go with him, but he spoke to him gently and told him to stay with me. Dempsey understood.

Bernadette was on her own, as Michael had gone to visit his parents. She lay back on the chair, her feet on a buffet, her hands on the bump in her belly. I had to take three dishes from the cupboard before I chose one that she agreed I could fill with water for Dempsey.

'I don't suppose you and Michael would consider—'

'No. I've told you. His mam and dad don't want me to have *this* one. "Babies and business don't mix," they keep saying Honestly, who would have thought it? If that got announced from the pulpit they'd never dare show their faces again.'

I sat at the table and looked through the documents Tommy had given me. I could not bring myself to read the school exercise book in which Heather seemed to have written messages for Leila. It gave me a shiver just to see them, wondering if she knew she might die. Tommy had put the marriage and birth certificates together, rolling them up tight so that they were the width of a hand-rolled cigarette. He had tied them with a piece of string. More saved ends of string and scraps of brown paper lay in the bottom of the biscuit tin. What caught my eye was a letter without a date, with an address in Garforth.

My dear friend Heather

You said you would write and you did and I am so glad. See I told you trying your luck would be a good thing and now you are a Leeds lass who can earn a bob or two and not a lost soul at the beck and whim of those old slavedrivers. I should have followed my own advice as work here is morning till night brushing, scrubbing, carrying kettles and shovels of coal, dusting, polishing, beating more rugs than you can count after sprinkling them with salt which takes as much getting out as the muck. Do not say I said this if you write back to me as I would not put it past them to read my letters as they think they own you body and soul.

Well what I can say is that the other servants here are good fun especially the gardener who is a young gardener on account of his father the old gardener dying. I can tell you he is more thought of by their nibs than we maids of work will ever be. He keeps the garden splendid and we are never short of vegetables as he has a private patch only he and me know about.

I would like to see you but I do not even get to see my mam and dad and the children much as it is too far to go and come back in a day except in the one week of the month when I have all of Sunday off.

I will close for now as they are ringing the so-and-so-ing bell for me again.

With the best of kind regards and wishes from your friend
Catherine Muston

Bernadette had her eyes shut. The clock on her mantelpiece struck two.

'I'm going to cycle to Garforth,' I said quietly, hoping not to wake her. 'I'll borrow your bike.'

'You are not,' she said, not troubling to open an eye. 'It'll be dark soon.'

'I'll be there and back. There's someone I have to see.'

Before she could argue, I picked up the biscuit tin. The whippet jumped to his feet. I was closing the door as Bernadette called, 'You're potty! Someone got knocked off their bike and killed by a motor car on York Road last week.'

A wizened old man standing by the Garforth war memorial pointed out the big house with its iron railings. A set of wide gates led onto a gravel drive. Now that I was there, I knew Bernadette had been right. It was fast growing dark. I hid my bike by some bushes and walked round to the side door where a light shone from the kitchen window.

From the sudden disappointment on her moon face, I guessed that the woman who opened the door had been expecting someone else. She recovered quickly, having one of those round, open faces that feels obliged to smile. Catherine Muston moved on ages ago, she told me. She married the gardener and they had got work in Gloucestershire, or was it some other place that sounded like Gloucestershire, she couldn't be sure.

'Come in a minute,' she said, opening the door and telling me to sit down. I must have looked weary because she poured me a glass of milk, told me she was called Dorothy, and offered me a buttered teacake, which I shared with Dempsey. Dorothy did not get to know Catherine very well as Catherine left shortly after she arrived, and she did not have an address. She thought the gardener was called Herbert, or was it Horace?

I wanted to cry. I wanted to cry because of how close Catherine and Heather had once been, such good friends. Now Catherine was somewhere else in the world, thinking fondly of the friend she had lost touch with, believing that Heather still walked the earth. It made me feel so sad. I asked Dorothy for paper and a pencil, and wrote my name and address, and that I was a friend of Heather, just in case Catherine ever got in touch, or someone else in the house knew where she had gone.

Dorothy took the paper from me and read it upside-down. She slid it into her apron pocket, promising to take good care of it. Somehow I felt sure that the next time the apron went in the wash, so would my address.

She walked down the path calling after me, 'I remember summat!' We stood on the gravel path. 'I remember the cook saying that your friend Heather came to see Catherine, about how long ago would it be? The Michaelmas before I come here, so that would be over three years. She come on a tandem with a young man, and made them all laugh by telling them she and the young man had sung "On a Bicycle Made for Two" the whole way here.'

Cycling home by palest moonlight, Dempsey sprinting like a ghost dog beside me, I kicked myself for not being more bold. The mistress of the house may have had an address; given references, or sent a wedding present. But it was too late to turn back.

Mam's fury boiled over. As I wheeled Bernadette's bike into our house, she screamed at me. Did I know the time? Usually we had to keep our voices down, so as not to let the neighbours hear even our laughing, and certainly no arguments. Mam was past caring. She threw a shoe at Dempsey and yelled that she wouldn't have the smelly thing in the house. The dog whimpered and looked for a corner to hide.

Dad sat at the table, a frown on his face, saying nothing. I thought afterwards he may have shifted his legs so that Dempsey could crawl under the table and try to disappear into the back wall.

Where had I been till this hour, Mam wanted to know, and my dinner turning to burnt leather in the oven?

I tried to explain calmly.

'You what? You what? You went where?' she kept saying. 'Well, don't think you're too big for a hiding. And your sister worrying herself sick that you'd been knocked down on York Road.'

Dad looked at the table. 'Are you listening to this?' she asked him. 'Is this how we brought her up, to think of everyone else first, to put everyone else before her own parents? Honour thy father and thy mother – what happened to that?'

I hadn't meant to say it, it just came out. 'Suffer the little children,' I said.

Something in her snapped. 'You'll bloody suffer. I'll make you suffer.'

She started to throw things at me, everything she could lay her hands on. A pan, a plate, the bread board, a box of nails. Every one of them hit me. Dad didn't move for an age. He just looked, his mouth open. I think he said, 'Dolly, Dolly, no.' Not until she picked up a mended shoe did he try to stop her.

She was thumping me, landing punches wherever she could, kicking me, saying things and crying, 'I had you down for dead.'

I think Dad took her by the shoulders and led her upstairs. I just sat by the table, not knowing what to think, my brain not working.

Dad came down. He filled a cup with water from the tap and went back upstairs. I could hear Mam sobbing and Dad talking quietly.

I didn't go to bed. I sat downstairs, wrapped in coats. When the fire had quite gone out, Dempsey crawled from under the table and sat beside me. I took my dinner from the oven and put it down for him. He did not mind it was burnt to a leather but ate it and licked the plate clean.

When I fell asleep I dreamed of Heather and Tommy. They stood in a boat on Roundhay Park Lake, and both were crying, their tears trickling down their faces. I thought a tear plopped into the murky water beneath them. I asked what was wrong but they wouldn't say, couldn't say, though I called to them as the boat passed by. In the dream I knew that they could not tell me because I could not shed tears. I woke up knowing that the person who took Heather on the tandem must have been Wilf, who had befriended her and sketched her when she worked at the Wright Shoe Company. It was just the kind of good turn he would have done. In a year, I told myself, in a year from now, Wilf and me will be married and Leila will come to live with us and everything will be all right. But I didn't believe myself.

My mind felt dull and numb. It seemed not to be me who went upstairs for a change of underwear and my bank book, into the cellar for the little seat to attach to my bike. I filled a bottle with water and spread bread with dripping. To the papers Tommy had given me, I added my own birth certificate and certificates from college, all rolled and tied with string.

I was at the Yorkshire Penny Bank when it opened. I did not withdraw my entire savings but left threepence on deposit. You always feel in that bank someone will tap you on the shoulder and demand to know if you have your mam's permission to make a transaction.

Did I mean to take Leila? I must have or I wouldn't have attached the little seat at the back of the bike. But I don't think I had quite decided.

At the orphanage, I said to Sister Ursula that I had brought some papers from Mr McBride. She held out her hand. I said. 'Oh, my papers are in the bike basket. Is it all right to see Leila first?'

She fingered the big black cross at her chest. 'I don't know. Father Flynn is with the children. He takes a special interest. We've got the child calmed down, I don't want her upsetting again.'

I could hear children saying their catechism. Father Flynn didn't see me peering through the glass in the door as he strode between the rows of little ones. All the children's eyes were on him. Except Leila's. She saw me. Like a little conspirator she looked away. Only two and a half years old, and she knew. I had come for her.

I walked along the corridor and waited by the door, listening for some change of sound that would tell me it was playtime.

She stayed behind in the yard when the others went inside after playtime, crouching in the corner, peeping at me through the railings. I walked over to her, took her hand, and she trotted beside me to the bike. I lifted her onto the seat. Then I pedalled like blazes, the whippet racing beside me as I headed for the road out of Leeds. I don't think I knew what way to go. I let the bike take me.

22

The Distempered Room

For the last ten miles Leila had made no sound. She could not have fallen out of the little bike seat. Could she? I stopped to check. Dempsey flopped down on the grass verge by the road, ears back, watching. Lulled to sleep by the ride, Leila opened her eyes and looked at me with a puzzled stare. I lifted her out.

'Let's stretch our legs.'

Sleepy and unsteady, she held my hand. Knowing that part of the road, I found a stream where Dempsey could drink. The poor dog might have running bred into him, but really he is a town dog and not used to such long journeys. I explained to him that he must stay close and keep an eye on Leila. Leila explained that as well. The explanation, and trailing her hand in the water, seemed to bring her back to life. When I fastened her in the seat again, she called to Dempsey that they were going to find her mammy.

I re-tied the ribbon on her plaited hair. A few more days in the orphanage and she would not have escaped the barber's scissors.

We reached Gargrave at a quiet time in the afternoon. I brought the bike to a stop outside Aunt Bella's house. Dempsey does not like to appear ignorant, and though I felt sure he had never set paw in Gargrave before, he pushed the gate with his head, walked to the doorstep and turned back, as if to say, *I knew all along we were coming here.*

Leila's head tilted at an uncomfortable angle onto her shoulder. I unstrapped her and lifted the dead weight of her sleeping body from the pillion seat. She started to wail softly before she opened her eyes, catching her breath; then another wail, louder and louder.

The door opened.

'I thought you'd be at work, Aunt Bella.'

'I were expecting you.' She took Leila into her arms. 'Come here, little lass.'

Leila's wailing lessened to a sob as Bella took her inside, wrapped her shawl around her, sat her by the fire and held a small cup to her lips. 'Have a drink of warmed milk, sweetpea, we'll get you changed in a trice.' Ignoring my surprise, my aunt said, 'Tea's mashed. I saw you cycling up.'

Dempsey nuzzled Leila. She reached out a tired little hand to stroke him. Then she looked all round the room and back to me. She started to cry, 'I want my mammy.'

'Bless you.' Bella stroked her hair. 'You don't know if you're coming or going. Jess, give the dog a drink of water out of that rice pudding tin. You'll find a bone under't sink. Put him outside with it.'

I followed her instructions while Bella took a digestive biscuit from the tin and broke it in half for Leila.

'Say thank you,' I said.

Leila snatched the biscuit. 'Thank you.'

'How did you know I was coming?' I asked.

'Just two places you would make for, according to your dad. Here to me or to Wilf in London. Only he thought you wouldn't have gone to London on the bike.'

'I won't go back.'

'Your dad went to Bill. They telephoned to the police house here. I had the constable knocking on the door of my place of work this morning, frightening the living daylights out of me. What a kerfuffle you've caused.'

'I'm not going back. If you'd seen her. If you'd seen her parcelled off to an orphanage, what would you have done?'

Bella sighed. 'There's teacakes in that paper bag. Make yourself useful and get the toasting fork.'

I sliced the teacakes and took the toasting fork from the drawer.

'Toast both sides,' Bella said. 'Your mam only ever does one side. We Prices are a toasted two sides family.' She gently touched the back of a knuckle onto Leila's cheek. 'Her little face is raw from't wind. No wonder she were bleating. Have you put owt on it?'

'No.' I pulled my sleeve over my hand to keep it from burning as I held the teacake near the fire.

She set Leila down on the hearth rug and took a jar of lanolin from the cupboard by the side of the range. Lifting Leila onto her lap again, Bella dipped her finger in the jar and spread grease on Leila's forehead, cheeks and chin. Leila screwed up her eyes and pulled a face. She held out her hand, wanting to put her fingers in the jar. Bella said, 'Go on, that's it. Jess'll change you in a minute and see to your bum.'

'She's taken to you.' I gave them each a piece of teacake. 'She doesn't usually go to strangers.'

Bella wiped butter from Leila's chin. 'Well, I'm no stranger, am I? She were here in the womb, when Heather stopped with me and I fed her up.'

'Heather came here?'

Bella didn't answer but spoke to Leila. 'We don't want to be mithering on about that now do we, little one?'

When we had eaten our toast, she said, 'Get her washed and changed before she drops off to sleep. Her bum's covered in shite.' She sniffed at her shawl and waved it about. 'What a pong!'

'I've no change of clothes.'

'Then it's a good job I've a sack or two of church jumble for sorting out. Look through that lot in't corner.' She set Leila down on the rug and pulled her shawl around her shoulders.

'Where are you going?'

'Over to the police house, make a call to our Bill's office, tell him you've arrived safe and sound, then he can get word to your mam and dad. Put their minds at rest.'

'Tell them I'm stopping here.'

'There's a bucket under't sink you can put her nappy in.' She left. I called after her, 'I won't go back!'

Dempsey took advantage of the opened door to come back indoors. He sat in front of the fire and let Leila put her arms around his neck.

Bella returned to work in the afternoon. She would not talk any more that evening, saying the child and I must rest after our journey, and that I should get myself upstairs. It would not do for the little one to wake and find herself alone in a strange bed. Leila had already fallen asleep. I carried her up the straight flight of stone steps, Bella following with the oil lamp. She talked as if to distract me from asking questions or making arguments. 'There's the pot under the bed, try and get her on it or she'll wet the mattress. I've put a rubber sheet on't bottom end.' I opened the door to the small plain room. The white walls hurt my heart as I remembered Wilf distempering the pantry for her only last August. She followed me into the room, her lamp casting its shadow, turning the walls a different shade, like a grey-blue sky. She set the lamp on the washstand while I arranged the pillows, sliding Leila in at the tail of the bed.

'Sleep in tomorrow. Rest.' Bella picked up the jug from the washstand. 'I'll take this down with me, and fetch you some warm water before I go to work in't morning.' At the door she turned back. 'I'm glad you made me your port in the storm.'

I fell asleep thinking that I had meant to look at Dempsey's paws, to see whether his poor pads were sore from all the running.

The morning light chinked through the worn curtains, weak sunshine from a pale blue-white sky. Leila had crept up the bed and lay beside me, looking at me. Waiting for me to wake up. I heard the post fall through the letterbox. Dempsey barked. I got out of bed, poured water, now cold, from the jug on the washstand into the basin.

I had a pair of soft leather ankle boots for Leila, the latest thing in children's footwear from the Wright Shoe Company. 'Look,' I said. 'Look what the fairies left for you in the night.'

She was delighted. After wearing clumsy orphanage clogs she did not notice the sixpence in the toe.

'Take that one off a minute. Feel for what else the fairies might have left.'

She held up the coin, her eyes wide.

'That's sixpence for luck. They must know you're a good girl.'

I found a big cloak in the jumble, and a man's trilby. It made Leila laugh to see me. 'This cloak will make me invisible,' I said, hiding my head, and she laughed. We made a tent of it using a buffet and chair. She tried on all the hats while I heated porridge and tried to press out lumps with the wooden spoon. She was well-wrapped in jumble clothes when we walked with Dempsey to the River Aire. Leila gazed at her boots as she walked. But soon, her lips moved to ask me the usual question. I got in first. 'You'll like the river.

Dempsey can swim. There're stepping stones. And you can paddle if it's not too cold.'

I had brought a towel and thought it wouldn't hurt us to get cold feet. 'Let's take our shoes and socks off, Leila.'

The water turned my toes numb. Leila stepped carefully. She flung a stick, but unsteadily, so Dempsey had to dodge out of the way.

A voice called to us. I turned to see the postman, a sharp-nosed man with thin lips, swinging the empty bag from his shoulder as if it got in the way of this talking. 'That's a fine dog. I have a whippet bitch myself. Can I tek a look at him?'

He crossed the grass. Dempsey took a few steps back, baring his teeth. 'It's all right, boy,' the postman said. 'Let me say hello. Let the postman see the whippet.'

He stroked Dempsey's head and felt his rib cage, ran a hand along his flanks. 'Does he have a pedigree?'

'What do you mean?'

'You know, giving his parentage, line of origin, whether he's come from winning stock.' He shook his head and clucked, as if I had given the wrong answer, though I had not answered him at all. 'It drops his value if he hasn't, but all the same, I could give you a few bob for him.'

Leila looked ready to cry.

'He's not for sale. He's the child's dog.'

'Pity.' He hitched his bag onto his shoulder. 'If you change yer mind, yer'll see me out and about, up and down.'

After that we dried our feet and walked around Gargrave, listening to the sound of the machines humming and singing in the cotton mill, peering in shop windows. A man on horseback stopped at the trough to let his animal drink. I came up with the idea as we walked around, standing by the railings as children played in the school playground, watching the woman with a basket climb on the bus to Skipton. The youngest children in the schoolyard were not much older than Leila. She could go to school here. I would get a job in an office, or any job. I hated leaving the Wright Shoe Company, after Uncle Bill had taught me so much and paid for me to go to college. What if no one would employ me, ever again?

In the afternoon, I heated two irons and stood at the table, ironing pillow cases, sheets, tablecloths, blouses – paying attention to cuffs and flattening the corners of collars – a skirt, tea-cloths and a pinafore with an edged border more tricky than a lace collar. We had eaten all the bread. Mostly I had watched Mam bake bread but had a go myself when she took badly, so I knew what to do.

We found the shop that sold yeast, and I bought Leila a two-ounce bag of jelly drops.

Leila weighed flour with me. While the bread rose in its earthenware bowl by the fire, I mopped up every crumb of flour and every drop of water we had spilt on the stone floor.

In other words, I made myself useful. Bella had not expected me to do so much. 'It's a great help, love. When you live on yer own yer've all to do, and it's a strain sometimes.'

I carried Leila to bed. Ever since I visited Wilf, I had kicked myself over something I'd forgotten to say. I know that artists do not earn much, and I had meant to say to him that we could have brought out our book of fairy tales. That might have made us some money. If it had, I could have afforded to stay in London and still wait to get married next year, and me and Leila would have lived off the fairy tales. I liked the idea of paying rent and buying groceries from the proceeds of glass slippers, pointy-toed goblin shoes, seven-league boots and red dancing shoes.

To send Leila to sleep, I told her the story of Rumpelstiltskin, picturing him appearing to the shoemender's daughter as she sat in the topmost room of the palace, trying to spin shoelaces into gold. I described Rumpelstiltskin circling the fire in the dark of the woods, in his scorched, sturdy boots. He skipped too close to the flames, singing to himself, 'A-ha, she will never guess that my name is Rumpelstiltskin, and I will take her child.'

'He won't?' Leila said.

'No, he won't. Because she knows his name, and anyway, his boots have scorched.'

When I went downstairs, Bella had made cocoa. She handed me a mug. 'There was no need for you to do so much today.'

'I want to stay here. I can get a job and pay you board. We won't be any trouble.'

'We'll see,' she said.

'It'll only be till next summer. Wilf and me are getting married.'

Bella raised her eyebrows. 'I hear you were on't train to London last week to arrange it all. Unbeknownst to anyone.'

'They knew I was off to London with Gladys Hardy,' I said.

'Not why. Thah didn't say why. Ticket must've set you back a bit.'

I hadn't told any of them, even Wilf, that Gladys Hardy bought my ticket.

'About me staying here,' I said, stirring the cocoa, taking a sip. 'I would pay you my board. I'm trained now. I'd get a job.'

'Folk round here don't let go of jobs that easy. They die in harness sooner than pass on a place.'

'You like having me here?'

'I won't say I don't.'

'I know Mam came to stay with you, when she was expecting. I didn't know other people came, like Heather, not family.'

'They don't,' she said. 'Not as a rule.'

'So why did Heather come? How did you know her?'

'I didn't know her, till she arrived.' She took the spoon from me and stirred her cup. 'That's the trouble with cocoa. If you're not careful, it stays at the bottom.'

'Is there some secret about why she came?'

'Heavens, no! She worked for Irene's firm, didn't she?'

I nodded. I had never heard anyone call the Wright Shoe Company 'Irene's firm' before.

Bella sipped her cocoa. 'I think what it was . . . I think Heather fainted one day when Irene was there, and one of the women said she were in the family way. Irene, being kind-hearted, thought she might need a bit of rest and recuperation. She paid the board and lodging for her to stop with me.'

'Did other women come, from the firm?'

She shook her head. 'No, never.' She rubbed her hand across her jaw. 'Do you know what, I was only thinking on me way home, I could do with someone to get them tweezers and pluck the hairs from me chinney chin-chin and top lip. I can feel them. I can see them in a good light, but I can't get them for the life of me. You can do that, while you're here.'

'So can I stay? I'll make myself useful. I will get a job.'

'We'll see.' Dempsey listened. Bella patted his head. 'That dog could do with a coat.' She fished out a blanket from the jumble bag and took her scissors from the drawer. 'I think we'll have tape fastenings for him.'

'What I don't understand, Aunt Bella, is how people can be kind up to a certain point, and then stop. If Auntie Irene was willing to send Heather here, why wouldn't she give Leila a home? There's someone in their house all the time. A maid, a cook. She said it's because she's not Catholic, but we could have made sure Leila got religious instruction.'

Expertly she cut and shaped a dog's jacket. 'It's not Irene's place to look after a child, not at her age. And she's got all her charity work to think on. That helps boundless numbers of young uns. People have their own lives, Jess. You have your life ahead of you. You don't want to be starting out saddled with someone else's child.'

I held Dempsey still while she gave him a fitting. 'I promised Heather.'

'I'm sure you didn't promise to adopt the bairn.'

It took me a long time to fall asleep. I knew they all had a point. Even Leila's dad had resigned himself to her being in the orphanage. But they were wrong and I was right. Something in me knew that Leila needed to be better minded than she would be in a child-factory of an orphanage wearing a graveyard uniform.

What I also knew, but could hardly put into words and would never to say to any of them, was that feeling I had had when Father Flynn glared at me in the house, Tommy not even noticing. Holding Leila made me strong, the protector. I couldn't let go of that and just be Jess again, the girl who was scared of bumping into the priest as he went about his rounds and called at our house, the girl who looked away, feeling guilty and humiliated. As I lay there in the darkness, I wondered, why I had done this. Was it for Leila, or for me?

Across the landing, Bella snored gently, like a kettle just about to come to the boil. Leila flung her arms and legs about the bed and ended up horizontal, her head lolling over the bed end. I picked her up and set her in a straight line near the wall so as to give myself room to climb back into bed. She felt heavy and hot. I dampened the corner of a small towel from the jug of water on the washstand.

A great pain of hurt and loneliness filled me up. I had to make myself shut my eyes and lie still. My brain stopped working. I couldn't think what I would do tomorrow.

I woke in the morning to see Leila lying beside me, watching me again. Downstairs I could hear Bella moving about, raking the fire, filling the kettle.

'Mammy?' Leila said, listening to the sounds. I wondered how long it would be before she stopped asking for Heather.

I did not want to let her see me cry, so on the riverbank I threw the ball and we all chased it, and I threw it again and again.

When we came back from our walk in the rain, the post lay on the mat. A letter to Bella in Dad's writing. Nothing for me.

Leila would not play properly, not with the scales and weights, the pencils or the jars, nor with the clothes from the jumble. Every time I showed her how to balance weights on the scales, draw a cat, make a tent from the cloak or play shops with jam jars she would want to do it her own way. Roll weights across the floor under the dresser where I couldn't easily retrieve them, throw pencils at Dempsey, try to shove a jumper in a jar or a jar in a hat. We were in a bit of a mess when Bella came in unexpectedly at dinner time, bringing pork pies.

She cleared a space on the table, reading her letter while eating pie. I heard Mam's voice in my head: *Don't read while you're eating, it's bad manners.*

Bella folded the letter. 'Your dad's coming for you on Sunday. You'll go back on the train. It's all been smoothed over with the orphanage and whatnot. Bill'll be glad to have you back at the office. The invoices have been piling up it seems.'

Poor Uncle Bill – I felt so bad. Mrs Crawford would be gloating.

Leila spat out her pie.

'Look at it this way,' Bella said. 'You and the little one have had a few days' holiday and you've got off lightly, by the sounds of it. Him at the police house said it could classify as abduction. We're fortunate he's a discreet kind of chap.'

I didn't answer. *Look at it that way if you like*, I thought. Next time they won't find me. All I have to do is hide out over the winter. Bide my time till me and Wilf can be together, and Leila, too.

'Read it, if you like,' she said, pushing the letter across the table to me.

You can come on Sunday, I said to myself, *but don't expect to find me here.*

23

The Cavalry

The call came to say Wilf could stop worrying. They had tracked Jess down. Paul would go to Gargrave to collect her on Sunday.

Wilf knew he must get there first, or he would let her down. He had been a fool to let Ralph and Jess persuade him out of marrying right away. Somehow everything would fall into place. If the award was withdrawn from him and he lost the travelling scholarship that was promised, so be it. There would be other opportunities, but only one Jess.

Moments after taking the telephone call he pulled on his leather coat. Flying goggles in his hand, he called up the stairs to Ralph to tell him he was going, asking him to make an excuse at college tomorrow. He would be back in time for his class on Monday.

By the time Ralph got downstairs, Wilf was revving the motorbike, switching on the single yellow light, pulling down his goggles and moving off from the kerb. Ralph called to him, but Wilf just waved and pulled away, his coat flapping, leaving behind the burning whiff of Wakefield's castrol.

Wilf dodged through the London traffic, heading for the road north. As darkness fell, the light of the motorbike picked out fewer houses. Trees loomed out of the darkness. A hedge would briefly flicker into life. The road seemed as open and full of promise as Wilf's own future. He put his foot down, revelling in the joy of a machine that was truly his and not property of the Wright Shoe Company for the purpose of deliveries.

No one would have expected a horse rider to be out at that time, suddenly to appear as Wilf rounded a bend. He swerved to avoid horse and rider, and shot across the top of the motorbike, landing in a ditch.

He woke in a hospital bed in Hertfordshire, not knowing how long he had been there. 'Is my bike damaged?' he asked the stiffly aproned nurse, who had not yet realized his eyes were now open.

'I don't know,' she said. 'You were concussed. We're keeping you in overnight, for observation. We don't have beds for motorbikes on this ward. Now, who can we contact?'

'If I can just get to my bike . . .'

She smiled and shook her head. 'You don't know our ward sister. She won't let you go until there's someone to hold your hand.'

Reluctantly, Wilf gave Ralph's details.

'We can't go haring off to Yorkshire just like that,' Ralph said as they left the hospital that Sunday.

Ralph's car and driver waited outside the main doors. The driver stepped out smartly and opened the rear door.

Wilf hesitated. 'Where's my bike?'

'Just get in! I've had the motorbike taken to a garage. The mechanic promises he'll make it good as new, but it'll take a while.'

'If we set off now—'

'Wilf, you're in no fit state. It'll have to be next weekend. I have train tickets. In any case, she won't be in Gargrave now. Her father will have collected her.'

Wilf groaned. 'I've let her down.'

24

Bolt Hole

I cycled through the entrance gates, past the large sign – Leeds Poor Children's Holiday Camp – and the visitors' bungalow, superintendent's house and store hut towards the long barrack-type prefabs where the holiday-making children stayed in the season.

Not a whisper of smoke escaped any chimney. The empty and shuttered superintendent's house looked cosiest, with a single rose still blooming on the bush by the wooden steps that led to the front door. But I did not feel right about going in there. The dormitory buildings stood bleak and forbidding. Each time I passed to look round, Dempsey stood stock-still and watched me. Released from the prison of her little seat, Leila ran across the grass and bobbed down by a tree for a pee. I wheeled the bike back to the visitors' bungalow. The door key still hung inside the letter-box on a length of string. Dempsey bounded ahead of us through the hall, sniffing. He nosed his way into the kitchen, asking for a drink of water. Water gushed strong from the tap, as if it had been waiting for release.

Neat, tidy and spotless, the place smelled damp and fusty. We explored the rooms, Leila holding my hand.

Dry foods had been left in the pantry in tins and jars – porridge oats, flour, raisins, sugar, tea – as well as black treacle. Gas spurted from the ring fixed to the calor container. I boiled the kettle and poured a cupful of warm water for myself and Leila. She drank and looked for more of something. The bread and cheese I had brought as we crept out of Bella's house before dawn did not go very far between the three of us.

Beds had been stripped and I could not see any sheets. I wrapped Leila in a rough grey blanket, and told her, 'Dempsey is very tired. You and Dempsey stay on the bed. Watch over him. Make sure he sleeps.'

She tucked the blanket round him. 'Where are you going?'

'To the shop,' I said, knowing that to explain 'foraging for food' would confuse her. It confused me.

But she set up such a yell and wouldn't let me leave her.

Across Morecambe Bay, the late-afternoon sun sparkled a weak pink, reflecting on pale ridges of sand. A squawking gull flew over the roof of the superintendent's house and perched on top of the wooden store.

'Let's go and see.' I took her hand and we ran to the store, rattled the padlock on the door. The sound scared her and she screwed up her face ready to cry. I lifted her so that she could look through the mesh-covered pane, at something in the shape of a pile of potatoes under sacking, but it was difficult to make out.

I walked round the long prefabricated building that Dad had said looked like an army barracks. The window nearest the ground was at the end of the building on the right. It would be easy to slide a knife through, flick the catch, push up the window and hoist myself in; find the kitchen, and perhaps some tins of food.

Then I had an idea. Everyone knows you buy cockles and mussels at the seaside, and how plentiful they are. We'd gather some. Leila would like that. I took a basin from the bungalow and went back past the superintendent's house and the main buildings. Higgledy-piggledy steps led to the shore. This time I knew not to stray too far, and to look for dry, firm sand. The wind blew hard against us. I made Leila walk beside me, holding my Gargrave jumble cape so she would not blow away like a ragdoll. Neither she nor Dempsey had ever seen sands and sea, and Dempsey would not keep close but raced about – dashing away from us and back, doing circles in the sand. He came back to us, something in his mouth – a dead gull. The crunching sound as he brought his jaws together made me shudder. When he realized we did not want it, he took it to a stony spot where he started to eat, feathers and all, I think, though I tried not to look too closely and kept Leila turned away from him.

We found a shallow pool where shells stuck to the rocks. I pulled some shells off and, sure enough, they had fleshy-looking insides that said 'food.' Into the basin they went. Leila rubbed her eyes when the sand blew.

'Don't rub,' I told her. 'Blink.'

She blinked, and though her eyes watered she said, 'I'm all right.'

Cockles popped up out of nowhere as we trod the sand.

'Boiled shellfish for tea, Leila,' I told her.

'I know,' she said. 'My mammy told me.'

The thought of food made us giddy. We ran back up through the camp saying, 'Food. Eats. Big eats,' and laughing. Dempsey got excited and began to bark. He chased off. I called him. Leila stood stock-still, listening to his bark.

'Talking to Mammy,' she said. 'My mammy is here.'

'Not today.'

'Yes.' She nodded her head, listening to the wind in the trees opposite the bungalow and the cry of gulls from the shore.

Dempsey came back to us, wagging his tail, carrying a rabbit between his jaws. He dropped it on the ground in front of me. It jerked once, twice, then lay still. For a moment none of us moved. 'Fetch it, Dempsey,' I said, not wanting to pick it up, but not wanting to leave it behind.

'My daddy skin rabbits,' Leila said.

I had never skinned a rabbit. I had no idea how to do it, or whether I could.

It was dark in the bungalow. I panicked for a moment, not remembering where I'd placed the matches. The first two matches wouldn't strike. Of course, you can't show that you are worried if you have a child by you who is likely to bawl at the least little thing. Fortunately, Dempsey kept Leila occupied while I got the matches, the calor gas ring and an oil lamp working. When I dropped the shells in water, there were not so very many after all. I boiled up our catch in a small pan, drained it and set it on plates, dribbling black treacle over my and Leila's portion. Dempsey turned his nose up. As we finished eating our strange little meal, the sky stayed light from the moon.

I tied the rabbit's legs together with a piece of saved string from the knife drawer and hung it on the back of the pantry door.

That night the rough grey blanket itched my skin. Leila was hot and her forehead damp. Each time I fell asleep I woke with a new fright. What if she got ill? Or what if I did? If I got up early in the morning and went into the long dormitory building, as I planned, leaving her sleeping, I might break my leg and not be able to get out. In the spring, we'd be two skeletons, she in the bungalow, or somewhere she wandered to, me on the dormitory floor. The fearful thoughts wouldn't stop. What had I done, bringing her here? Maybe I was wrong and everyone else right. At least in an orphanage she would have food, shelter and attention when she took sick. I wasn't even sure what cockles and mussels looked like in their raw state. Maybe we'd eaten something else altogether and would die. Soon.

Then they'd all be sorry, I couldn't help thinking. Oh, would they be sorry then! But so would I.

In the morning, she wanted to run outside with Dempsey, but I wouldn't let her out of my sight. When we ate our porridge, she asked, 'Are we like the three bears?'

'Yes.'

'Am I Goldilocks?'

'Yes.'

'Who is Goldilocks's mammy and daddy?' But she did not seem so upset this time.

We ran across to the small wood, by the camp, crunched over dry leaves, looking at the ground and up at the tree tops, hoping to see something edible. Leila picked up a conker. Chestnut, she called it. Her dad had fetched chestnuts home from the fruit shop. Not knowing the difference between a chestnut and a conker put me at a disadvantage, but we picked them up and put them in our sack. Beyond the stone wall at the edge of the wood stood an apple tree. The stones on top of the wall looked wonky so we walked the length of the wall towards the road until we came to a spot where the wall had fallen into disrepair, stones lay in a heap and we could clamber over and reach the apple tree. Leila picked up apples but they were brown, soft and maggoty, except for one. I climbed up the tree to shake a branch. Leila stood below, looking anxious, picking up each apple as it fell, a serious look on her face as she grasped each one with two hands and placed it in our sack. She gripped so tightly that a brown gungy mass of rotten apples covered her fingers and spread to her wrists.

I liked being in the tree, feeling the wind blowing against me, hearing it disturb the branches and the few remaining leaves. But I heard a crack and felt the bough move with my weight, so I quickly slid down again.

From there we walked to the road. I had a little money and could have gone to the village shop, but what if people asked questions? For all I knew, someone at home might guess where we had come to hide and there would be a poster outside Silverdale police house: 'Wanted – Dead or Alive.'

We went home and stewed the bits of the apples that seemed all right. Even the ones I had shaken from the tree were full of grubs, and there was not much left by the time I cut out all the bad bits. I drizzled treacle onto Leila's, and a touch of sugar onto my own, for they were quite sour. Afterwards I washed the pan and dishes and put them away, fearing someone might come to check on the bungalow and, like Mammy, Daddy and Baby Bear, say, 'Who's been sitting in my chair? Who's been burning my pan?'

'Come on.' I reached for Leila's hand. 'We'll leave Dempsey on guard here and I'll show you all the clogs the children wear when they come on holiday.'

I picked up the sack, hoping there might be tins of food in the camp kitchen. Perhaps there would be evaporated milk in a tin. Dempsey would not stay on guard. He ran along beside us.

I opened the dormitory window catch with a knife, pushed up the window and lifted her onto the sill. I climbed up after, lowering her down.

She didn't like the gloom. I raised the blinds to let in the last of the evening light; soon the sky would turn black. On either side of the long dormitory stood iron beds. Above each one sat a plaque remembering a fallen soldier from the Great War. I hoped the children who came on holiday would not read the words, which might cast a gloomy shadow over their fortnight's stay.

We clattered along the wooden floor. At the end of the dormitory, a door led into a passageway. Off either side, and beyond, were more doors. On one side of the hall was a room stacked to the ceiling with bedding, sheets and blankets on different shelves, and an overpowering smell of mothballs. The next room held a sad smell of rainy days, soggy children and misery. Row upon row of clogs sat side by side on wooden slatted shelves, in order of size, the smallest nearest me, the clogs growing as they stretched in a line to the farthest end of the shelves. I took down the smallest pair. As I held them in my hands, I remembered Dad making them and saying, 'Some of the bairns are like little dolls.'

Beyond the hall was a dining area with long scrubbed deal tables, and benches set either side. The whole place felt so cold it made me shiver. It was chillier inside the building than out. I wondered what it must be like for the children who visited. I imagined they never got warm. But did they eat well? If so, what? And might something have been left behind for us?

The kitchen seemed almost cosy, with its huge polished black range and large ovens. Two long flat sinks ran half the length of the wall on my right. Cupboards held scales, huge pans, giant-sized dishes, tin plates and cups.

Finally, I found the pantry. As I took the lid from a tall earthenware jar I half expected a genii to rise. One jar held oats and another flour. Two smaller jars contained salt and black treacle. I could make treacle pie, I thought, or some other kind of pie, if I could think what might go in it, and if you could make pastry without lard.

A cupboard held tins, but none of them with labels. Still, what did that matter? Food was food. It cheered me up to see it. We wouldn't starve. Not if I could help it.

Leila had started to cry. Again. I'm sure I never cried half as much as a child.

'Dempsey. Dempsey wants to come in,' Leila said. 'My mammy says.'

I climbed out. With difficulty I lifted the wriggling dog through the window and heaved myself back in again after him. Why didn't I just say no? I asked myself. Or that he had to stay outside. Because. Because I felt so bad about bringing her to the edge of the earth, rummaging among pauper children's food for leavings.

Even the smallest pair of clogs was too big for Leila, but she wanted to put them on, and tried to pull off her boots without undoing her laces so I had to help her. 'We haven't come for this,' I said. 'We've come for food.' But it amused her.

She took my hand, pulled me back into the room where the iron beds stood in rows. 'Sit down,' she ordered. I sat on the end bed. She started to dance. 'Mammy showed me,' she said.

I clapped and sang while she stamped her little feet, thumping out her clog dance, shoulders straight, arms stiff by her side. She looked at me without a smile, listening to my clapping, keeping time in a way that surprised me for one so little. She put her hands on her hips and twirled, stomping a circle.

'That's enough,' I said.

Her face turned red with effort, her eyes shut tight.

'Mammy says keep dancing.'

'No, stop now!' I said gently, reaching out to her.

She danced as if driven by demons, as if trying to break through the floor into hell below.

'Stop, Leila, stop it.'

Dempsey barked. Leila suddenly stopped dancing. She opened her eyes, and stood motionless, frozen to the spot, looking beyond me, to the end of the room.

Dempsey barked again. Leila let out a howl of fear and ran to me.

I turned to see who or what had caught her eye.

A tall man stood between the window and door. He seemed to block all light from the room. In his hand he held a rifle. He looked at us as if we were ghosts or fiends. I hushed Dempsey and made him sit. Leila stayed close beside me, hugging my leg. Slowly, the man walked past us, up to the far end of the room, to the open window, his footsteps hobnailing across the floor. The window rattled as he shut it. I held Leila's hand and Dempsey's collar. We waited.

He turned back to face us. I thought of running and glanced at the door.

'What are you doing here? Why do you make a sick bairn dance?'

'She not sick. I'm not making her dance.'

I would not say I had tried to stop her, or that would make me look a fool and her a fiend. She clung too close to me and did not want me to talk about her, that I knew. She hid her face in my skirt. Dempsey sensed danger and struggled to break free.

The man lay the gun on the bed nearest him and took off his cap. When he did that, I knew he was what Dad would call One of Nature's Gentlemen. I hoped he was.

'Don't be afeared,' he said, keeping his distance from us.

We could not have run away from him then, or at least that was how it seemed. Even in the dusky light his face glowed, sun-burned. He had thick black hair and eyebrows. A shining, brown-skinned mortal. He must have a wife, I thought, someone of his age must have a wife. A rhyme came into my head: *Ee-aye-adio, the farmer wants a wife.*

Leila held my hand tightly. Dempsey sat close, growling. The man spoke again. 'You'd better come with me.' I could not tell what he said next.

I caught a word. War-rum. War-um. The man was saying we should get warm. And we were cold, so cold in that dormitory. I put Leila's boots back on, taking my time, fastening the laces slowly, trying to think.

Dempsey stopped growling.

'I never saw but one whippet before. Across in Morecambe in the summer.'

'He's valuable,' I said. 'A valuable dog.' I don't know what made me say that, except I did not want him to think us paupers. I pulled my jumble cape around me and stuck the trilby on my head. 'His name's Dempsey. He has a pedigree, only we haven't got the certificate to prove it. I was offered ten shillings for him, which is nothing for a dog like him, and of course I said no.'

'You talk well enough,' he said. 'And she dances well enough.'

Well enough for what? I wondered. Did he have some devilish plan?

'You're from Leeds?'

'How do you know?'

'By your twang.'

Outside the dormitory building, a sheepdog waited for him. It wagged its tail, then made to growl at Dempsey. 'Shurrup, Madge,' he commanded. 'Yon's a valuable dog.'

Because his boots were stout, well-mended and had a bit of a shine to them, and because I thought him a married man, we listened to him when he said he would take us to get war-rum, and that he would feed us. We walked with him along the cliff path, out of sight of the holiday camp. To our left the sea roared. The sun hung on the far horizon like a penny slotted halfway into a money box.

'Carry me, carry me,' Leila whispered.

I lifted her. She looked over my shoulder at where we had come from, showing no sign of caring where we went.

We walked a narrow, bumpy track alongside a field of burnt

stubble. As we neared a yard and buildings, animal sounds came from a shed.

'What's that?' Leila asked, hiding her face on my shoulder.

'Cows,' I whispered, because I did not know for sure whether the sound that floated on the wind came from a cow or some other animal.

The writing on the stone lintel above the door had worn away. I was going into a house that stood alone, with no name, number or date.

I could tell as soon as we went in that there was no wife. You could not see yourself in the mirror on the wall by the kitchen door – it was covered with dust and grime. As if he read my thoughts, he said, 'I live here alone. But you are safe.'

I didn't answer. He jerked his head back towards the yard. 'My worker is a married man, with bairns. You can go there if you wish.'

'The little one's tired.'

'Does she have a name?'

I had decided to tell him she was my sister, but I did not say it. 'She's called Leila Catherine.'

I thought she would not speak to him when he bent down to her and said hello. She turned away from him saying, 'Mammy, mammy!'

'And you?' he asked.

'Jessica.'

He held out his hand to me. 'Isaac Dennison.'

'How do you do, Mr Dennison?' I said, taking off my trilby.

I thought he was going to laugh at me, but he turned away, took a taper from the holder on the mantelpiece, lit it from the fire and touched it to the oil lamp on the table.

'There's soup,' he said, nodding to us to sit at the table. He took a pan from the hob by the fire.

Fairy tales came into my mind. The evildoers do not strike straight away but lull their prey into feeling safe. Hansel and Gretel, fattened up by the witch. The wolf making polite conversation with Red Riding Hood.

It was mutton stew with pearl barley, which Mam often made in winter. Leila took one spoonful then shut her lips tight. 'Yon fetched it,' he said, nodding again in the direction of the yard.

While we ate, he went upstairs. I heard him moving about, a chair scraping across the floorboards.

'Drink of water,' Leila wailed. I went to the sink, piled high with dishes, rinsed a cup and looked for a tap. There was none. I poured water from a jug. She took a sip.

'Don't like.'

'What's the matter?'

She tried to get down from the chair, hurt her leg and began to cry, holding out her arms to be picked up.

'You have to be good,' I said.

She cried and would not stop.

When Mr Dennison came down, he carried two chamber pots, one a child's.

'Outhouse is down yon. You passed it coming in.' From the wall he pulled down a bed. 'You're best here. It's war-rumest.'

I tried to shush Leila. 'You'll fright Dempsey with your crying.'

He took a small pan from the sink, scrubbed at it, rinsing it with water from an enamel jug, then poured in milk from a blue pot jug and set the pan on the gas ring, lighting it cautiously. 'We have no mains but calor gas in containers,' he said with some pride, as if he had only just got calor gas.

While the milk heated, he closed the blinds and pulled the curtains shut.

Leila fell asleep after she had drunk the milk, sitting on my lap, quiet finally. I lay her on the bed.

'She sickening?' he said slowly.

'No. I don't think so.'

He nodded. 'You know her best.'

I felt my cheeks turn red, realizing he thought her to be my child.

He looked away from me, towards the shelf on the wall alongside the kitchen range. 'Only there's a *Virtue's Household Physician* set on that there shelf, two volumes onnit. If she's a-sickening, that'll give chapter and verse, more'n most folk'd need to know.'

He said goodnight and turned to go upstairs. I called him back.

'Mr Dennison, I'm looking for work and somewhere to live, for me and the child.' He came back to the hearth, sat in the chair by the dying fire and waved his hand for me to sit opposite him.

'What kind of work?'

'I can type, do book-keeping, wages. I have certificates in them, and in commerce.'

He raised an eyebrow. 'You have a lot of certificates, excepting the dog's that got lost. You'd have to go to Lancaster or Morecambe for your kind of employment.'

'I can cook, bake and sew,' I lied. 'I had a job as a housekeeper once.'

'You've done a lot for one so young, just a bit of a lass.'

'I'll be eighteen in March.'

'And what fetches you so far from home. From Leeds?'

I knew it would be taking a risk, but I had to say something, not too much. 'No one would have Leila. If I went back they'd put her in the orphanage.'

'You're weary. Let's sleep on it.' He got up from the chair. 'See what the morrow brings.' He threw something to each of the dogs. 'Goodnight, Jessica.'

'Goodnight.'

As I undressed, I heard his boots drop on the floor in the room above. I climbed into bed beside Leila, pulling the curtain around the bed.

The tall clock by the door tick-tocked, though I could not see its face and had forgotten to notice the time. I heard his footsteps moving about above us, pacing to and fro, then stillness. A murmuring sound came through the ceiling above me. Prayers. He was saying his prayers. I lay still, listening to his murmur. A movement, a small sound, like the faintest of creaking. I guessed he had climbed into bed.

One of the dogs whimpered in its sleep – his sheep dog, I think. After a few moments the house went quiet, except for the clock, a spark and crackle as the fire died, and the steady breathing of the dogs.

When I woke, I didn't know if it was day or night. I heard the sound of water hitting a kettle bottom. I opened the bed's curtain an inch to see.

'Is thah awake?' he asked.

'Yes.'

'It's early rising. The tides tell us when to stir.'

I didn't understand what he meant but said nothing.

'I'm making a flask of tea for me-sen. On the gas ring. Take good care if you use't gas. Light match first, switch on and keep well back.'

By holding the blanket to my face and the curtain open a little, I could watch him without being seen. He shaved by candlelight. He mashed a pot of tea and poured himself a mug. 'I've left thee some,' he said, as if he knew I was watching. 'There's bacon to fry when you get the fire going.'

We never had bacon for breakfast at home. I could not think what to say. Perhaps he would think I had gone back to sleep.

He pulled on his coat. 'We go out shrimping now. I'll tell yon you're here, then she won't be wondering.'

'No! Don't tell anyone about me!' It came out before I could stop myself.

His old dog stood beside him, wagging her tail, ready for anything.

'Nay, Madge,' he said to her. 'You don't come shrimping, that you know. Stay here with the gir-ruls.'

After he had closed the door, I went to the window to watch him go. The morning was so dark I could just make out the direction he walked, off to the left. I heard a horse neigh and guessed he must be harnessing it into a cart. So perhaps he would not tell 'yon' about us after all.

I wanted to get back into bed but knew I should light a fire and start some breakfast. Little Leila looked so pale and done in.

As the room grew light, I knew for sure that there had been no farmer's wife here for a long time. And yet there had been someone, perhaps a child, too. Among the dirty but neatly set out china on the dresser was a child's dish. On the cup rack hung a tiny mug with a picture of a little boy and a cat.

With the heel of my hand I cleaned a space in the centre of the mirror on the wall. Someone had looked at herself in this mirror, patted her hair before leaving the house. A fright looked back, hair all over, a scratch on her forehead. Me.

As I looked round the room, Leila woke and said, 'I want my mammy.'

'I'm going to light the fire.'

'I want my daddy.'

'You stay there and keep warm.'

She needed to use the potty and then would not go back to bed but kept close to me as I raked the ashes, screwed newspaper into balls and set sticks on top. 'This is what Cinderella did, Leila. And a fairy godmother came and magicked her into a beautiful dress and glass slippers.'

I missed my dad. Fires never failed when he put a match to them.

Leila wouldn't eat the bacon, just a bit of bread dipped in fat. After we had breakfast, I found cloths, hard soap, a scrubbing brush, bucket and mop. The sink had no tap, but through the window I saw a pump in the yard. I tried to make her stay in the doorway, but she followed me out. The pump handle made a clanking sound and she turned and ran back into the house, calling to me to stop.

How long it took me just to wash the dishes in the sink I don't know because she wanted to help, then she cried, then she wanted to help. I tidied and cleaned the room a little, and swept and scrubbed the floor, which was not an easy task with Leila trying to help me, wanting to hold the brush and dustpan, spilling the dirt and crying when she hit herself on the head with the brush handle.

As I looked where to put away the plates and cups, I heard pails clanking in the yard. A woman's voice called. Straightaway, Leila perked up. She ran to the door. Knowing what she thought, I lifted her and carried her to the window. The woman had her back to us. Leila wriggled free. She ran, trying to reach the latch to open the door. I had to open it, knowing she would be disappointed, but I held the waist of her dress to keep her from running into the yard. As we stood there, the woman scattered grain for chickens that appeared out of nowhere. She half turned, not looking in our direction. We saw her face, and the fair hair that fell from under her scarf. Leila's body seemed to go loose with disappointment. I picked her up and closed the door.

'Your mammy has died, Leila. She has gone to heaven and won't come back.'

'I want to go to heaven,' Leila said. 'You fetched me here. Fetch me to heaven.'

'I can't.'

'On the bike.'

'We don't go to heaven till we die. You can't die till you're old.'

Then she cried and cried and wouldn't stop. When I wanted to fetch the bike and our things from the bungalow, she cried again and I had to carry her all the way there, the two dogs running with us.

She cried to go into the dormitory again and dance in the clogs, so I opened the window, lifted her in and climbed in after. Putting on the little clogs and dancing her heart out between the empty iron bedsteads made her smile at first, until she got out of breath and her cheeks turned far too red. After crying to go in, she cried at having to go out.

'You must be a good girl, Leila,' I told her as we walked up to the bungalow. 'How can I look after you and how will we manage if you cry all the time?'

In the dresser drawer at the visitors' bungalow, I found pen and ink, paper and envelopes. Certain that Wilf would guess my bolt hole, I wrote a note telling him where we had gone. If he cared for me at all, he would search us out. I wrote his name on the envelope and set it in the centre of the table, anchored by a little stone Leila had found on the beach when we were gathering shellfish. It was a grey pebble, flecked with red. She had turned it this way and that, saying, 'This stone is bleeding.'

I put what little we had brought with us to the bungalow into my bike basket and wheeled it to the farm, with her on the seat looking more miserable at every bump. It was only later I remembered that I had left a dead rabbit hanging on the back of the pantry door.

25

Virtue's Household Physician

When we came back from fetching our few belongings from the bungalow, I tried to get Leila to sit by me on the bed. How could I know if she was sickening for something, as both Bella and now Isaac Dennison thought? Travelling on the bike, looking for food, sleeping in strange beds, without the two people she loved best – all those things would make any child heartsick and weary, or any adult. But could it also have made her poorly?

From our spot on the bed, I saw the books Mr Dennison had mentioned, bound in dark maroon. She whimpered as I moved away to fetch both volumes, not knowing which I would need.

The first book seemed to open itself at 'Female Diseases'. I looked at the colour plates and black and white drawings, at a picture of a woman, curtains on either side of her pulled back to show her kneeling in an exercise position, head on the floor turned away, bottom in the air, her insides showing in shades of grey and black. The page heading read 'How to Replace Fallen Womb'.

I snapped the book shut. 'You want a drink of water, don't you, Leila?' I escaped across the room.

She took a sip and sat back against the pillow. I kept still, hoping she would fall asleep. I found 'Care of Children and their Diseases,' but before I had a chance to begin reading I heard the horse's hooves clop-clopping through the yard, and cart wheels rattling over cobbles. Going to the window, I saw Mr Dennison and another man. They had led the horse to a low stone outbuilding and, with the cart near the door of the building, lifted something off the cart. They exchanged a few words, then Mr Dennison strode across the yard. I turned away quickly so he would not think I was spying on him, though I did see him lift a pot from the cart and guessed someone had made him a stew.

He came inside, nodding to me. It was a good thing I had emptied the sink and boiled a kettle of water. He poured hot water into a basin, rolled up his sleeves, turned down his shirt collar and began to wash.

'I know I should do this upstairs at my washstand,' he said, 'to be a gentleman.'

'It's your house,' I said, shuffling up the bed, picking up volume one of *Virtue's Household Physician*. 'I'm not watching you.'

I pulled the curtain round the bed, which was not a good idea because I could not see to read. I thought I heard him chuckle and I saw through the chink in the curtain that he had taken off his shirt, which reminded me of Dad, washing at our sink. I thought of Wilf, after we had made love. He had stood just so and washed himself, before dresing again to walk me back to the hotel.

Closing the curtain seemed to quieten Leila and she fell asleep, which was a great relief and my first peace and quiet of the day.

When I knew Mr Dennison had finished washing, I drew the curtain back. He wore a clean shirt.

'I'm off to see someone, Jessica.' He ran a comb through his dark hair. 'Then we'll speak of what's best to do, for you and the child.'

He picked up his coat and did not give me chance to answer, although I wanted to say again, *Don't tell anyone we're here.*

He popped his cheery face back round the door. 'That there's a stew on the fire, if you're hungry afore I come back.'

I decided I had better not be hungry before he came back as I did not want him to think we would eat him out of house and home.

When I started reading about childhood ailments, sitting at the table for the better light from the window, I could not stop. I never knew so many children died before the age of five. They could be destroyed within weeks of birth by impure air; later by mumps, whooping cough, diptheria, erysipelas, meningitis, poliomyletis or falling off a chair. I felt dizzy at the thought of what could go wrong.

And there seemed to be so little advice. Give her a warm bath, it said, nurse her, keep her still, don't let her get too close to the fire.

While Leila slept, I filled a pail with water from the pump in the yard, topped up the big kettle and put it on the fire. I did not know what time Mr Dennison would be back, but I hoped not before I had a chance to follow the book's advice and give Leila a bath.

She woke whimpering. Perhaps the sound of the pump had disturbed her. I put my hand on her forehead; still hot. That was when I noticed the rash on her head. When I undressed her, the rash was on her tummy, too.

'Good girl,' I said, trying not to let my panic show. I put her in the bath when it was ready, and just at that moment there was a knock on the door. I dashed to the door, telling her to stay still, but in the moment it took me to take the loaf of bread from the little boy at the door, she had slid down into the water. I lifted her up, patted her on the back, cupped water in my hands and let it fall over her. I had no idea where Mr Dennison might keep a clean towel.

When I finally got her back to bed, I looked again at the book. She had either chicken-pox, smallpox, scarlet fever, or something worse, not illustrated in the book.

I mended the fire and set the stew pan on the hob. Then I remembered the room should be cool for an invalid, so opened a window. Mr Dennison was just walking through the yard, whistling to himself. Dempsey jumped up. I had to open the door and let him go running out to meet him and the sheepdog.

'What's wrong?' Mr Dennison asked.

'Leila's ill.'

He looked at her, then put a hand on her forehead. 'I'll fetch the doctor.'

She never got ill for Heather. As soon as I took over, she caught something. 'How did she catch it?' I asked the doctor, half expecting him to say she got it by travelling too far too fast on the back of a bike behind an idiot.

But it was chicken-pox. She caught it not from a chicken but from some other person. I tried to think who. Perhaps one of the children we watched playing in the school yard in Gargrave when I thought that village would hold our future. The germ travels through the air, invisible, and it is just Leila's and my luck that it took a fancy to her.

After Mr Dennison went for the doctor, I didn't know what to do. She would not be enticed by the little cup showing the boy and cat having a jolly time together, whether I put water in it or milk.

'Not thirsty,' she said, looking ready to burst into tears.

'You'll upset Dempsey if you cry.'

That stopped her tears for a while. 'Dempsey's named after a boxer,' I told her, 'A boxer man who puts up his fists like this. Put your fists up like a boxer. Show Dempsey how you can do it.'

'Can't,' she wailed.

'Boxers drink their milk, that's why they can make a fist.'

I was too busy trying to get her to drink something and did not hear Mr Dennison come until he was almost behind me saying, 'Doctor's on his way.' He put his hands in his pockets and produced two bars of Fry's chocolate, one from each pocket. 'What do you say to this?' He handed one to Leila and one to me.

Leila went shy and wouldn't say thank you. I saved one bar and broke three pieces, one for each of us. We had still not touched the stew that sat on the hob.

The doctor inspected Leila's scalp and body, took her temperature, examined her tongue and asked me had she vomited. She hadn't, but did so in moments, as if to oblige. 'Where does it hurt?' he asked her.

She rubbed her legs. 'Headache.'

'Headache in your legs?' the doctor asked kindly.

She nodded.

'Where else do you have a headache?'

'All over,' she whined, and I'm sure was about to demand her mammy and daddy and lead me into awkward explanations, but that was the moment she threw up. The doctor was quicker than me at dodging. I wiped her face and chest as he announced chicken-pox and told me what I should expect.

'The rash will turn to a red or purplish lesion and fill with fluid like a blister. A crust will form and last a week or two before falling off. She'll want to scratch, but keep her from scratching. She might break the skin, cause an infection and a scarring that would last for life.'

I had a sudden picture of the once perfect child I had abducted turning into a scar-face because I would not be able to keep her from scratching. A rescue party would come from Leeds, headed by priests and nuns, stare at her in horror and mark her down as fit for the order of nuns that scrubbed churches and prayed silently and out of sight. Tommy would come to visit her, having made his fortune in the south of England and he would return in triumph, which would turn to ashes in his mouth when he beheld his scarred and miserable daughter.

'How am I supposed to keep her from scratching?' I asked.

'Watch her. Talk her out of it. Oh, and keep her fingernails clean.' He took a bottle of calamine lotion from his bag. 'This will help. You could also rub honey on her spots if you have a jar.'

Mr Dennison, standing by, nodded vigorously. 'Arnside honey – an untouched jar in the cupboard.'

The doctor closed his bag. 'Sponge her down with a solution of bicarbonate of soda – four teaspoonfuls to four pints of tepid, not cold, water. That will help the spots dry and heal.'

I expected him to do something else, give some medicine. 'How long will it go on?'

'A fortnight perhaps. Did you have chicken-pox yourself as a child?'

'Yes.' I suddenly thought of my mother yelling, 'Don't scratch!' But I was older than Leila and could understand the instruction. Couldn't Leila have waited? I wondered. Got sick when she was older, or at least given us chance to settle somewhere?

When Mr Dennison came back from walking the doctor out to the yard, I said, 'I'm glad you were able to fetch the doctor for us, Mr Dennison.'

'So am I.' He ladled out soup into two large dishes and one small. The small was a child's dish, with a picture of a rabbit. 'There's a rabbit at the bottom of this dish, Leila.'

Her stew sat cooling while we ate.

'I'll try her with it.' He picked her up and carried her to the big chair, tucking a tea-cloth under her chin. 'You must eat, little one. Make you strong and better.'

'She won't have anything,' I said.

But Leila opened her mouth like a little bird and let him feed her.

When she fell asleep in the chair, he and I sat at the table and drank tea.

'You mustn't worry, Jessica. What we talked about, you looking for employment, with all your certificates. It will not be much of a place for you, but you and the child can stay here and you will be housekeeper.'

The very word housekeeper made me feel slightly sick. He looked at his tea carefully, seeming to know he had said the wrong thing. 'It will be above board. You must feel safe here. I won't vex you or meself by saying what-like I was as a lad, but these days I sing in church every Sunday. This afternoon, when you saw me put on a clean shirt, that was where I went.'

'About me?'

He held the mug of tea between two hands, as if to keep it warm, turning it this way and that. 'I am a religious man these days – well, all my life long in my bringing-up – and attend chapel. For a long time, since my wife and then my little boy died, I have lived alone.'

He went silent and I did not know what to say, but somehow thought that he blamed himself for their death.

'A woman used to come from the village and clean and cook for me, but she's too old now. I make do as best I can and sometimes this neighbour or that will bake me a pie or a pot of stew, for my mind is a deal on my work.'

So I would have to bake and make stew. I wondered how I would manage that while keeping Leila from scratching herself to bits. But I said nothing.

'I did a wrong thing once and afterwards wondered whether the loss of the two I loved might be a kind of retribution. When I saw you that day, after I'd gone to the camp on seeing smoke from the bungalow chimney, when I saw you ... This will seem fanciful. I looked through the open window, and heard the sound of the little one's clogs, and saw you sitting at the bottom of a bed. I came round so quiet like, half thinking you to be a dream. Yon's a desperate place in the dark weather, with the sounds of the sea and the building that creaks and groans like a living thing. You give me the chance to make amends, you and the child straying in from I know not where. My chance to make up for the wrong I did in my life.'

'I'll be glad to stay,' I said, not looking at him, fearing I would see a question in his eyes, demands for explanations I had not the energy to give just then. 'I wouldn't want to have to move again too soon.' It seemed to me that perhaps he did not really see me and Leila, but only the chance to do a good deed. If he knew he was harbouring runaways, would he feel the same? I wondered.

He spoke quietly. 'I did not jump in straightly and make the offer because it might not be thought proper, a man alone and a young woman.'

'Is that why you went to see the minister?'

'Yes. That was my reason. But on my way there, walking along the lane with the day drawing in and the sky turning grey, I realized I was not going to ask him, but to tell him. Because I know it is the right thing. See that bag over there? His wife has sent some things that you and the little one might need.'

'So now all the village will know I am here?'

'No. They keep a confidence. But you must be weary. If there's a day when you want to tell your story, then do so, when you are ready. I reckon you had good reason to come, and the Lord guided your way.' He got up to go.

I wanted to make sure this was not charity. He had not asked for references, and I had none to give. 'What are my duties to be? Housekeeping duties?'

'I suppose as you see fit, as you did before when you were a housekeeper. Oh, and my name is Isaac, not mister. On the mantelpiece you'll see a dish with money. Take what you need for yourself and the child.'

I felt sure my housekeeping here would be a world away from life in the priest's house. But Leila stirred and moaned in her sleep, so I did not get a chance to think how different it might be. I carried her to bed, as he wished me goodnight and went quietly up the stairs.

When his boots dropped on the floor above, she did not stir. More blotchy rash had appeared on her arms and neck, making me itchy just to look at her. I lay there, listening to Isaac Dennison above me, murmuring his prayers like a child.

In my dream, Heather spread a picnic rug on just-mown grass in the shade of an oak tree. She sniffed in the scent and did not seem to mind that cut grass stuck to the rug, though I tried to clear it away with my hands. Strapped on her back, she carried a baby boy, and I knew she would carry him into eternity. Leila scooped up acorns from just beyond the picnic rug and carried them in cupped hands to her mother. Heather took an acorn between her finger and thumb. Neither of them spoke, but agreed on this as the world's perfect acorn. This was why they had come, and now Heather rolled up the picnic rug with Leila lumped inside, to be taken away, floated away with Heather, who seemed to glide just above the ground, beyond my reach. As fast as I could, I ran after them, calling. Heather didn't understand that Leila must stay. No matter how fast my legs moved, I could not catch up. Some pressure stopped me, an invisible something pushing my chest, hurting me.

Waking with a jolt, my heart beating fast with fear, I opened my eyes expecting Leila to be gone. She lay snuggled into me, her little mouth clamped on my nipple, sucking. That was the sensation that had woke me.

Gently as I could, I prised her off. Sliding out of bed, I felt my way to the table and lit the lamp. Still half asleep, I poured milk into a pan. Leila stirred and made a little cry. I wondered if she was dreaming of her mother. And if Heather came for her, would she go? As I struck a match to light the calor gas, I thought how Isaac Dennison treated it as if it were a dangerous firework. Light the blue touch paper and stand back.

While the milk warmed, I looked at the money he had mentioned, on the mantelpiece in a dish. There would be no point in my taking anything. Leila and I had nothing and it would need more than a dish of coins to change that.

26

Search Party

The station master blew his whistle. Wilf folded his overcoat and placed it carefully on the luggage rack beside his Gladstone bag. As the engine spluttered into life and the train jerked forward, the carriage door opened. Wilf turned to see who had cut it so fine. There stood Ralph Moxon, like a great streak of whitewash, wrapped in a tweed cape. He pulled off a deerstalker cap. His ridiculous red hair bounced to life on either side of his head. Wilf could have sworn the bald patch in the centre had grown since yesterday. Ralph placed a food hamper on the seat between them.

'I told you to stay out of this,' Wilf said.

'I just happen to be going in your direction. When the country and the arts are in the doldrums, someone has to give things a shove. I'm part of a consortium, old chap. We're building a grand hotel in Morecambe, to be called the Midland Grand Hotel. We shall be wanting to commission artists and sculptors so I'd stay on the right side of me if I were you.' He opened the lid of the picnic basket. 'Did you manage breakfast? Only I have a flask here, and one or two choice items.'

It was ten o'clock, and dark, when Wilf stepped onto the platform at Silverdale station, Ralph at his heels. The station master marched up smartly and slammed the carriage door shut. The porter beside him swung a lamp, flinging a glow of light across the platform. No one else embarked or boarded, but still the station master called in a booming voice, 'Lancaster to Barrow, boarding for Barrow.' He blew his whistle.

Torn between shedding light for his superior or for the alighting passengers, the porter hovered mid-platform, giving light only to himself.

Wilf strode towards the way out, Ralph ambling beside him.

'What's the plan, Wilf old chap?'

'If you wanted Morecambe, you took the wrong line,' Wilf said, but not sorry now that Ralph had tagged along. Wilf had thought of walking to the holiday bungalow to search for Jess there. This late, in the dark and driving rain, that no longer seemed a good plan.

'I suggest the Silverdale Hotel,' Ralph said. 'Unless we're to strike out straightaway for where you think she might be. In fact, let's do that, eh? If she and the abductee are holed up somewhere, they'll be pretty chilly on a night such as this. King Lear on the heath sort of night. We could ride in like white knights. Who comes to Lear's rescue? I can't remember. Gloucester or the Fool?'

'You'll be wanting transportation, gentlemen?' the station master asked. 'The porter here will attend on you in a sheep's shake, if you'll be kind enough to avail your good selves of the welcoming fire in our humble waiting room.'

They stood on either side of the fire.

Wilf said, 'If she's where I think she is, she won't be going anywhere on a night such as this. Morning will be best.'

'Cold feet?' Ralph said sympathetically. 'You suddenly think you've steamed yourself up all this long way on a wild goose chase, and you want to delay the disappointment.'

The station master swung open the waiting-room door and held it wide. 'Transportation at your service, gentlemen. To the Silverdale Hotel?'

'Exactly my thought, station master,' Ralph said, making for the door.

Wilf followed, turning up his collar against the rain.

The transportation turned out to be a handcart on which the porter pushed their luggage. Ralph, as the taller of the two men, held the station master's copious umbrella above their heads. 'Couldn't have been much of a public school they sent you to.'

'Leeds grammar school. What's that got to do with the price of fish?'

'You don't hide your feelings very well, Wilf.'

'Why should I? Do you know what? I think you want Jess for yourself. Is that why you're tagging along?'

'I'm being a chum, that's all. Any chum would do the same.'

At eight o'clock the next morning, the sun shone brightly into the dining room of the Silverdale Hotel. After kippers, toast and tea, Wilf felt more kindly towards Ralph. Having long given up all hope of shaking him off, Wilf satisfied himself with the thought that Ralph had promised faithfully that once they found Jess, or not, he would make his way to Morecambe and leave Wilf to his own devices.

They walked through the town and past the churchyard. Leaves that had resisted autumnal winds had fallen under last night's downpour and made the road slippery underfoot.

As they trudged up the hill towards Arnside Knott, Ralph took a deep breath and surveyed the fields and hedgerows spread with silvery cobwebs. 'Atkinson Grimshaw wasted his palette on Leeds. The man should have migrated to this side of the Pennines.'

Wilf laughed. 'If you feel so strongly about capturing this landscape, do it yourself instead of wasting your time with portraiture for vain idiots with more money than sense.'

'Ah, there we differ. You don't like people, Wilf. I do. Good, bad and indifferent. I've yet to meet a person I don't take to and half fall in love with.'

'You don't have to paint them all.'

'I do, you see. It's as simple as that. I was put on this earth to paint everyone who'll stay still long enough. And to help you search for your girlfriend.'

'Fiancé.' Wilf turned and, through the trees, caught a glimpse of the shore and, way out beyond, the grey sea.

'All right, your fiancé then, which means it is even more careless of you to lose her.'

'You didn't give me an answer last night. Have you fallen in love with Jess yourself? Is that why you wanted to paint her?'

'I wanted to paint your charming mother, too, and one day I'll paint you.'

The shut gates of the holiday camp seemed such a part of the grey landscape that Wilf almost walked past them.

Ralph stared at the sign: 'Leeds Poor Children's Holiday Camp. They have a holiday camp especially for poor children?'

'Yes. I thought you knew everything about this area?'

'This impressive little enterprise passed me by. And are they here now, these poor children?'

'No. It's deserted. A perfect place to hide. We came here, in the summer, and had use of that bungalow.'

'It's locked,' Ralph announced, trying the door.

'The key hangs inside the letter-box.'

Wilf looked round. 'Don't see her bike, or any tracks. I'll just check round the back.'

Ralph bounded in first. 'What a jolly little spot for a tryst.'

It had rained. Wilf saw no tyre tracks. He followed Ralph into the bungalow. Never had a place seemed so empty.

Ralph stood at the table, with his back to Wilf. Heavy with disappointment, Wilf sat down at the table, picturing Jess opposite him, smiling as on that August day.

Ralph had something in his hand.

'What is it?' Wilf asked.

'Just a pebble.'

'Let me see. Where was it?'

'On the table.'

'It's unusual. Little red flecks. It's what Jess would do. We used to find pebbles and fossils for each other when we were kids. She's been, Ralph, I'm sure.' He jumped up. 'There'll be a note.' He looked on the mantelpiece, the sideboard.

Ralph looked around the room. 'Everyone picks up pebbles. Just because there's a pebble on the table doesn't mean she's been here. Look, that ashtray's full of pebbles and shells visitors have brought up from the beach.'

Ralph stepped from room to room, opening and closing doors, looking for signs of life. He paused in the pantry, then came out in a rush, carrying something.

'What is it?'

'Don't even look, and hold your nose.'

Wilf glanced once more around the room. On an impulse, he took his new monogrammed hanky from his top pocket and placed it in the centre of the table.

Ralph came back a few minutes later. 'Some idiot left a rabbit hanging on the pantry door. It couldn't have been Jess. It's running wick. Must have been there for months.'

'Are you sure?'

'I've been shooting the blighters since I was six years old, I ought to know.'

Wilf walked down the path to the superintendent's house. Finding no key when he reached his fingers into the letter-box, he lifted a flower pot and found it there. The chalet was cosily furnished with chintz cushions and covers. A dark oak table stood bare in the centre of the room. From the silence and musty smell, Wilf knew that there would be no trace of Jess. But still, he looked.

The accommodation for the children was locked. Through a chink in the curtains he saw rows of stripped-down beds in the dormitory. Wilf peered through an outhouse window at potatoes under sacks.

Ralph stood beside him. 'Bit bloody bleak. Spiffing view of the bay from here, though. And look, a rainbow!' The rainbow arched off towards Arnside Knott and beyond. 'Jess is at the end of it.'

'Don't be ridiculous.' Wilf shuddered. 'The gold at the end of the rainbow is buried. Jess is alive and well. I'm sure of it.'

'I'm sure, too. We'll find her.'

'Not if she doesn't want to be found,' Wilf said. 'You don't know her. If she wants to keep that child out of the damned orphanage, she'll do it.'

'Go back to London,' Ralph said sympathetically. 'She knows where to find you then. There'll probably be a letter waiting.'

'You're right.' Wilf brightened. 'She's bound to get in touch.'

27

True North

On those November nights, I sat by the crackling fire at the day's end. Leila slept soundly, recovered from her chicken-pox. The silence between Isaac Dennison and me was not a pained silence, for the dogs sat with us, and they talked in their way to each other and to us. Sometimes Isaac would tell me how things went for him that day, and how he must earn his living according to the season – farm and seashore, seashore and farm.

One fine Sunday, when the sun shone almost like a spring day, he asked if I would like to bring Leila for a walk. He was smartly dressed in his Sunday suit and coat. Leila wore the little red coat I had salvaged from the bag of clothes sent by the minister's wife.

As I drew my old cape around me, I felt very shabby. Isaac must have read my mind. 'Shall we see if anything upstairs will fit you?'

I followed him up to the bedroom opposite his own. A deep closet held women's clothes.

'Whose are these?' I asked.

Leila pushed her way between the clothes, hiding.

'Some are my mother's, some my late wife's. I put them in here together, meaning to do something about them. Perhaps you would do that one day. I should get rid of what you may not think worth keeping. But if there's anything . . .'

'This coat looks warm.' I touched a brown tweed.

He slid it from its hanger and held it for me. 'Try it for size.'

'Whose was it?'

'My mother's.'

Somehow a mother's coat seemed more acceptable than a wife's. I put it on.

'It'll keep you warm.'

'Which clothes were your wife's?' I asked.

'Those . . . on that side. Why?'

'I just wondered.'

A few minutes later, we walked the cliff path, the dogs running ahead, Dempsey wearing his blanket jacket made by Bella.

Leila saw the camp buildings. She wanted to clog dance again. Isaac had the keys with him and opened the dormitory door.

'Have you been to check on any of the buildings recently?' I asked, thinking of the note I had left for Wilf. Isaac had told me since that he'd been entrusted with care of the camp out of season.

'Not since the day I found you here.'

'Are you afraid you might find other waifs and strays?' I asked.

He laughed. 'Something like finding you two happens once in a lifetime.'

'Will you watch her while she dances? I want to look at something.'

He nodded.

I walked to the visitors' bungalow and pulled the key through the letter-box. First I went to the pantry. At the oddest times, when I could do nothing about it, I had remembered the rabbit hanging behind the door. I expected to smell it now. But there was no smell, only a cold fustiness. No rabbit behind the door.

I went to the dining-sitting room. A folded handkerchief sat in the centre of the table. It had an embroidered W on its corner. Wilf's handkerchief.

I picked it up. So he had been here after all, had found my letter and done nothing. But why leave a hanky? To say he had been?

A loneliness surged through me. He had come to find me and, having found a note telling him I was safe, that was it. This hanky was his message to say that he wouldn't follow me. He would forget me. Go on with his life, and let me lie in the bed I had made for myself. My breath came fast. My hands trembled. I pushed the hanky in my pocket. If that was what he wanted, if he didn't have the courage to go on loving me no matter what, then let him get on with his damn carvings. I would be better off without him. I didn't need him. I sat for a while, because I couldn't help but cry. At least I had his hanky to blow my nose and wipe my tears. Not even a note. He could have left a note.

Isaac was watching through the dormitory window. He turned away and I guessed he would be telling Leila to take off the clogs and put her boots back on.

We walked up the lane to Eaves Wood – which Isaac had told me was the name of the little wood by the camp. He carried Leila on his shoulders. In the wood she wanted to run ahead, crushing fallen leaves underfoot, bobbing down to pick up leaves and crackle them in her hands.

'What's wrong?' Isaac asked. 'You seem so sad.'

Since I was wearing his mother's coat and living in his house, it seemed all right to tell him. I had no one else to confide in.

'The boy I loved doesn't love me any more.'

'Then he's a fool.'

'He's an artist. I think that will always come first.'

We watched Leila, kicking her way through the leaves.

'I've never met an artist,' Isaac said, 'but to my way of thinking if he were anything of an artist, a true artist, he would want you in his life.'

I wished he hadn't said that. It made me want to cry again.

'I'm sorry, Jessica, did I put my big foot in it?'

'No.'

'Don't answer me if you don't want to, but is this fool of an artist Leila's father?'

'No!' I felt myself blush. I had forgotten the mistake he made when he first found us, when I guessed he thought I was her mother. I didn't get chance to explain because at that moment Leila saw an animal stirring, took fright and came running back.

That night, I saw my chance to speak and thought I had better set things straight.

While I tucked Leila in and kissed her goodnight, Isaac stretched and walked across the room to wind the tall clock.

I had thought all through our supper about how to say it.

He turned to say goodnight.

'Isaac, before you go up, there's something I want to show you.'

I had rolled my own certificates and Leila's birth certificate together in a cloth shoe bag. I took it from under the bed, peeled off

Leila's birth certificate, and handed it to him. He read it, and read it again.

'She's not your child?' He sat in the armchair by the fire.

I took the opposite chair. 'She's my goddaughter.'

'When you first came, and you said you wanted to keep her from the orphanage, I thought she was to be taken from you.'

'I know.' I explained about Heather's death and showed him the letter Tommy McBride had written, giving me permission to take care of her.

'Bless you. You left home, you left everything, to take care of someone else's child?'

'I had no choice.'

'We always have a choice. Perhaps that's a curse or blessing of being young, that you don't see choices – only the one direction.'

He handed the birth certificate and letter back to me. 'Is that what came between you and your sweetheart?'

'I think so. He said we could be together, but at the bottom of him I think he feared a child would get in the way of his work.'

'So he let you down?'

'We knew each other from childhood. I begin to think we only came to care deeply for each other when we knew we were going to go our separate ways.'

'That could be it. But it's hard to fathom. And your folks, they must be achin' for news of you.'

'I'll have to write to them, but not say where I am. I won't go back.'

For a long time, he sat without speaking, his head in his hands. Then he said, 'Once, long ago, I did a wrong thing myself. Perhaps that's why I thought the same of you. I thought my life would go by, without the chance to atone. You and the little one give me that chance to make amends, balance up the scales of good and evil.'

The wind blew down the chimney and sent a gust of smoke at us. 'Sometimes life deals you a hard blow,' he said. 'You spin and spin, and when you stop spinning you're facing another way altogether and may never find true north again.'

At first, I didn't see how you could make a mistake about north when you had the sea in the west right next to you and had only to stand with it on your right-hand side to have north behind and south in front. Then I realized he was talking in the abstract way that in poetry you learn is a metaphor.

'We used to spin and spin,' I said, 'for a game in the street. When you stopped you felt dizzy and had to sit down. It was a way of getting outside of yourself.' I don't know what had made me think of that. What I was trying to say was, I can't go back, and I'm afraid about going forward in case someone appears and accuses me and snatches Leila back.

He got up and went to the dresser. From the drawer he took something and placed it on the hearth rug between us.

'Come take a look.'

It looked like a big heavy watch. We sat on the rug. 'Have you seen a compass before?'

'Yes, but not one so big.'

'Look. See how it finds true north.'

We watched the pointer move.

He picked up the compass, put it in my hands and closed his hand over it. 'It's yours. Think of it as an early Christmas gift.'

At the foot of the stairs, he turned as if to say something more. 'Goodnight, Jessica.'

'Goodnight, Isaac.'

I began to undress in front of the dying fire. I took my time undressing, warming my nightie on the oven door. I could hear him upstairs, the murmur as he said his prayers. I shivered into my nightie. The loneliness I had felt at the loss of Wilf had lessened after talking to Isaac. In all my life, he was the only person other than Wilf who seemed to listen to me with real attention, as though what I said mattered more than anything. I carried the compass to bed and held it for a while before setting it on the little table.

28

Cockle Pickers

That month long, Isaac and his shrimping partner had set off early with their nets, but the next day they were not going out. He said he would go cockling just down in the bay.

I could hear by the question in his voice that he wondered if I would want to come. Perhaps he wanted to divert me given that he had seen me near tears over Wilf.

Although I had made myself useful in the house, useful does not bring in a living. Useful does not give you independence, or take you nearer to making your mark, buying a good coat and driving back to Leeds in a motor car in ten years' time. I said that we would go. We left the dogs in the stable, as neither Isaac nor me thought cockling a good occupation for dogs, especially Dempsey, who feels the cold in spite of his jacket.

It was not the coldest of days and I thought the sea air might do Leila good. I wore my cape and trilby. We followed Isaac into the stable. He lifted a thick seesaw plank of wood which he called a jumbo. It was almost five feet long and an awkward thing, a foot and a half wide, with metal handles on top. I offered to take an end but he said I should fetch the cramb which stood next to it. Just longer than a school ruler, it looked like a fork I'd seen Neptune hold in a pantomime at the Grand Theatre where a wonderful underwater scene took place on stage and even the smell floating up to our seats in the circle made you think you had gone under the waves. I unhooked a couple of baskets from the stable wall and gave the smallest one to Leila.

'I'll fetch the horse and cart round by the road with the big baskets,' Isaac said as he leaned the cramb against the stable door. 'You two can cut across the field – it's not too muddy. I'll see you by the path.'

The tide was far off, leaving a great wide stretch of shore. We joined Isaac at the edge of the path. He had brought a little homemade cart and blankets, so Leila could rest and be kept warm if she tired. He tucked it in a crevice between the rocks and the cliff foot.

'This is our own special seesaw,' Isaac told Leila, showing her the jumbo. 'Jess and me will take it along the sand, one of us at either end, and you'll see what creatures appear for us.'

We each of us took an end of the jumbo and placed it on the sand, rocking it this way and that with our weight. Sure enough, when we moved it, there sat the cockles. Leila stared as if some magic had taken place, but soon she began to pick them. I used the cramb, wanting to get the hang of it, though it was not so easy at first. Isaac almost cleared the cockles before I gathered half a dozen with my Neptune fork.

We worked our way along the sands, the jumbo bringing cockles to the surface. As we filled our baskets, we would take them to the cart, tip them into the larger basket and start again. Isaac called to me over the wind, telling me about the sands, the high banks and the low, the rivers and paths that were safe, but I must not take a risk or trust to walking across without him because I would never read the secrets well enough to understand the bay's treachery.

'See,' he said, as the morning wore on, 'how far away the sea was when we came and what it does now.' We turned about and started to work our way back to the cliffs, Leila playing as we went, looking in pools for fish and crabs when she grew tired of gathering cockles.

By the time we got back to the rocks the sea had cut off the beach where we had worked, like a pair of scissors closing.

I handed Isaac my basket to tip into the bigger one. 'What do you do if you see the waves coming in like that?' I asked.

He took the basket from me. 'You run like the devil.'

When we got back, the dogs went mad at us for being left in the stable. Dempsey has almost learned to talk and gave a high-pitched bark as if to say, *Where have you been?*

I looked forward to the fire and a rest, but it was not to be.

'We need to rinse the cockles in cold water,' Isaac said. 'I'll show you. They're all sand and seaweed else.'

After I had given Leila her warm milk, we went to the outbuilding, followed by the dogs. I put Isaac's mug of tea on the draining board and held my own, to warm my hands. He stood at the big sink, working the pump.

'What are you smiling at?' Isaac asked.

'That you have no tap in the house, but a pump in here, so the cockles are more important than the people.'

'You could say that.' He took a sup of tea. 'When I have the time, I will put a tap in the house.'

If gathering cockles is cold work, it is nothing to having your hands in icy water for so long that you lose track of time, but he would not let me do it for many minutes that day, saying I must go back inside, keep war-rum, and he would be in for supper when he had done.

As we ate supper, he said, 'If you like, you can go on the train to Carnforth tomorrow and take as many cockles to sell as you can carry. The cash to be for yourself and Leila.'

'I'm not sure I'd dare go selling in the streets.'

'You don't have to call out, you can knock on doors. I'll draw you a map of where to go.'

When Leila had gone to bed, we sat at the table. We did a practice of what I would say when I knocked on doors: 'Fresh cockles for sale.'

'Be sure to say fresh,' Isaac said.

He drew a map and said which streets to go along. I must measure out the cockles into the dish that a woman would bring to the door, using the tin jug for my measuring, and be even and fair. He told me what to charge and to accept no hard luck stories. 'The cockles aren't yours to give tick. Them as pays gets, them as don't, don't. And keep your money belt covered by that cape of yorn.'

The next day, Isaac and his cockling partner set off with the horse and cart to cockle at Hest Bank. I went to the outhouse while Leila slept. I saw that Isaac had already filled the basket that would strap to my back. The cockles had settled there and so I was able to put in some more, as many as it would hold. In the bag at my waist, I carried newspaper, cut into neat rectangles, and a tin jug for measuring. On my arm I carried a smaller basket so that I would not have to unstrap the larger one from my back each time I made a sale.

Leila thought it a grand adventure. We walked to Silverdale railway station to catch the Barrow to Lancaster train that stopped at Carnforth. She soon complained about her hurting legs, and it was awkward to know how to carry her under one arm with a basket on the other, until I worked out how I could hold her, and she could grasp the basket.

On the train, I practised making a cone of the newspaper, just in case I made a sale in the street. I did not think I would have the nerve to call out loudly enough, 'Cockles, fresh cockles for sale!' so I would probably just go for doorstep sales. It gave me a new admiration for people like Tommy, who had taken a barrow round and cried out, 'Fresh fruit', or the chestnut sellers and newspaper vendors.

I decided I would keep my trilby pulled well down; not that anyone in Carnforth would know us.

It is harder than you think to walk through the street with something to sell. You have the feeling that people look down on you. Once I got my nerve up and called – when there was no one about – 'Cockles, fresh cockles!' Leila did not like it. 'Shhh!' she said, until I encouraged her to join in and call out with me.

When I knocked on a door and a rude woman glared at me and said, 'I'm not buying eatables from a creature done up like Guy Fawkes,' I wanted to turn and run. I spent two streets thinking of what answer I should have given her, and wishing I could remember the door so that I would never knock on it again.

We did well enough at our selling, and celebrated with a cup of hot sweet tea and a toasted teacake in the café on the main street, though I felt self-conscious, like one of the poor tramps who had knocked on the priests' door for a hunk of bread.

Leila slept on the way back. I thought I would have to carry her up the hill, but Isaac met us at the station with the horse and cart, and the two dogs leaping off the back to bark a greeting and lick as much of us as they could reach.

I counted the money, and put it in a jar on the mantelpice. Isaac insisted that I keep the money separate, for myself and Leila.

He said, 'You look so much better for having earned a bit of brass.

But it must have seemed a peculiar way to earn it, you with your certificates.'

My certificates and my other life seemed almost unreal. Leila sat on the buffet in front of the fire. I dried her after her bath and told her the story of Rumpelstiltskin.

Isaac joined in, telling stories. He told of the time his father first took him fishing as a boy, how the cold chilled him to the bone. When he came back to the house, his mammy hugged him war-rum.

'Where is your mammy now?' Leila asked.

'She is dead this long while ago and in the churchyard.'

Leila said nothing. But I know her so well. As I plaited her hair in lots of little braids, taking them to a whisper at the end, I knew she had stored away that word. Churchyard. There is a reel of thread in the drawer but I do not tie the ends of her plaits. It is our amusement to see how well I can do them, to make the braids stay in until morning. Each morning, we check to see whether some have come undone. I like to make her hair curly, because she is tiny, like her mother, and there is so little to her that giving her curls makes her seem more substantial somehow.

Under my hands I could almost feel the word seeping out through her scalp. Churchyard. Churchyard. I could tell she was saying it over and over to herself. Sometimes she goes silent, knowing we have a secret, but unsure what our secret is. A month ago, we knew nothing of Isaac Dennison or what he does and how lives. Now we know that the fields to the south and south-east of this house are leased to him. He grows wheat and barley in the spring and summer, and these feed the three cows in the stalls of his stable. He would keep more if he could feed them. Major, the horse, came to Isaac and his father at the end of one long-ago summer. We listened as he told us about Major, and how they chose her.

He said, 'Everyone has one animal they love best. For me it was Major, and for Major it was me. At the end of the summer season, when I was about ten years old, Dad and me went to Morecambe to choose a horse. We had been before, while the season was at its height, to watch horses take holidaymakers to and fro, trotting along the promenade. We looked for a big strong horse with a bit of spirit, and we saw Major. He took to us straightaway, and was good at the work, having no fear on the sands and not taking fright at the waves.

Once he saved my life when I was young and reckless and strayed too far.'

When he had finished his story, the horse seemed to be in the room, the scent of him, his hooves on the flagged floor. In listening to his tale, I had forgotten Leila's hair. I finished the plaiting.

Leila put her hand around her head, to feel the braids. 'Want to see Major.'

'Major is long dead, these many years.'

'In churchyard?'

'No, horses don't go there.'

'Where is he?'

'Nay, little one, you ask too many questions. It's time you went to school. They'll knock it out of you.'

'Want to see Major.'

'He went to a farm.'

'Take me there.'

'He's not there now. He died, and when he died, he went to the knackers' yard.'

'Say it.'

'To the knackers' yard.'

'Say it.'

But I picked her up and carried her to bed, knowing that tomorrow she would be asking to see the horse, the churchyard and the knackers' yard. Dempsey jumped on the bed and lay at her feet.

She was tired but would not close her eyes. A clatter from above startled her. 'What's that?'

'Only Isaac moving about above, taking off his boots.'

'Jess?'

'What?'

'Will my mammy come? Just to tuck me in.' Her gaze was steady, holding me, demanding an answer I couldn't give.

I tucked the bedclothes to cover her shoulders. 'Your mammy couldn't stay with you, or she would have. She can't come back to you. But she knew I'd look after you. She and your daddy wanted me to look after you.'

I remembered Heather telling me about her childhood, how she missed her mam and dad. When children at the village school said, 'my mam' or 'my dad' with such ease, she felt even more bereft. She had told me that sometimes, when she was alone, she would say the words aloud to feel them in her mouth. Mam. Dad.

I spread Leila's plaits across the pillow. 'I'm going to be your mammy now, if you'll let me. You and me, we'll take care of each other.'

'I know.' She let out such a little sigh.

I leaned down to kiss her goodnight, then closed the curtain around the bed.

'Leave it open, Mammy.'

I pulled the curtain back a little way and knew that she watched my movements as I took down the jar and counted my cockle takings. This would be my first Christmas away from home, and Leila's first Christmas without Heather and Tommy.

I wanted to find some way of getting word to Mam and Dad and Bernadette, to say that we are safe and well. But how to do it without letting them know where I was?

I lay awake going through all the possibilities. Even if I went as far as Lancaster or Barrow to post a letter to Mam and Dad, they would be on the train and searching.

Was there someone I could write to who would pass on a letter and not give me away? The Treasures might believe it their Catholic duty to get back at me for taking the child they wanted. Perhaps, given her interest in where creatures went when they died, Leila would have been a perfect candidate for them. Gladys Hardy had been kind to me. Something told me she would feel obliged to keep my counsel. But they would get it out of her. Auntie Irene would chip and chip away if she thought Gladys knew. Given her connection with Silverdale, she would recognize the postmark. She knew the area too well and might find me, to give me good advice, or put me on the right track. I would not write to Wilf, since he clearly wanted to forget me.

As I fell asleep, faces came into my head, faces of no one I knew, some grotesque, some smiling. Faces of horses. Faces of ghosts. One more face floated before my mind's eye, a long face, with bright eyes, wiry red hair and a bald patch that made the temples and forehead look grave and thoughtful. Ralph Moxon. He had given me his card on the day I sat for my portrait.

I was up first the next day and lit the fire as quietly as I could, keeping the raking to the barest of sounds, clearing out the ashes with the soft brush and leaving the pile to shovel up later.

I washed my hands. From the dresser drawer I took paper, envelopes, pen and ink.

Dear Mam and Dad

Just to let you know we are well and have a good place to live. Do not worry about me.

I am sorry I had to go away without telling you but I could not bear to see Leila in the orphanage. Sorry to Uncle Bill for leaving a pile of invoices undone. I hope he and Auntie Irene – and Aunt Bella – all have a good Christmas.

Wishes and love to Bernadette for Christmas.

Jess

P.S. Someone is posting this for me so don't go looking in London as that would be a wild turkey chase.

I wrote their address on the envelope, folded it in two and put it inside an envelope to Ralph.

I do not know who else to ask to send this note to my parents. I cannot ask Wilf. I do not want him to feel obliged to me out of guilt. You told me when I sat for you that you believe Wilf to have true genius and that is why you were anxious to protect his future. I am glad he has you to look out for him.

Thank you for forwarding my letter. Please keep my confidence if you have any regard for me.

With good wishes

Jess Price

PS Do not you go by the postmark, either! I am not to be found.

The strange thing was that when I had finished, I felt glad. It puzzled me because here I was, so far from everyone who had cared for me, and yet this light-heartedness spilled through me. Upstairs, I heard Isaac moving about. I was glad I had put the kettle on and would make us some tea, for he works so hard and deserves a little looking after. As that thought came to me, I suddenly knew. The reason I felt happy and not sad was because in a moment Isaac would be in the room with me.

The minister's wife kindly said she would keep an eye on Leila while I went to Lancaster to buy sugar mice and chocolate pennies for Christmas, and to look round the shops. If she guessed there was more to it, she asked no questions.

I bought stamps and posted my letter to Ralph shortly after getting off the train.

I wanted to buy a Christmas present for Isaac because he had been so kind to me. In a wool shop window I saw a man's scarf in dark blue, with a lighter blue contrast, the colour of Isaac's eyes. The scarf was displayed in order to sell the pattern and the wool. The assistant seemed a little disapproving when I wanted the scarf and not the knitting wool.

'You could do it in an evening,' she said, looking at me critically, as if I were too poorly dressed to be asking someone else to labour over clicking needles for me. But she sold it to me. Even though it finished off my cockle-selling money, I was glad.

How free I felt, walking about without a child. I love wandering alone, but for years and years, I shall always have Leila. That is the choice I made and I am stuck with it.

29

Bleak Midwinter

An inch of light snow covered the yard and the fields beyond. If Dempsey had seen snow before he must have forgotten because he sniffed, snuffled his nose in it, stretched himself, inviting Madge to play, and bounded about the yard as Leila watched through the window.

She wanted to run outside without getting dressed. Quickly as I could, I got her into her clothes, including mittens, hat and wellington boots. Snow began to fall again. She put out her tongue to catch snowflakes. We scooped snow from around the pump and made snowballs.

Isaac came from the barn, pushing a cart with fodder.

'I want to come!' Leila called, as he pushed the cart towards the lane.

'I'm going to feed the sheep. You can both come if you want.' He lifted her onto the cart. She wanted Dempsey beside her, but the whippet raced along, still trying to make Madge play, which she does not always want to do.

We turned onto the path that runs by the drystone wall to the cliff top. Isaac opened a gate and pushed the cart through. I shut the gate and followed him to where the wall meets a circle of trees.

The flock of sheep huddled together between the wall and the trees.

'How did you know they'd be here?' I asked.

He lifted the fodder from the cart and put it down for the animals. 'This is their shelter spot when it snows or blows.'

As I leaned forward and helped him tug at the tightly packed fodder to make it easier for the animals, I felt as if I had known Isaac all my life.

'See this one? She'll let you feed her.' Isaac pointed out a creamy chubby sheep to Leila. 'She's tame. She was hand-reared by Mrs Shaw in the spring. Try stroking her.'

Leila touched its side, stroked it as she would Dempsey or Madge. 'What's her name?'

'Mary.'

It was the afternoon of Christmas Eve. Later the three of us walked down the lane to attend the children's carol service.

'I won't know any Protestant carols,' I said.

'Yes, you will. Listen.' He began to sing 'In the Bleak Midwinter' in his fine baritone voice.

In the chapel, Leila looked wide-eyed at the stable tableaux, spread with sweet-smelling straw. The carved figures of Mary and Joseph looked down on a jolly, kicking baby Jesus in the crib, and a far greater number of carved animals than I have ever seen in one place looked on.

Isaac did not join in the carols, preferring to listen to the children and saying that he sang enough on Sundays and did not want to drown out the little voices. The minister's wife brought out bars of chocolate for each child, and gave me one, too. It was not like being in a church at all. For one thing, it was all in English, not a word of Latin. The minister never turned his back but faced us all the time. The biggest surprise of all to me was that a woman got up to speak, and told the children the Christmas story. We always used to feel a sort of pity for people born into the wrong religion. Now I saw that they may have been onto something after all. I felt glad there was no Catholic church in Silverdale, to call out to me at midnight, or to have some bishop's letter naming me as a black sheep to look out for and herd back into the flock.

Leila ran ahead as we walked up the lane, shyly tagging along with a little family of children. The biggest girl made a great fuss of her before they all turned off and cut through a narrow lane whose branches hung low under the snow. Leila ran back to me, to dash the snow from her collar before it slid down her neck, and for me to wipe her nose, as I had told her not to use her sleeve.

'You have to see this place through the seasons,' Isaac said, 'before you can tell whether you will feel at home here.'

'It's the stillness and the quiet I find strange, after being in the town. And the pitch-darkness on a moonless night without house lights or street lamps. The fresh air hurt my nose at first, but I'm used to it now.'

I did not say how content I felt. At home, for so long I had the worry of seeing Father Flynn. There was always the least thing that might draw down Mam's wrath, her criticisms that all our efforts went for nothing and we had not even Premises to show for years of hard work. Perhaps her lameness and the pain from her insides made her bad-tempered sometimes. But when you are constantly on edge because you can be in the wrong at any moment, or see the person you dread in the church or in the street, it somehow gets in the way of being yourself. Here I could feel free and safe with Isaac.

'It suits me well enough here,' I said.

Leila came running up, her legs hurting, wanting to be carried up the hill. Isaac hoisted her onto his shoulders. She liked to be up there, to reach and rattle tree branches as she passed, and dodge out of the way, turning her head to see showers of snow fall behind her.

When we got back, Leila went in to the Shaws to have mince pies. Isaac said he would milk the cows, to save Mrs Shaw the job. I could have stayed for mince pies, but I went with him into the milking shed. He put on a long white overall.

'Show me how you milk a cow.'

'All right. You can watch me.'

He sat on a three-legged stool by the cow. 'This one is the hardest, so I'll do her first.'

He patted the cow, spoke to her gently, then took hold of her teat. After a moment, milk squirted from his fist into the pail. 'I have a good finger grip, which you need for this one. Come closer. Watch.'

The cow flicked her tail. I could feel the warmth of her massive body.

'They say if you sing to them, it improves the milking.'

'And is that true?'

'I wouldn't be surprised. Depends who's singing.'

When he had finished, he moved the pail and picked up the stool.

'This is the action you want for the teats,' he said, holding my wrist in his fingers and thumb, pressing, pushing, stroking. 'But are you sure you want to try? It's hardly the kind of job for a young woman with certificates.'

I was not sure at all. 'Yes, I want to try.'

He set the stool down for me, and a pail. At first no milk came.

'Try again,' he said softly. 'She's not used to you; be coaxing with her.'

I tried again, pressing her soft teat. Milk squirted into the pail. 'Well done,' Isaac said.

As he milked the last cow, I sat on a stool and watched.

A cup hung on a nail by the sink. He dipped it into the pail. 'Here. See if you've ever tasted sweeter milk.'

As I tasted, he poured the milk from the pails into the container, then washed the pails.

'Jesicca,' he said, as we turned to leave.

I waited by the door, leaning against the doorpost. The white-grey light of the dying day made everything in the milking shed seem shadowy and half a dream.

He stood opposite me in the doorway. 'We've got to know each other well in this short time.'

'Yes.'

'When you have been here through seed time and harvest time, through cold and heat, summer and winter, then you might know if you want to stay,' Isaac said. 'You will know me better, too. Then, if it seems right, I will ask you something – for it might be a secure and a good thing for all who live under our one roof to have one name. I'm not an old man yet, and there could be a son who would take over and provide for you in old age.'

I didn't know how to answer, and since it was not really a question, I said nothing.

'I'm saying this now, Jessica, out here where words can blow away across the fields so that you don't have to think about it when we go inside. Indoors it will be as if I haven't spoken. Forget my words, till this time next year. And if you want me to speak, I'll know. And if you don't, I'll stay silent.'

But I couldn't forget his words. I lay there that night listening to him moving about above me, then murmuring his prayers. I wanted him. I had never expected to feel that way.

The next day as he filled the pail at the pump, I watched him. I did not know how I could wait a year for him to speak again.

30

The Man in Black

Easter came at the end of March. I turned eighteen, Leila turned three and started school in the infants' class.

On a fine afternoon, I waited in the school yard for her. I stood with Dempsey, by the gate.

He strode briskly from the direction of the station, carrying a small bag. Many people wear black, but there is something about a priest's black that darkens the day. The old dread I thought I would never feel again swept through me.

He looked neither right nor left, but even so had about him a terrible, sharp alertness, as if he were breathing in the business of the village and everyone in it. I tugged at Dempsey and we went further into the school yard. Dempsey gave a low growl as Father Flynn walked by.

Feeling trembly and weak, I leaned against the wall by the window, telling myself, *He's not here to search for us. He's here because Leeds children have started holidays at the camp and he wants to be sure the Catholics go to mass on Sundays.* Sure enough, he headed in the direction of the camp. It struck me that it would be a good idea to keep Leila off school the next day, for he would likely stay the night and may be on the prowl tomorrow. It would only take some chance remark to prick his ears and send him searching. Someone might say, 'Oh, we've a little girl from Leeds who has started school.'

Seeing Father Flynn made me feel I had found my way into one of those dreams that starts out so gently and turns into a nightmare.

Over and over I told myself he had come about the Catholic children at the holiday camp.

The children tumbled out of the school door, and Leila ran to me. I know it makes her feel important that Dempsey comes to meet her, as he has many admirers. Leaving others behind, we cut through the ginnel and down the path that led to Jenny Brown's Point. On the flat rock Leila sat in the centre of my spread-out cape and drank from the bottle of water. She ate her slice of bread and dripping, saving a piece for Dempsey.

Although she only started school after Easter, she has stopped telling me what she did, saying, 'I can't remember,' or 'Nothing.' So I sang the song I heard through the classroom window and she joined in, singing, 'One two three four five, once I caught a fish alive . . .'

On our way back, we began to fill our basket with cockles, keeping to the dry sand, looking for the tiny round marks that would tell us a cockle lay buried. Leila found a small piece of rock, grey-brown streaked with dots of red. 'This stone's bleeding like that other one,' she said. 'Shall I throw it into the sea to make it better?' She was always looking for a reason to run down to the sea, although I had told her so many times she must not.

'No, we'll keep it.' I put it in my pocket. 'We'll make it better at home.' It no longer pained me so deeply to remember that I had left just such a pebble for Wilf with my letter to him. Now I was glad he had decided to part with me. Because otherwise I would not have been free to love Isaac. And I did love him, even though neither of us had declared our love.

Our basket was more than half full when I saw him striding towards us across the sands from the direction of the holiday camp.

I set the basket down on the rock and held Leila's hand, watching him come nearer and nearer. He could not get a firm footing. He edged this way and that, avoiding rock pools, making his slow way towards us.

'I knew it was you,' Father Flynn called, the wind carrying his voice to the sea. 'I recognized your stance in the playground. A bold hussy stance. That's not a Catholic school!'

I said nothing. He looked ridiculous in his black suit, the turn-ups of his trousers wet and sandy, his reject Oxfords covered in sand. My chest rose and fell too quickly as my heart pounded. Leila's hand grew hot in mine.

It is odd how our minds work at times like this. I imagined Isaac standing beside me on the rock, urging me to be strong. *You spin and spin and believe you will never find true north again.* We stepped up onto the rock and watched him come towards us. No one would snatch Leila from me now.

He came to a halt, the toes of his shoes touching the rock, water rose around his feet. The pressure of his weight raised a cockle from the sand by his left heel.

'Well, young woman, I think you had better step down from that rock and give me an explanation.'

'There is nothing to explain.'

'There is nothing to explain, *Father*,' he hissed. 'Oh, but there is a great deal to explain. Do you know how much distress, how much anguish you have caused? How much trouble you have put your poor parents to?'

Something came back to me from a retreat we had at school, when a Jesuit priest terrified us with stories of hell. He had asked question after question, never expecting answers from us, and sometimes not answering the questions himself. Each question led to another question. *Do you know how hot are the fires of hell? How many aeons hellfire burns throughout eternity? How brimstone eats the flesh?*

'And do you know, *Father*, how much distress and anguish you caused me?'

'Don't you cross-examine me, you young hussy. Get down from that rock.'

'Why don't you like to see us on a rock? Do you think you'll slip on the seaweed, or do I remind you of Our Lady of the Rocks, or the Star of the Sea—'

He looked as if he would explode. 'You are a bold and disobedient girl.'

'Oh, I'm a girl now. I was a girl when you sleepwalked into that nasty, smelly attic room. I was a girl when you blamed me for what *you* did.'

'Not just bold and disobedient, but deranged and digusting. I'm taking you back with me, and the child to the orphanage.'

Leila let out a yell. Dempsey, who is not a brave dog, made a dash, as if trying to bite Father Flynn's ankles.

I held Leila close. 'She's going nowhere. I'm guarding this child, as I promised I would.'

'Come down from that rock, or I'll drag you down. There's a train in an hour. We'll be on that train.'

'I'd rather be under a train than on one with you.'

'Call yourself a godmother!'

'Call yourself a priest!'

He reached out to grab Leila. His slippy soles would not let him get a footing on the rock. I hit out at him with the basket of cockles, thumping him in the chest. The cockles spilled out as the basket fell and he tripped. I leaped from the rock, holding Leila's hand. As soon as my feet touched the sand I picked her up and lifted her over my shoulder, yelling back at him as I hurried along the shore, 'Don't follow me!'

Dempsey was glad to be away from him and ran ahead, looking back now and then and waiting for me to catch up.

The priest followed. I glanced back and saw him stumbling and hurrying along. All the while he called to me to stop, torrents of words, ordering me to listen to him, to be obedient to the Church, my parents, God. It was as if his words gave wings to my heels. Never have I hurried so fast. I ran for a dozen steps, I walked fast for another dozen, I ran, again zig-zagging on the dry sand. His voice told me that he could not keep up.

Isaac would know what to do. He would help me. They would not take us back, none of them.

As I reached the pebbles by the edge of the beach where the path led up to the lane, I turned back to see how much distance I had put between myself and him. What he was doing stopped my breath. He had not followed my footsteps but took what he thought to be a straight path through the dunes. He was about to step into soft sand.

'Stop!' I called, but he did not listen, trying to keep me in his view. 'Not there!' I called again, waving my hands at him and shaking my head, but the wind carried my voice away.

He had stopped moving. His feet struck fast. I watched him tug, his body moving one way and the other, trying to free himself from the sand. Slowly but surely, he began to sink. I felt rooted to the spot. The beach and cliff were deserted. Not a soul in sight that I could call to for help.

I kept Leila turned from him so she wouldn't see. I should go back and try to save him.

'Help! Help me!' His voice carried on the wind. I set Leila down in the dunes at the foot of the cliffs. I took a few steps towards him, but I knew there would be nothing I could do to save him. His legs were under the sand, then his waist. He held his arms aloft as if someone might reach down from the sky and pull him free.

I turned and, carrying Leila, ran back to the farm. Even so, I saw not the path and the cliffs and the horizon, only the horror-stricken look on his face, his desperate, clutching hands, his clawing fingers disappearing under the sand.

31

The Witness

How we got back to the house I do not know.

'Don't like that mister.' Leila stood by the table, ready to burst into tears.

'Shhh. It's all right now.' My hands shook. I had things to do – hot-pot to stir, clothes to iron. I burnt my fingers on the pan. The iron slipped from my hand and bashed my toe so hard that my eyes watered and the water turned to tears. I felt so cold, so shivering cold. It was no use trying to do anything. I sat on the edge of the bed.

'Come on, let's rest.'

Leila climbed up beside me. I wrapped the eiderdown around us and she fell asleep.

We were still there when Isaac came home.

He could not get me to speak for a long time, and gave me hot sweet tea.

'Jessica, what's happened? Are you ill?'

I couldn't answer.

'You're exhausted. You've taken on too much.'

Guilt sickened through me. I had killed the priest. Made myself an outcast.

'Shall I send for the doctor?'

I shook my head.

'Is it a woman's thing? Do you want Mrs Shaw to come across?'

'No.' I found my voice for that. The fewer people to read my face, the better.

'What happened? Did something bad happen to you?'

My tongue clung to the roof of my mouth and would not let me speak.

'On the sands . . . a priest.'

'What?'

'Swallowed up.'

'Jessica, Jessica.' He put his arm around me. 'That's terrible. What a shock.' For a long time, he held me. 'I saw a horse die once, a young horse, but a man . . .'

'I killed him.'

Lifting my foot, he undid first one boot then the other. He rubbed my cold feet with his big hands. 'You must rest. No more talking.'

'I didn't save him.'

'Shhhh. I'll report it.'

'No!'

It came out in such gasps and gulps that I do not know how he pieced the story together.

He said, 'You didn't kill him. A grown man should know the teachery of them sands. You think you know them, but it's the grace of God that you're still here yourself. Even I, brought up to the sands, need to take care. They change by the day, by the hour. We have to use every sense in our being, every nerve in our bodies, to watch and listen and find the path across. You weren't to know, you're not a sand guide for priests or any other body.'

'They'll take us back.'

'No one will take you where you don't want to go.'

'Don't let's tell.'

'We must. A man's life . . . You were the witness.'

'They'll blame me. Take us back, put Leila in the orphanage.'

For a long time he did not speak, but held me, rocked me. 'Have no fear of being taken back where you and the little one don't want to go. No harm will come to you, not while you're under this roof.'

Slowly and quietly, he talked to me until somehow I fell into a sort of half-sleep. He must have gone to the Shaws and asked them to keep Leila there. When he came back, he said that Arthur Shaw had gone to report the death.

'Tell me once more exactly what you saw. If it will ease your distress, I'll say I witnessed it. You keep silent.'

It was dark when the constable knocked on the door. Isaac looked grim-faced. He motioned me to stay where I was, resting on the bed.

'It's a bad business, Mr Dennison.' The constable took off his hat and nodded to me.

The two men sat at the table.

'You stay there, Jessica,' Isaac said, 'I'll give the account of what passed.'

But I knew I couldn't leave it to Isaac, how hard it would be for him to lie, how much against his grain. I swung my legs from the bed and walked across to the table.

The policeman took his notebook from his inside pocket. Isaac pulled out a chair for me, saying, 'There's no need—'

'I was the one who saw the priest die,' I said.

I left out what I had told Isaac, that I knew the priest's name and that he was chasing me across the sands. I had let Isaac think it was purely because of Leila and the orphanage. I made no mention of my own fear and dread so far as Father Flynn was concerned. To even think of it overwhelmed me with guilt.

I tossed and turned most of that night. I got up and washed the dishes, and washed the floor, too, just to try and stop my thoughts. My thoughts would not stop. I went back to bed in the early hours, and fell asleep as I heard Isaac getting up.

Before he left for the fields, he brought me a cup of tea and set it on the little table by the bed. I pulled back the curtain to take it and he was still standing there. Without a word, he picked up the cup and saucer and put it in my hand.

I took a drink. 'Isaac, on Christmas Eve, you said you would one day ask me a question. My answer is yes.'

His mouth opened slightly in surprise. The deep breath he took seemed to swell his chest. Then he let out his breath with a sigh as he leaned down and kissed the top of my head so gently. 'You have such soft, such beautiful hair. I've never known a woman have short hair, it seems so strange.' He touched a finger on my cheek, stroking from my cheekbone to my chin, raising the finger to my lips but stopping. 'Thank you. But, Jessica, it's too soon.'

'No. It's not too soon.'

'You're grateful to me for giving you a place. You've had a bad shock. I would hate it if, in a few years' time, you realized you mistook gratitude for love.'

'I won't. I don't mistake it.'

'This place offers a hard life.'

'I like it here. I like this house, and whenever I go out of the door and see the wide open sky, and the fields and woods in one direction and the beautiful bay in the other, my eyes love what they see.'

'And so do mine,' he said. He leaned towards me, then drew back. 'We know so little about each other. There are people who'll be missing you, that I'm sure of.'

I looked up at him, and though I had not gone to sleep planning this to happen, I knew I wanted it to come true now. If I let him draw me back into the past my resolve might weaken, and so I would not speak about the past, only about the future. 'You would miss me, too, if we went back.'

'Of course I would miss you. You and the little one have got under my skin. But there are things you should know about me. I did a wrong thing once. I loved two lasses and let the wrong one go. I married the one I was told to marry, to grow the farm. God knows I suffered and prayed for it, and when you came I thought here was my chance to make amends.'

It did not seem to me a comfortable thing to be viewed as a person to be charitable to, to make up for a wrong. 'And do you think that still? Am I a penance?'

'Jessica, you would make me the happiest man alive, and I would worship you, but we mustn't be hasty. You must be sure. I couldn't let you say yes when you are in a state of shock after what happened yesterday. We'll talk about this on Sunday, and not before.'

32

Eaves Wood

When Isaac came home from chapel, I had our picnic ready – boiled eggs, cold ham cut from the bone, slices of bread. I packed the basket, along with bottles of water, cold tea, a small fruitcake and a knife.

We walked down the lane under a clear blue sky. Masses of white blossoms bloomed on the hawthorn bushes, reminding me of May Sundays cycling in the Dales with Dad, Bernadette, Uncle Bill and Wilf. Then as now, tides of wild flowers bustled for attention – tall-stemmed garlic mustard, buttercups and daisies, cowslips, and above them the heavy blooms of lilac bushes with their powerfully sweet fragrance. Last May seemed a lifetime ago. Leila and the dogs ran ahead of us, Leila chasing an orange butterfly. It flew out of sight and she stood beneath a horse chestnut tree at the edge of the grass meadow, trying to see where the butterfly hid.

'Look!' Isaac pointed to the cone-shaped flowers in the horse chestnut tree. 'We used to call those flowers candles when we were children, and the leaves giants' hands.'

'I know,' Leila said, still looking for the butterfly. Not that she does know much, but it is a little phrase that she comes out with now. You say something to her and she says, 'I know,' meaning yes, or I see, or I understand.

Isaac knows which tree was stuck by lightning a decade ago; where pheasants shelter from the rain; the clearing where a wild doe gave birth to her fawn last year; which part of the limestone pavement in

Eaves Wood has a bowl-shaped place where the rain runs down and deer, or our dogs, will stop to drink.

The wood was full of pungent garlic flowers and a mass of sweet-scented bluebells. I held Leila's hand as we crossed the bare rocks, some slippery with moss. The dogs ran out of sight, up tracks and through the undergrowth. Leila worried about them, saying, 'Where's Dempsey? Where's Madge?' Isaac whistled them back, to reassure her.

The path rose, till we reached an area of flat rocks and a stone tower with a sort of pointed hat for a roof.

'It's called the Pepper Pot,' Isaac said, 'built almost half a century ago to mark Queen Victoria's Golden Jubilee.'

It seemed an odd thing to build for a celebration, and I asked if the queen had come to see it. But I didn't get a chance to hear his answer because Leila got excited at finding giant footsteps in the rocks and yelled at me to come. When I had marvelled over the footsteps, I took her to where Isaac stood at the edge of the hill, a steep drop below.

We could see the shore, sands sparkling in the sunlight, glinting rivulets of water in the channels, and the distant sea reflecting the blue of the sky.

'Look,' Isaac said, lifting her up. 'You can see from Barrow to Blackpool.'

And she repeated it, like a little parrot, as she repeats so much of what you say, and I knew she thought Barrow was a wheelbarrow so explained to her that it was the name of a place, like Leeds.

'So,' Isaac said, as I opened the basket and began to set out our picnic on the cloth, 'what shall I tell you, and you tell me, and how will we begin?'

'We're a bit close to the edge, Leila. You must be careful. You would fall a long way. It's dangerous.'

'Don't worry.' Isaac took my hand. 'No one will fall. No one will get hurt.'

'The dogs . . .' I couldn't see them.

'The dogs have more sense than to jump down there.'

Then the dogs appeared, smelling food, coming to join the picnic. But I could not stop myself from feeling anxious, and even when I made myself look at the cloth and share out bread, part of me still saw Father Flynn disappearing into the sands. It set me all on edge, so I felt like some twitching half-mad creature.

As if he knew what I felt, Isaac took over setting out the picnic, uncorking the bottle of cold tea and giving me first drink.

Leila said, 'What's wrong?' She sat beside me and put her hand on my thigh.

I took her hand but could not reply straight away.

Isaac answered for me. 'Your mammy is a little tired.'

He knelt beside me and stroked my hair, once, twice, but then he did not stop at my hair. His palm smoothed its way down the back of my neck, all the way down my spine, then he started again at the top of my head and stroked me again.

'I can't talk, Isaac,' I said. 'I don't know what you want me to say.'

'Then say nothing. Just pay attention.'

He stroked a line across my shoulders, down my spine and round to my waist.

'What letter did I just draw on your back?'

'A letter J?'

'Yes. Pay heed to my fingers.'

He drew on my back, all the letters of my name.

'Now eat your lunch, Jessica. Trust in time and the passing of days. There'll be a day when the horrors of this week will be like a nightmare from another life. If we do what we think we might, I will make you glad.'

As we ate, he told me that although he was a tenant farmer and owned no land, his lease was secure, having been held by his father and grandfather before him. And that though the life was hard, he had labouring men to help him, and the living was not a bad one. He would see to it that I had some help in the house if I wished and asked me if I had any questions.

'Yes. I have a question. What am I to do when I feel ashamed for people to look at me? Selling cockles in Carnforth, waiting in the school yard for Leila, wearing an old skirt and blouse that would disgrace a tinker.'

'Go to Lancaster tomorrow. Buy yourself a dress, two dresses. A coat. Shoes, whatever else you need.'

'And Leila?'

'For Leila, too.'

We walked back another way, down a steep slope past a stone seat where we sat while Leila picked bluebells. As her back was turned, Isaac put his arm around me. 'You're still a mystery to me. I need to know something.'

I turned to him.

'I won't kiss you,' he said.

A wave of disappointment flooded through me.

'I won't kiss you indoors. Not yet. It wouldn't be right.' Then his lips touched mine.

The only kisses I had known till then were Wilf's and I had expected to be disappointed. But his mouth felt right on mine, nothing awkward or strange came between us in that moment, as if this was meant, to be, as if we were coming home to each other after being apart too long.

When he stopped, I felt light-headed and wanted more. Leila had come back with a straggly bunch of bluebells, some with long stems and others with no stems at all.

'You still haven't asked me,' I said.

He got up from the stone seat. 'Leila, go fetch us more bluebells.'

She ran off eagerly.

Isaac knelt on the ground before me, picked up a bluebell and held it to my lips.

'I still feel I'm stealing you from your other sweetheart. What was he, an artist?'

'Wilf? He once said that he could not bear it if he met me again in the future and we would not be as close. I think we must have both known that was what would happen. We had different lives ahead of us. My life is here now, with you. His life was always going to be in London, an artist's life. That wouldn't suit me and Leila at all. My feelings have changed. It's not fair of you to make me say these things.'

'I have to know. And what about your family?'

'I will go back and see them. But I won't go back as Miss Jessica Price. Can I say it any more plainly than that?'

'No, that's plain enough.' And before Leila had time to come back with her bunch of bluebells, he said, 'Jessica, will you do me the honour of becoming my wife?'

'Yes, Isaac. I will.'

33

A Wedding

Every bride must have flowers for her wedding and in spring there's such a wonderful choice. But I would not have thought of a posy if Isaac had not mentioned it days before, saying old Mrs Prentice, who used to clean for him, has asked what flowers I would like. He brought pinks and carnations from her garden, to see if they would please me. The scent recalled May processions setting out from school, when we wore white dresses and veils, and walked to the church behind the statue of Our Lady. Bernadette was crowned Queen of the May one year. Mam stood the framed photograph on our sideboard, three inches to the left of the brown glass vase of silk flowers.

'Not pinks or carnations,' I said.

'Why not?'

'Wild flowers would be just the thing. I'll gather them on the morning.'

He frowned. 'You'll forget. You'll be busy getting yourself ready, and little madam Leila.'

'She'll help me.'

But, taking no chances, the next day he brought home anemones, which looked so neat, sweet and prettily turned out with their bright petals and black centres like a dark heart. So it was agreed. I would carry anemones. Leila would bear wild flowers, and Isaac a buttonhole of golden forsythia.

On the last Saturday of May, in the early afternoon, the three of us walked along the lane under lilac blossom heavy from rain. The soaked branches hung low.

'It's such a sad, sweet scent,' Isaac said, as a few petals floated to the shoulder of his black jacket.

I wondered whether his first wedding took place on a May day and if his wife had carried lilac. That would explain why he wanted to know what flowers I would carry.

'Do you think lilac is unlucky?' I asked.

He just smiled and said he hoped I wouldn't be running to a fortune-teller to see how long his love would last.

Arthur Shaw, Isaac's cockling partner, and Mrs Bradley, the minister's wife, stood witness for us.

How slowly the minister spoke his words, breaking them into small chunks as if he thought us idiots who could not parrot back more than a mouthful of words at a time. It reminded me of standing godmother to Leila and I wished it hadn't for then I needed to tell myself: *This is your wedding day. You have moved into a different world.* But the voice in my head talked on over the minister's words. *Here you are in a Protestant church, surrounded by chapel people who won't so much as toast you with a glass of sherry.* So deep in me was the feeling that if you did not marry in a Catholic church you did not marry at all that I felt a kind of distance. Yet a deep sureness held me, and the certainty was my love for Leila and Isaac. We had a place in the world, with each other.

When the ceremony was over, we went into the large room of the minister's house where Mrs Bradley had set out scones, buns and an iced fruitcake. Isaac and I sliced the cake with a bone-handled knife.

Only when we stood behind the table after cutting the cake did the people from the church, our well-wishers, take on separate identities. The Bradley's curly-headed son whispered that our cake was left over from Christmas, 'just in case'. Leila's teacher made a fuss of her and admired her flowers. The old woman who used to clean for Isaac came up to wish us well. I thanked her for the anemones. She said I must come and see her garden.

When I told Leila she must be good for Mrs Bradley and I would see her tomorrow, she more than cried, clinging to me and screaming for me not to leave her. I tried to calm her and wished I had not agreed to a night in a hotel without her.

'I promise we'll be back tomorrow.'

I turned to Isaac to ask him could we take her with us, for it seemed to me not a good start to a marriage to see her breaking her heart. But he bobbed down to her level, whispered to her and gave her chocolate. The curly-haired Bradley boy and the teacher led her away. To look at some kittens, the boy said.

I wanted to go after her, to see she would be all right, but Isaac took my hand. Arthur Shaw waited outside with the horse and cart, decorated with ribbons and garlands, for our ride to the railway station to catch the Morecambe train.

'You look so young,' Isaac said as we bounded up the steps to the hotel. 'It's a good thing we're booked in as Mr and Mrs Dennison or you'd be mistaken for my daughter.'

'Don't say that.'

He tapped the bell on the desk. 'Didn't you see the looks we got on our walk from the station?'

'That's because we're such a handsome couple, Isaac.'

From somewhere along the corridor a balding, paunchy man appeared, smiling a good afternoon.

Issac signed the register with his own pen pulled from his top pocket, making him seem such a man of the world.

From our window, we looked across the broad bay where afternoon sun glistened on the sands. We watched a horse trotting proudly along the promenade, pulling its carriage of seaside visitors. Isaac stood behind me, his hands around my waist. He kissed the back of my neck. 'I wish we could have the week here. Perhaps after harvest we might manage a longer time. There's a brand-new hotel that they're putting up.'

I opened drawers and cupboards, unpacked our small case, tried the taps on the sink, both hot and cold.

'There's a bathroom along the hall,' Isaac said. 'I noticed it when we came up.'

Sure enough, there was, and a bath that looked big enough to go to sea.

We walked along the promenade twice, looking in the shops, then made our way onto the sands. Isaac said the beach was safe enough for children to play and we must bring Leila one Sunday. She could make sand castles.

I wished I didn't have my stockings on, as I love the feeling of sand under my feet, between my toes.

'Take them off,' Isaac said. 'No one's watching.'

I said no because I wouldn't get them on again, not with my feet covered in sand, and we planned to go to a café for our evening meal.

We walked up to the sea wall, and Isaac shielded me from the few other people scattered along the beach. 'Do it now. Never wait till tomorrow for some small pleasure. Give yourself the pleasure today.'

So I undid my suspenders and peeled down my stockings. Isaac put them in his inside pocket and held out his hand to carry my shoes.

'You must take yours off,' I said, 'and carry our own shoes.'

So he did, and rolled up his trousers, and we walked towards the sea, which was far off but had left its hard ridges and pools on the shore.

A dog rushed by, chasing a piece of driftwood thrown by its owner.

'Have you noticed,' Isaac said, 'when people come visiting, they always stand looking out to sea?'

After a long walk, we reached the sea. Waves lapped our toes, covered our feet and splashed our legs.

'I'll make a fine mess of these trousers,' Isaac said, rolling them up further onto his calves. 'I've not brought another pair, neither.'

'Take them off, then.' I said. 'Do as you told me. Never wait till tomorrow for some small pleasure.'

'Cheeky!' He picked me up and ran out with me into the waves, and how we laughed, and the waves beating around us and the sun shining golden.

By the time we had walked hand in hand back to the sea wall, I felt hungry and ready for the café meal of steak and kidney pie.

'I'm sure I'm the only female in this café not wearing stockings,' I whispered.

'I won't tell anyone,' Isaac said, 'or we might be thrown out for being improperly dressed. This is a very respectable café.'

When we got back to our hotel room, the last of the sun's rays danced through the window and gave a strange light to the room.

Isaac took my stockings from his inside pocket and hung them across the back of the chair.

'Perhaps I'll try that bath,' I said.

'Later.' He sat on the bed. 'Come here, Mrs Dennison.'

I went across to him.

'There's something about a dress with buttons down the front, something I've wanted to do all day.'

He undid the top button on my dress.

'They're not easy buttons. The buttonholes are a little on the small side.'

He undid the next one. 'Yes. I see what you mean.'

Soon, all the buttons on my dress were undone.

He slid the dress off my shoulders and hung it across the back of the chair over my stockings.

'My shirt buttons are not a bit hard to undo. Will you try?'

Without speaking, I undid his shirt, took it to the wardrobe and hung it on a hanger. When I turned back, he had stripped off his vest. He had a broad chest and strong arms, tanned from working outdoors.

'Come back, sweetheart. You're too far away.'

When I didn't go to him, he came across to me, slid the straps of my petticoat off my shoulders and tugged it down.

'It goes over my head,' I said, thinking it wouldn't slide over my hips. But it did.

I had not expected this. I had thought I would go to the bathroom and change into my nightgown and robe. It looked as if we would both soon be naked, and the curtains were still open. He saw my gaze at the window.

'We're too high up for anyone to see us, and we have no need to be ashamed.'

'Close them just a little,' I said. 'It's still so bright.'

He pulled the curtains halfway shut.

I stayed by the wardrobe and he came back and turned me towards the mirror.

'Look at yourself. You're so beautiful, my golden girl.'

'Pick me up, like you did on the sands.'

He carried me to the bed, lifted back the sheets and set me down so gently. In a moment he was beside me, naked, and kissing me on the mouth so hard that he took my breath away. I had feared that nothing between us would match what I had felt for Wilf when we had been close, but Wilf slid out of my mind as though he belonged to another life.

Isaac did not try to take off my vest but lifted it above my chest so it felt tight under my arms and I wanted to be rid of it, but forgot when he kissed my breasts, stroked them and said, 'I can't tell you how long I've wanted you.'

'Yes, you can.'

'Since the first day I saw you.'

I wriggled out of my vest.

'Tell me how long you've wanted me, Jessica.'

'I'm not sure yet that I do, Mr Dennison.'

'Then I shall have to make you want me,' and he tried to wrestle me and I wrestled back, then pushed him away and pulled the sheet to me, not that I wanted him to stop, but to give me time.

'You liked this, I think, when we had our picnic.' He turned me over and took the sheet away, kissing the back of my neck, spelling my name on my skin, then kissing around my shoulders and all the way down my spine.

And it was when he had kissed me all over and I had stroked his chest, his back and arms that he whispered, 'Do you think you might want me now?'

And I said, 'It's possible.'

'I knew you would drive me wild, Jessica. And I promise I'll do the same to you.'

34

Spinning Blue Hornton Stone

Each morning since arriving at the summer-rented house in Norfolk, Wilf rose early. By the time Ralph stirred, Wilf had been sitting cross-legged on the lawn for a couple of hours, like an Indian shoemender who worked and meditated on the infinite all at once – according to Ralph, who took his oils and canvas onto the terrace.

Wilf started each morning wearing a thick sweater, which he would discard as the July morning grew warm. In front of him stood a sturdy slab of wood supporting his work: a block of Blue Hornton stone. For hours, he held his pose, shifting only to lean a little further forward or back, sometimes tilting the stone this way or that, half closing his eyes, running his hands over the grooves he had chiselled, feeling for that perfect transition between one layer and the next.

Slowly over the long days his piece took shape. When the sun said noon, he would stretch himself out, stand back from his precious work, looking at it as the light changed.

Wilf carried the piece in this thoughts. He imagined he saw it spinning through the sky like a meteorite. A tingle of certainty from scalp to toes told him this piece marked an important shift in his development as an artist. Though just two feet high, it had the lightness of a child's spinning top, or of the child itself, turning and turning to a state of dizziness. Natural and organic, it was also a made thing, fusing man and nature. When someone looked at it, they would say, *Yes, that's it. That's exactly it.* It would give back to the viewer the emotion they experienced when spinning a top as a child, twirling in a back street or rolling down a grassy hill, watching the world go all out of kilter.

He was not in the least bit tempted by Ralph's proposed trip to Norwich to see the cathedral, but then tore himself away from his work and was glad. It was worth the trip.

He left Ralph sketching the cathedral from the front while he went to the side, fascinated by the open way in which the buttresses were built between the roof of one storey and the top of the next, giving a graceful support and rigidity but still allowing space for the elegant windows.

Going through the west door, Wilf thought of Jess that long-ago day in Leeds, holding the newly christened baby, lighting all those candles with the shilling he had lost. Always, wherever he was and when not lost in his carving, he would see scenes of their time together, a glimpse of her on her bike, at the outdoor pool, or up close to him as he held her in his arms. Then he would think of what he should have done differently.

Ralph interrupted his thoughts. 'Come and see the bishop's throne behind the altar.'

Dutifully, Wilf listened as Ralph explained that the throne and surrounding apse preserved the plan of the Christian sanctuary, dating back to the beginnings of Christianity.

Sanctuary. Where did Jess find sanctuary? Wilf wondered. No one had heard from her since that letter with the smudged postmark around Christmas time. Anything could have happened since then.

'The plan probably pre-dates Christianity, Wilf. If, as some say, it's based on the pattern of the Roman law courts, that bishop's throne is where the judge would have sat, surrounded by his officials.'

A sanctuary. A place of judgement. I'd be judged and found wanting, Wilf told himself. I should never have let her go.

They walked out into drizzling rain.

'There's talk of adding another chapel and restoring the cloisters. Could be some wonderful work for sculptors.'

'I'll leave that to the believers,' Wilf said. 'How about you lead the way to a hostelry?'

It was when they left the pub, revived by pints, pie and peas, that

Wilf noticed the bookshops. The centre of the window displayed several copies of the fairy-tale book that Jess had scribed, opened at different illustrations.

'I told you it would be a huge success,' Ralph said. 'Come on. I'm sure they'll want you to sign some copies.'

Wilf had agreed reluctantly to the book's publication. Only when Irene said that Jess may see it and get in touch did he agree. His hesitation came from being associated so early in his career with nursery drawings of fairy-tale characters.

The bookshop owner beamed when Ralph introduced Wilf.

'It's the novelty of emphasizing the boots and shoes of the stories – and your spectacular drawings, of course. Please do sign all my copies. I shall put a note in the window, "Copies signed by the artist". I don't suppose the author is with you to sign, too?' He looked past them at an elderly woman who had just entered the shop.

'I wish she were,' said Wilf.

The next morning he finished his carving. Ralph helped him wrap it in old army blankets and pack it in a tea chest surrounded by wood shavings, ready for its journey to the London gallery.

'Do you know,' Ralph said, as he stuck an address label on the side, 'this is the first piece you've carved for a long time that doesn't have a great hole in it à la Hepworth.'

'The hole's in here.' Wilf struck his chest with mock drama. 'And it will be until I find her again. I felt sure she'd get in touch with me around now. We said, didn't we? This summer.'

Ralph cleared his throat. 'The thing is, Wilf, the thing is that the letter she sent at Christmas—'

'What about it?'

'Here, give that hemp to me. I'm good at knots.'

Ralph wound the rope around the tea chest and tied a knot.

'What? What were you going to say about Jess's letter?'

'Her letter?'

'Don't be annoying. Spit it out if you have something to say.'

'She didn't write to you, did she? It was addressed to her parents. She's never been in touch with you, Wilf. Doesn't that say something? I'm sure she's fine. A girl like her will always be fine. I think, the thing is, what I think . . .'

'What? What do you think?'

'That she didn't want to stand in your way.'

'Only because you told her about that damned award. We would have managed. I could have swallowed my pride and asked Bill for money. Promised him a sculpture of a dirty great boot for the outside of his new factory. Anyway, what do you mean "a girl like her"?'

'I mean lovely, in every way,' Ralph said quietly.

'Were you in love with her yourself?'

'I won't say she didn't impress me.'

'And you've hung onto that painting of her.'

'For sale, if you can afford it! I suppose what I'm trying to say . . . What you have to tell yourself, Wilf, so you'll stop worrying so much, is that attractive girls have a way of landing on their feet.'

'You're thinking of the girls of your own class, Ralph. They also have money and influential families behind them to make sure they land on their feet. It's not the same for Jess. There's never a day goes by that I don't worry about her.'

Ralph looked as if he would say more. Wilf waited.

'Help me pack my painting.'

Ralph's work showed jockeys in stables, getting horses saddled before a race. It did have a certain life and movement, but Wilf wondered why Ralph bothered. An excellent technician, he broke no new ground. His work came from life without, for Wilf, imagination, or evoking emotion. You saw it, you knew it. There was no mystery, no heart of the matter.

As if he felt Wilf's criticism, Ralph looked at him steadily. 'People like it. It gives pleasure, Wilf. That means a lot to me. And they pay.'

'Never said a word. What are we packing it in?'

'For people who know that world, it takes them into the moment in a way no photograph ever could. That's what they say.'

'It's the best. No one's saying it isn't.'

Ralph basked in the praise, not knowing that Wilf added, in his head, 'The best − of its kind.'

The packing of the picture was interrupted by the postman. Ralph picked up the post − forwarded from London. He passed two letters to Wilf, who scanned the envelopes eagerly, hoping still for Jess's familiar round script. One was typed, the other in a long, looping, old-fashioned hand. Wilf opened them. 'I've got two commissions.'

He stared at the letters in astonishment. 'As a result of the fairy-tale book. One's for a mural in relief at a public school in Hertfordshire. The other's for a sculpture at a municipal park in Wiltshire. It's thanks to Jess, Ralph. I never would have done that book without her.'

'Splendid. Congratulations! You see, I knew you'd be a great success. You'll have so much work you'll be employing minions to do the preliminary chipping.'

'Anything exciting for you?'

'One cheque, one bill. Oh, and this one's for you, too.'

Wilf snatched the envelope, for a moment seeing just the colour of the ink and thinking of Jess.

It was from Bill, telling him about Irene.

'I have to go back to Leeds,' Wilf said. 'Irene's had a heart attack. Bill says it's a mild one but how can you have a mild heart attack? Where's that train timetable?'

'I'll come with you.'

'No, you won't. It's family. You'll do me a big favour if you see to the shipping of my piece to the gallery.'

'Leave it to me. And give your mother my good wishes.'

35

Mothers

Wilf stepped into a waiting taxi outside the station.

'Blenheim Square, please.'

In City Square and along the Headrow, couples and knots of friends strolled by on their evening out, sharing umbrellas. Solitary figures, hurrying home from shops and offices, headed for tram stops.

Not wanting to ring the doorbell, in case Irene slept, Wilf went round to the back of the house and let himself in through the unlocked kitchen door. He looked first in Irene's sitting room, her preferred spot.

Quietly he climbed the stairs and tapped on her bedroom door, which was not quite shut. Looking pale and so much older than a few short months ago, she sat up in bed, propped against pillows, wearing a pink lacy wool bedjacket.

'Hello, Mother.'

'Wilf!' Her face lit with pleasure at the sight of him, at his kiss on her cheek.

Only then did he properly take in the figure in the basketweave chair at the other side of the bed. For a moment, he froze, then, as if Irene had sent him a silent message – *Remember your manners* – he walked round the bed and extended his hand.

'Hello, Miss Hardy.'

She gripped his hand, but not too tightly, and in a low, even voice returned his greeting.

When he released her hand, she said, 'Wilf's come all this way to see you, Irene. I'll leave the two of you to talk.'

'No, you won't, you'll stay!' Irene ordered. 'Wilf, pull up that little straight chair, and don't put your full weight on its back. Bill mended it last week.'

'You mustn't go on my account,' Wilf said to Gladys Hardy, as he sat awkwardly on the spindly chair, wishing he had sought out the maid who would have told him his mother had a visitor.

Irene rang the bell for tea. 'Bill shouldn't have worried you, Wilf. It was a very mild heart attack, according to Doctor Jensen – a warning for me to slow down a little, that's all.'

She insisted on hearing his news, and both women smiled with pleasure at his success and the commissions for the sculpture and mural relief. He did not mention his forthcoming exhibition because he felt sure Irene would want to come, and equally sure that she would not be up to the journey.

He waited for the moment when he could ask for news of Jess. It came after the maid brought tea.

Irene frowned. 'Nothing since the letter at Christmas.'

'What do the police say?'

Irene's hands moved listlessly on the white candlewick bedspread. For the first time, Wilf thought how old her hands looked – veined, wrinkled, dotted with liver spots.

'She's on the police files. But she's eighteen now. That's the age Leila's father, Tommy McBride, got a solicitor to arrange for Jess to have custody of Leila. He should have known better, but people do strange things when they're grieving. It makes us think she may show her face again soon, feeling safe about keeping the child. No one knows where else to look, Wilf. Dolly and Paul wait every day for a letter that never comes. It eats them up. Whoever she's with, you think they would know someone's missing her.'

The slight change in her voice, the tightening of her jaw, made Wilf want to say something reassuring, but what?

'The diocese has had Leila's name circulated, in case she turns up at a Catholic church asking for help, or tries to put the child into nursery school.'

Somehow Wilf did not think Jess would turn up at a Catholic church. He was grateful when Gladys Hardy changed the subject.

She had come to collect some correspondence that Irene had been about to deal with before her attack, writing thanks for the contributions in kind to the Leeds Poor Children's Holiday Camp and the Society for Friendless Girls. Among the many useful gifts in kind, such as supplies of dripping and a bushel of apples, were odd and useless items. Of all the committee members, only Irene had the knack of seeming grateful for a hand-worked needle-case or stockings produced by a trainee knitter. She somehow managed to point the givers in the direction of more serviceable presents for the future. Wilf smiled as he heard Irene's letter-writing tips to Gladys, who feared she would lack the necessary tact.

He had the idea of donating copies of the illustrated fairy-tale book he and Jess had produced. Both women thought that a wonderful idea. It touched Wilf to hear them, for he realized that such small things would make them so very happy.

Gladys gathered up the cups and set them on the tray, saying it was time for her to go and for Irene to rest. 'You're looking so much brighter today,' she said as she left the room carrying the tray.

'Have you eaten, Wilf?' Irene asked.

'Yes. On the train.'

'Then go down to my sitting room. You'll see a bundle of letters in the right of the escritoire, tied with red tape. They're for Gladys to take. And you must see her to the tram.'

'All right. I'll walk her to Woodhouse Lane.'

'Or Sheepscar, as she chooses.'

Wilf nodded.

'Pass me my diary and pencil. I might write something.' Irene shut her eyes. 'Don't worry about me. I'm going to rest now. I'll be all right. Your father will be glad to see you. He's at some golf club event this evening. I suppose that's one advantage of being ill. I get out of that!'

Wilf smiled and closed the door gently.

Gladys was coming back from the kitchen, having returned the tray. Wilf led her into the sitting room and retrieved the bundle of correspondence. She popped it into her bone-handled velvet bag.

'Let me walk you to your tram, Miss Hardy.'

'There's no need, Wilf. You stay with your mother.'

She said it without hesitation or a hint that they both knew she was his natural mother.

'She's resting.' He almost added that he had his orders to escort her, but he guessed she knew that.

He picked up a large umbrella from the hall stand. 'This should see us right.'

'I don't catch the tram. Woodhouse Lane is out of my way, and by the time I cut through to Sheepscar I'm almost home.'

'Sheepscar and home it is, then. So we'll go out by the back door, it's nearest.'

What on earth would he talk to her about? he wondered, as they stepped out of the yard and he opened the umbrella. He remembered that Jess had told him how frequently Miss Hardy's boots needed mending because she strode around the poor districts of Leeds, visiting families, arranging holidays, taking an interest in mothers' welfare. She strode out like a person wearing seven-league boots. It made him smile to realize he did not have to shorten or slow his step.

'I should have come to meet you sooner,' he said. 'I knew I was adopted from an early age. When I was about thirteen, I think, they told me you lived in Leeds. And I've known who you were for ages. I'm sorry.'

'Don't be. At least I knew where you were and that you had a good home. A lot of mothers who give up their children never know where they go or what happens to them in life. You've done well at art college. I couldn't have sent you there.'

Her words took Wilf onto what seemed like safer ground. 'A few of us are going to have an exhibition soon.'

'I'm glad.'

'I didn't mention it to Mother because I'm sure she'd want to come and she won't be up to it.'

'You should mention it. She'll be delighted, and she'll know whether to come or not.'

'Yes. Would you like to come?'

Gladys laughed. 'Just because you probably heard of me going to London for the children's charities conference doesn't mean I'm a great traveller. I don't get much chance. But if I can, I will. Thank you.'

They had reached Sheepscar library and he had not once had to rack his brains for something to say.

'Mother said you draw and paint, too. She thinks that's where I got my talent from. If so, I should thank you.'

'Should you?' She smiled. 'God must have added quite a bit to it for my artistic talent is very slender. It was good enough for a school teacher—'

'You were a teacher?'

'At the school, in Silverdale.'

For the first time he sensed a reluctance in her, a kind of withdrawing, almost physical. She slid from under the umbrella. 'You can close the umbrella. It's stopped raining.'

As they walked along Roundhay Road, past the tightly grouped streets of redbrick back-to-back houses, she said, 'I'm used to this walk. You don't have to trek along to Bayswater Road.'

'Is that where you live?'

'Just off Bayswater Road.'

'Then it's no distance.'

They walked in silence for a while, but not an awkward silence. Eventually Wilf said, 'I didn't mean to start asking you awkward questions. I was interested, that's all.'

'I'm not putting you off. But not today. And this is my street. So thank you.'

'I'll see you to the door.'

She put the key in the lock and turned to him. 'You may never be here again. Come inside. There's something I want to show you.'

He walked into a small room, crowded with heavy furniture. A large, almost completed jigsaw puzzle sat on the table. She saw him looking at it and said, 'Yes, your mother and I both do jigsaws. Here's one I meant to pass on to her.'

She gave him a box showing a picture of a little boy blowing bubbles.

On the mantelpiece stood a row of carved soldiers.

'My father did them. During the war. Afterwards his hands lost their steadiness.'

Wilf picked up the figures one by one. 'Where did he learn?'

'He was self-taught.'

Wilf held a tiny figure of an Australian soldier in the palm of his hand. He turned it this way and that. For a penknife carving, it was good, very good.

'He gave them all names.'

'Who's this?'

'Do you know, I can't remember. I always thought he changed the names according to his whims, but he swore he never did. Can I get you something. A glass of water? Tizer?'

'Water would be fine.'

'And I'd like you to choose a couple of soldiers. We haven't much of a legacy for you, but perhaps your grandfather's carving represents what we had to give.'

'I'll treasure it.' He slipped the soldier into his pocket.

'Only you've taken one of ours so you must take this one, too. I think he's called Fritz. Dad never had a bad word for the German soldiers.'

She put his glass of water on the table. He sat down when she did. It surprised him how, after dreading this meeting for so long, and sometimes feeling sick at the thought he must one day speak to her, everything seemed all right.

'You've done this house out very smartly.'

She laughed again. 'There's no need for that. It's respectable, which is what we strove to be, Dad and I. Quite a lot of striving, I can tell you.'

'I like you,' Wilf said. 'Do you know, I didn't think I would. Isn't that terrible?'

'Because I gave you up?'

'Possibly. But I'm not sure why, to tell you the truth. Perhaps because you worked for one of Mother's charities.'

'You'd be surprised how many people dislike me for that. Particularly the recipients of charity who don't like do-gooders and lady bountifuls.'

'Then more fool them. Now I'd better go. I'm sure you're tired.'

'It has been a long day.'

'I'll send you details of the exhibition, just in case you can come.'

'Thank you.'

He turned at the end of the street and saw her still standing by the door. She waved and he waved back before turning the corner.

As he climbed the hill towards home, the rain started to pelt down. He had left his umbrella behind – leaning against Gladys Hardy's kitchen table.

Back in Blenheim Square, he hurried through the back door, locked it behind him and kicked off his wet shoes. He wanted to tell his mother that he was back, and to say how much he liked Gladys Hardy, and how Irene had been right all along in wanting him to meet her. He would give her the jigsaw puzzle and help her make a start on it.

Irene's bedroom was dim. He did not want to switch on the light. Her diary lay fallen open and the pencil had rolled down the counterpane. Her head tilted a little to the right and her eyes were shut. He moved the diary and pencil and went to lift the counterpane, to cover her arms and shoulders, as the room had grown cold.

Afterwards, he could not have said what made him feel for her pulse because she was still warm.

There was no pulse.

He sat on the bed to get his breath, to catch his thoughts. The diary lay open with a single line of writing.

'Wilf met his mother today.'

36

The Wise Child

In the days following Irene's death, Wilf learned to find his way to the doctor's surgery for a death certificate, to the coroner's office and to the registrar of births, marriages and deaths. He sat with Bill in Irene's sitting room while funeral directors took instructions and the minister from the Unitarian chapel arranged the order of service for the funeral.

A severe, pin-striped solicitor with a snuff-taking habit came to read the will. Wilf heard that Irene had been more generous to him than he might have expected since he had turned his back on the business. She was equally generous to her two favourite charities, the Leeds Poor Children's Holiday Camp and the Society for Friendless Girls. Bill benefitted most. She had signed the firm over to him years ago and the house and all investments and monies went to him.

Bill walked around the house like a lost soul. Sometimes he would stumble into a room where Wilf sat, and look surprised to see him. Once, as they sat at their breakfast boiled eggs and toast, Bill said, 'I didn't marry your mother for her money, you know. Some people said that, but it wasn't true.'

Wilf realized that there was no wrong or right thing to say. Sometimes when he said the tactful things, they fell flat. He let his curiosity get the better of him, feeling it would make no difference.

'Where did Mother's money come from?'

'Her grandfather owned mines, in South Yorkshire. Abroad, too. Her father got shot of them and invested in other things, not very successfully, and developed the shoe factory and so on, just to be bloody-minded, I think.'

Wilf wanted to ask about the 'and so on' but decided against it when Bill turned his complete concentration to trying to spoon egg from a shell that had no more to give. This action, the refusal to waste a morsel of food, gave Wilf a sudden insight into Bill. He was brought up poor.

Only when Paul arrived later did Bill seem a little more like his old self, pressing his brother to smoke a Capstan and take a glass of brandy.

Paul did not need much persuading. A fire had been lit, though the evening was not cold. The two of them sat there, remembering their childhood and their weddings. They had each acted as best man for the other, and it had been expected that Paul would stay on, working in the firm, when Bill married the boss's daughter. But Paul had other ideas.

'Perhaps you'll come back in now, join me in the firm,' Bill said softly.

'Nay, it's too late for that,' Paul said.

The talk turned to Irene's father, and how he came to rely more and more on the two brothers. Always when they talked, Wilf felt he was missing something important, a secret or a rivalry, but if so they did not let him in on it, though Paul stayed till after midnight and Wilf sat with Bill till two in the morning.

In all the years they had gone out cycling together on Sundays, Wilf had never seen them act in any way that suggested they were close or cared for each other. Their outings seemed more like a habit than an enjoyment. But at the door, when Paul left, they hugged each other and Wilf knew that whatever it was Bill got from Paul, it was something he could get from no one else.

Visitors came. Some gushing, some awkward. Professional men from Irene's committees; the wives of professional men from Irene's committees; clever spinsters with the right turn of phrase; business associates and a handicap of golfers. Dolly came with Bernadette whose baby stayed sleeping in the pram in the hall. Wilf was sent to peer at the baby and while he was out of the room heard Dolly complain to Bernadette, 'I could die and Jess wouldn't know. Wouldn't care, either, like as not.'

'Mam!' Bernadette said with only a sigh to convey whatever else she could not or would not express.

Gladys Hardy did not come.

But at the packed service in Mill Hill Chapel, as Bill and Wilf followed Irene's coffin, Wilf saw Gladys at the end of a pew halfway up the aisle. They caught each other's eye. She looks almost sadder than I feel, Wilf thought with surprise.

The funeral cortége made its slow way from the chapel to the cemetery. Along Beckett Street people lined the pavements, men with their hats in their hands, women in shawls, many openly weeping; children kept off school for the day. Wilf recognized some of the workers from the shoe factory, which was closed as a mark of respect.

As he watched Irene's coffin being lowered into the ground, a huge feeling of loss almost overwhelmed him. She had always been such a good woman, such a fair person, trying to do right by everyone, and now he felt he hardly knew her. He pulled out his handkerchief and blew his nose.

'It's all right, son. She knew,' Bill said. 'She knew.'

But what did she know! Wilf wondered. And did I love her, or just take her for granted? You have to know someone to love them.

When he turned from the graveside, people he had no recollection of ever meeting shook his hand, patted his shoulder, spoke words. It made him feel such a fraud.

A familiar voice said, 'We all think our parents will live for ever.' It was Gladys Hardy. 'Take care of yourself, Wilf. Irene was so thrilled with your success.'

'Will you come back with us?' Wilf asked.

Her look was towards Bill. 'No. Take care of Bill today.'

'I'll do my best.'

'I know this is the worst time, but I don't know when I'll see you again. There might be a day when you're curious, and want to know who your father was.'

She slid a folded sheet of paper into his pocket.

37

Harvest Time

I only ever heard of flaxen curls in fairy tales, describing the colour of a girl's fine head of hair. Now I know flaxen curls belong to the corn growing in the fields and make a graceful drooping show. The corn is cut and bound, and the sheaves arranged in a tunnel shape so the ears will dry. People worked in pairs, Leila and me together, so we were not much of a team. It entertained her no end to know that corn has ears. People came from the village to help. No one asked me questions or mocked my accent, partly perhaps because I took a cue from the Shaw boys and said nothing.

The sky got a great deal of attention as we went from farm to farm, field to field over the weeks. A fierce rain could ruin all efforts. But the sun smiled. After the corn, we got in the barley. I liked touching the feathery sheaves together to clump them and make them one.

We sat in the corner of the field, in the shade of a beech tree, to have a bite and a drink. A boy from the village had come without his drink. I passed him our bottle of cold tea. 'Thank you, Mrs Dennison,' he said, and with such respect.

People's conversation is different here. They do not wonder about each other as much as those of us who have lived in a town, belonged to a lending library and been to the flicks and the theatres.

The work sends you into a kind of stupor. Leila found it hard but she enjoyed herself, and she and the other children played as much as they helped. I thought of our history lessons at school, when Miss Maloney stopped telling us about the kings and queens to say that little children, our age and younger, had worked beneath factory looms, catching and fixing loose threads. Their unemployed parents carried the little ones in the early mornings across Leeds Bridge, the children half asleep and crying, to start their long, miserable days.

Leila could not help in the field of wheat because the sheaves are stiff and hard. She liked to walk the path through the tall wheat before it was cut, and seemed sorry to watch it fall, as if saying goodbye to an enchanted forest. Wheat sheaves will scratch your hands and arms, especially if you do not spot thistles bound up with them. Isaac found me a pair of gloves and so I managed well enough.

When we stopped work for our break, talk centred on the harvest supper they would have, and when it would be, and of the suppers in other villages. Some would go to Arnside Knott, some to Silverdale, some to both. Those who had gone to both in previous years compared them. They knew who made a pig of himself, or drunk too much, and who fell in a ditch on the way home.

Mrs Broderick, whose son Abe is in Leila's class, said, 'Eh, look at our two young uns picking up acorns. They'll leave none for any poor creatures that come seeking food.'

From the way she said it, she thought I was Leila's mother. It is best for them all to think that now.

Those harvest days left we three tired out. We'd brush our teeth, tumble into bed and be fast asleep. In the early morning, Isaac pulled me close to him and we made love so gently, and sometimes fiercely. Every morning he got up first, fetched me a cup of tea and a jug of warm water to wash myself.

Leila had the room across the landing, and since the start of harvest had not once come across crying that she could not sleep without me beside her.

Isaac fitted a swing to the branch of a tree and she loved to be on it at all hours, ordering one or other of us to push her higher, which we did not always have time for. She was laughing, stretching out her legs as she swung forward, looking at her new boots, bending her knees as she swung back. I stood beneath the tree in the shade, and pushed her out into the sunshine, all glorious and confident. I kept pushing because so long as she stayed on the swing she would not dirty her gingham dress.

But Isaac came out, nattering me to get ready for the harvest supper. After he went to the expense of the two dresses I bought in

Lancaster, I did not like to say I don't feel right in them. My dress with all the buttons feels so special since I wore it for my wedding. No one has a dress so new and fine. I felt they would all look at me in it and say, Who does she think she is, wearing a bought dress? Or, Don't you know she wore that dress for her wedding? Though really I know in my heart they will not because they do not seem alert enough to things, or curious. It is what people in a town who know you well might say among themselves. My other dress was plain and simple and would have done nicely except for the shape of the sleeves, which made my shoulders look so big. Isaac said I looked perfect whatever I wore, so he was no help at all.

Leaving him to push Leila on the swing, I decided on the big shoulders dress. I wished I had one of the outfits Bernadette and I had worn to be Vilma Banky and Agnes Ayres. Or just a bright scarf to take the attention from my shoulders. I combed my hair and looked at the strange reflection in the sparkling mirror. Perhaps if I had not given all Isaac's first wife's clothes to Mrs Bradley for poor people, I would have found a scarf. He had told me to look through the clothes that had been his mother's. Though they were all so very old and stinking of camphor, some were good, including a cardigan and a grey dress that did for working in after a good wash and iron. But no scarf. Perhaps there would not be a scarf in the world such as the one I was thinking of.

Leila came running in to fetch me. As she dashed through the door, her dark curls catching the light, she reminded me of her mother. Heather always looked perfect to me, but not to herself. She had that wild gypsy look even without dressing up as a Rudolph Valentino leading lady. In her gingham, Leila looked like some dark flower fairy that had crept from a forest to cast spells. She ran ahead of us in the lane, wanting to catch up with two children she knew, and when she had caught them up, ran back to us.

Isaac chatted to one and all at the supper, laughing and joking, though he drank only lemonade. I tried not to keep myself apart, but when I looked at them all, so easily pleased at a trestle table of food, jugs of beer and cider, comic turns and fiddlers, I longed for a trip to the flicks, the Empire or the City Varieties, the excitement when the lights went down, the scent of plush seats, perfume and cigarette smoke.

When I took a glass of cider, he said, 'Jessica! That's alcohol.'

It was sweet like summer apples and I told him so.

'It's fermented. You know I'm tee-total.'

'But I'm not,' I said, although I could not remember ever having a proper drink before, except Aunt Bella's cider or a sip of sherry or port wine. 'I don't expect to fall down drunk on one glass of cider. It's rude to refuse when you are offered something.' I held the glass to him.

'I can't. I took the Pledge. And it depends on what you're offered whether you should refuse it or not.'

The cider made me feel witty. I said, 'Next you'll tell me that if God had intended us to drink cider he would have a cider press on top of every apple tree.'

He answered but I did not catch what he said because someone had brought a gramophone and a record by Caruso began as Isaac spoke. All the company sat in silence listening to 'Your Eyes Have Told Me What I Did Not Know'. The moment the song ended and the record scratch-scratched, a great round of applause rose to the ceiling, as if Enrico Caruso himself would stand on the table and take a low bow.

Next came a dance with a pianist thumping out a tune, and Isaac pulled me to my feet and whirled me round the room with smiles saying, 'See, you don't have to drink to be merry.'

Next, the boy from the village who had come to the field without his food and drink one day, stood and recited 'The Boy Stood on the Burning Deck', with all the actions, and drama and sadness in his voice, so he got a great round of applause.

Isaac was pushed from his seat to stand by the piano. Someone called to him, 'Sing "Scarborough Fair",' and another called, 'Let's have your "Annie Laurie"'. He said a word to the pianist, then turned to us all but looked directly at me and sang:

> Daisy, Daisy, give me your answer do,
> I'm half crazy, all for the love of you.
> It won't be a stylish marriage –
> We can't afford a carriage.
> But you'll look sweet upon the seat
> Of a bicycle made for two.

251

He smiled as he sang, in his rich baritone voice, and he expected me to smile back. I did, when he had finished.

How they applauded him, and me, too, though I had done nothing. They called for another song, and he obliged. When he came back to me he said, 'Are you enjoying yourself?'

'Yes. I've never heard you sing that before.'

'It just popped into my head. You did come to me on a bike, so it seemed the right tune to choose.'

Then I was the one to be pressed for a song or recitation.

'I should have warned you,' Isaac whispered.

I'm sure people thought I recited 'The Owl and the Pussycat' because of being newly wed, but it was the only poem I could remember that night, and I had difficulty even with that because 'A Bicycle made for Two' went on playing in my thoughts, sung by Isaac, sung by Wilf.

We walked home by moonlight, Isaac carrying Leila on his shoulders. Behind us a small group of people were laughing and singing. Then they lost one of their number and had to go back, calling out and peering in ditches.

'See what drink does,' Isaac said sternly.

'Oh, Isaac! Don't be so straight-laced. I'm sure they're doing no harm.'

He didn't speak for a while.

'I've a mind to go into Lancaster soon and buy myself a red scarf.'

'That's the cider talking,' he said, but making a joke of it so we both laughed.

He was a long time coming upstairs. I had put on my wedding nightgown with its silky feel against my body. I stroked the silkiness, hoping he would come to bed soon.

When he did, he knelt by the bed to say his prayers, which he did most nights.

'Are you angry with me?' I asked when he slid in beside me, for I could feel he was keeping himself from me.

'No. It's not you. It's me.'

'What?'

But he would not tell me.

'Are you thinking of some other harvest supper, when you were with someone else?'

He paused too long before answering, then rolled over towards me, hugged me tight and said, 'I love you, Jessica.'

'I love you, too, Isaac.'

'Jessica, what is it you're keeping from me?'

'I don't know what you mean.'

'There's always something I think you mean to tell me, and then you don't. You hold back.'

But I could not tell Isaac about Father Flynn sleepwalking to my room, and where that led. Some days I believed the priest had ensnared me and tried to bring me under his power. That I could bear. What froze me inside was when everything turned inside out. I ensnared him, and destroyed him.

When I didn't answer, Isaac said, 'Perhaps one day you'll tell me.'

38

Packing Whiting
for Market

He had expected to see more activity. Fields stood bare with only a covering of stubble. Here and there, crops not yet taken into barns stood draped with tarpaulin sheets. The land held an eerie quiet, as if hedgerows hushed their breath. Wilf imagined his mother and father walking this lane. It was hard not to take against the man. Why hadn't his father married his mother? Wilf tried to imagine the life he might have had as a country boy. Would he still have found his way to the Royal College of Art? Somehow he doubted it. So he could not entirely hold onto his anger towards the man whose indifference or callousness had led Gladys Hardy to the anonymous city and himself into a new life.

He followed the directions given to him by the man at the post office and turned down a track towards a yard and buildings. A passing gull disturbed the still air. Somewhere not far off, a cockerel crowed. Wilf tried to read the house's date, but the lintel above the door was worn. How long had his forefathers lived here? he wondered. Why did he feel no spark of recognition, no dream memory for this place?

No one answered his knock, but a dog barked from behind the door. He turned his back on the house and began to explore. Slowly he opened doors, gazing at farm equipment and machinery, wishing he knew what was used now and what had been long abandoned. A rusty scythe hung on a nail in the barn. Near it stood a long broad plank, like a seesaw, and next to it a Neptune's fork. It irked him that he could not name the equipment his father must know so intimately. What was that thing with the big blades, like an over-sized lawn-mower?

In the stable, a lonely-looking horse turned its head to him, neighing plaintively. He went to speak to it, stroked its mane. Daringly for Wilf, he put the noose-like rope around its neck and led it out of the stables and around the yard, clip-clopping, to the horse trough. He watched it drink. Being so close to a horse and in new surroundings gave him an insight into what Ralph Moxon chased after in his paintings. Though Ralph's work was too busy for Wilf's liking, and too close to life to be art, Wilf now saw an equilibrium between the animal and the trough. The horses Ralph painted were like something out of a Stubbs portrait; sleek smooth creatures, owned by showy individuals and ridden by neat, small men in colourful shirts. Maybe all artists were after the same thing. A kind of balance. The peak of a moment. The horse looked at him, finished with its drinking. He led it back. In his pocket he had an apple. He offered it. The horse took the apple and munched.

Feeling eyes on him, Wilf turned to look, thinking someone had returned. From the stable doorway the dog barked. It was a black and white sheepdog. Perhaps it expected someone else. Its tail fell between its legs as Wilf approached. He saw that it was old. Its milky eyes gazed on him, then it barked again. He patted the dog's head and felt the sharp bone of its skull under his hand. It moved away, and looked back at him. When Wilf did not budge from the yard, it ran on a few paces, then back to him, barking again. Wilf followed the dog. It led him across the yard, past the house to a long low stone building.

The dog stopped by the entrance. The top part of the door swung open. A stench of fish hit him full on. A woman stood at a long low sink. She worked a noisy pump and did not hear him say, 'Excuse me.' He heard running water and a slap-slap sound as she washed something and set it aside.

The bottom half of the door had a bolt on the inside. Wilf reached over, undid the bolt and stepped inside. He coughed. 'Good afternoon.'

She turned.

She seemed not to know him for a moment. She reached for a

cloth, dried her hands, touched a hand to her hair, which was hidden by the folds of a scarf. She wore a long apron over a grey dress, as if she had gone back in time and was another Jess altogether.

Jess? However he had imagined her, it was not like this, in a dim shed, wearing dull clothes, her fine blond hair hidden. Jess, washing fish? It couldn't be. He walked towards her; she stood motionless as a statue, looking at him as if he were a ghost.

'Wilf.'

Her voice broke the spell. He took her into his arms and for a moment she responded, then pulled away.

'Jess! I thought I'd never find you. Why didn't you write to me? I didn't mean to lose you. Oh, Jess.'

She was shaking. She pulled free.

'You look well, Wilf. But . . . you'll smell of fish if you come in here, if you touch me. Go outside.'

He took her hand. She shook it from him. 'I must finish what I'm doing. This stuff's going to market. It's got to be boxed and taken to the station to catch the train. It has to be done.'

'What tyrant has you doing this?'

'No tyrant. It's our living.'

'Jess, leave it!' But she turned away from him and continued rinsing fish in cold water as if her life depended on it. He stood beside her, not knowing what to do.

She did not look at him. 'It's going to Burnley or Bury or one of those Lancashire towns. They all begin with B. Perhaps it's Bolton or Blackburn. They like fish there. It's whiting.'

'Then let me help.' He laid some fish into a box.

'Leave it alone,' she said, her eyes on her work. 'I'm quicker on my own. Go outside, Wilf. I'll come to you when I'm done.'

He would not leave but watched as she layered the fish into wooden boxes, placing them on top of each other, putting a lid on top of every third box.

Outside in the yard, Wilf heard a horse's hooves, and footsteps.

'Sorry to leave you to it, Jess,' a woman said. 'But we're both here now.'

'It's done,' Jess said.

'Then we'll have the boxes on the cart in no time. Arthur!'

'This is my cousin, Wilf,' Jess said. 'Wilf, this is Edith and Arthur Shaw.'

'Pleased to meet you, sir,' said a man with big red hands. He offered one. 'I've just washed them.'

The man and woman each picked up boxes. Wilf went to help.

'Oh, young man, don't you pick none up,' the woman said. 'You don't want to go round smelling of whiting or no girl will look at you, eh, Jess?'

But Wilf carried three crates of fish into the yard and set them down on a cart. The horse nuzzled him.

'Beauty likes you,' the man said. Wilf had forgotten their names already. He just wanted them to go away, so he could talk to Jess.

'Have we seen you before?' the woman asked. 'Only you look right familiar.'

Jess stood in the doorway. She had never looked so beautiful to him. He wanted to grab her, run all the way down the lane and get the first train out of this damn place that had kept her from him for so long. Of course they would have to take the child, but Wilf had got used to the idea now. It would not be so bad to have a little girl in tow. He took Jess's work-worn hand.

He felt a ring on her hand. Of course she would have to wear a ring. People would think that the child was hers.

'How did you find me, Wilf?'

He thought he heard reproach behind her words, not just *How did you find me?* but *Why did it take you so long?*

'I did search, Jess. Believe me. I came last year. I thought you might have headed for the bungalow.'

'When did you come?'

'Not so long after you left Gargrave. I would have got there sooner but toppled off my motorbike.'

'Then you did see my note.'

'No.'

'Liar. You left a hanky with your initial to acknowledge it. Well, I understood your message clear enough. You have no business to come back again.'

'I saw no note. There was a pebble on the table, that was all.'

'A pebble. Yes, I put a pebble from the beach on top of the envelope.'

'Jess, there was no note. One of us would have seen it. We both looked, Ralph and me.'

'It doesn't matter now. It's for the best. You shouldn't have come.'

He could not lie, not to Jess. 'Why I came here . . . to this farm or fishery or whatever you call it . . . I didn't expect to see you. Miss Hardy, my natural mother—'

'I know who Gladys Hardy is.'

'I know you always said I should have spoken to her ages ago, and you were right. But there's a moment, isn't there?'

'For some people it's a very long moment,' she said. 'There was a moment for me when I had to take Leila from the orphanage.'

They were still standing just outside the low building, breathing in the stench of fish. He wondered where she lived, and where they could go to talk. She made no move.

He felt glad she was cold and angry towards him. Without the anger, it would mean she didn't care.

'Are you saying Gladys told you to come here?'

'Not exactly. I told her I'd been over this way to look for you last year. She said Isaac Dennison keeps an eye on the camp during the winter months . . .'

'Yes, he does.'

'Jess, can we go somewhere and sit down? You look as if you're going to pass out.'

She nodded, but didn't move.

He took her arm. 'Where? Where shall we go? Don't say back in that fish place. I can't stand the stink.'

'We'd better go inside.'

She led him across the yard, to the house he had knocked on earlier.

'Is this where you lodge?'

'This is where we live.'

She opened the door and a whippet rushed at her, wagging its tail. She patted its head absent-mindedly.

Wilf looked round, admiring the low-beamed ceilings, the polished hearth, the well-scrubbed deal table. 'Very rustic, Jess. I never pictured you in such a setting.'

'Sit down, Wilf.'

He sat at the table. She took the chair opposite him.

'To tell you the truth, it'll be a relief for me not to meet Mr Dennison today.'

'Why?'

'Why?' Because I'd rather be with you.'

'It's strange to hear your voice after all this time. Strange to see you sitting in here.' She spoke as if something puzzled her. Yet it was not that long since she had seen him.

'I've missed you, Jess, every day, every hour.'

She didn't answer at first, then said, 'He'll be here soon.'

'I don't care about Isaac Dennison now.'

'Why did you want to meet him? To find me?'

'He's my father, if you must know. But I'll meet him another time. I don't want anything else to happen today that will distract me from having found you. We said we'd be married this summer. We promised. Summer came and went. Why didn't you get in touch?'

She spread her hands on the table and seemed unable to speak.

A scraping sound came from outside the door, a man cleaning the mud off his boots.

'I got all the hay in,' said a deep voice as the door opened.

Jess stayed where she was, very still, looking across at the man who came through the door, smiling.

Wilf stood up and turned, ready to shake hands.

'Isaac, this is Wilf from Leeds. Wilf Price.'

'A relative of yorn?' Isaac asked, striding the short distance from the door, holding out his hand. 'This is an honour.'

'We're cousins – that's to say, cousins by Wilf's adoption. Wilf, this is the man you came to find. Isaac Dennison, my husband.'

Wilf could not see her face because Isaac Dennison still held his hand and seemed not to want to let go. But the man's expression had changed. He looked from Wilf to Jess and back to Wilf.

'And what's brought you all the way from Leeds?' Isaac asked, as if he dreaded the answer.

Jess got up from her chair. 'You'd better sit down, Isaac,' she said, touching his arm. 'You, too, Wilf.'

They did as she said. Isaac looked at Wilf, waiting.

'Miss Hardy. Gladys Hardy . . . she told me about you. She's my mother. She thought I'd better know who was my father.'

For a long time no one spoke. Isaac looked dazed. 'She . . . your mother did the right thing to tell you. And I'm right glad you've come. Only how strange. Jessica's cousin.'

Jess stood a little way off, looking at the two of them together. She came closer, put her hand on the back of Isaac's chair as if to steady herself.

'Jessica? Sit down,' Isaac said.

'I have to pick Leila up from school.'

Wilf looked past Isaac to Jess. 'You knew, didn't you? You knew I was his son.'

'No.'

'Gladys befriended you. She must have told you.'

'I had no idea. No idea.'

'I should have insisted I met your family,' Isaac said, reaching back and snatching Jess's hand. 'Then it would have come out.'

'I'm not Jess's family, though, am I?' Wilf said bitterly. 'I'm yours.'

Jess pulled her hand free. 'I'm going to pick Leila up from school.'

Wilf wanted to leap and grab her, keep her from leaving the house.

Isaac said, 'It's not time yet.'

She seemed not to hear. At the door she turned and spoke to Isaac, not meeting Wilf's look. 'We'll ask Wilf to stay for supper, Isaac, dear?'

'Yes, yes.'

When she left the room, the dog bounding after her, Wilf thought that the light had gone out of his life.

For a long moment neither man spoke.

'You're the artist, Wilf?'

'Yes.'

'And you love Jessica,' Isaac said flatly. 'You were childhood sweethearts.'

Wilf looked at him in disbelief. Childhood sweethearts. Was that what she had said, or was that what this man chose to believe?

'Are you really married to Jess? Properly married, not just—'

Isaac frowned, his jaw tightened. 'She's my wife.'

Wilf got up and made for the door.

'Wait! Wilf, come back!'

Once he left the yard, Wilf had no recollection of what way he had come. He stumbled along the lane, just walking where his feet took him. He followed a path that he knew was wrong, but what difference did that make?

Wilf wanted to get out of this place. Soon. Back to London. To kill Ralph Moxon. To murder him slowly. For he saw that visit to the bungalow again – remembered Ralph going inside while he looked around the building for bike tracks. He saw Ralph standing by the table, holding the pebble. What had he slipped in his pocket the moment before? Wilf had known there should be a note. But why would Ralph do such a thing? Why would he conceal Jess's message?

Something else came back to him as he walked. When Dolly and Paul got the letter at Christmas, the postmark was smudged. Everyone said so. But Dolly and Bernadette swore it said London. Bernadette had grilled Wilf mercilessly on New Year's Eve. Was he holding something back? Did he know where Jess was?

Jess knew only one other person in London: Ralph Moxon.

When he got to the station, the last train had left. It was too late. The train companies and the whole universe conspired against him.

If he turned up at the hotel, looking as he did, feeling as he did, the manager would call the police. Wilf felt sure his murderous feelings showed in his eyes, his every movement. If he was going to commit one murder, he could commit two. Isaac Dennison first. He'd throttle, strangle, squeeze the life out of him.

He thought of going back to the farm and howling at Mr and Mrs Dennison as they took to their bed, probably smiling about him. Poor Wilf. Still carrying his torch. The childhood sweetheart.

He could go to the holiday camp bungalow. Smash the table where Jess had left her note and he his monogrammed handkerchief. He was by the camp gates now. He stopped outside the bungalow. No. It would be too painful to go in there.

He walked down the path, passed the superintendent's house where a light shone from the window. With his penknife, he slid back the latch on the dormitory window, raised the window, climbed in and closed it behind him. There he curled, sleepless and cold, on a child's narrow bed, waiting for morning.

39

Rumpelstiltskin

When I came back with Leila from school, Isaac was standing in the doorway. He seemed relieved to see us and it suddenly came to me that perhaps he expected we would not come back.

'Wilf's gone,' he said quietly.

'He wouldn't stay to supper, then?'

'I thought you may have passed him on the lane.'

'We came back around the shore.'

'Ah.'

Leila grabbed his hand. 'Push me! On the swing.'

'It's too cold,' I said. 'Come in and get warm.'

I expected Isaac to say he had to go back to work. But neither he nor Leila took any notice of me. From the kitchen window, as I mashed potatoes and fried whiting and onions, I watched Leila swinging higher and higher, Isaac pushing her.

'Everything's going to be all right,' I told myself.

And I wondered why I had never seen the likeness before. Isaac and Wilf. Wilf and Isaac. Perhaps I had and that was why I always felt right in Isaac's arms. And the night he sang 'A Bicycle Made For Two' and made me shiver. Though it's such a silly song.

I called them to supper.

Only when Isaac said he would put Leila to bed did it come to me that he was being distant. All that evening he had talked to Leila but not to me at all. I could not ask him what had passed between him and Wilf, not trusting myself to speak on the subject. I didn't want him to speak either, fearing words. My longing was for him to take me to bed, make me forget everything.

We sat by the fire. He put on another log.

'I won't stay up,' I said. 'I'm going to bed.'

'Wait. Don't go yet.'

Still he didn't speak. I thought perhaps he wanted to talk about the past, but didn't know how to begin. I tried to help, thinking of something to say. 'It must have been strange meeting Wilf. No one in the family ever knew who you were. His mother never said.'

'You knew her?' he asked.

'Yes. My aunt was active in the charities that she worked for.' I didn't say that my dad mended her shoes. It seemed too personal somehow.

He nodded.

'Perhaps you're sorry now that you didn't marry Gladys,' I said.

'Don't rub it in. I did a wrong thing, I know, in loving two lasses. I was a young man in my prime, and flattered to be cared for. I've learned patience since, Jessica. But I didn't deserve you. You're too young for me.'

'Isaac, don't say that. Twenty years is nothing between a man and a woman. But is that what you think, that you should have married Wilf's mother after you were widowed?'

'Gladys deserved better. I did ask her after my wife died. She said no. It was too late.'

'Then you offered.'

'Offered? Jess, you don't offer yourself like you offer a cup of tea to a passer-by No one takes love that lightly, do they? Do they? Do you?'

'No.'

I had never seen him like this. He leaned forward, his head in his hands.

'Isaac, come to bed.'

Leaning down, I kissed the top of his head. He pulled me to him.

'You still love him, don't you?'

'Who?'

'*Who*? My son. Wilf.'

'No. Did he say that? Because it's not true.'

'He didn't say a word. He didn't have to. His eyes when he watched you go.'

'I can't help it if he loves me. Isaac, come to bed.'

I moved away. He took my wrists, hurting me, pulling me close, looking up at me, the flames from the burning log lighting his face. 'Tell me the truth, Jessica.'

'He's a boy.'

'The truth.'

'We were close, of course. I told you that.'

'How close?'

'We thought we loved each other.'

'Thought. Only thought?'

'Feelings get mixed up. You should know that.'

'Did he make love to you?'

'No.'

'Are you sure?'

'Stop it.'

'Because if he didn't, who did?'

He stood up and grabbed me, holding my arms, gripping me too tightly, his fingers pressing into my flesh through the sleeves of my dress.

'You're hurting me.'

'Did he have you? Did you sleep with him?'

'Don't be like this.'

'No. You're right. I'm sorry. Sorry.'

He began to kiss me with such urgency and a kind of hardness that I hadn't felt from him before. I felt so relieved and began to kiss him back. He pulled at my dress to get at my breasts and I drew him close, knowing if we made love he would forget all his doubts and questions. Then we were by the table, he was lifting my dress, pulling at my underwear, pushing himself into me, and I wanted him to go on and on and not stop, and never speak Wilf's name again. And we did not go upstairs that night because climbing the stairs would have taken too long. We made love again, in the corner bed.

'I always wanted you in this bed,' he whispered. 'When you first came here, how I wanted you.'

'You have me now,' I said.

'Do I? I never knew jealousy, Jessica. Not until now. It eats me up.'

'Don't be jealous.'

'On our honeymoon, you didn't bleed.'

'Isaac, you've been married to one woman and you've had a son by another. I don't know who else you might have loved. And you say I didn't bleed.'

'You know who I've loved, their names, who they were – just two of them, until you. Talk straightly, Jessica. Was it Wilf?'

And there was no point in lying. He knew. He could not see my face because we were too close and although it was almost morning, the room was still dark.

'Yes. It was Wilf.'

'And he still loves you?'

'He thinks he does.'

'And he came looking for you, not for me.'

'No!'

'And you love him.'

'I love you, Isaac. I only love you.'

He got out of bed slowly and began to pull on his clothes.

'What are you doing?'

'Going to work.'

'Don't just leave me like this. And it's too early. It's still dark.'

'I must make it worth your while, having married an old man. I'm good for earning money, to buy dresses and scarves, and put food on the table.'

Something must have disturbed Leila. She appeared at the bottom of the stairs as Isaac opened the door and went into the yard. I slipped on my coat and boots and went after him.

'Isaac! It's the middle of the night. Come back!'

Leila ran after me in her bare feet. I picked her up and pulled my coat around her. We caught up with him, but he shook me off. I called, then took Leila back in the house, put her in the corner bed, and went after him again, seeing a movement by the track. But it was a sheep that had strayed down from the fields. Isaac was nowhere to be seen.

I climbed into the corner bed myself. Not having slept all night, I closed my eyes expecting to be too exhausted to sleep.

Leila woke me.

'Go back to sleep,' I said. Uncle Isaac will be back soon.'

'I can't see him.'

'Who can't you see?'

'Uncle Isaac, and Rumpelstiltskin.'

'Go to sleep.'

'The world is on fire.'

The dogs whined. I groaned, just wanting my sleep, feeling worn out. I felt a gust of cold air and realized she had opened the door.

'Leila, you weren't born in a field. Shut that door.'

'Rumpelstiltskin has set the world on fire.'

Then I smelt the smoke.

'Who made the sky red?'

I jumped from the bed and ran to the door. Scarlet sparks flashed and lit the black sky. I guessed it must be around dawn but couldn't tell for sure whether it was day or night. The fire came from the direction of the fields. Straightaway I knew Isaac had set fire to the stubble. I wet my finger and held it up to the wind as he had shown me.

'You stay here. Keep the dogs in. The fire won't come this way.' I pulled on my boots.

'Don't leave me!'

Trying to appear calm, I sat her on the bed, set the dogs there with her and grabbed a blanket. 'I won't be long. Promise. Look after the dogs. You're in charge.'

I could not cut across the burning fields. I ran to the lane, holding the blanket to my face to stop myself choking on the smoke that seemed to curl after me. I thought I saw him on the lane and called. It was Arthur Shaw.

'What the hell . . . Who's set fire to the stubble in this wind?' he said as I caught up to him.

'It must have changed.' Even at that moment I had to defend Isaac's idiocy. The state of him, I would be surprised if he had held a finger to the wind.

'It's more than the stubble.' Arthur held a muffler to his mouth and it was hard to hear him. 'The camp buildings are alight. I saw the flames – too high to be stubble.'

Sure enough, I looked over and flames licked the sky above the holiday camp.

'Pray to God the superintendent and his wife have got out.'

'I thought they'd left for the season.'

'Not till tomorrow.'

The bungalow stood intact but the superintendent's house blazed.

So did the dormitory building. The whole end surrounding the window I had climbed through that day last year was a mass of flames.

The superintendent, wearing striped pyjamas, called to us from near the dormitory building. 'Help me!' He was wrestling Isaac.

'Stop them!' The superintendent's wife stood on the path in her coat, but wore no shoes. 'Farmer Dennison's gone mad. He said he saw a face at the dormitory window.'

Isaac broke free and ran into the burning building. I called to him but he didn't hear. I raced towards the building, calling his name, pushing my way past the superintendent through the doorway into the storage area. The heat was unbearable and I couldn't see. 'Isaac!' I tumbled against him. The fire was just beyond us, in the dormitory. Isaac grabbed me roughly and threw me out of the building. 'Stay back, Jessica!'

Arthur Shaw held me. 'Don't be a fool. Think of your child.'

Someone stumbled from the building. I ran to him, and he put his arms around me. Half choking, he said, 'I couldn't see for the smoke. Isaac saved me.'

And I saw it was Wilf. I screamed as I heard a crash inside the building. Isaac stumbled blindly towards us, clothes blazing. I ran to him with the blanket, burning my hands as I beat at the flames.

'Let me,' Wilf said.

And when Isaac was covered with the blanket and carried to the bungalow, Wilf came along, coughing, trying to explain.

'Just go,' I said.

People came, an ambulance, but that was a long time after. A doctor or ambulance man gave me something to drink and after that everything seemed to swim.

I woke in our downstairs bed, Leila kneeling over me, looking into my face.

'Isaac?' I asked.

Someone else appeared behind Leila. It was Mrs Bradley, the minister's wife. 'He's in the infirmary at Lancaster.' Her face looked drawn and grey. 'Rest now.'

My hands hurt under the bandages, my arms and face, too.

Mrs Bradley said, 'Go out and see if you can find a fresh-laid egg, Leila. Your mammy could do with an egg.'

Leila went outside. Mrs Bradley held a glass of water to my lips.

'A young man who missed the last train had gone into the building for the night. Isaac saw his face at the window. He got the young man out but . . .'

'How is he?'

'The young man is fine. He left. You'd think he would have stayed to see how his rescuer fared.'

'I don't mean him. How is Isaac?'

'Not good. They wanted to take you to the infirmary, too, but little Leila went near crazy at the thought of you being taken away. I said I'd look after you here.'

'Thank you.'

'The superintendent and his wife are safe. Fortunately she was able to telephone for help before the fire reached their house. The buildings are gone, except for the playroom and the visitors' bungalow.'

'I must see Isaac. I must get to Lancaster.'

'You're in no fit state.'

'I'll need my fingers. Would you change my bandage to let my fingers free?' But she would not let me stir that day, or the next, and I had no strength to argue.

When I did go, on the third day, it was not visitors' day at the infirmary. When I asked to see Isaac Dennison, the porter looked at my bandaged hands and took pity on me, I think. He spoke with the matron, and it was agreed to let me through.

There was not much of Isaac to see, through the bandages. He lay very still and I could not tell whether he was alseep or awake. I said nothing, but sat quietly beside him. After a long while he said, 'Is that you, Jessica?'

'Yes.'

'I waited for you to come.'

'I came as soon as I could. Mrs Bradley practically held me prisoner.'

'They're good people. They'll take care of you.'

'Do you have much pain, Isaac?'

'I'll not deny it.'

'Is there anything you want me to do?'

'Yes.'

'Tell me.'

'Listen to me carefully. I have not got long.'

I started to protest.

'Shhh. We may not have told each other everything, Jessica, but we meant well. We loved each other, perhaps too much.'

'Don't talk as if—'

'I know my time is short.'

I wondered whether to give him some hope that might help him live. 'I do love you, Isaac. You must believe that.'

'Yes,' he said. 'Or you wouldn't have followed me. Is Wilf safe?'

'Yes.'

'Good. Tell him not to worry.'

'I won't be telling him anything.'

For a long time he did not speak, and I thought he slept.

'The farm will be re-let. I daresay Shaw will make a go of it if he can. Pity his sons aren't older.'

'Don't think about the farm now.'

He gulped and it struck me how dry he must be, as I was myself. There was no water to be seen. I walked up the ward and asked the nurse for a glass of water. She was about my age, and looked uncertain. 'Is he meant to have it?' she asked.

'Yes,' I said. 'He is.'

She took a glass and filled it with water from the sink.

It was hard to get it to his lips as he lay on his back, unable to move, and I feared he might choke. I dripped the water from my finger into his open, bird-like mouth in tiny drops and drips.

'In our room, the trap door I showed you in the floor.' His voice had a painful rasp.

'Shhh. Rest.'

'There's savings, a blue bank bag. I wish it were more. Keep it for you and Leila. Don't let the agent get a hold on it.'

'Isaac, you're going to get well.'

'And the farm stuff, the tools, let Arthur take what he wants, and the horse.'

The ward sister told me it was time to go. 'Just give me a while longer,' I said, knowing I must say something to him but not knowing what.

'Two minutes,' she said. 'And you can come back in the morning to see how he is.'

'Go back to Leeds,' Isaac said, 'to your people.'

'I'm going nowhere. I'm staying by you.'

'Bless you. I wish it could have been different.'

'Leila sends her love,' I said.

The ward sister touched my shoulder. 'We need to give Mr Dennison his medication now.'

You don't know where to kiss when a person is wreathed in bandages. I touched his hand. 'I'll come tomorrow.'

I saw no point in going back to the house that night, just to catch the train again the following day. I sat in the ladies waiting room at Lancaster station, and pretended I had missed my connection. The next morning I washed my face as best I could with bandaged hands, and walked back to the infirmary.

This time the porter would not let me through. He ran a stubby finger down a sheet of paper, cleared his throat and asked me if I would please sit down. Even before the matron came to the door, so solid in her blue dress and starched apron, I knew. But when she said the words I could not stop my tears.

'I'm sorry, Mrs Dennison. Your husband died at three o'clock this morning.'

I stood up to go, but she was in my way, put her arms around me and held me as I cried. 'You come with me,' she said. 'I'm going to find you a cup of tea and a boiled egg.'

40

Last Week's News

Scorched and brown, the earth all around the farm and down the fields to the camp would not let us forget, even for a moment. As I walked Leila to school, a terrible quietness held the lane. 'Have the frogs died?' she asked.

'No. They'll be safe. They'll have leaped and jumped as frogs do.'

'Why didn't Uncle Isaac leap and jump?'

I didn't know what to say but turned her attention to a green bird flying across our path.

The land agent called while Leila was at school. I sat at the table, not knowing what to do. Isaac had taught me to milk the cows but Arthur and Edith Shaw seemed to be doing everything, as if proving that I was not needed and could slip away as quietly as I had come, so far as they were concerned. People sent pies and cakes and a ham, so I did not have to think about cooking. I picked up the broom to sweep the floor, and that was when he knocked.

Isaac's dog, old Madge, lay by the door, or sometimes outside the door – waiting. She knew the land agent and wagged her tail. He is a youngish man, having taken over from his father. Well-spoken and polite, he sat at the table with me and offered condolences. He knew Isaac well, and admired him, as one who knew how to get the best from both the land and the sea. He asked me about the arrangements for the burial, and when it would take place, saying that of course he would be there. He hoped I would ask if I needed anything.

Perhaps this was not the best time, he thought, but there would be no good time. He brought out a book, to show me when the rent is paid up to. It seems that if Isaac had lived he would have been liable to pay compensation for burning down the Leeds Poor Children's Holiday Camp building, and he regretted to ask me but must. Did Isaac have a bank account and had he made a will?

I looked through Isaac's papers, but there were no bank books and no will – just receipts for items bought and a book recording sales of produce, with a separate book for sales of fish and shellfish.

Since the smoke got into my lungs from the fire, a cough would come over me without warning and I began to cough and choke and had to pour myself a glass of water.

He waited until my coughing had stopped. My eyes still watered.

'It's awkward for me to ask this, Mrs Dennison, but do you know where he kept his money?'

Until that moment I had not remembered. I did not answer, only shook my head.

'There is insurance, of course,' he said, 'but that isn't immediate and is unlikely to cover the full loss – the re-building of the camp.'

He rubbed at his shirt collar, and asked me for a glass of water though the room was not warm. When I had given him the water, and he drank then cleared this throat, I realized there was something else. I knew we would not be able to stay on.

'I suppose we must move out at the end of the rent period?'

'Actually, the thing is . . . we do have another tenant who is ready to move in, and to buy the machinery and tools and so on. We can't leave the farm empty and untended.' He looked round the room. 'You've made the place smarter than it's been in years.'

'So when will we have to move out?'

'I can give you until the day after the burial. You do have somewhere to go? Your family?'

Since I thought it would make little difference to him whether or not we had somewhere to go, I told him I had other things to think about. He nodded and got up from the table saying, 'I'll take a look round outside, if that's all right.'

I walked him to the door. Madge came with us, hopefully, looking out into the yard after him. He had a fine horse, harnessed to the post by the gate. It threw back its head, and breath from its nostrils made small clouds in the chill November air.

Leila stayed in school during the burial. We stood in the cemetery in drizzling rain, a mound of clay and grey soil piled close by. I had never seen the stone that marked the grave of Isaac's wife, Emily, and their little boy, but that was where he would rest. It seemed right in a way that he should go back to them, since he had been mine for such a short time.

Afterwards Mr and Mrs Bradley ushered us into the manse where she had set out a funeral breakfast. Mrs Bradley asked me what I would do now, and I could not answer. Leaving Mr Bradley talking to the land agent and the neighbours to each other, she led me into the hall and gave me back my coat, saying, 'I've somewhere to show you.'

She took my arm and we strolled along the road, as if on an outing, and down a lane to a small cottage with a neat garden. 'You could live here, in exchange for cleaning the chapel, the hall and our house.'

We went inside, to one room that was kitchen and living room, with a single rocking chair, a straight chair at the plain square table and a stool tucked under it. Up stone steps was a bedroom, exactly the size of the room below.

'The pump is out the back,' she said, 'and the privy, too. It's been well kept, though without a fire in the grate you can see it gets damp at this time of year.'

'Thank you.'

'You'll take the job?'

'Yes. Thank you.'

'I'm glad. You needn't start the work until Friday. You'll clean our house on Fridays, the chapel on Mondays, with a dust round on Saturday. You can fit in the hall on a day to suit yourself, by arrangement.'

I looked round the cottage room with its neat window sill, still holding a small vase of evergreen leaves. 'Who was here before?'

'The woman who had it previously, Mrs Prentice, she's too old for the work and a vacancy came up in an almshouse. She was at the funeral today, the old lady. Very fond of Mr Dennison, as we all were. Perhaps you can speak to her about the work. Of course, it's just the rent that is paid. You would need to find some other work to feed yourselves, but Mrs Prentice did clean for others and once it's known you've taken on the cottage, I'm sure there'll be approaches.'

When we went back to the funeral breakfast, the old lady had left. As soon as I could excuse myself, I did the same.

Our clothes did not take much packing. It was Edith Shaw who came bustling in, bossing me and saying. 'What else will you need? Don't be leaving foodstuff behind, and good sheets and blankets.'

She made me go round with her, packing everything she thought we might need and telling me that if I didn't need it, she would take it off my hands.

'I want to go now,' I said. The agent wanted us to be out the next day, but I could think of no good reason to spend another night there.

So we took the horse and cart down the lane, with more stuff than I would ever need on the back of the cart, and Dempsey running along behind. Mrs Shaw lit a fire in the damp little cottage while I went to fetch Leila from school. It was Leila who missed Madge. Mrs Shaw said the dog would be somewhere about, in the stables probably. She would look when she went back up by the farm.

But Leila would not settle without her. She cried until I agreed to walk up to the farmhouse and find her. She was not with the Shaws, or in any of the buildings. We went in the house and Leila ran from room to room in the evening gloom, calling her. The house had never felt so empty. I walked around, saying goodbye to the place – for Isaac as well as for myself.

In our bedroom, I remembered what he had said about the trap door in the floor. While Leila was in her old room, I knelt down and pulled the brass ring on the trap door. I reached in and found a blue money bag that weighed heavy in my hand, and also a bank book for the West Lancashire Bank.

I gave the bank book to Leila. 'Put that on the table.' The land agent could take it towards the fire damage.

At my waist under my skirt I had the linen money belt that had belonged to Isaac's mother. I put the heavy blue bag inside it.

All the way back down the lane, we called for Madge. Dempsey darted about the bushes, raising our hopes as he pretended to find her.

Dempsey did find her by leading us to the cemetery. She was lying in the clay at the side of the grave, her coat heavy with the rain. We coaxed her to come with us. I built up the fire to try and warm her, but she would not eat. She let us dry her, rubbing at her with an old sheet and towel.

It was strange for me to have time on my hands, as I did the next morning after taking Leila to school. One of the mothers gave me a pot of stew. When I got back to the house someone else had left a wrapped cake and flagon of cider on the steps. The kindness of people made me want to cry. I knew I must do something, get out of the house.

A little silver pencil had rolled out of sight under the table, found by Leila, and I decided to take it to the old woman in her almshouse, along with some evergreen leaves cut from her garden.

A stout woman in a faded dress and heavy, cable-knitted cardigan opened the door. I remembered her from our wedding. She had supplied my bunch of anemones and his buttonhole of forsythia. I presented the leaves, returned her silver pencil. I could not remember whether I thanked her for the wedding flowers. She said I did thank her, and right prettily, and began to cry. We sat at the table together, roaring our eyes out until she wiped her face, made us some tea and opened a tin of homemade biscuits.

I told her I was in her old cottage. She explained to me how you go about keeping a chapel clean, and Mrs Bradley's little require-ments and fussiness regarding her house, and how she would keep a body talking far too long and then complain that the work was going too slow and should be done before Mr Bradley came in for his dinner.

'But why are you doing that?' she asked. 'Isaac was that proud of marrying a young woman who had certificates as you do and could have got a job in Lancaster, or Manchester even.'

'I have Leila to take care of. We need somewhere to live. She's at school and has had enough upheaval in her little life.'

'If I were young and had certificates, I wouldn't take up where the old me left off. I'd be into the world, trying to make my way. I'd be buying a newspaper, searching for a job for meself.'

'But there's Leila—'

'There's Leila whether you have a good job or are on your knees cleaning up after folk who'll dirty the place again an hour after. Don't wear your bonny self out scrubbing other folks' floors. Getting arthritis in your elbows and knees, and nobody to heave you up and down or care, so long as a floor is polished.'

'I'll think about it,' I said.

'Well, don't think too long.'

'Mrs Bradley's been very good to us, right from the start.'

'Oh, Mrs Bradley's very good all right. Very good indeed.' She got up and went to the cupboard. 'But I'm in heaven here right enough, in this house with none to see to but meself and a bit of a pension to keep body and soul together.' She brought out a bottle of port wine and two small glasses. 'Now then, this was given to me by someone I cleaned for and I won't say who, not to give the game away.'

I was glad I'd called to see her. As I left, she pushed the local weekly paper into my hand. 'Here, I know you won't be up to shifting yet, but it doesn't hurt to look.'

'What for?'

'What I said – a job! Somewhere fresh.'

It was too early to collect Leila from school. I took the dogs and walked them round the village. They stayed outside the grocer's while I bought candles and tapers. The grocer wrapped the candles in newspaper, tied with string. As I watched his fingers tie the knot and make a small bow, I suddenly filled up with tears and felt such a fool. When he handed me the package of candles, I couldn't hide my face. I reached into my pocket for the money and a hanky but had no hanky, so stood there, sniffling and waiting for my change.

Outside, I found the hanky up my sleeve, wiped my eyes and blew my nose. Dempsey followed me into the post office where I bought writing paper, envelopes and stamps. I had forgotten to bring a pen from the house and so had to buy pen and ink, too. On the way back, Madge stopped by the gates of the churchyard. She whined and looked at me, her tail down but wagging, wanting to go back to where Isaac lay.

Mrs Bradley strode along the street carrying a basket of shopping. She smiled, 'If you're at a loose end and work would help, I've no objection to you taking up your duties earlier than planned.'

Madge saved me from answering as she had disappeared and I made the excuse of going to fetch her.

After Leila and I had eaten, I got her washed and brushed her teeth. She sat in her nightie by the fire with the dogs, playing with the scales and brass weights from the cupboard.

Since my hands got burned, I stroke on ointment that the doctor gave me, and draw white gloves over at night. With my white gloves on, I set myself to write letters. I could not seem to get the wording right, though, and wasted paper on the wrong way of saying things, trying to find a way to tell Wilf his father had died without saying, 'And it's your fault. And my fault, too.'

Should I ask him to tell Gladys Hardy? But of course she would know. The charity had lost its accommodation for all the poor children. Auntie Irene's committee would have to start fundraising all over again.

Even harder was to write to Mam and Dad.

As I wrote, I could picture Dad coming to fetch me, trying to drag me home. But Mam would not want the disgrace, so I added to my letter, explaining that I married in the local chapel, to make sure she would not want to try to force me to go back. I did not give them my address.

I sealed the letters and stuck on the stamps, thinking about going to post them quickly so as not to change my mind. Then I did change my mind and decided to post them from somewhere else, or not at all. Suddenly it occurred to me that I had given away too much and so I unsealed the envelopes quickly, before the glue set fast, and took the sheets out.

I put the letters on the fire.

There was a tap on the door and a familiar voice called, 'Jessica!'

Mrs Bradley opened the door before I had time to get to it. 'May I come in?'

Since she was in already she did not need an answer. I moved the envelopes as she seemed to be peering at the upside-down addresses. 'I wondered whether you'd given any more thought to what you might want to do tomorrow? I know it must be hard to be on your own all day, and perhaps you would like some task for idle hands?'

I placed my white gloved hands on the table, looking at them, as though they belonged to someone else. 'I'm not ready to start yet. My hands.'

She peeled off her own gloves and sat down at the table. 'Glad to see you're following doctor's orders. Of course, gloves won't get in the way of your working. Poor old Mrs Prentice had eczema and wore gloves as many days as not.'

Leila came to stand by me, as she often did when strangers came. She would stand and hold onto me, hiding herself a little, peeping at them.

'Hello, little Leila! Goodness me, aren't you up late?'

Leila did not answer.

Mrs Bradley tipped back her head and sniffed the air noisily. 'I think it's Madge that stinks to high heaven.'

Very slowly, because I had to be careful not to lose my temper, I said, 'I'm grateful that you've let us stay here before I've started work, but I have more letters to write, and matters to deal with – regarding the land agent and so on.'

'Of course, my dear,' She smiled and touched my arm reassuringly.

I hoped my words let her know I was not some silly young girl to be bossed around according to her whims.

She picked up her gloves. 'Only you mustn't lose your nerve for work. Work is a great healer.' She moved to go, then the flagon on the table caught her eye. 'What's that?'

'People have been very good, bringing me food and drink. I haven't needed to cook since—'

She picked up the flagon of cider, uncorked it and sniffed. 'You poor girl. How irresponsible of people! It's alcohol.'

'Cider.'

She took it to the sink and poured it down, shaking her head. 'There are people in this village who ought to know better. They know this is a chapel house.'

'I'm not chapel,' I said. 'Isaac was tee-total, but I'm not.'

'This house is.' She smiled and leaned to catch Leila's eye. 'Goodnight, you two. God bless.'

When she had gone, I lit the gas lamp and began to look at the newspaper, which old Mrs Prentice had seemed to think would be teeming with jobs.

I pushed it away when I saw it had an account of the fire and damage at the Leeds Poor Children's Holiday Camp at Silverdale.

'Come on, Leila. Let's get you to bed.'

We climbed the stairs, Dempsey running ahead of us.

'Tell me a story,' Leila said.

'What story?'

'Rumpelstiltskin.'

I told her the story of the shoemender's daughter, locked in her tower charged with turning shoelaces into gold, and Rumpelstiltskin turning up making his demands. Dancing in his sturdy boots that never scorched no matter how close to his own bonfire he danced.

'Another story.'

I told her the story of Rapunzel, trapped in another tower, who let down her long hair for her rescuer in his spiky-soled shoes to clamber up to her.

She looked worried as she reached out and touched my bobbed hair, which I had persuaded Isaac to cut for me when he wished I would let it grow. She tested the length of her own braids.

'Don't worry. We won't get trapped in a tower. If we did, we wouldn't let down our hair. We'd use a rope, or tie the sheets together and climb out. Now go to sleep, because Dempsey's tired. I'll be coming up soon.'

The newspaper article about the fire talked only of 'casualties', not a death. The paper had come out before Isaac died. I wondered if that was Mrs Prentice's real reason for giving me the paper, because here was my history now. And the following week, when the story would tell of Isaac's death, that would be my history, too. I made myself read on. Towards the end of the article, the words shocked me, and I had to read them twice, three times: 'This will be a severe blow to the children's charity, following as it does the recent sad death of the chairman of the Leeds Poor Children's Holiday Camp, Mrs William Price.'

Auntie Irene dead.

When? Wilf hadn't told me. He must have known when he came to find Isaac. I had taken it for granted that when I left Leeds, everything would go on exactly as before. I sat down beside Madge on the hearth rug. She was the only one who felt as bereft as me. The tears came from nowhere and turned into great sobs. Madge licked my hand. I lay prostrate on the rug crying my eyes out, my head on the dog's back like a pillow.

41

The Midland Grand Hotel

When I woke that first morning in a different bed, the one Mrs Prentice had slept in for fifty years, it was with the very definite thought that cleaning the chapel week in, week out for the rest of my life would not be such a good idea after all. Cleaning it once would be once too often.

All I wanted to do was Nothing. I had woken in the middle of the night from a dream where Isaac lay beside me. I reached out for him. The emptiness swelled inside me so I had the strange sensation of being in someone else's body. Every bit of myself seemed awkward and uncomfortable, not belonging. Only the hands were mine, the hands that still hurt.

I let the dogs out into the back garden while I brought in water and emptied the slop bucket. There was no calor gas in the container to light the ring. I got a fire going to boil the kettle and heat milk for Leila before she went to school. The newspaper with the account of the fire still lay on the table. Something else caught my eye. An article about the opening of the Midland Grand Hotel in Morecambe. If a hotel is grand, and that certainly was, then it would need staff. And if a manager were important, he would definitely need a secretary.

Leila was still sleeping. I sat on the bed, wondering whether to let her sleep and miss school. My two good dresses hung behind the bedroom door, my wedding dress and the long-sleeved dress that made my shoulders look big. I could not go looking for a job in November in a wedding dress worn in May, but the sleeved dress would do well enough, with the coat Isaac bought me. To look respectable, I needed a hat and gloves. Leila opened her eyes. We went downstairs so I could dress her in front of the fire.

I cut Leila a slice of bread to dip in her milk and we sat at the table. While busybodying herself emptying the flagon of cider, Mrs Bradley had left her leather gloves on the table. I would need a hat to go hunting for a job. I would also have to get to the railway station without Mrs Bradley spotting me and demanding her gloves. I slid them in my coat pocket.

Leila likes the dogs to walk her to school, but that morning we fastened them in the house. I waved to her as she went in.

Old Mrs Prentice seemed surprised to see me as she cleared her breakfast things. But I knew she had a suitable hat because she wore it to our wedding and to Isaac's funeral. She asked me in and took the hat from the hook in her little hallway.

'It's not much of a hat for someone looking as fine as you.'

Black and small, it sat on top of my head in a jaunty way and did the trick.

'Good luck,' she said, when I told her of my mission to go to Morecambe and find work. 'You're doing the right thing. And I'll say nothing to no one, but let me know if there's some way I can be of assistance.'

'If I get a job, would you be willing to take Madge in, give her a home?'

She shook her head. 'I'm not sure about that. I wouldn't be able to walk her overmuch.'

'She wouldn't mind. She's not so active as she was.'

'Well, it's against almshouse rules to have children, but there's no forbidding of animals. Bring her along. See if she takes to me.'

A fierce wind blew from the bay as I walked from Morecambe railway station towards the hotel, one hand holding the hat on my head, the other clutching my certificates in their envelope. I approached the back of the hotel. The building had not been finished when Isaac and I came to stay in Morecambe for our one-night honeymoon. Now it stood in all its grandeur, a white, curved, three-storey building with smooth lines and tower-like shapes in the centre and on either end. The central tower contained the entrance. It seemed to me more like a magical castle than a hotel, something out of a fairy tale or a film. I could imagine a modern Cinderella dashing out of that door and losing her glass slipper as she hurried towards her carriage. On the right was a circular café. I was tempted to go for a cup of tea but told myself to get on with my business and be brave. First I had to see the beauty of the whole building. I walked round past the café to the front. It was even more glorious viewed from the promenade, like some great liner ready to loose its moorings and set sail. For a few minutes I stood back to admire it, and walked along the front, still holding onto my hat. Finally, I took a deep breath and mounted the hotel steps.

I remembered the way in which salesmen had called at the Wright Shoe Company, walking with a swagger, smiling, everything about their voice and manner announcing that they were expected and welcome, even when they were not.

But I forgot my intention to swagger even just a little when I walked into the lobby. It was like stepping onto a film set. I expected Douglas Fairbanks to sweep down the grand staircase.

Treading across a huge beautiful rug with a pattern of waves, I walked to the desk and asked to see the manager.

The desk clerk was a young man, a little younger than me, his face covered in red spots. I was glad he was young, because an older person might not have been so obliging. I flashed my best smile.

'Is he expecting you?'

There are only two answers to that, and I chose the salesman's answer and said yes, and gave my name, Mrs Dennison, suddenly remembering as I did that my certificates all said Jessica Price.

He moved further along the desk, picked up a telephone and dialled a number. Putting his hand over the mouthpiece after he had spoken a few words, he said, 'Are you sure you're expected?'

'Unless there's been a mistake,' I said. 'I've come specially.'

'What is about?'

'I'm recommended for the job of . . . secretary.'

He spoke again into the phone, and then hung up.

For a moment I thought that was it and I would have to trail round Morecambe, knocking on the doors of solicitors' offices and the newspaper, and anywhere else where a female office worker might have a chance of being taken on. But the young man rang a bell and beckoned to a porter whose uniform flashed with gold.

'Come on, miss, this way.' I followed the porter past the winding staircase to the lift. He pulled back the doors for me and I stepped into the lift with its mirrored sides, decorated with seahorses. At the top floor, he opened the door and let me step out first, then led the way down a corridor.

'Mr Oliver's in there, miss.' He tapped on the door and a voice called for me to come in.

A man about Isaac's age stood up as I entered. He said good morning and shook my hand.

His age was the only thing about him that reminded me of Isaac. Where Isaac was dark-haired and weather-beaten, this man was fair, with a pale, owlish face and tortoiseshell glasses framing light-blue eyes.

'You don't have an appointment, do you, Mrs Dennison?' he asked.

I had not thought beyond my first lie, to try and see someone, and so it seemed best to speak straightly, as Isaac would have said.

'No. I read about the hotel. I saw it being built when I was in Morecambe last, and I felt sure you would need staff.' I took my certificates from the envelope and offered them to him. 'I'm qualified in office work, and I have experience.'

He looked at my certificates. 'These certificates belong to Jessica Price.'

'I'm Jessica Dennison now.'

'If you're a married lady . . .' He looked puzzled, as if I could not be a married lady and looking for a job.

'I'm a widow. I'm hard-working. I can do book-keeping, wages, shorthand, typing, anything at all to do with running a busy office.'

He opened his mouth, took a gulp of air, looked at my certificates again and back at me. He didn't believe me.

'I'm recently widowed. My husband died in a fire.'

I wanted to take off the gloves and show him my ring, but beneath Mrs Bradley's gloves I wore the white ones that protected my sore hands.

A flicker of belief came into his eys. 'The fire? It was reported in the paper?'

'Yes.'

'Further along the bay?'

'Between Arnside Knott and Silverdale.'

'I'm sorry. Isn't it too soon . . . ?'

'Not too soon for me to be turned out of our house, which goes with the farm.' This was not going how I had planned. I had not meant to reveal anything about myself.

He seemed not to know what to say next. He got up and looked out of the window towards the bay. 'What do you think of our hotel?'

'It's the most beautiful building I've ever seen.' I did not say that working there, looking at the splendour of it, walking its staircase, would be like a soothing balm to me.

He slid a shorthand pad and pencil across the desk. 'Let's try a letter.'

I took down the letter. Once you learn shorthand by rote you do not forget it. The white cotton gloves made me feel self-conscious but did not hamper me.

It is easier to take shorthand in white cotton gloves than to type wearing them. I set the shorthand pad on the desk beside me and took a sheet from the drawer. The typewriter was the same Remington I had used before but it was a long time since I had typed. I turned round to him, so he would not think I was beginning the letter straight away.

'A practice sheet,' I said, 'because this typewriter is different to the one I used before.' That would cover me if I made mistakes; a machine takes time to get used to.

I tried the practice sheet wearing my gloves. My hands hit the keys in a clumsy way, sometimes the keys locked and I had to release them.

When I rolled the letter-heading, carbon paper and copy sheet into the machine, I knew I would have to peel off my gloves. My hands still felt sore but I shut my mind against the pain as I typed, thinking only that I must have work.

I found an envelope in the drawer and typed the name and address on the envelope, then separated the top copy and the carbon. I put my white gloves back on.

I pushed the letter and envelope across the desk to Mr Oliver. He read it, signed it and was about to fold it.

'Not like that,' I said. 'It's best to fold a sheet of paper so that it exactly fits the envelope.'

I took it back, folded the paper, slid it in the envelope and returned it to him.

He thanked me. For a moment I thought he would lick it and seal it, but he left it on the desk in front of him. 'You type a perfect letter.'

'Yes, I do. Every time.'

He looked at my gloved hands. I looked past him to the view through the window.

'When can you start?' he asked.

'Next week.'

'Monday?'

'Yes, Monday.'

'I'll see you at nine o'clock. Thank you for coming in.'

'The wages?'

'Oh, yes, yes. Look, let me find out what's a fair wage round here.'

'What's fair to you might not be fair to me, sir.'

'Oh, I assure you, Mrs Dennison, it will be.'

He handed me back my certificates and walked me to the lift. I pulled on Mrs Bradley's gloves.

At the lift door, he shook my hand. 'Till Monday. I look forward to working with you. I'm sure we'll get on.'

'Thank you. I'm glad I'll be working here.'

As the lift door slammed shut, I felt that my life was about to begin again.

In the lobby I took another admiring look around. The young man at the desk called to me. He held the phone in his hand.

'Mrs Dennison! Mr Oliver wants to know, would you like accommodation in the hotel? People not from Morecambe do stay here in the staff quarters.'

Just for a second I imagined the joy of staying in such a place, but I did not think they would cater for a child and a whippet.

'No. Thank you. I'll make my own arrangements.'

First I treated myself to a cup of coffee and a bun in the café, feeling glad to be part of a brand-new world with such smart people in it. If only Isaac could see me from wherever he had gone. I hoped he could, and that be would be glad for me.

With the confidence of coffee and a bun inside me, I looked in the shop windows and asked where I might find accommodation.

The first three I tried said no. One wanted a gentleman. Another would not consider a child. The third had an aversion to dogs. Reckoning there would be just enough time to try one more address before my train back to Silverdale, I knocked on the last door on my list. The woman was a widow, Mrs Cynthia Tully. She asked me in. Her grown-up children had gone to work in the mills in Darwen. She said she would be glad to have a child and a dog in the house, to bring a bit of life back to the place. For an extra amount she would mind Leila for me and seemed obliging enough.

'We'll have space enough in the winter,' she said, showing me a large upstairs room at the front of the house. 'We might have to squeeze up in the summer, when visitors come.'

As I was leaving, she gave me a smile and said, 'Just wait till I tell my daughter in Darwen I have a young lady staying who works at the Midland Grand Hotel!'

I got outside, turned round, knocked again and left a deposit, just to be sure of her saving the room. For it occurred to me that a great many miserable people must rent out rooms in Morecambe, and there might not be so many will give you a smile and be glad to have you.

Walking back to the station, I spoke aloud to Isaac, just in case he was listening: 'We have somewhere to live, and we'll have money coming in. We'll be all right, Isaac. Don't worry about us.'

A delivery boy going by on a bike looked at me as if I must be a mad woman. And perhaps I was.

Back in Silverdale, I called and returned Mrs Prentice's lucky hat and told her my news.

'Good girl! If you've got certificates, you must make use of them. I knew you had it in you when Isaac told me a lass had turned up with a bairn, all the way from Leeds on a bike. That takes gumption, and with gumption and certificates you'll go a long way.'

When I got back to the cottage, Dempsey went mad to see me and I let him out in the garden. A note on the table told me that Mrs Bradley had called for her gloves and couldn't find them. The stupid woman had let Madge out.

Leila's teacher came out with her to speak to me, and I thought at first Leila had got herself into trouble. But she is a kind-hearted woman, in her twenties, and the children all love her. She gave me a bag of daffodil and tulip bulbs for Isaac's grave. Her friendliness made me want to tell her that Leila will be leaving soon, but I kept my own counsel and thanked her for the bulbs. She turned to go back into the school and I called her again, but couldn't think what to say.

After we had eaten and Madge had not come back, we walked down to the graveyard, taking the bulbs and a trowel from the shed. 'That's where Madge will be,' I said. 'Don't worry, we'll fetch her home.'

She was there, lying across Isaac's grave, not moving.

'Make her get up,' Leila said.

Dempsey backed away, keeping his distance.

'Come on, Madge, Madge.' Leila leaned over.

'She's dead, Leila.'

Leila's wail should have wakened every long-gone person in that churchyard. It brought the old gravedigger, his trouser bottoms tied with string above his boots, hurrying from his hidey-hole, snuffing a cigarette as he came.

'Oh, dear. Well, she's come to the right place,' he said.

'Come here, little darling.' I picked Leila up, holding and rocking her. Really she was getting too big now to be lifted, rocked and nursed.

The gravedigger realized he had not been tactful. As Leila hid her face on my shoulder, he mouthed to me from his position at the top of the grave where the headstone had not yet been placed. His lips said, 'I'll fetch a sack.'

In a moment, he came back with a sack and slid Madge into it.

'Can you bury her with Isaac?' I asked.

'Oh, no, Missis Dennison. That's more than my job's worth. I'll find a place for her, don't you worry. I'll do it now, then you can show the child where the old dog lies.' He disappeared, saying he would be back in ten minutes.

Getting dirt and clay on her hands took Leila's attention for a while. We planted the bulbs at the foot of Isaac's grave so they would not be disturbed when the headstone was put in place.

When he had dug a dog's grave on the field that edged the graveyard, the old man came to fetch us. He lowered Madge into the grave as if she had the best of coffins, then put soil in our hands to throw in after her.

'She were the most faithful dog what a man could have and now we commit her to the great dog in the sky,' he said with terrible solemnity, holding his cap at his chest.

It struck me that gravediggers do not often get chance to officiate at a funeral. After he had filled in the grave, we planted daffodils and tulips. I am almost sure Madge got more bulbs than Isaac because we could place them all across her grave as there would be no headstone to disturb our planting.

So long as I was with Isaac, I felt confident no one would take Leila from me. In Morecambe, the old anxieties returned. I was in no hurry to find a school place for her.

She took it in her stride that we had flitted yet again. Our first-floor front room had two beds as well as a dressing table and hooks for our clothes. She would be able to play safely in the garden when the weather grew warm. Cynthia Tully had an easy-going manner, and was patient enough to let Leila help her as she baked, cooked, washed and cleaned.

Every morning I walked to my job in the Midland Grand Hotel, full of delight at the place itself, and at the respect I received from other staff, being the manager's secretary. Each time I rollered a sheet of paper into my typewriter, added a column of figures, or even looked out of the window across the bay, I felt such relief at escaping the drudgery of a life cleaning the chapel.

Mr Oliver, a bachelor gentleman, meticulous in his dress habits and very proper in his dealings, was always courteous to me. Although he called me Jessica, he was not familiar in any way, which was a great relief.

One afternoon, when I knew Mr Oliver would not be coming back for the rest of the day, I knew I should not put off writing to Wilf any longer. I told him about Isaac's death as plainly and as briefly as I could. I said I was sorry that I had not known about Auntie Irene's death until I read in the paper. It upset me greatly that the camp dormitory had burned beyond repair, especially when I thought of the hard work carried out by Irene, Gladys Hardy and all the others over the years.

Every autumn and winter Isaac had kept such a careful eye on the place. It seemed too cruel that his stubble fire should burn it to the ground. With an income from my job, I did not need the money in Isaac's blue bank bag. At the post office in my dinner hour I changed the cash into a money order and asked Wilf to send it to be put towards the re-building of the camp. In the end I could not bring myself to write another letter, so asked Wilf if he would please tell them at home he had heard from me, and although I gave him my address I asked him not to pass it on. I put the money order in the envelope and felt sure Isaac would have been glad of that.

Only after I posted it did it occur to me that Wilf may not have stayed at the address I had for him – Ralph Moxon's.

That night I lay in my bed. Leila slept soundly in the opposite bed, Dempsey curled at her feet. Their breathing disturbed me. Our landlady's movements in her room disturbed me. Someone walked by outside, calling to another person across the street. Whatever way I lay, I could not get comfortable. I felt too hot and tossed the covers off. Then I felt too cold. Events spun in my mind. If only I had said something different to Wilf, before he met Isaac, so that he could have concealed his feelings more. Isaac would not have jumped to such a conclusion, that he had taken me from Wilf. Or was there something I could have said to Isaac to persuade him that wasn't so and I had no regrets? Smelling the smoke, waking up five minutes earlier, I would have got to the camp in time. In time for what, though? If I hadn't tried to stop Isaac going into the dormitory, perhaps he would have saved Wilf and himself. A minute could have made the difference.

If I had given Wilf more time to talk to me, he may have told me Irene had died. That must have upset him greatly and left him not able to hide his feelings when he discovered I had married Isaac. Now Wilf had lost the father he had only just found. My fault, again.

When I could not twist those events any further to hurt myself, or imagine a different outcome, I began to think about Mam and Dad. Here I was, concealing my whereabouts, when for all I knew they could be dead. Or have stopped caring where I was. Several different ways of keeping them off my track had come into my mind. Asking my landlady to get her daughter to post a letter from Darwen. But then I would draw other people into my deceitful web, and what if Dad got the train to Darwen and searched high and low for me, knocking on the doors of cotton mills, visiting schools to see if they had a child called Leila McBride on the register? Would they even believe that I had married and been widowed in such a short time? I had heard of women being committed to asylums for odd behaviour, and I felt sure some people would think me odd for snatching a child from the orphanage, marrying a man I hardly knew and then starting a completely new life as if I did not care one jot for the tragedies left in my path.

I tried lying on my right side, my left side and my back. Dempsey gave a great sigh from where he lay by Leila's feet, as if my tossings and turnings disturbed him excessively and made sleep difficult.

'It's all right for you, Dempsey,' I told him. 'You can sleep tomorrow while I have to work.'

He gave that little yapping sound dogs make when they are dreaming, so even he was not keeping me company in my sleeplessnes. Trying to sleep made me think of Father Flynn and his sleepwalking. I had left two dead men in Silverdale, one of them my worst enemy, the other my best friend, husband and the only man I felt I would ever truly love.

Sleep would not come. Without my wanting them, pictures came into my mind. Dad polished a pair of newly mended shoes. Mam took bread from the oven. Bernadette picked me up in the playground when I fell. Auntie Irene brought dressing-up clothes from the cupboard in her bedroom.

When I finally fell asleep, the sky outside had grown light. What seemed only moments later, Leila was jumping up and down on my bed, and downstairs Cynthia filled the kettle from the noisy tap.

My tiredness made me sick. After I had eaten my breakfast bread and dripping and taken a few sips of tea, up it all came in a great rush. Tidying myself up, I was almost late for work and had to hurry the last few yards, for I have never been late yet and did not intend to be.

That evening, after Leila had gone to bed, Cynthia made up cups of cocoa. She is very good to me, irons my blouses and has made me a costume from the good suit of a lodger who left without paying his rent.

She sighed, building up to say something.

I felt too tired to listen, because she tells me when her sons do not write, or when her daughter sends a postcard instead of a letter. But it was not about them.

'How many times have you been sick these past ten days or so?' she asked.

'A couple.'

'Not sick at work, then?'

'Once.'

'Such a shame, and you with your grand job and everything going so well.'

'What do you mean?'

She stirred the cocoa round the bottom of her cup. 'I'm guessing you've had no monthly visitor in some while.'

'No, but, the change of air and a new job and—'

'You need well put your head in your hands, lass, and you widowed.'

For a long time neither of us spoke.

'How long gone do you think you might be?'

'I don't know.' It took me a while to work out, and even then the events of the past weeks all merged into each other. 'I haven't had the curse since before the harvest supper.'

'What is doesn't always have to be.'

'What do you mean?'

'There are ways of bringing on your bleeding.'

'What ways?' I had a sudden picture of chanting spells at midnight and throwing pebbles in the sea.

'Well, for one, sitting in a hot tub with a strong drink of gin.'

'And what would that do?'

'It could bring your bleeding on. I've known women throw themselves down the stairs, but of course you don't want to break your arms or you won't be able to type. There are other ways, but if you want to try it, the hot tub and the gin would make a good start. It's worth a go, if you want to carry on with your job and earning, and looking after Leila. Don't let your cocoa go cold, you need to keep up your strength whatever you decide.'

For yet another night, I did not sleep.

42

Glass Boots and Seven-League Slippers

Cold, tired, hungry and wanting never again to stir, Wilf had fallen asleep on the hard, narrow bed in the dormitory building. A crackling sound woke him. A smell. Heat. He opened his eyes and saw that where he had pushed open a window to gain entry, the whole wall blazed, flames leaping to the ceiling. The nearest window was opposite the bed, but the curtains were alight. He'd better get to the other end, away from the fire, smoke and the noise.

But by the time he reached the centre of the building, everything behind him was on fire. Too late, he realized that the fire came from the other direction, too. He was caught, with locked doors between himself and the outside.

Someone called. He tried to make himself heard but had nothing to hold to his mouth except his arm. He thought he heard Jess. A figure caught him, pulled at him. Wilf couldn't see for smoke, couldn't get his bearings. He was pushed, half thrown into the open. Something behind him, a beam or wall, made an ominous cracking sound.

Jess embraced him, then let go. She looked past him to the figure stumbling from the blazing doorway, his coat in flames. She had a blanket around her shoulders, whipped it off and, as the screaming figure tripped and fell, Jess was by him, putting the blanket on him.

Wilf went to help. He couldn't remember now what she had said; did not want to remember.

He made his way back to the railway station. Everyone was talking about it. How did it start? Was anyone hurt? It would not have been Farmer Dennison burning stubble, never in this wide world. Did you see it? someone asked Wilf, looking at his gaunt, blackened face. He did not answer.

On the train to London, he tried not to think about the fire. Impossible. He had lost all hope of Jess.

'Moxon!' Wilf yelled up the stairs as he charged towards Ralph's studio on the top floor of the house. He pushed the door and marched in. No Ralph. Jess's portrait stood in a frame by the window, and on the window ledge sat the pebble Wilf had first seen Ralph hold in the Silverdale visitors' bungalow, a small grey pebble dotted with red markings. Wilf picked it up and put it in his pocket.

He turned the frame round and prised off the clips with his penkife; slid out the canvas, and rolled it. He met Ralph coming up the stairs.

'What's up, Wilf?'

Wilf charged at him, not knowing where to hit him, torn between wanting to keep the portrait intact or use it to do Ralph some injury. 'Bastard! Why? Why did you do it?'

'Do what?'

'You know what.' Wilf took the pebble from his pocket. 'This was the only thing on the table, was it? No letter?'

When Ralph didn't answer, Wilf grabbed him and shook him, shoved him till they were on the landing. Ralph wouldn't fight, wouldn't hit back. In exasperation, Wilf tried to thrust the pebble down Ralph's throat.

Ralph escaped, half choking, coughing out the pebble. Wilf chased after him. Ralph stopped, picked up the portrait of Jess that Wilf had dropped and held it between them as if holding a crucifix to a vampire. 'Here, then. Have it.'

Wilf grabbed the canvas. 'I didn't want the painting, I wanted her.'

Ralph didn't let go in time. The painting ripped.

It hung in Wilf's hands, torn down the middle. Wilf let it fall. He looked at Ralph with scorn. 'You loved her yourself, didn't you? But you hadn't the guts to do anything about, so you just got in my way. She wouldn't have had you in a million years.'

Wilf went downstairs and began to pack.

When he had almost finished, Ralph tapped on the door. 'Let me explain.'

Wilf was not given to swearing and cursing as a rule. But he made an exception. Ralph went away.

As he left the house, Ralph's butler appeared. 'May I be of any assistance, Mr Price?'

'Someone will come for my things.'

'And where are they to be sent, sir?'

Wilf pretended not to hear. He got on his motorbike and set off to see a painter he knew in Hampstead. That would be a reasonable distance to put between himself and Ralph Moxon.

Not until he had found a ground-floor flat and sent for his belongings did Wilf let himself think about Jess, and about Isaac Dennison. He hardly knew the man and liked him less. The fire had left such a sense of confusion and pain. Still, Wilf hoped Isaac Dennison was recovering. Who wouldn't recover with Jess waiting to take care of him? Wilf wasn't needed. She had made that clear enough. He wished he could find out how she was. How long would it take Dennison to recover, and would that affect Jess? It was bound to. The drudgery of her life did not bear thinking about.

His visit to Silverdale, and the discovery that Jess had married, removed all doubts for Wilf about where his energies would go now. He would follow his instincts and his ambition, throw himself into his work and stay there.

The book of fairy tales called *Glass Boots and Seven-League Slippers* – from Jess's title story, in which all the boots and shoes get mixed up and go to the wrong characters – had led not just to two commissions, but a lot of interest in his work. The two commissions had led to a third. This and his teaching contract made him feel confident about looking for a place where he would have the space to work outdoors in the summer months, with room for a sculptor's workshop.

Irene's legacy gave him additional funds. Although the will was not finalized, Bill had said he would advance some money.

Wilf would follow his own path, without Jess.

He visited the country house whose owner had commissioned his work. He explored the spot where his sculpture would be placed; made sketches and took measurements, developing an awareness of space and dimensions. He needed to absorb the atmosphere, and get a sense of the people who would see and, he hoped, enjoy his work. At different times of the day he visited, seeing how the light played and who inhabited the space. Each time he made new sketches.

His week followed a regular routine of teaching and working. On the weekends he polished his motorbike and rode out to different parts of the country, scouting out a place that he might be able to afford to buy. It should be near a railway line, so that he could transport his work. A quarry nearby would be a bonus. Wilf wanted a landscape with hills. Part of him ached for the Yorkshire Dales, but he needed to be near London.

Occasionally he was persuaded to a party, or a student dance, and for a while he would forget himself. He even found a girl he could talk to and kiss. But she wanted to come with him on his weekends looking for a place in the country. Once she did, but he realized her search was for a house, home and husband. *I can't*, Wilf thought. *I can't do it*. And so he went alone and left her wondering what she had done wrong.

The house Wilf found in the country had stood empty for a year. Once he signed the documents, he engaged a builder to turn an outbuilding into a studio, enlarging its windows to improve the light. The walls were to be reinforced, to allow the addition of new doors large enough for the delivery of materials and the transit of sculptures to be transported to the railway station for the journey to their final destination.

When he got back, feeling pleased with himself, riding his bike into the back yard of the Hampstead house, he saw Ralph.

Ralph sat on the back doorstep, a large painting, wrapped in brown paper, standing beside him. Wilf knew at once what it would be.

'Bugger off.'

'It's Jess,' Ralph explained. 'I painted her again.'

'I don't care.'

Ralph continued as though Wilf had not spoken. 'I wouldn't call her beautiful, not entirely. She's striking. Once in a generation there are a tiny number of young people, female and male, who have what I call The Look. She captures whatever it is, the right feel, for the time we live in. It's the cheekbones, the profile, the swing of her hair.'

'I've lost her, Ralph, thanks to you. I don't need her picture to remind me of that.'

'She's written you a letter. I should have brought it sooner but I thought you might get violent again. I didn't love her. You were wrong about that.'

'What then?'

'It's starting to rain. I spent a long time on this portrait. Give it to her if you don't want it, or to her family.'

Wilf did not ask Ralph in but did not shut the door in his face either. They walked into the kitchen. Ralph set the painting, still in its brown paper, by the dresser. He handed Wilf Jess's letter. Wilf could not read it with Ralph in the room.

'How long were you waiting outside?'

'I don't know. I decided not to go without seeing you.'

'Why? Why did you come between us if you didn't want Jess for yourself?'

Ralph shrugged. 'Look what you've achieved in such a short time. There'll be no stopping you, Wilf. I knew that from the first day we met, when you showed me your work. Some of us are good, but you're better than good.'

'That's not a reason.'

'She would have stood in your way. Do you think with a wife and child you'd have come this far this quick?'

'It's thanks to Jess's fairy tale book—'

'No. If you did the kinds of things Jess inspired – giants' shoes and fairy slippers – do you think you'd be on the verge of building an international reputation?'

'It was up to me to know whether Jess would be good for me. Not you. You'd no right to interfere.'

Ralph pulled out his cigarette holder and slid a cigarette into it. He offered the case to Wilf, then lit their cigarettes. 'When I was a boy, I chummed up with a young chap my age. He was the head keeper's son on our estate. The smartest boy you could imagine. Naturally clever, you know? Full of promise. I came back from prep school to find he'd been shipped out to labour in Australia. He deserved better, Wilf. It made me value talent when I see it.'

'What happened to him?'

Ralph shook his head. 'No one would tell me. Not a good

friendship, you see, not the right sort of thing at all for a boy of my class and background.'

He took the stub of his cigarette from its holder, threw it into the fire grate and got up to leave.

'Thanks for bringing the letter.'

'Don't mench.'

Through the window, Wilf watched Ralph open his umbrella and then the gate.

Wilf ripped the brown paper from the portrait, to see Jess again. After he had looked at her for a long time, he opened her letter.

43

Blooming in Morecambe

A tall Christmas tree stood in the Midland Grand Hotel lobby, tastefully decorated with silver trimmings, blocking Wilf's view of the large Portland Stone relief carved by Eric Gill. It showed Odysseus being welcomed from the sea by Nausicaa. *Why didn't I get that commission?* Wilf thought with a pang of envy. *If they'd waited another five or ten years to build this hotel, perhaps my work would have sealed its style.* Gill had also designed the circular ceiling panel over the spiral staircase. His sea god Triton was gloriously painted – by Gill's son-in-law, if Wilf remembered rightly.

Now that he was here, directed by Jess's landlady, Wilf felt reluctant to ask for her. He wandered the lobby, hoping she would materialize, sweeping down the stairs or stepping from the lift.

He went outside again, examining at close quarters the Eric Gill seahorses that were said to look like Morecambe Bay shrimps. A sharp breeze blew sand from the beach. Wilf took refuge in the rotunda café at the north end of the hotel, superbly decorated. He wondered how the afternoon Christmas shoppers could bear to sit comparing purchases when the walls rivalled an art gallery in their depiction of seaside scenes. The astonishing mural, everything about this building, made him think Jess was fortunate to have found herself here. He remembered what Ralph had said, that she had The Look, the modern look. Now she had a setting that fitted her perfectly.

Suddenly his journey seemed pointless. He was not even sure why he had come. Only because he did not know how to write to her.

But even less did he have any idea what to say. What an idiot he would feel if he sat in the café, or hung about in the front lobby, while she left by the back door.

An idea came to Wilf. He returned to the entrance lobby, to the main desk, and booked himself a room. Now he felt legitimate. Signing the register he said, as casually as he could, to the young man with the fiery spots on his cheeks and chin, 'Would it be possible to speak to Mrs Dennison?'

'I'm not sure, sir.'

'Could you tell her it's Wilf Price? Of course, if it's inconvenient, I'll wait until she's ready to leave for the day.'

'If you take a seat, sir, I'll see if she's in.'

The clerk waited until Wilf was out of earshot. Wilf watched him pick up the phone and knew he was speaking to Jess.

Moments later, Wilf turned, knowing she was there even before she began to make her way down the stairs.

She looked blooming, in a soft sweater and dark skirt. Her hand lightly touching the bannister, she came closer. He went to meet her at the bottom of the stairs, such a public place. Yet he had to make some gesture, and took her hand.

She thought about smiling, and said his name. He sensed a wariness.

'You look so well, Jess. Morecambe must suit you.'

'Yes.'

'I didn't mean to interrupt your work. What time do you finish?'

'I could finish at five today.'

'Will you have a meal with me? I'm staying at the hotel.'

'On business?'

'Yes. I'm here to ... I wanted to see the place, and Eric Gill's work, of course. See what other sculptors are up to. I have a couple of commissions myself.'

'My landlady cooks me a meal, and there's Leila.'

Someone passed by and nodded to Jess. Wilf knew she did not want to stay by the staircase chatting to him.

'Why don't I walk you back to your digs, and see Leila again?'

'All right.'

'Don't let me keep you from work. I'll see you at five. I'll be sitting over there admiring the scenery.'

'Meet me at the rear entrance. Five o'clock.'

Wilf splashed his face and glanced at his reflection in the ornate mirror in the men's room. Before meeting Isaac Dennison, Wilf could look at his own shock of black hair and think of no one but himself. Now something intangible seemed to cloud and swell around him, as if he might be caught in a net, waiting to be scooped out of this unfamiliar element in order to become himself again. The man who had passed on some of his looks, his colouring, his way of spreading his fingers as he talked, had met the most dreadful, lingering death Wilf could imagine. Wilf shuddered.

A few minutes before five, he went out of the hotel's front door and walked round to the back where he stood in the grounds watching the rear door, unsure whether Jess wanted to keep their meeting from prying hotel staff eyes.

She fell into step with him, walking back towards her digs.

'Jess, we won't be able to talk there. There are things I need to ask you, and to tell you.'

'Let's walk, then.'

'Where?'

'Anywhere.' She seemed impatient to be away from the hotel. 'Let's walk the streets up away from the promenade, out of the wind.'

'I want to be able to look at you when we talk.'

'You want, you want. Too bad, Wilf. There were things I wanted you never did. I wanted you to marry me and help me take care of Leila, and I'm glad you wouldn't because I found a man I loved.'

'I wasn't the one who said no. You did. You didn't want to spoil my chances, risk my losing the bursary.'

'And who was the one who could have said to hell with the bursary? But you didn't.'

'I did!'

'And you really and truly meant it?' she said fiercely. 'That's why we parted. And when you came across me in the outbuilding, getting the fish ready for market, I asked you to go away, but you wouldn't. Oh, no, not you. You always have to jump in and do what you think.'

'Oh, really, do I? Not like you, then. Not like abducting a child and making off with her and leaving everyone worried sick.'

'And you conveniently didn't find my note in the bungalow.'

'Only because Ralph saw it first. I half-killed him when I found out.'

'That I believe. Because if you hadn't come sticking your nose in, Isaac would still be alive.'

Wilf grabbed her arm and pulled her off balance halfway along a street of terraced houses. Through open curtains gas lights were lit and fires glowed.

'Do you think I don't know that?'

She waited until he let go of her arm. 'It wasn't your fault. It was mine. He knew I was holding something back. He thought you and I still loved each other. Not true so far as I'm concerned, but I didn't make him believe me.'

Wilf leaned against a house wall. Inside the house, someone closed curtains. The pool of light disappeared from the pavement by his feet.

'I killed him,' Wilf said softly.

'No.'

'Poor Isaac. Poor Jess. Let me hold you.'

She pushed him away. 'Don't touch me. Don't ever touch me.'

He hadn't noticed until then that it had started to rain. 'Let me walk you back.'

'No. I can find my own way. Go back to the hotel. You probably didn't see all of the Eric Gill sculptures. There's more in the children's room. That's why you've come, isn't it, for your work?'

'Which way do we go?'

Jess paused. 'I don't know. I still don't know my way about properly.'

'Well, Morecambe's not that big a place.'

'You find the way then, big city boy.'

They retraced their steps back to the hotel.

'Now, let me walk you back, Jess. Let me see this amazing child that you had to love more than you loved any of the rest of us.'

Jess seemed to grow tense beside him. 'Have they told you to try and take us back?'

'No. I haven't told anyone where you are. You asked me not to. What are you afraid of? You've got a job, a place to live, someone to take care of the child.'

'You don't know, Wilf. You're a man. People think they have to make sure women don't think for themselves, act for themselves. Parents. Priests. They don't give up on a girl that easily.'

'I never thought of that.'

'There's no reason why you should. Just because I'm a widow, that won't make any difference. What would a chapel wedding count for out of ten for Catholics?'

They had reached the street where she lived.

'I didn't come to see the Grand Midland Hotel. I came to see you. I was worried about you.'

'There's no need. You can see how I'm doing.'

'And to tell you about our book. It was published. There's some income for you when you want it, royalties. But I expect Isaac left you well provided for if you were able to send me a money order for the charity.'

A child smiled through the window, a little elf with black curly hair like a gypsy girl.

Jess opened the door. 'You'd better come in.'

In the hallway, the child ran to Jess to be picked up, twirled, kissed and receive a hotel biscuit from Jess's pocket.

Mrs Tully had prepared a meal of sausage, mash, peas and thick onion gravy. They sat at the table by the warm fire and tucked in. It was a long time since Wilf had enjoyed a meal as much as this one. With the landlady and the child, the tension between Jess and himself seemed to lessen. She smiled more, and asked Wilf about the book. He said he had meant to bring a copy but had left it at the hotel. Jess wanted to see his drawings again, and how they looked in print.

'So you'll both be rich, then?' Mrs Tully asked.

Wilf said that there had not been much money yet, but what there was would come to Jess because it had led to commissions for him, and that was reward enough.

He told them about the cottage he was buying, and what a good place it would be to work outdoors in the summer months.

When Cynthia Tully produced an apple pie, and Leila clapped her hands, Wilf realized that perhaps they were eating more than they normally would on a week night.

'Do you have other guests here?' he asked.

'Not in the winter.' The landlady seemed cheerful about her lack of lodgers. Wilf wished he had asked for a room from her instead of making his great gesture of booking in at the Midland Grand. If he had not asked for Jess at the time he made his booking, he would have cancelled. But then staff might have said that the manager's secretary had unreliable friends who booked a room and then scarpered.

'Of course, I have my regulars,' Mrs Tully said, 'especially from Darwen, in the summer.'

Leila followed the conversation, looking from one of them to the other, listening to every word. She started to speak, holding her spoon on end as if it would help her get her words out.

'In summer I have a baby brother.'

Silence.

Wilf looked at Jess. She picked up a blue jug and poured evaporated milk on Leila's apple pie.

Mrs Tully passed the jug along to Wilf saying cheerfully, 'Well, we'll have to see what summer brings.'

'Weren't you going to tell me, Jess?' Wilf asked.

'I did think of climbing on the rooftop and shouting about it, but I changed my mind.'

'This cottage you're buying,' Mrs Tully seemed to be changing the subject, 'will you be living there all on your own, then?'

'Not if Jess will come. And Leila.' Wilf hadn't meant to say it.

'Wilf, don't be ridiculous.'

He leaned across, took Leila's spoon from her and scooped a small piece of pie for her. 'Jess, I'm not used to living in the middle of nowhere. You could give me a few tips.'

'I don't want to move again.'

Mrs Tully concentrated on her pie.

Wilf took a spoonful of pie and paused with his spoon resting on the dish. 'How about if I come back in the late spring, when the house should be ready, and see how you're getting on?'

44

Motorcycling

The house on the side of the hill suited Wilf. Workmen had re-plastered the interior. He would give it a few months to dry properly, and then do something to the walls – decide whether to leave them plain, or to create some extraordinary mural that would bring the world of nature into the cottage.

He rose early, while a May mist hung over the valley concealing the hamlet and the village beyond. All the day long he worked on his sculpture for the Rutland country house, chiselling and shaping, working from his model, stopping to take measurements and to get the sense of the stone. So far he had not come across a fault in the material that would force him to adapt and change. From time to time he would stand back from the work. The hill rising behind and falling below allowed him to imagine it placed in the grounds, where children might climb through its centre, or jump from the stumpy shape on its side. On fine days, Dempsey came to watch, patiently, uncritically. Wilf maintained the dog had been a patron of the arts in a previous life. Jess said Dempsey simply wanted male company.

Sometimes he caught Leila looking at the sculpture, but she kept her distance, near the house, religiously feeding the hens that Jess had insisted on having so that Leila would have an egg each day. They ate a lot of eggs.

One day, when the stone did not want to be carved and rain trickled down Wilf's hair onto the back of his neck, he went into the outbuilding where wood had been delivered from the local timber yard. He carved a seat for Leila, in the shape of a boot, based on one of his illustrations from the book.

In the middle of the day he would go in for lunch, usually eggs, cooked by Jess. He had persuaded her to come here when she was seven months pregnant and could no longer hide her condition at work.

Never had she looked more radiantly beautiful, or seemed more distant. Her hair gleamed, her skin glowed and her eyes sparkled. Wilf's sketchbooks were full of her, sometimes alone and sometimes with Leila beside her.

They did not talk about his work, but each evening, after Leila had gone to bed, Jess would stroll up the path across their acre of land and walk a wide circle around it.

'It's grand, Wilf. I don't want them to have it in Rutland.'

'I'll make us something else,' he would say.

One such night, when they got back indoors and closed the door, he said, 'Can I hold you, just hold you?'

She stood very still, like a sculpture herself, not moving. He let her go, and away flew the thought of asking if she would share his bed.

One night he heard her crying and went across the landing. He stood by the door but did not go in. The next day he said, 'What's the matter, Jess?'

'I dreamed of Isaac. He came into the room and climbed into bed with me. He was as real as you are now, more real.'

Without asking, he took her in his arms and held her close, the huge bump in her belly pressing against him. She put her head on his shoulder and he stroked her hair, her neck and shoulders. For a moment she sighed as if some spell had been broken and she would be his again. But she quickly drew away.

As he pulled on his big sweater and boots to march across to his work, Wilf wondered how men lived if they did not have some task like his own, something that would take every ounce of attention and devotion, that you would never properly master.

It was arranged that before Jess went into the cottage hospital, the daughter from the nearby farm would come, get to know Leila, and what to do and how to look after Leila and Wilf while Jess was away. Though Wilf said he could look after himself.

The girl came each morning, a big bouncing young woman with braided hair tied in loops. While Jess rested on the battered chaise longue, Ann swept and washed the floor, fussed over Leila, took her outside and tried to teach her to skip. As Wilf worked, he could hear them laughing and turned to watch. For a moment, he wished he could find a big country lass, for whom love and sex would be no more complicated than skipping in a rope, who would climb into his bed and never tire the night long, as mad for sex as he imagined he might be himself given half a chance. It was one thing to be devoted to his art, and another to live halfway up this hillside, like a monk.

Jess wrote to her parents, to Bernadette, to Bill and to Gladys Hardy. She did not tell Wilf what she said, and he did not ask the details.

He took the letters and walked with Dempsey to the post box in the hamlet, buying tobacco and a newspaper while he was there, and a book for Jess, though he did not know what she wanted. Anything, she had said, a detective story. On his way back along the lane he met Ann.

'I would have taken the letters for you, Mr Price,' she said, giving him what he thought was a teasing look. 'You only have to ask.'

'I needed the exercise,' he said.

She looked as if she might speak again, but he hurried on.

Jess stood by the back window, watching him approach the house. She looked enormous and said she could not get comfortable, but stayed where she was when he reached for his sketch book to draw her. He drew her again as she stretched on the chaise longue reading *The Hound of the Baskervilles*.

'Jess?'

'Mmm?'

'What makes you think the baby will be a boy?'

'I don't know. Perhaps because Isaac wanted a son, to take over the farm. And to look after me in my old age.'

'He must have been a very kind man. I'm sorry I didn't get to know him.'

'You're a kind man, too, Wilf.'

'Rubbish. Not every sculptor can find a pregnant unpaid model. I'll probably get a Madonna and child out of you as well.'

'You did once say I was your muse.'

'I used to talk a lot of nonsense.'

Jess let Sherlock Holmes slide to the floor. 'What were you saying to Ann, on the lane?'

'Nothing. She said she would have posted the letters, that's all.'
He changed the subject quickly. 'What made you decide to write to them all now?'

'To make my peace. Women die in childbirth. I read the figures in Isaac's medical book. Good thing I can't remember the numbers.'

'You're not going to die.'

Jess laughed. 'You might be an artist and a great creator, Wilf, but even you don't have the power to hold up your hand and say halt to the Grim Reaper.'

'Jess, don't let the baby hear you say that.'

'That's not the only reason I wrote. I woke up one morning thinking Mam or Bernadette might want to rush here to help me. Some hope.'

As he lay awake that night, Wilf guessed what must be worrying Jess. He tiptoed across the landing.

'Jess? Are you awake?'

'Yes.'

'Can I come in?' He pushed the door open. It was too dark to see her.

'I'm too uncomfortable to sleep. I can't get in the right position.'

He followed her voice and felt for the bed, sitting on the edge. 'Don't worry about a thing. I'm sure you'll sail through this. In another couple of weeks you'll be nursing the new baby.'

'Can't be soon enough for me. I'm fed up of waiting.'

'The minute you say, we'll be on our way to the hospital. I'm not leaving you alone till then, not even to post a letter.'

'Thanks, Wilf.'

He went back to his room and wondered whether what she had wanted was some other kind of reassurance, given her fears of not pulling through. What if he was left to look after Leila and a baby? How would he possibly do it? Marry the bouncing Ann, who would be sure to lactate for the infant at the swish of some mysterious herb across her ample nipples. He could have his way with her every July and August and leave her to bounce in the cottage while he escaped back to London for the rest of the year.

Why had Jess reminded him that women die in childbirth? He wanted to sleep, and couldn't, not until the sky grew light.

He washed in cold water, took Jess a cup of tea and went to work. After he had chiselled and smoothed for a couple of hours, with no thought of the piece ever coming to an end, the sculpture took him by surprise. *I'm almost finished*, it said. *You can stop.* Sure enough, as he walked round it, looking at it from every angle, running his hands over its curves that slid into flatness then rose again, he could find nothing else that needed to be done.

Through the space in the centre of the piece, he saw Leila and Dempsey ambling towards him.

Leila climbed on the sculpture, through it and round it.

'Do you like it?' Wilf asked. 'It's finished.'

'Will you make me a swing? Uncle Isaac pushed me on the swing.'

Jess came to inspect the piece. 'I'll be sorry to say goodbye to it.'

He was not sure whether she was talking about when it would go, or when she would.

That night, Wilf slept soundly, knowing his work was done. It only remained to have the piece transported and set in place, which he would oversee himself. In his dream, he watched the sculpture slide into its setting. His dream-self took on the dimension of a giant, for he placed it without help from anyone.

'Wilf!' He woke to the sound of Jess calling his name.

She stood on the landing, fully dressed, a bag beside her. 'It's time.'

'Are you sure?'

'Yes.'

'Right. Give me one minute.'

Wilf pulled on his shirt and trousers, fastening his belt as he hurried back to the landing. 'Hold on, let me help you.'

He walked backwards down the stairs, holding her hands.

'Wilf! I can manage.'

But he would not let go. He manoeuvred Jess to the chaise longue. 'Sit there, Jess.'

'Did you borrow the pony and trap like you said?'

'I've done better than a pony and trap. Don't you worry.'

Wilf pulled on his boots. He ran to the outbuilding, ready for this moment. He wheeled the Scott Squirrel motorbike – with its newly welded sidecar – to the front of the house and flung open the door.

He came back in and took her arm. 'Can you manage? This is my surprise.'

Jess looked at the sidecar. 'In that? Wilf, I won't fit.'

Wilf looked at her and at the sidecar. 'What shall I do?'

'You said you had it all under control. You're supposed to know about dimensions.'

'All right. Don't panic. I'll cycle there and fetch the doctor back.'

'Don't leave me. Hitch me on the back of the bike, Wilf,' Jess ordered.

'I can't do that.'

'Yes, you can. And put Leila in the sidecar. She'll be terrified if she wakes up in an empty house. Hurry!'

Wilf ran upstairs, picked up the sleeping, wriggling Leila, and carried her to the sidecar, putting Jess's bag in beside her.

'Come on, Jess. Let's get you on.'

She stepped gingerly towards the motorbike. 'I can't. I can't heave myself across.'

'I'll help you.'

'I daren't open my legs, Wilf. I'm sure the baby's going to come any minute.'

'Sit side-saddle then.'

'Are you mad? I'll fall off. I'll tip the bike.'

'If you have to lean, lean away from the sidecar. I'ts no distance, Jess. We can do it.'

'Help me astride the pillion seat. I'll just have to hold on.'

Wilf helped her. He then mounted his seat as carefully as possible, trying not to touch Jess. 'Hang on to me.'

'I can't. My bump is in the way.'

He undid his trouser belt, put it round his waist with the ends in Jess's direction. 'Take hold. How's that?'

'It'll do.'

'Hold tight!' He kicked the engine into life.

She leaned into him, pulling on the belt. 'Just go steady, steady as you can.'

'Sorry, sorry, sorry!' Wilf called every time he bumped across a rock or pothole.

There were three steps up to the nursing home. Wilf asked Jess if she could manage them, but she would not speak, keeping her lips closed, as if any excessive movement would bring on the baby.

The night porter took one look at her and hurried for a trolley. Soon, Wilf watched her being wheeled away, her lips still tightly shut. She raised a hand to him.

He would have fallen asleep with Leila beside him on the bench in the waiting area, but a no-nonsense ward sister told him to go home, let the poor child get her rest, and come back tomorrow.

Back at the cottage, he carried Leila to her bed, then went to his own. Not expecting to sleep, he did – and soundly.

45

The Visitor

Wilf brought my letters to the cottage hospital. Only one person wrote to me. Since he does not go in much for writing letters unless another person types them, perhaps it was not surprising that I did not hear from Uncle Bill. Maybe Mam and Dad did not know what to say to me, or had cut me off. I thought Bernadette would have taken the trouble to answer but she did not.

The only reply came from Gladys Hardy. She had a holiday due and proposed to visit me and Wilf. Feeling done in after the birth, I asked Wilf if he would write to her and tell her about the baby. In my thoughts, I called him Isaac, but had not yet named him.

Wilf called the baby Little Fellow, just because I could not make up my mind. He said that it was nothing against Isaac Dennison, but Isaac would be a difficult name to hang around a little fellow's neck. Isaac was the character in the Bible willing to sacrifice his own son. He thought the name old-fashioned, not at all suitable to give to a 1930s boy who would become an adult in the second half of the twentieth century. We tried out so many names. If Mam and Dad had written back to me, I would have called him Paul after Dad, with no hesitation. If Bill had replied, I might have called him William.

'He should have a name all his own,' Wilf said. 'Don't call him after anyone.'

Wilf brought Leila to see us. I asked her what names she liked for a boy. In the school at Silverdale, she grew fond of a child called

Jimmy. So we named him James. When the registrar came round, I gave him that name, with Isaac as a middle name.

Two weeks seemed a long time for them to keep me in the little hospital. I only saw the baby when they brought him to feed, so could do and think nothing for hours and hours on end. No need to pay anyone attention – Leila, Wilf and his sculpture, Ann and her cleaning and busying about, even Dempsey when he would jump to sit with me and crush my cramped legs. Only the nurses' activities marked the passing of days. The doctor prescribed a glass of water every morning, which sat overnight with a slice of lemon in it. Each day began with the lemony water.

Never in my life had I spent so much time doing nothing but looking out of the window, into a garden full of roses. I strolled the corridor to where the babies lay, in a row, only to be told off for stirring too soon. I watched nurses busy with their routines, read magazines passed on by other mothers, and marvelled at the cleverness of Sherlock Holmes.

And never did I have so much time to wish things could be different; that Isaac would be alive to see our baby. I pictured myself back in the farmhouse, the two of us choosing a name together. In Morecambe Bay it would not have mattered if a name seemed too old-fashioned for the twentieth century. What mattered there stayed the same, decade after decade. Seed time and the harvest, heat and cold, time lived by sunrise and sunset, the change of seasons and the bringing in of the catch from the sea. Thinking of what I had lost made it hard for me to imagine a future, a future built on shifting sands.

By the time Wilf came to collect us, I was able to squeeze into the sidecar with baby James, and this time our journey felt stately. The July sun shone for our return to the cottage. I kept the sidecar hood attached all the same, to protect the little fellow from any breeze or blowing of dust from the fields. When we reached our gate, Wilf stopped the motorcycle, peeled down the hood and told me to look as we drove back through our one acre of ground to the cottage.

His sculpture for the country house was gone. But all around me were extraordinary creations in wood and stone – boots of different sizes, single and alone, two giant red shoes, a spindly pair of heeled slippers carved from what looked like marble, a Puss in Boots, and a great shoe that contained an old woman, with little heads peeping up around her. It was like riding through fairyland. 'Look, Jimmy,' I said to the baby, but he kept his eyes tightly shut, not at all ready to pay heed to his amazing surroundings.

'Have you done all these since I went in?'

Wilf laughed. 'No! I've been working on them for ages. They were in the workshop, hidden.'

Leila rushed out to meet us. Behind her stood Gladys Hardy, still wearing her old, much-mended boots, a shawl around her shoulders. She took the baby from me so I could climb out of the sidecar.

Leila wanted Jimmy to wake, but he only screwed up his face in his sleep as Gladys placed him in the cradle. When she looked up she said, 'It's been a long time since I held such a young baby.' She took something from her pocket, an envelope. 'Wilf, I wrote this to you, on the day I gave you up. It's a poem, and if I don't give it to you today, I'm not sure I ever will.'

Wilf took the envelope, and went outside with it to his workshop.

'I can't imagine having to give up my baby, Gladys. It must have been terrible.'

'It was. It would have been worse, except that I knew where he was going – to Irene and Bill Price. And over the years the regrets seem to get smaller. Except one Mothering Sunday, when I woke from a dream. Children were bringing me flowers, and I woke with my heart breaking. After that it was never quite so bad.'

She made me cry. I couldn't help it, just roared my eyes out. Then Gladys started to cry, and so did Leila. When Wilf came back, he looked ready to fall to pieces. He didn't say much, just kissed Gladys on the cheek.

Fortunately Jimmy woke up at that moment, demanding to be fed. Leila watched for a few minutes then bullied Gladys into going out to play with her on Wilf's sculptures.

'It's good to have you home.' Wilf said. His sketch book and pencil sat on the table near to hand, but I was glad he didn't pick it up to draw us.

Later Gladys gave me news of the family. Dad still mends her shoes. Mam went into St James's for a hernia operation, which proved successful. Bernadette is expecting another baby.

'Why don't they write to me?'

'These things fester in families. Animosities go on for years. People behave as if they have forever.'

'But I wrote to all of them.'

'They'll come round. Give them time.'

'How much time?'

46

Stepping Stones

That part of the country was still strange to both of us. When Gladys said she would take care of the children, we had a chance to explore. I left some of my milk to be given to baby Jimmy and we slipped away, telling Leila she must mind her Auntie Gladys and be good for her and Ann.

I was glad to sit in the sidecar. After giving birth, straddling a motorbike seemed something I would never want to do again. We explored the countryside a little, Wilf driving all the way across a bumpy lane to a huge tithe barn. Walking its length was like wandering around a great deserted railway station or a scooped-out cathedral. Wilf pointed out how the builders, unable to read or write, had left their mark on certain stones, to show where they had finished a day's work, so it could be reckoned how much pay must come to them. It seemed amazing to me that such a magnificent place, built to last a thousand years, could be created by illiterate people. Wilf said the craftsmen didn't need to read and write to know what they were about. Now that he has two days' teaching a week at his college in London, he would like to bring his students to look at the grandeur of such a barn, as glorious in its way as a fine church.

The riverbank nearby was overgrown with nettles so we walked a little further on, to a spot where stepping stones led across the water. I used to leap across stepping stones and perhaps would do so again, but that day we went gingerly, Wilf not wanting me even to try, but a river is there to be crossed if there's a way.

He went first and turned back to me holding out his hand, but I would not take it. It is feet that matter when finding your way across stones, and I had taken off my shoes and stockings. On the other side Wilf placed the cushion for me, so I could sit comfortably and stretch out my legs, with a boulder as a backrest and Wilf's sweater folded behind me.

While I watched him leap back across the river, to fetch our picnic, his shadow long across the stepping stones, the most awful pains shot through me like blades in my stomach. The agony made me turn cold and start to sweat. He came back, carrying our picnic bag, then rushed to me, saying, 'Whats wrong?'

'Something's happened to me, to my insides.'

He sat beside me, put his arm around me. I could feel the sweat running down my face, my body hot and clammy. The blades in my stomach stabbed and churned, making me feel sick. I raised my knees, to try and ease the pain, but nothing helped.

'I'm going to die, Wilf. What a place to die.' And even as I thought it, I knew there would be worse places to die than sitting by a river, listening to its water-music, seeing a white cloud move across the sky, and Wilf there.

'You're not going to die. You'll be all right.' He put his arm around me.

'The children. Wilf, the children.'

'I'll take care of them.'

'You won't be able to, not on your own. You've your work.'

'Jess, you're going to be all right.' He placed his hand on my stomach. 'Don't scrunch up. Breathe. Take it easy.'

I knew this would be the end. No one could have such pain unless something terrible had happened inside. Why couldn't it have happened in hospital? I thought. Someone could have helped me more.

'Gladys. She'll help you look after the children. Don't marry anyone who won't love them.'

'Jess. Shhh. Stop. Let me get you back to the sidecar. We'll find a doctor.'

'I can't move. Just let me sit.'

'I can carry you.'

'No.'

The birds must have been singing all the while, but they seemed to get so noisy, as if they sounded an alarm.

He wiped the sweat from my brow. Cupping his hands in the river, he brought me water. I tilted my head back and some trickled onto my mouth but most was lost, dropping through his fingers onto my throat and the front of my dress.

He stroked the back of my hand, rubbed my palm with his thumb, rubbed each of my fingers, my arm, then my other hand and arm. Lifting my foot, he massaged each toe, the ball of my foot, the sole, my heel and my ankle. I knew he was trying to take my mind off the pain but the stabbing went on and made me double up.

I felt suddenly cold. 'Hold me, Wilf.'

He edged down beside me, put his arm around me.

'Tell me how you'll look after the children. Don't let them go into an orphanage.'

'Jess, you'll look after them, we'll do it together.'

'Don't marry anyone who won't care, not that girl with the dark hair.'

'I don't know who you're talking about.'

'Yes, you do. She was at your second-year exhibition. You were laughing together.'

'I can't even remember her name.'

'Promise me . . .'

'I won't let you down.'

Later Wilf said he knew, from how the sun moved and the shadows shifted, that we sat for about an hour. The agony passed. Whatever moved around inside me, stabbing and churning, just stopped.

He didn't let go of me for a long time.

'I'm all right now,' I said.

He stroked my hands. 'Feet and hands are so hard for some artists, Jess. If you look at William Blake's work, he makes a right mess of them.'

He made me smile because saying 'a right mess' makes him sound so young. He has spent the last three years having the edge polished off his way of speaking.

When he uncorked the cold tea, I took a drink but did not want to eat.

'You must,' Wilf said. 'Keep your strength up. Shall I take you to the doctor?'

'No. If I go home and rest, I think I'll be all right now. It's passed.'

'You scared me, Jess. I thought I was going to lose you.'

'I scared myself.'

When we got back to the cottage, I went to bed to lie down, just for half an hour, but fell asleep for ages.

Gladys brought me soup. 'Wilf said you had a bad turn.'

'I'm over it now.'

Wilf brought Jimmy and sat with me while I fed him. From the window I could see the tops of the trees along the lane, and the sky darkening a little. There was none of the wind and wildness of Morecambe Bay. Propped against the pillows, I felt so peaceful. And, after my fears of dying, relieved and surprised to be alive.

'Jess, I'll need to go to London soon. I don't want to leave you.'

'I'll be all right.'

'This is no place for you to be on your own with two little ones. When you said you'd stay here through the winter, I didn't want to upset you by disagreeing. But it's not a good idea.'

'There's the money from our book, that'll see us through the winter. Ann will come over to help.'

'I'd worry about you.'

'Wilf, I can't start finding somewhere else to live.'

'Come back to London with me, not tomorrow but in September when I start my teaching.'

'We'll be in your way.'

'Don't say that. Not after today. That was the most unnerving picnic of my life.'

I meant to say something about it, but instead I said, 'Isaac proposed to me on a picnic. In Eaves Wood.'

Wilf's jaw snapped shut, as tightly as a poacher's trap.

He went away without speaking again. When he came back, he carried a shoe box.

'I sent for a present for you. It was meant to be a coming-out-of-hospital gift but took a while to arrive.'

He handed me the box. It was a pair of red shoes, of soft calfskin leather.

'To step into your future, Jess. Whatever it is.'

'Thank you.'

But he had turned and left.

I put Jimmy in his cot and tried on the shoes. Something touched my toe in the right shoe. A sixpence, for luck.

47

Assemblage

On the day after Wilf took Gladys Hardy to the station for her journey back to Leeds, he bumped back across the same road to meet the art gallery assistant who was coming to photograph his work.

The person who strode down the platform was not Oscar's assistant, but Ralph Moxon.

'What are you doing here?'

'That's a fine welcome for a fellow artist. Oscar's protégé took sick. I volunteered to step in. Don't worry, I'm very handy with a Box Brownie. Oscar just needs to see what you've been up to.'

'Just let's get one thing clear: Jess is with me, and Leila and baby Jimmy. If you dare say one word out of place—'

'As if I would. I hold Jess in high regard.'

'You'd better.'

'Exhilarating!' Ralph cried uncertainly from his pillion seat as they rounded a bend on the country lane, and, 'Slow down!' as Wilf drove across the last acre towards the cottage.

Ralph's eyes were fixed on the sculptures dotted around the field, the slippers and boots, the old woman who lived in a shoe. He leaped off the bike before it came to a halt. Wilf walked him round the sculptures.

'Amazing, Wilf, but not what I'd come to expect from you.' After walking three times round the sculptures and viewing them from every angle, he whipped his Box Brownie from a capacious inside pocket. 'I was at the gallery yesterday. Oscar said you'd told him you only had one piece down here to show him.'

'These aren't for sale. They're for Jess. Come and see her. You'll have time for picture-taking later.'

'Quick peep at your workshop first, Wilf. I'm dying to see it.'

But Wilf caught a glimpse of Jess taking a cake from the window sill where it had stood to cool covered by a white cloth.

'Time for that later.' He wheeled his bike down the path, Ralph keeping pace, admiring the view, asking about his working schedule. 'I don't suppose it's easy, with your adopted family waiting in the wings.'

'It's like this.' Wilf brought the bike to a stop. 'I go out of the house in the morning and into my studio, and I stay there until the end of the day. Like any man who goes out to work.' He threw open the door. 'Come and see Jess.'

Jess wore a pale-blue blouse, and a skirt made for her by Mrs Tully in Morecambe. She sat at the table, urging Leila to be patient. They would cut the cake soon.

Ralph strode in, talking over her surprise, speaking in his heartiest, jolly voice, shaking hands with her. He patted Leila on the head, admired the sleepy baby, stroked Dempsey and praised the scones and sponge cake, which Jess then cut.

'Oscar's sorry he couldn't come himself,' Ralph said. He's delighted with the response to the Rutland work. Since the stock market crash, people losing their shirts and all that, Oscar says the gallery's pretty quiet. But I tell you what, those pieces out there – your magic boots and shoes – I could see certain Americans who've played it clever taking a shine to your shoe sculptures, pardon the pun.'

'Told you. They're absolutely not for sale.' Wilf grabbed a slice of cake and stood up. 'Ralph, I'll leave you with Jess, and to take a look round the place. I'm going back to the studio while there's still some light.'

'Thanks very much, old chap, glad to see you haven't become hospitable or developed any such bourgeois habits as politeness to your guest.'

Jess topped up the teapot. 'Ralph, if you fetch your luggage in, I'll pour you another cup of tea, and show you where you'll be sleeping.'

When Wilf finished working for the day, he saw that Ralph was again looking at the sculptures in the field. Leila and Dempsey were running about. Jess, carrying the baby, sat on the seat formed by the base of a seven-league boot.

'I was just telling Jess. Oscar has a client who lives in one of those buildings overlooking Central Park. He's deliberately buying up art because he says it's safer than the stock market. He'd love these.'

'They belong to Jess,' Wilf said simply.

'Jess wouldn't mind, would you?'

Wilf glanced at Jess. She looked puzzled, as if she knew something more was going on between Ralph and Wilf, but she did not know what. She moved the baby to her other arm.

'Don't be proud,' Ralph said. 'There's nothing wrong with pleasing people, especially if it brings in the dough, as the Americans say. You don't have to rank yourself with Moore and Hepworth, you might be better off cutting out a new turf, as it were.'

'Let me take him. You must be tired.' Wilf reached out his arms, and Jess passed him the baby.

'A pity the light's fading.' Ralph glanced around, trying to judge whether he could take another photograph.

'If you show photographs of this stuff to Oscar, make it clear they're not for the gallery.' Wilf settled the baby on his arm.

'Pity,' Ralph said. 'I know he'll think the same as me.'

'I hope not.' Wilf said. He turned to Jess. 'Ralph is saying that my art has dropped a peg. From abstract and modern, he thinks I've turned into someone who'll create garden ornaments.'

'I didn't say that!' Ralph protested. 'That's you being a terrible snob.'

Jess called to Leila and Dempsey. As they came back, she said to Ralph, 'You didn't see the piece Wilf did for the people in Rutland, or you wouldn't think that. These are for us, only for us.'

Ralph had brought wine. Over rabbit stew, potatoes and cabbage, he brought them up to date on all the gossip from London.

Wilf spooned more stew onto Ralph's plate.

After they had eaten, Jess went upstairs to feed the baby. Wilf followed her after a few moments. 'Do you feel embarrassed feeding Jimmy in front of Ralph? Should I have got him to stay in a hotel?'

'It's not that. Another damned artist, isn't he? If he sees me sitting there with a baby at my breast he'll whip out his sketch book.'

'When you've finished, there's something in the studio I want to show you.'

'Won't it wait till tomorrow?'

'No. I want you to see it first, and I don't know how much longer I can keep Ralph at bay.'

Wilf waited until Ralph gingerly stepped outside to find his way to the privy, carrying the small oil lamp.

'Come on, Jess.' Wilf lit the larger lamp and she followed him out to the studio. He pushed open the door, lit a second and a third lamp, and led her to a large sculpture at the end of the room, placing the lamps around it so that she could see its outline and shape, which cast long deep shadows across the ceiling.

After a moment the newly lit lamps grew a little brighter. Jess's eyes adjusted to the gloom. The seated adult figures were oval-headed and sharp-shouldered. Their lower legs seemed like pillars forming a protection around two smaller figures set between them, a child and a baby lying on its back, feet in the air. But they were universal shapes rather than particularized individuals. She could not see their eyes.

'I didn't know,' Jess said. 'It's extraordinary.'

'It's called assemblage. You create each piece separately, then bring them together.'

'They look as if they were always together.'

'That's the art.'

Wilf waited as Jess walked all around the sculpture and back to him. 'Jess, what did you mean when you said you didn't know? What didn't you know?'

She stood very close to him. 'That you were working on this.'

'Oh.' He sounded disappointed.

'What did you think I meant?'

'I thought you meant, you didn't know that I feel what this piece says.'

Outside, an owl broke the stillness. Wilf heard Ralph's footsteps as he walked back to the house. Still, Jess hadn't spoken.

One of the lamps spluttered and died, leaving just two burning on either side of the sculpture.

'Jess?'

'What?'

'Come closer.'

323

'I can't come much closer.'

He put his arms around her and kissed her on the mouth. When she kissed him back, he still did not feel sure he had her again. He kept on kissing, harder and harder, waiting for her to give herself away, to remember Isaac, to draw back from him. He was the one who stopped.

'I didn't think we could, Wilf, not after everything.'

'Shhh. Only say you'll marry me.'

'Ask me, then.'

'Jess, will you marry me?'

'Yes. Thank you.'

'And we're going to set a date, as soon as we can. I won't lose you again.'

He extinguished one of the lamps and picked up another. They walked into the garden and stood by the fence. Looking at the light coming through the window, Wilf said, 'There's no rush to go in. Ralph will come and find us if we're needed.'

'Die out the lamp, then, or he'll spot it and track us down.'

The cloud had moved from the moon and lit the scene, giving the sculptures in the field an eerie, otherworldly look.

Ralph came to the door.

'He's seen us,' Jess said.

Wilf sighed. 'We'd better go in.'

'Shall we tell him?'

'Why not?'

'Because,' Jess said, as they walked arm in arm towards the house, 'he was throwing down a gauntlet to me today. He believes if you take me and the brood on, you'll lose your way as an artist.'

'I know he thinks that. He looked at our magic boots and shoes and was prepared to believe I'd lost the battle.'

When they went back inside, Wilf said, 'Can we open that other bottle of wine, Ralph?'

'Thought you'd never ask. Didn't want to seem like a solitary sot.'

When Ralph had filled their glasses, Wilf said, 'Jess and I are getting married.'

Ralph raised his glass. 'Am I still to be your best man?'

They spoke together. Jess said yes. Wilf said no.

'It's a yes, then, Ralph said.

As Jess slid into bed beside Wilf, he said, 'I don't think it's very wise to have Ralph as best man.'

She snuggled up to him. 'Since when have we been wise?'

48

Not an Ounce of Filth

The day after his proposal and Jess's acceptance, Wilf ushered Ralph to his workshop and presented his assemblage. Ralph took a deep breath and let out a whistle. 'I take it all back. You'll give Moore and Hepworth a run for their money all right.' He went back to the house to fetch his camera.

Wilf booked the register office for the earliest date. Ralph took on the organizing of a reception, and delegated it to his butler.

'What about invitations, Wilf? Are we inviting Oscar and his gallery assistant?'

'Yes.'

'And colleagues? Fellow students?'

'No. Jess won't know them. She'll get to know Oscar, so he might as well come, but I don't want her to be faced with hordes of strangers.'

'And family?'

'I'll know when I get back from Leeds.'

Carrying his overnight bag, Wilf walked from Leeds central station to the tram stop. He had not quite decided where to go first. When the tram conductor came calling 'Tickets, please,' Wilf knew. He asked for the Roundhay Road stop near Bayswater Road, and hoped that Gladys Hardy would be at home. It seemed only right to call on her first since she was the only one who had responded to Jess's letter by getting herself on a train and taking the trouble to visit.

Gladys took some time to get to the door, calling out to ask who it was. A key turned. A chain rattled. She opened the door.

'Sorry,' Wilf said. 'I shouldn't just turn up.'

'Of course you can turn up. I was soaking my feet in salt and water. I've been on the tramp all day.'

'Don't stop for me.'

'It's all right. The water had gone cold.'

'Let me do that.' Wilf picked up the bowl and tipped the water gently into the long shallow sink. 'I've come to invite you to my wedding. Mine and Jess's.'

'That's wonderful!'

'You'll come?'

'When?'

He told her.

'I'll have to get permission to have time off work, but I don't see why not.'

'We'll pay your fare.'

'Don't be silly.'

'It's the least we can do.' Wilf wished he could call her 'mother', but feared he never would.

As if she read his thoughts, she said, 'You never call me anything. So call me by my name – Gladys. Gladys will do just fine.'

She insisted he drink a mug of tea, and eat a cheese sandwich and slice of seedcake before his walk up to Blenheim Square.

Bill sat in the dining room, smoking a Capstan, looking into the fire. The *Yorkshire Post* billowed across the floor, as if he had abandoned each page after reading it.

'Wilf!' The delight on his face lasted only a moment. 'Is something wrong?'

'No. I know you think I only come to see you when I want something.'

'I never said that.'

'Mother told me.'

'She had no business. A little bit of truth goes a long way, too far sometimes.'

'Well, I'm not here to ask for anything – only to invite you to my wedding. I'm going to marry Jess.'

'Are you, by jove? I hope you've asked Paul about it.'

'Dad. She's a widow now, taking care of two children. I shall be going to tell Paul, not to ask him.'

'I hope you know what you're letting yourself in for.'

'Yes. I think I do.'

'Of course I'll come. Though I would have been just as pleased if you'd said she was after her job back. She wrote to me, you know – keep meaning to reply – and it did strike me. If she wanted to come back, we could always hire a nursemaid.'

'No, she won't want her job back. We're going to live in London most of the year, and spend a couple of months in the country each summer.'

'All right for some. Now then, you'll want to eat.' He reached to ring the bell.

'No, but if you want to toast our health, happiness and success, I wouldn't say no to a drop of something.'

First thing the next morning, Wilf braced himself to visit Paul and Dolly. Paul held no fears for him; it was the thought of Dolly that made him take time over his shave and dawdle over breakfast.

When he reached Benson Street, Wilf wished he could just call into the cellar and take Paul to the Eagle. Dolly opened the door.

'Well, this is a surprise. Step inside, Wilf, don't be a stranger.'

Wilf spent as long as he could listening to news of Bernadette, her little boy, her new baby girl, and what miracles she worked in the Mooneys' shop in between the duties of motherhood. Not until Paul came up from the cellar, shaking hands and enquiring about his nephew's work, did Wilf pluck up the courage to say that he and Jess had named the day and hoped they would come to the wedding.

Dolly went very still.

'Well, now, our lass has a way of taking us by surprise, eh, Dolly? We were still working out how to answer her letter. How is she?'

Wilf told them that Jess had a baby son, and was well, though he felt sure Gladys would have already given them the news.

'I'm right glad,' Paul said. 'Something inside me said she'd land on her feet.'

'Wedding,' Dolly said. 'Where's her wedding to take place this time?'

'In London.'

'I mean, what manner of place, what manner of person will conduct the proceedings?'

'It's to be in the register office.'

'Why am I not surprised?' Dolly asked no one in particular. 'And what makes her think I shall want to attend?'

'Nay, Dolly. She is our lass. Wilf's right to come and ask us.'

'You go, then. I'll chase after her as much as she's chased after me, which is not a jot. She weren't married the first time. Bloomin' chapel. And she certainly won't be married in the eyes of God in some London register office.'

Wilf wrote down his address, and the date, time and place of the wedding. He stood the note on the mantelpiece.

'I hope you'll change your mind, Auntie Dolly.'

Paul shook hands with him, and wished them well. As Wilf left the house, Dolly called after him, 'And don't go nattering to Bernadette. I won't have the Mooney clan pawing over our dirty linen for their amusement.'

Paul had gone back in the cellar. He spoke to Wilf through the grate. 'Bernadette's shop's on Cherry Row.'

Wilf watched through the drapery shop window as Bernadette folded a pink corset and wrapped it in tissue paper. She smiled at the woman who handed over a note and waited for change.

The moment the customer left the shop, Bernadette walked into the back room.

A weary look flitted across her face, as she turned back from the house door when the bell rang announcing another customer.

'Wilf!'

She took him to the back to see the children; a sleeping baby and fractious toddler behind the bars of a playpen.

'Is Michael still working in the corporation offices?' Wilf asked.

She shook her head. 'He's meant to be here with me, but he likes to tell me how capable I am.'

Wilf stopped himself from asking where Michael was. When he changed the subject and talked about Jess and the baby, Bernadette seemed relieved.

'Tell her I would have written, but . . . well, I didn't know what to say. The truth is I was feeling very low when she wrote to me, and I couldn't think how to answer in a cheerful way.'

When Wilf invited Bernadette and Michael to the wedding, she looked doubtful. 'I'll ask, but we're as surely imprisoned here as any convict in Armley gaol. The shop only closes on Sundays and at

Christmas. Keep an eye on the children a minute, and listen for the bell.' She went upstairs and came back five minutes later with a bag bursting so full she could hardly close it.

'She might want my wedding dress, and one or two other things besides. I'm not supersitious so I won't say it's the wedding dress that brought me ill-luck. I hope you and Jess make a good go of it, Wilf. Take care of her. Give her my love.'

Wilf felt a rising anger towards Michael Mooney. 'Where is he, Bernie? Why are you here on your own?'

'It's a race day,' she said with a forced lightness in her voice. 'And if it isn't a race day, then there'll be a card game somewhere. He's right. I can manage. Because I have to.'

The shop bell rang. Wilf waited until Bernadette had served two more customers, then he said goodbye to her and the children and left.

'Your Aunt Bella won't come,' Bill announced as he watched Wilf write his letter. 'Furthest she's been from Gargrave in twenty years is Skipton, and that was too lively for her taste.'

'Well, then I won't have left her out and she might knit us a fancy tea cosy as wedding present.'

When he had posted the letter, Wilf had one more task to do before returning to London. He retrieved the small swimmer statues he had carved from the marble headstone before he left to start his studies at the Royal College of Art. Carefully he wrapped each one in beef sheeting and placed them between the dresses Bernadette had given him for Jess. The case he would take back was much bigger than the one he arrived with.

On a drizzly day in late September, a small group gathered at the register office. As best man and witness, Ralph and Gladys radiated calmness. Wilf and Jess looked more confident than they felt; Wilf, anxious that everything would go smoothly; Jess, wishing her mother would suddenly appear, since her father was there. But although Dolly had come to London, she was too sick to attend the ceremony.

'Take no notice,' Wilf whispered. 'She's not sick. She just wants the attention. Do you think your dad would be here if she really were poorly? Don't let her take the shine off our day.'

And Jess knew he was right.

330

Dolly put in an appearance the next day, at their Hamptead flat, trying not to look too impressed. They had all come to see where Jess and Wilf would live.

'You've done well for yourselves,' Dolly said gruffly, turning her eyes from the two nude statues on the mantelpiece.

Ann, who had come up to London with Jess from the country, took the children for a walk. Paul, Bill and Gladys tactfully went to see the sights of London, leaving Dolly alone with Jess and Wilf.

'It's a pity Bernadette couldn't come,' Dolly said, as Jess showed her round the flat. 'She'd have something to throw in the Mooneys' face. They're lucky to have her. I might not have had a son, but I've two daughters who I knew would go far.'

Wilf tried not to smile when he heard her. He could imagine Dolly boasting about her married daughter in London, and because she had not attended the wedding, she would never have to admit that it was in a register office. She would always be just a little vague and say, 'Oh, they married in London, you know.'

Wilf excused himself to go back into his workshop in the garden. As he walked away, he heard Dolly saying to Jess, 'It were your fairy-tale book that was the making of Wilf, giving him chance to show he can draw. And there were no mucky pictures or nudes in that book. Not an ounce of filth between the covers or on them.'

49

Mentioning
Unmentionables

It was our first Christmas together, just me, Wilf, Leila, Jimmy and Dempsey. Ann went back to her family for the holidays, and although I missed her help, it was good to have the place to ourselves.

Wilf had worked so hard during his first term teaching at college, so I wanted to make it a special time for all of us. This made me far too extravagant. I bought nuts, dates, candied fruit, sugared almonds and chocolate pennies. Wilf's present from me was a small African carving I got through Oscar at the art gallery. I also had a go at knitting him a long thin scarf that would look sufficiently Bohemian to suit him among his artist friends.

We trimmed the tree with silver balls and tinsel. All the trees that can be seen through the Hampstead windows look so tastefully done, some with hardly an ornament on them but prettily placed candles and red and white ribbons.

The London shops are magnificent. I wish Bernadette could see them; she would appreciate the sights even more than I do. So I have written to her about them in great detail. My present for her is a dark-red scarf, silk and velvet, which was absurdly expensive and, I'm sure, like nothing that would ever be stocked in Mooney's drapery shop. Wilf has bought Leila a proper doll with a porcelain face, rag body and blue dress.

I love to be with Wilf. After we have made love, we lie and talk for hours, and there is nothing we can't tell each other. We discussed what I would say to Leila about Christmas. At four, she is old enough to understand the Christmas story, and yet I have a deep reluctance to tell her it as a gospel truth, as neither I nor Wilf believe in that any more. In the end, I told it as I would tell her any other story. When she is old enough, I had better keep my vow and send her to a Catholic school, but until then I will keep the stories simple. Wilf said if we send Leila to a Catholic School but not Jimmy, then they won't grow up with enough in common. He has heard of some progressive schools that he thinks might suit both children. But we will cross that difficulty when we come to it.

At midnight on Christmas Eve we exchanged presents. He slid a silver bangle on my arm and I never want to take it off, though I am not sure when there will be time to read the complete works of Sir Arthur Conan Doyle which he also gave me.

Christmas Day was madness, trying to roast a goose, which neither of us had ever done, keeping Leila entertained and Jimmy happy. Wilf took Leila and Dempsey for a walk on Hampstead Heath and fortunately met an acquaintance who knew how to cook a goose. You pierce the skin so that fat drains away because a goose is a very fatty bird. So now we know.

We went to Leeds for the New Year and stayed with Uncle Bill. With his black hair, Wilf was in great demand as the dark haired first-footer who would bring good luck for the new year. He went into half a dozen houses wishing them all the best, downing a drop of something and moving onto the next. It seemed to me very risky of Gladys to allow him to walk her home and it did not surprise me that he was still not back at two o'clock in the morning.

Bill and I sat in my favourite room – the one that was Irene's sitting room. It still has the William Morris wallpaper and the pretty covers. He lit a big cigar and poured me a huge glass of sherry wine. The smoke from his cigar wound its way towards the fire.

'What do you reckon to all this arty business of Wilf's?'

There was no easy to answer to that. 'I don't know really. He does well.'

'Does he? Does he indeed? If you say so. Would he have been able to buy that place in the country if Irene hadn't left him something to be going on with?'

'Perhaps not. But he could have put down a deposit.'

'A beggar can put down a deposit.' He sighed. 'I worry about him. He could have had a good life in't firm.'

'We don't go without.'

'Living above your means, I don't doubt.'

'No.' I tried to sound convincing, but this was not exactly true. We had spent far too much on the flat, and on our splendid Christmas.

'Look, lass, don't let on I said this, but if everything goes belly-up, you're always welcome to come back.'

'Wilf won't want to—'

'Listen to me. I mean you. You and your bairns. If he can't keep you, you can have a job with me and get a nursemaid. I miss you in that firm.'

'I'm not going to leave Wilf.'

'I'm not asking you to. He could come with you. What's the difference whether he sculpts in London or on the outskirts of Leeds? I know where I'd sculpt if I were that way inclined.' He swayed towards the sideboard and refilled his glass.

I thought he must get lonely on his own, but I steered him back to his heart's delight – the business. With so many people out of work, orders for shoes are down this past year or so, but Bill felt sure sales would pick up again. I let him refill my glass, too.

'People will always need shoes, Jess. Just remember that. They won't always need a statue for the mantelpiece or a decoration to plonk outside a building. That happens when all the other needs have been met.'

'But Uncle, there are lots of people where we are whose other needs are met ten times over, so I think Wilf and I will manage.'

I had not convinced him, and perhaps that was because I was not entirely convinced myself. But I was sure whatever life threw at us, Wilf and I would make a go of it.

On New Year's Day, Wilf borrowed Bill's car. I wanted to visit Heather's grave. A cemetery on 1 January is not the best place in the world for children, so we agreed we would not stay long. Wilf carried Jimmy and took Leila's hand, leading her to see a Christmas rose.

I knew Heather was buried to the left of the chapel, between the path and the wall. I walked along, looking at the stones. But Heather did not have a headstone. I could only guess which grave it might be.

A freckled, ginger-haired boy of about nine years old appeared from nowhere and startled me. A girl of exactly the same colouring appeared, both dressed in grey serge coats. If she had not had plaits and the boy a basin cut it would have been difficult to tell which was which.

'Who are you looking for?' the boy asked.

'Heather McBride.'

'Oh, she's here. Between three O'Neils and another unmarked.'

'Thank you.'

'You were quite close,' the girl added.

I looked around but saw no adults. 'How do you know Heather's grave?'

The boy shrugged, as if he had been born knowing and therefore could not explain it.

Someone called. The children looked across to the chapel. A couple had just come out, wearing the same grey serge. She wore a black felt hat and he set a bowler back on his head. The Treasures. If I had recognized them, they had recognized me. I went over, feeling slightly guilty and awkward.

'Miss Price hmmmm!' Mr Treasure extended his hand.

'How lovely to see you.' Mrs Treasure beamed, as if it truly was lovely for her to see me.

I hoped Wilf would not re-appear too quickly, as I did not want to have to explain that I was no longer Miss Price but Mrs Price and that in between I had been Mrs Dennison.

'These are our two adopted children, hmmm-humm twins, and as bright as the knobs on a new hummm coffin.'

The children grinned.

'Home to a slap-up dinner, eh?' Mrs Treasure took the little girl's hand.

Mr Treasure extended a bony claw to the little boy.

We said our goodbyes, and the Treasures and their two small apprentices trotted off, as happy as farmers under little white clouds and a blue sky.

Wilf appeared from behind the chapel.

I had half hoped there would have been a headstone which would have told me that Tommy McBride had prospered and been able to afford to mark Heather's grave. We walked across to the mound the child had pointed out.

'This is your mammy's grave, Leila.'

Leila looked at the hard ground. 'Are we going to do gardening?'

'Not today. Another day, when we come again.'

Fortunately Mam had not just invited us to tea. Bernadette and Michael came as well, with their two children. So we sat where we could, squeezing round the table on chairs, stools and a couple of buffets brought up from the cellar.

Of course Mam objected when I asked Dad to let me see the cellar again. It smelt just the same, of damp brick walls, distemper, leather, glue and blacking.

'Dad, I didn't want to ask in front of Leila. Has anything been heard of Tommy McBride?'

Dad shook his head. 'I thought you'd want to know that. No word of him round here. I asked Bernadette to quiz the nuns from the orphanage, just in case he got in touch. They've heard nothing of him.'

'I'm surprised they'd be willing to give anything away, after I snatched Leila from them.'

'Bernadette's well in with the nuns. She supplies their unmentionables.'

The cellar was in its spic and span Saturday night and Monday morning state, with only a couple of pairs of shoes keeping each other company on the shelf.

'We're not doing too badly,' Dad said, reading my thoughts. 'It's the good shoes that come in from the high-class shops that save our bacon these days. Poor folk are cobbling their own as best they can, or sticking in cardboard soles and praying for a dry day.'

'So you won't be moving to Premises just yet?'

'Doesn't look like it, love, though I would have liked to, for your mam's sake. The only advantage from her point of view is that these days there's just the one bike in the doorway for her to fall over.'

50

Coming Home

August, and we were back in the country. Sitting in the upstairs room that faces south-west, I asked Leila to drop the olive-green canvas blind a little way. It slid down at a slant, cutting off the tops of the trees. A pale leafy shade dimmed the room to suit the summer afternoon.

This time I would not leave it so late to go to the hospital. Tomorrow would be soon enough. Wilf had arranged to borrow a horse, to be harnessed into a trap that he is assured has good suspension. We'll see.

Jimmy had fallen asleep beside me, curled like a cat, thumb in his mouth. Dempsey was somewhere outside.

'Look out of the window,' I told Leila. 'See if Dempsey has found a shady spot.'

Whether it's cold or hot, a whippet has so little between himself and the elements. She couldn't see him.

I heard a noise from Wilf's workshop; perhaps stone being delivered, or wood from the timber yard across the valley.

Downstairs Mam was doing something and I didn't know what, but noisily.

It surprised me at first that she wanted to come. But then I saw her in my mind's eye, at the baker's, the greengrocer's, the butcher's, in the church porch, saying, 'You won't see me for a few weeks. Paul will be eating at Bernadette's. I'm going to Jess's house in the country.'

A compensation for not finding herself in Premises. If a daughter has a house in the country and a flat in Hampstead, then surely, some day soon, that daughter's mother and father will find themselves in better circumstances. With Premises. Or without the need for Premises even.

For as long as I could, I wanted to keep the children by me. Mam offered to come. I would not have asked her. I wanted to write to Gladys. Mam would do her impatient duty by the children; Gladys would love them. But Mam made it clear she would not stay if Gladys were here. I did not have the energy for a fight.

When she arrived she asked me if Jimmy had been christened.

Later, I heard him cry and looked out of the window. Mam stood by the pump, dropping water onto Jimmy's head. That was why she came. She will baptize the new baby when I'm not looking.

I was uneasy at leaving Leila and Jimmy with Mam, but Wilf would be there, and Ann.

Only Ann had fallen in love with George who lived across the valley. She had always known him, but at the New Year dance, they danced. George's friend then asked Ann's friend if Ann would meet George the following day, on the corner opposite the post box. Ann's friend said Ann might. And she did.

Now she takes Wilf's binoculars and looks across the valley. George has his own borrowed binoculars and looks back. They exchange signals by pre-arranged codes involving scarves.

When the baby first kicked, I held a pillow close so it would know that there would be other things out in the wide world besides me and Wilf that might be worth investigating. A sister, a brother, a pillow, a dog. Even when the baby didn't kick, out of habit I sometimes held the pillow to me. It annoyed Mam.

Leila now knows that the words in the notebook on the shelf were written by her mother, Heather. She brings it to me, to read to her. Always I must resist the temptation to say something that is not there, something full of hope and dreams, or a set of instructions in which Heather tells Leila how to read a clock or fasten her shoes. (There are some lines I do not read to her.)

She likes to hear how her mother lived as a child in a horse-drawn wagon, travelling the highways and byways. And when she and her sisters and brothers had to, they lived off hedgerow berries, wild rhubarb and drank from a sweet stream.

I do not know whether I am doing the right thing when I mention

338

Tommy McBride, and how Heather met him across his barrow of fruit when he handed her an apple, their fingers touched and he would not take pay. Leila is almost ready to think of Wilf as her father, and I hope she will. Should I tell the children everything, or nothing, or hope they will never ask?

This one in my womb will have a simple story to understand.

We have taught Leila to say please and thank you. When I read to her again what Heather wrote, she said, '*Gracias.*'

'What?'

'*Gracias.*'

'Who taught you that?'

She wouldn't say.

This is the passage that I do not read to Leila, the passage that Heather wrote to me, in indelible pencil, the point dampened, so it wrote purple:

Bring her up in the faith as you promised, with Latin, French and Italian so she will have knowledge and thoughts beyond any gypsy, and beyond you, too, Jess, champion swimmer, who understands that money makes the world go round.

Leila saying words in Spanish makes me dizzy. Sometimes I dream of Heather, and she is watching, to see that we treat Leila right. Once in the night, I woke and heard Heather say, as plain as can be, 'Don't let her play with candles.'

In the cottage hospital, the youngest nurse, Alice, with auburn hair and speckled eyes, comes on duty after our daughter is born. Alice remembers me from last year. She asks if I am to be a regular customer, every summer. I hope not.

Wilf comes to see me, bringing flowers. We both begin to cry, because we are so happy. Our baby has dark hair, a red face and tiny slits for eyes. Wilf says she has eyes from a Mexican carving, the kind that see everything and will always see enough.

Mam will not come to visit me here. She does not believe visitors should disrupt the routine of a hospital, which is no place to take children.

Wilf brings Leila anyway. She says good morning to me and the baby in Spanish, though it is afternoon.

'Why have you taught Leila Spanish words?'

339

'For when we go to South America. I want to see for myself how they did it, those old carvers, how they made those eyes.'

'You already know. You told me.'

'I won't know until I see, until we see.'

'We can't take babies to South America.'

'South America is full of babies.'

'You haven't asked me,' Leila says. She reaches out her hand to get my attention, to take my attention from Wilf and South America.

'What haven't I asked you?'

'The baby's name.'

For a horrible moment I think she is going to call the baby Rapunzel, or Rumpelstiltskin.

'It's Heather,' she says.

Silence.

She knows Heather not just from my stories of her, or the words in Heather's exercise book, but from Wilf's drawings of her when she worked at the Wright Shoe Company. A Heather for ever young. I do not want to name my baby after a dead mother.

'Your middle name is Catherine,' I tell Leila.

'I know.'

'What about if we call the baby Catherine Heather?' I look at Wilf for a reaction.

'That's a good name, eh, Leila?' he says.

'Yes, Daddy.'

It is the first time she has called him that.

The nurse distracts Leila, so that we can have some time alone.

'Does she think that's her job in the family? To name the children?'

Wilf shrugs. 'She's quicker off the mark than we are. We couldn't make up our minds.'

'Thanks, Wilf.'

'What for?'

'For the flowers, for everything, for waiting for me.'

'Just come home soon.'

'Whenever I'm with you, I'm at home.'

He smoothed my hair with his hand. 'I've felt like that about you all my life.'

I was glad no one else was there, to see us both roaring our eyes out.